Only For You

by

Genna Rulon

Only For You

The Cataloging-in-Publication Data is on file at Library of Congress
ISBN: 0615868401
ISBN-13: 978-0-615-86840-0

Cover design by G. Relyea
© Genna Rulon, 2013

Cover Image Copyright © Viktor Kunz
Used under license from shutterstock.com

Dedication

To my loved ones *(you know who you are)*,
You supported and encouraged me to follow this
dream. Without you it would still be nothing more
than an idea in my crazy mind. Thank you for
having faith in me and giving me faith in myself.

An extra special thanks to my three incredible men.
You sacrificed your time with me, allowing me to
achieve this goal and didn't complain...much.

𝕹𝖊𝖜𝖘𝖉𝖆𝖎𝖑𝖞

VOL. CLXII . . . No. 56,141   © 2013 Newsdaily

Hensley Students Live in Fear

By: Matthew Smith

Hensley University students have been afraid for their safety after a string of brutal attacks on campus began this past October. "Seven violent offenses have already been reported over the past six months," Suffolk Police Det. Lt. Ray Cartone confirmed.

Although the Suffolk County Police Department (SCPD) refused to release any details pertaining to the attacks, presumably to discourage copycat behaviors, there are indicators that the same assailant perpetrated all of the assaults to date. "We are currently investigating the crimes that have occurred at Hensley, and we hope to apprehend the culprit expeditiously to prevent future attacks," Det. Lt. Cartone said during a news conference on Monday.

The female student body is concerned, demanding Hensley take more aggressive preventative action. Sophomore Marilyn Stokes said, "It's my job to come to college and learn. It's the University's job to provide a safe environment for me to do so. They are failing." Another student,

junior Kelly Selonitakis, stated, "I have fun, but I'm careful. I make smart choices. That's not enough anymore. I am scared. I don't want to be next."

Hensley is taking its turn in the hot seat, at a time when universities across the country are being scrutinized for their lack of response to rape and sexual assault claims from students. Schools are often accused of suppressing the volume and severity of registered complaints.

The Night Is Ours, a local women's advocacy group, is pressuring SCPD to dedicate additional resources to the investigation stating, "They can't sit back complacently in the hopes the epidemic will subside." They have also called upon Hensley to be proactive in preventing violence against women, including increasing security throughout campus and providing free self-defense classes for students.

We will continue to follow the events at Hensley University and report developments as they occur.

Hensley University had no comment at the time of printing.

Chapter One

"The world is not full of assholes. But, they are strategically placed so that you'll come across one every day." -Unknown

"Uggghhhhh!" I groaned and dragged myself from the warm cocoon of my bed, giving the alarm my most scathing stare. The red numbers illuminating the face mocked me as I finally registered the time.

"Sam! It's 6:30 in the morning! Have you lost your damn mind?" I shouted to my scheming roommate, who was undoubtedly responsible for my rude awakening.

My bedroom door slowly creaked open, allowing my favorite coffee mug to materialize through the crack. Sam hesitantly followed, waiving her hand above the mug, wafting a heavenly aroma of freshly brewed caffeine in my direction. I sniffed dramatically, a bloodhound scenting the kill, as I made my way toward her.

"No, no, no. You need to forgive me before I hand it over." She raised her hand in an effort to ward off my attempt to steal the coffee.

I stared at my best friend as I debated my options. She undoubtedly deserved punishment for her cruelty, but she possessed the steaming mug I craved. It was a difficult decision.

"Alright. You're begrudgingly forgiven. Now gimme!" I swiped the coffee from her unprepared hands and hastily swallowed a sip, reveling in the rich flavor.

I eyed Sam resentfully. "Care to explain why you snuck into my room last night, moved my alarm, and set the bloody thing to scream me awake at 6:30? The sun isn't even up yet! Why am I?"

Sam ignored my resentment, unaffected. Having known me fifteen years, she was well aware of the consequences of waking me. She waited until I had ingested the majority of my mood stabilizer before offering an explanation.

"You remember the self-defense seminar that Hensley University is sponsoring?" she paused, retreating a step before announcing, "I registered us for this morning's session at 7:30 am."

I opened my mouth to protest, but Sam continued hurriedly.

"It's only ninety minutes once a week."

I shook my head. "Are you serious?"

"The seminar's only six sessions, and we even get credit from the University for participating. A credit we don't have to pay for; it's free money. You know how much you love free stuff."

I continued to scowl at her, unimpressed by the single credit that I didn't need to graduate this May.

Sam's shoulders sagged as she looked at me with sincere eyes. "I'm scared, Everleigh, for both of us. The police haven't succeeded in preventing the attacks. Every week another girl is beaten and dumped on campus. We need to do something to protect ourselves."

Her concerns were valid, and I was scared too. The brutality of the attacks and frequency continued to increase.

Although few details had been leaked to the public, the tidbits we heard through the campus grapevine were frightful. I released an exaggerated sigh, wishing it wasn't necessary to agree, but knowing I should participate. "Alright. I'll do it *if* you promise to be my partner."

"Deal!" she quickly agreed, clearly relieved she would not attend the class alone.

"And I'm going to find a way to pay you back for the early wake ups."

"I know you will," she smiled, evidently unafraid of my threat. "We need to leave in twenty minutes, so hurry up and get ready. There's more coffee in the kitchen—your current mood is bad enough without adding caffeine withdrawal to the mix."

I looked around my room formulating a plan of attack. I wanted to participate in self-defense classes about as much as I wanted to slam my hand in the car door. I was tempted to bury my head in the sand and pretend everything was normal, but ignoring the danger wouldn't remove the threat. If I didn't take the initiative to protect myself, who would?

I glanced at the clock again 6:40 in the morning and I was awake. I glanced back at my bed longingly, struggling to contain my frustration with Sam. I reminded myself that she was my best friend, regardless of the inconvenient enrollment she made on my behalf.

Samantha Elizabeth Magdalena Whitney, Sam, grew up in a mansion on the North Shore of Long Island surrounded by every amenity. She wanted for nothing, other than her parent's attention and understanding. It was the same old story—her father was absent physically and emotionally, and her mother tried to micromanage her life. Sam emerged unscathed, no longer expecting her father's regard and disregarding her mother's propaganda. She followed her own path—living life joyously and without pretension.

My mother was a 'domestic' at the Whitney estate, a title synonymous with housekeeper. It was an ideal position for a single mother, permitting her to work while I was at school and only required the occasional babysitter when the Whitneys hosted a special event. The salary was conservative, but she was provided with a car and her compensation included health insurance for us both.

Mom and I shared a small two-bedroom apartment in an older complex—we only lived fifteen minutes from the Whitney estate, but we were worlds apart. My mom strived to provide all of my needs and as many of my wants as was manageable. She understood the importance of appearances to a young girl's self-esteem and creatively protected me from peer scrutiny. I wasn't outfitted in designer labels, but I never had to hang my head in shame, either. When we couldn't afford store bought costumes, she sewed my Halloween costume from old clothing she found at garage sales until I had a couture masterpiece—I always had the winning costume at the school parade. As I grew older, she would find incredible vintage pieces at thrift stores, which my girlfriends coveted. I can only imagine the hours she must have invested to find each discounted treasure, motivated by her love for me. She even squirreled money away, enabling me to receive haircuts at a trendy salon, so my hair would 'do its job to frame that beautiful face.' She loved me fiercely and proved it not only in words, but also in actions. It was only in recent years I fully appreciated how blessed I was—what I lacked in trivial possessions was inconsequential compared to her steadfast love and devotion.

Sam and I met shortly after Mom was hired by the Whitneys. The school called the Whitney estate to advise Sam was sick but her mom had plans to go shopping in New York City, so she sent my Mom to collect Sam from school and care for her. Since the school day was nearly over Mom brought me along, unable to arrange a sitter on such short notice. I spent the afternoon keeping Sam company, and we had been best friends ever since.

The following week Sam demanded I join her dance class— according to Mrs. Whitney it was imperative that Sam study dance—and with no alternative to coax her participation, the Whitneys paid my tuition to accompany Sam. It was Mom who taxied us, watched our rehearsal, and brought us home. In fourth grade, Sam agreed to study piano *if* I joined her. Unbeknownst to me, piano was another critical life skill that Sam must acquire, which meant I would acquire it as well. In eighth grade, Sam refused to attend a prestigious enrichment summer camp unless I accompanied her. It was quickly understood that if the Whitneys wanted Sam to endure any extracurricular activity, it best include me to gain her cooperation.

Sam's choice to attend the same university as me was the natural progression. She could have attended any college in the world with her intellect, grades, and familial resources. We applied to the same Ivy League universities. Sam's dream was to move as far from her parent's oppressive shadow as her admittance letters could take her. My enrollment would be determined by the university offering the greatest amount of financial aid as I was unwilling to burden my mom or myself with student loans. I was accepted to all schools I applied, and Hensley was the highest-ranking institution to offer a full scholarship. Sam was accepted to the same universities, with the exception of Yale—a slight she would never forgive. When Sam learned I committed to Hensley, she shocked me by following suit. She wanted to share the college experience with me and, after fifteen years of friendship, virtually sisters, separating would be akin to losing a limb.

The Whitneys were appalled at the prospect of Sam living in student dormitories. Consequently, they bought a two-bedroom condominium in the most prestigious complex near to the school. It was small, as all the apartments near school were, but luxurious. Ever generous, Sam insisted I room with her rent-free to eliminate on-campus housing expenses. I never could have foreseen Sam's decision would be my saving grace.

Two weeks prior to our departure for Hensley, my mom passed away—hypertrophic cardiomyopathy, sudden cardiac death. I was working at a local deli, one of my last days before school began, when Sam came in. She marched to the back without looking at me and spoke with my supervisor. When she returned with my belongings, she took my hand and guided me out. I didn't ask questions, if Sam needed me I would be there. In her silence, I speculated a confrontation with her parents was the cause; a litany of possible disputes circled my mind. I knew enough to give her space until she was prepared to share what troubled her. She drove a few blocks to the beach, we walked along the shore until finding a relatively desolate section where she sat, and I followed her lead. After a few minutes, Sam turned to me and revealed what transpired. My mom had died at the Whitney estate while working. Mrs. Whitney had found her on the kitchen floor and called an ambulance, but she was gone by the time paramedics arrived. She was gone...just like that. Perfectly healthy and happy that morning; over breakfast we planned a shopping trip to purchase the final supplies I would require for school. Sam held me as I sobbed for hours, inconsolable and adrift. I stayed at the Whitney estate until school began, unable to face my apartment knowing my mom would never return. Mrs. Whitney was kind enough to arrange the funeral on my behalf. Sam and her brothers emptied the apartment, packing everything I would need for school, and placed the rest in storage for me to sort when I wasn't as vulnerable and raw. I have spent every school break and holiday with the Whitneys since. There was no replacement for my mom, and the Whitneys were not nurturing, but at least I had a place to go when I would otherwise be alone. I will always be grateful to them for that gift.

If not for Sam, I would have shattered irrevocably. She was like a sister, mourning the loss of her surrogate mother while helping me find a way to survive crippling grief. She pushed me when I struggled to maintain the grade point average my scholarship required. She brought me ice cream on the nights I cried with longing for my mom. She partied with me when I finally accepted I was not betraying my mother by enjoying life again. She was selfless and patient when needed, tough and bitchy when required, and entertainment director once I was able. I may never find the words of gratitude equal to all Sam did. I attempted once, but she cut me off.

"I've done nothing for you that you haven't or wouldn't do for me. You have been my shoulder to lean on enough times—it was my turn. I loved her too—I lost her too. Helping you helped *me* heal, and it was the last gift I could give in honor of the love she gave me."

We were both orphans in our own way; the only true 'family' either of us could rely on was one another. I prayed I never had the occasion to repay Sam, but I would be there to hold her together if ever the need arose.

I broke free of my melancholy and walked to my dresser to find a black sports bra, which I wrestled on. The battle was close, but I triumphed. I quickly dressed in my workout clothes and sneakers, ready to spar.

In the kitchen, I refilled my mug with the rich black coffee I loved. Armed with my tonic, I headed to the bathroom to finish my preparations. I raked a brush through my medium blonde locks, taming the tangles, and then wrangled the mass into a convenient ponytail. I glanced in the mirror again and noticed my pale skin-tone. Late-January in New York didn't lend itself to a golden tan.

"All done, Sam," I called while heading to the living room.

In return, Sam bellowed, "I need ten more minutes."

I sank into the couch and turned on the news. The anchor was reporting on the escalating assaults at Hensley University over the past sixteen months. Joining mid-broadcast I missed the details, but assumed there was another attack last night. Spring semester at Hensley began today, offering a smorgasbord of potential victims to prey upon.

The attacks began in October of my junior year. Initially they were believed to be isolated incidents of abuse, but as the frequency and severity of the attacks escalated, the connection became evident. What began as bruised faces became broken arms, which became internal injuries, and finally savage beatings with debilitating consequences. There had been no confirmation that victims had been sexually assaulted, but many assumed including the media outlets. All of the victims were female and students at Hensley, but no other commonality among the victims had been identified; the police suspected they were selected at random. Of the thirteen women attacked, three victims sustained injuries so severe they would suffer permanent physical disabilities. I was certain all thirteen would bear permanent psychological scars, even after the physical injuries healed.

Hensley University's enrollment consisted of over 6,000 undergrads, to whom they were obligated to provide a safe environment, conducive to learning. In response to the attacks, Hensley significantly increased security and pledged cooperation with the police task force. Hensley was harshly criticized for their passive response after each incident. In the last year, 37 percent of the female students had transferred due to parental concern, and new student enrollment was down 68 percent. Understandably, Hensley was desperate, needing the violence to cease and the panic to recede. The self-defense seminar was their latest attempt to appease concerned students and parents, and mitigate the current public relations nightmare. Specifically developed for Hensley, the seminar was supposed to ensure our safety, or at least foster that illusion.

Suddenly, I was tackled to the floor under Sam's dead weight.

"Ha! You totally need this class," she smirked, "you didn't even see me coming! Didn't even protect yourself."

"Come on ninja girl," I rolled the petite body off me and onto the floor, "let's get this over with."

"There's the enthusiasm I was looking for," she deadpanned while rising from her prone position.

Sam headed to the door until I called out, "Wait a minute." I scampered into the kitchen and grabbed the travel mug from the dishwasher, filling it with the remains of the pot.

"Okay, now I'm really ready to go."

Snatching my purse from the kitchen table, I headed for the door. Sam eyed the coffee in my hands dubiously. "If you wet yourself when I take you down because of your excessive coffee consumption, you will regret it," Sam warned.

I pretended to ponder for a moment. "I hadn't considered that method of self-defense...it has potential."

We walked to my blue "hand-me-down" Honda with the rising sun at our backs. I opened my door and tugged the purse from my shoulder to my lap, rummaging for the keys.

"Do you ever lock your car doors?" Sam commented disapprovingly.

"Not all of us drive a Mercedes, Sam," I sniped, "who would want to steal Papa Smurf? He's a twelve year old no-frills Accord," I asked after locating the keys in the black hole I called a purse. "Got' em!" I shouted triumphantly.

Within five minutes of leaving our apartment we arrived at the athletic complex and entered Studio A. Fifteen unfamiliar girls sat on the thick floor mat looking as apprehensive as I felt. Sam and I quickly joined them after depositing our personal items to the side.

At the front of the room was an attractive woman in tight workout attire, which intentionally displayed her ample assets. Her shiny brunette hair was atop her head in a high ponytail, and she was wearing full supermodel makeup.

I rolled my eyes while muttering, "Are we recording an exercise video? Did I miss the memo?"

Sam laughed while she studied our specimen her further.

"Is she wearing fake lashes? They match her fake—" she trailed off as the buxom brunette eyed the doorway behind us and purred, "Hunter, you're here."

I turned to the door along with everyone else and froze. The man who entered was arresting, breathtaking. He appeared to be mid-twenties, at least six feet two with broad shoulders that tapered to a narrow waist, creating the idyllic masculine V-figure. He wore a fitted black tee that hinted at a patchwork of muscles hidden beneath. I forced my reluctant eyes to his face, the sight I encountered compelled me to whisper, "My, oh my...it just keeps getting better. Damn."

His defined bone structure was deliberate, but not sharp, with a squared jaw and prominent cheekbones. Shaggy ebony hair, slightly longer in front, framed his face and contrasted his bottomless aquamarine eyes in such a way they seemed to radiate light from within. His jaw was dusted with dark stubble that called attention to his lips, which were wide and appeared alluringly strong yet soft. Those same lips were currently raised on one side in a knowing smirk. I watched as he walked, his gait confident and fluid, the stride of a man who knew his effect on the occupants of the room. I subtly attempted to track his journey; as he passed me I was rewarded with an unhindered view of his brawny back and muscular butt, beautifully showcased and begging to be bitten. He was the human equivalent of a perfect piece of fruit featured on a magazine cover—impossibly succulent, such perfection couldn't be real. The difference in this case being a picture could be doctored until it no longer resembled the original, but merely an idealized representation. He was no altered ideal—he was authentic sex incarnate.

I snapped back to reality when he reached the Jane Fonda fitness model wannabe. She raised her arm to stroke his cheek, murmuring, "No chance to shave this morning?" She made her approval obvious as her hand lingered longer than was appropriate.

"Thanks Crystal," he replied neutrally while stepping back, increasing the space between them. He was neither discouraging nor encouraging her blatant advances, accepting her actions as par for the course. Directing his attention outward, he addressed the group.

"Are we ready to begin?" Of course his voice was as sexy as his body, a rich, deep baritone, reverberating through the air seductively. Double damn.

The command his voice wielded over my body was disconcerting, tingles danced across my skin in response. Was he a cyborg of masculine perfection created to test the restraint of earthly women? It seemed a viable explanation for my responsiveness. I licked my suddenly dry lips.

Fighting my alarmingly wicked thoughts about this man, I shifted my gaze to observe the condition of my classmates. Evidently, every female in the room was as mesmerized by him as I was. Faces ranged from slightly flushed to carnal red, most still gawking wantonly. Turning to Sam, keen to assess his effect, I found her mouth agape, eyes still locked on the eye candy. I nudged her to break the trance, causing her to shake her head several times as if dispersing the fog.

Chuckling softly I teased, "You okay, Sam? I think you may have swallowed a fly."

Sam's eyes regained focus and snapped to me.

"Don't even pretend you don't see that prime cut of meat. I'm quitting food and becoming a manivore," Sam smacked her lips to emphasize her point. "In fact, when I'm forty with three screaming kids it will be *him* I visualize when I close my eyes to pretend I want to have sex with my husband, instead of getting the sleep I would prefer." Sam rubbed her hands together wickedly like a villain from the silent movie era, enjoying her evil plan.

"Wow, way too much information. Please, don't think you need to filter your thoughts to spare my mental health. Just go ahead and pollute my mind with your carnal daydreams. I'm sure I will scrub that image from my brain in another ten years or so." I tilted my head to the side, banging my hand on top as if trying to knock loose the image she painted.

Sam rolled her eyes at my theatrics. "Whatever. Even you can't deny that man is a god."

"True," I conceded, "but I'm pretty sure I saw Miss Abs-of-Steel peeing on him to mark her territory. I'm afraid if we don't take the hint she may start humping his leg and that is a horror I would never forget, so try to control yourself."

Getting a laugh from Sam cleared the lustful haze that had lingered about her.

"Alright everyone, let's get started. My name is Hunter Charles, and I'm honored to be your instructor for the next six weeks. I have been studying martial arts for twenty years, and I hold varying degrees of black belts in Karate, Aikido, Tae Kwon Do, Krav Maga, and Brazilian Jiu-Jitsu. Since this is not a formal study of martial arts, please feel free to address me as Hunter instead of Sensei."

He sidestepped and gestured to Exercise Barbie. "With me is Crystal Duvall, she is the liaison between the Suffolk County Police Department and Hensley University."

"Hello ladies, I'm happy to be here with Hunter to teach you how to protect yourselves." Crystal placed her hand on Hunter's lower back as she spoke, clearly trying to reiterate her claim of him.

Hunter stepped forward slightly, dislodging her hand, and addressed us again.

"Crystal will spend the first thirty minutes of each session outlining safety awareness and prevention strategies. The remaining sixty minutes I will instruct you in physical defense techniques. You're all to be congratulated on taking the initiative to participate in the seminar. It's the first step in protecting yourselves and, by doing so, you have substantially increased your odds of avoiding or escaping an attack." Hunter then stepped aside allowing Crystal to take control without his distracting presence.

"Can anyone tell me what your best weapon is in preventing an attack?" Crystal looked around the room as people called out answers.

"A gun." "Mace." "A Taser."

Crystal shook her head. "Those are all tools you can use to protect yourself *during* an attack, but they will not prevent an attack. Any other guesses?"

No one said anything. Crystal continued to stare at us, unwilling to give us the correct answer. I groaned inwardly.

In the interest of expediting the lecture, I answered, "Our mind or intuition?"

Crystal nodded her approval, "Exactly. Your brain and your gut are your best weapons to prevent an attack. Be aware of your surroundings, think about safety measures, and assess the risks you're taking. Your gut is your intuition or sixth sense. It's imperative that you listen to it; if something feels wrong, don't ignore that feeling. We all have innate self-preservation instincts, and we need to heed to them. Here are a few general safety points to remember—always be alert to your surroundings. At night, walk in well-lit, heavily traveled areas. Use the campus escort security service or walk with a friend. Be cautious of strangers who approach you trying to engage in conversations. Never hitchhike or accept a ride from someone you don't know. In regards to your home and car—always lock your doors even when you're home or in the car. Make sure your cell phone is always nearby and accessible."

Crystal paused to assess our attentiveness. "Don't worry; you will receive a packet at the end of each class that includes the information presented." She gentled, "You must be scared, that's why you're here. Fear is a potent protector and will help you remain vigilant." Crystal hardened her tone, "And most crucial, do not impair your awareness by using alcohol in excess or taking any sort of drugs. If you're going to imbibe, make sure you're with friends you trust and stick together, no matter what. Just like you should have a designated driver when drinking, you should have a designated sober friend to remain aware and ensure the safety of your group."

I quickly caught Sam's eye.

"Well there go my plans for picking up random hitchhikers this weekend. Newsflash—I have appointed you the 'sober friend.' I'll order your tee shirt as soon as I get home...or perhaps an embroidered sash would better highlight your status."

Sam struggled to contain her laughter.

When I returned my attention to the front, Hunter's arctic glare pierced me, "Are you finished now Miss—"

"Ev," I blushed, caught being my usual snarky self.

"Ev?" he questioned in return as if my answer was incorrect.

"Everleigh," I replied dispassionately. He continued to stare at me as if I was a suspect withholding information. I sighed my displeasure, "Everleigh Carsen."

"Are you finished interrupting the seminar now Miss Carsen, or shall we plan to be inconvenienced further?" he scolded as if I was an errant child.

"I do believe I'm finished," I responded tartly, burning with anger at his reprimand. As he redirected his attention to the rest of the class, I couldn't help but add, "For now at least."

His captivating eyes shot back to me and turned glacial with his anger.

"Miss Carsen, everyone is here of their own free will and at no expense to themselves. Most are here because they are justly afraid for their safety. You are belittling their concerns, diminishing the seriousness of the threat, and minimizing the suffering of the victims with your flippancy."

I stared at him open mouthed, for once, rendered speechless.

"You're wasting my time, Crystal's, as well everyone else present. I believe this would be an appropriate time for you to leave," he ordered firmly with no room for negotiation.

"I...I'm sorry. I didn't mean—" I began, stuttering in my shock, but he cut me off.

"I thank you for your apology, presuming it's sincere. You may return next week, provided you join us with the intent of learning, participating, and extending everyone in this room the respect they deserve." He turned away from me dismissively. I had been deemed unworthy of further consideration.

Mortified and disoriented by what transpired, I rose from my seated position and collected my belongings before silently exiting without a backward glance. In the hallway, I struggled with my coat and haphazardly wrapped my scarf around my neck. As I opened the front door the wind stung my eyes, exacerbating the tears that were fighting to escape. I stomped to the car, jumped in, and slammed the door. Tears prickled the back of my eyes and a telltale itch began in my nostrils.

Damn it! I was not going to cry. I *never* cry, not since my mom died and I learned what true pain was. I would not give some pompous, condescending muscle-head that type of power over me. My humiliation before fellow students and the Sports Illustrated swimsuit imposter was no excuse for tears. How dare he? Who does he think he is? My righteous indignation swept aside my momentary weakness. I inhaled deeply, held it, and exhaled slowly, attempting to calm my rage. I would never intentionally disrespect the victims; my heart ached for what they had survived. If I met any of them personally, I would have been the first to offer support during their recovery. Yes, I'm extra snarky when I'm afraid, a common coping mechanism. Who wouldn't be scared living in the danger enveloping Hensley?

I had considered transferring during winter break, what sane person wouldn't? After exploring the possibility, I found I would be required to repeat some courses to earn sufficient credits to graduate and my graduation would be delayed by at least a year. I weighed the risks of remaining against the loss of a year, torn. When it became clear I would not be able to obtain comparable scholarships and grants on such short notice, I put the matter to rest.

Perhaps Mr. High and Mighty decided to single me out because I was *slightly* heckling his girlfriend, how gallant of him. Okay, I may have outright mocked Ms. Silicone, but I limited my commentary to Sam's ears while he harpooned me before an audience.

I grabbed my iPod; music would be required to exorcise my anger. As if by magic, the first song to pour from my speakers was "Sweet As Hole" by Sara Bareilles, or as many fans refer to it—"That Guy's An Asshole." I smiled at its timeliness; I swore there was a genie that lived in my iPod. Provided I instilled my trust in her infinite wisdom, demonstrated by selecting random shuffle, the mystical imp saw fit to grace me with the perfect song when I needed it most. Grateful, I sung along, relishing the lyrics, shouting the final lines of the chorus like a mad woman.

Chapter Two

"One of the greatest victories you can gain
over someone is to beat him at politeness."
-Josh Billings

I arrived home and proceeded to make a pot of coffee, finding solace in my drug of choice. Feeling more like myself, I headed to the bathroom to restart the day.

Once showered, I applied make-up while examining my reflection. An oval face with blue-green almond shaped eyes, slightly upturned nose, and full lips greeted me. No one part was exceptional, but the effect of the whole was pleasing. I had been called pretty or cute most of my life—except when I glam-up on special occasions—then I was elevated to "beautiful" status. While beautiful was an appealing compliment, it also required far more effort than I was willing to invest on a daily basis. I had learned to be content with cute and pretty in recent years.

Needing comfort after my trying morning, I selected my new dark wash skinny jeans before sneaking into Sam's room to steal her cream Merino wool sweater; it was chunky, soft, and warm, just what I required. It was a rarity I could borrow Sam's clothing as she was five feet one and slender, compared to my five feet seven hourglass figure. I returned to my room and zipped my knee-high brown leather boots. I loved these boots—if an equestrian and a motorcycle boot had a baby, these would be their chic offspring. Discovering it was already 9:40, I hustled to make my 10:00 class. With luck, I found a spot in the metered lot near my destination. Happy with the pleasant turn my day had taken, I smiled as I headed to class, stopping to obtain yet another coffee from the cart inside.

Thankfully this would be a small class of thirty students at most. The benefit of being an upperclassman was most of the advanced courses were intimate when compared to introductory level courses that often exceeded one thousand students.

I selected a seat in front, learning long ago that all professors granted higher marks for class participation to those seated in the front row. The drawback to this ploy was you could never be late or skip class without notice.

Placing the coffee on my desk, I pulled my laptop from my oversized purse. After booting up *my precious*—yes, that sounded like voice of Smeagol from the Lord of the Rings in my head—my desk was jarred as someone settled in behind me. Receiving no apology, I was prepared to scold the ill-mannered culprit, but Dr. Forster entered the room, derailing my reprimand.

"Good morning future corporate giants. It's a pleasure to see so many familiar faces. Welcome to Business Strategy."

As Dr. Forster distributed the syllabus, he briefly recounted the course description. Following his first lecture of the semester, he thanked us for our attention and kindly dismissed us twenty minutes early—I loved when professors wrapped early the first day. The sound of students preparing to depart echoed behind me until the professor spoke.

"I'm sorry everyone. I neglected to take attendance, a consideration in your final grade. Before you depart, allow me to correct my oversight. Feel free to respectfully exit once I have called your name."

As the roll call began, I shut down my laptop and slid it into my purse. I was poised and ready when he called my name—"Carsen, Everleigh."

"Present," I responded as I quickly reached for my belongings. In a moment of sheer clumsiness I knocked over my coffee, groaning at my inelegance while assessing the damage. Mercifully, the cup was nearly empty, but enough spilled to require minor clean up. Frustrated I hunted through my bag for the tissues playing hide-and-seek. I considered feigning ignorance and leaving, but I would feel guilty if I left the mess—stupid conscience.

At the exact moment my fingers connected with the crinkly rectangular package, I heard the unthinkable—"Charles, Hunter." I halted all movement as if I had looked directly at Medusa and turned to stone, not a muscle or hair shifted. From the seat directly behind me, I heard, "Here," in the same low baritone that chastised me earlier.

I was reeling, a slight wheeze escaping just before the chorus of "Sweet As Hole" began playing through my mind, causing an unsanctioned laugh to spring forth. I slapped my hand across my mouth desperate to stifle the sound. Unfortunately, the hilarity of the song coupled with how apropos it was for the man seated behind me would not be contained. Hell, I was tempted to turn around and inquire if he had ever met Sara Bareilles personally as it clearly was her ode to him. At that thought, the last of my composure crumbled. With effort I managed to remain silent, but my shoulders shook with muted laughter. Wiping the desk with shaking hands while caught in clutches of my humorous musing proved challenging.

"Are you having a seizure? I don't see a medic alert bracelet," he whispered. His tone was staid, but I also detected a hint of amusement. No, that couldn't be. Any humor I heard must be at my expense, he was mocking my clumsiness. What a jerk!

I immediately lost the mirth that possessed me moments ago. Satisfied the desk was sufficiently dried, I rose with my belongings in hand and fled for the door projecting serenity, but internally it was an emergency evacuation mission. As I exited, I detected his presence tailing behind me.

"Would you like to tell me what brought on your epileptic fit?" he inquired smugly.

It was the perfect set-up—a gift given to me to redeem all that had gone awry today. I spun around to face him, forcing him to stop abruptly.

It was cruel. How could he be even more enticing than before? His hair was damp from a recent shower, though he still had not shaved. He wore a thin knit sweater that emphasized his expansive shoulders, defined pectorals and developed biceps. His jeans showcased the powerful thighs beneath, temptingly. I wished for the superpower to freeze time, allowing me to behold his derriere, confident it would be awe-inspiring. A black leather racing jacket dangled from his right hand where I spotted a wide hammered silver band on his middle finger. Why was that stupid ring obscenely sexy?

Regaining my composure—despite his penetrating crystalline eyes—I asked the question that would not be refused.

"Have you ever met Sara Bareilles?"

He shook his head, puzzled. "Who? I don't think so."

"Are you certain? I would have bet every dime in my savings account you knew her." Granted, my savings account was pathetic, but it was all I had.

"I'm positive." He was thoroughly perplexed, mentally reviewing the entire catalogue of women he had ever met. He shook his head again assured there was no Sara Bareilles in his memory bank.

"Why did you think I knew her?"

"Perhaps I was mistaken," I replied sweetly, feigning innocence. "Sara wrote the most remarkable song, and after meeting you, I was positive you were her muse. The description was so precise, it seemed logical that you knew her personally."

He eyed me skeptically, "What's the name of the song?"

"Nevermind. If you don't know her, it's not relevant."

I abruptly turned on my heel and headed for the exit. I was feeling sassy after the exchange, triggering an extra sway in my hips as I sauntered away.

Following my second and last, class of the day, I was in need of a restorative cup of coffee. I debated my options, deciding on Cup O'Joe, the small University owned coffee shop, which offered the best on-campus coffee. I entered to the voice of Meg, my favorite barista, greeting me.

"Hey Ev. Want your usual?"

"It has been a rollercoaster of a day. Dark Brazilian Santos is necessary for recalibration," I replied after careful consideration.

"What size?" Meg inquired.

I stared silently until she made eye contact and chuckled. "Right, Ph.D. it is."

"Unless there is a larger size available now? The B.A. and M.A. only serve as an appetizer for me," I replied sharing her delight in my well-known addiction. When speaking of coffee, amongst other things, bigger is always better.

"I tried to persuade them to sell gallon size jugs for you. I even suggested we keep the plastic milk containers in lieu of a cup. Management thought I was kidding," Meg shrugged, "Black?"

"You know it. I don't see the point in selecting the perfect bean just to dilute its luscious body and flavor with milk and sugar. It's sinful, I tell you."

Meg smirked at my usual rhetoric. When she directed a pointed look to the new barista beside her, I realized I had been baited. My reply must have been the evidence necessary to verify stories she shared about my epic love affair with coffee. Oh well, if I had to be remembered for something at least I wasn't reputed for kicking puppies or stealing candy from babies. I grabbed my twenty-four ounce Ph.D. and headed next door to the buffet.

With a grilled chicken sandwich and soup in hand, I searched the tables and found Sam by the windows.

"I knew I would find you here," I declared proudly as if I had just mastered nuclear fusion. "It was a safe bet," she replied while taking a bite of her pizza. "Are those your new skinny jeans?" "They are," I answered, quickly confessing, "along with your sweater." She nodded, not minding my thievery. "Those jeans are killer. I love the combination with *my* sweater and those boots."

I smiled at her approval. Sam was as opinionated about clothing as I was about coffee. She taught me much over the years, *taught* being a generous description. To be accurate, she beat her will into me over the last fifteen years. Now I wouldn't dare go out in public in my flannel pants and worn sweatshirts, having learned that lesson the hard way. When caught trying to sneak out freshman year, Sam withheld coffee until I returned to my room and removed the offending clothing from my person. Many people subscribe to the theory—dress for the job you want. Sam concurred, but her real mantra was, "Dress for the man you want...and make the bitches jealous." Clothing didn't have to be designer, but every outfit must be strategized to convey a message. Yes, she is crazy, but everyone has their hang-ups, so I overlooked her clothing tyranny.

"How were your classes? You're done for the day, right?" Sam asked.

"Yep, I'm working a swing shift at Higher Yearning from three until eight." My job in a top-notch coffee shop located adjacent to campus was not work to me. It was a veritable playground filled with fragrant coffee beans, my idea of heaven. "My classes were okay," I stalled to generate suspense for my big reveal, "and the Karate Kid was in my Business Strategy class."

Sam paused, pizza halfway to her mouth. "You're kidding. That must have been awkward."

"Actually it was invigorating," I replied cryptically, wanting a dramatic reveal for my triumph. "We had an *exchange*."

"Spill it," Sam demanded, losing patience.

"Actually, that is how it all started," I mused before continuing to give her the blow-by-blow.

Sam gasped. "It was...it was...perfection," she paused to collect her thoughts. "I think this may be one of your finest verbal altercations to date. He doesn't even know you were insulting him," she marveled.

Content with the knowledge my best friend appreciated my duplicity, I sighed. Only a true friend can revel in your achievement as if it was their own.

"It was the least he deserved after berating me. I'll have to see him in class for the rest of the semester; I couldn't employ a direct strike, it had to be the Trojan horse of retaliations."

"What if he figures it out? You just called him an asshole in the guise of a compliment. I can't imagine he would appreciate the sentiment, despite its brilliant delivery and execution," Sam worried.

"He probably isn't bright enough to figure it out."

"He's attending Hensley, he can't be an idiot," Sam reasoned, "I haven't seen him on campus before. You?"

"Nope. He seems a bit old to be an undergrad. Maybe he is auditing courses in return for teaching the seminar. There's enough space in the classrooms with the mass exodus of female students."

Sam nodded in agreement. "He mentioned his family owns Higosha Dojo—the big chain of martial arts schools across the East Coast. He is probably taking business classes for the good of the family empire."

"Which reinforces my point that he won't clue in to my insult. His family probably bought his way into Hensley," I concluded confidently.

"Whatever you say. The class was actually decent—challenging but instinctive. You should try again next week; you would enjoy it if you gave it a chance."

"I would enjoy it if He-Man and She-Ra weren't the instructors, and if I hadn't been disrespected. My pride is worth more than free self-defense training."

"Pride goeth before a fall," Sam returned in a terrible Scottish accent. "Seriously, nothing has changed since this morning—the bad guy is still at large. If something were to happen to you—God forbid—I would never forgive myself for not forcing you to return."

Sam played on my conscience to get her way. She rarely wielded guilt to manipulate me, but when she did, it had a one-hundred percent success rate.

"Fine, but don't expect me to become teacher's pet."

"Yay!" Sam clapped her hands in approval. "Besides, Hunter was a terrific teacher, professional and patient."

"I already got a taste of his professionalism in class. I'm not sure I can take much more."

"In all fairness, you *were* interrupting," she gently reprimanded.

"You're defending him?" I asked disappointed by her lack of backing.

"I find your caustic tongue absolutely hilarious, but there's a time and a place."

"From the girl who says anything that crosses her mind, no matter how personal or graphic."

"Guilty as charged," Sam affirmed proudly, "but I do switch on my filter when required, such as in a professional or educational setting. You never switch your filter to the 'on' position."

Dang, she had a point and, by the smirk on her face, she knew it.

"You may have a point," I conceded. "I might have been slightly disrespectful in choosing to share my thoughts at that precise moment." Sam was about to praise my admission, but I continued, "However, it didn't warrant being ejected."

Sam sighed dramatically, "You're right. He was probably making an example of you to stress the seriousness of the situation."

I was about to launch into another rant about Mr. Hunter Charles' behavior when Sam cut me off.

"It's over. You need to let it go so we can start with a clean slate next week. Give the seminar a chance; it's important."

Chapter Three

"My sexual orientation? Horizontal, usually."
-Unknown

When I arrived on campus Thursday morning, I obtained my mandatory cup of coffee before heading to class. Several students were already present, but my customary front row seat was vacant. Business Ethics, my final undergrad course; I couldn't believe graduation would arrive in four months, and I would finally have my Bachelor's degree in Business Management.

The person coming down the aisle on my left stumbled over my purse protruding in the aisle. I raised my eyes to offer my apology and stiffened. Not again, this could not be happening to me. I blinked repeatedly hoping my eyes were deceiving me. Just to be certain, I blinked again. He was sinful in navy wool trousers and a light blue shirt. Damn him and his supermodel gene pool! Recognizing I must address the interloper, I pasted a fake smile on my face.

"Hello, Mr. Charles. Fancy meeting you here." Cheesy, but it was the best I could do in my current condition. Was fate toying with me? Had I committed some grievous crime unaware, for which I must now pay?

"Hello, Miss Carsen." He returned my greeting while occupying the seat behind me...again, "I'm surprised to see you, too. Although there are a limited number of advanced business courses offered in the morning, so odds were high we would share a course or two. You're a business major, I presume."

"Yes, I am. Are you?" I asked him suspiciously.

"No. I already have my Bachelor's from Columbia in Sociology. I decided to enroll in several upper level business courses that I regret not taking during my undergrad studies."

"You already completed your degree and returned for more by choice?"

He shrugged casually. "It's beneficial to my family's business interests for me to have the extra classes. I don't mind. I've always enjoyed learning."

"Aren't you the overachiever," I retorted, frustrated that he had disproven my dunce theory.

Then it happened—his million-watt smile hit me full blast. His lips quirked slightly higher on the right side, permitting me to see a row of straight pearly whites peeking out. Am I drooling? I stealthily wiped the corners of my mouth. I asked again—what deity had I offended or profaned resulting in this torture?

"Did you have braces?" I blurted suddenly, searching for any imperfection, willing to settle for one that was no longer visible.

"No," he answered puzzled, "I do have three implants from competition injuries though."

"That's something I suppose." I sullenly clung to the image of him missing his four front teeth. You would think this would extinguish the fire of my lust. Apparently, Hunter would be smokin' hot even without teeth.

His astonished gaze met mine, undoubtedly prepared to ask for an explanation to my peculiar comment, but I was saved by Dr. Kull's arrival. I whipped around, temporarily rescued.

At the end of the lecture, I roughly shoved *my precious* into my bag, grabbed my possessions, and dashed for the door.

I succeed in covering half the distance to the exit when he called me. I pretend not to hear as I clumsily pulled on my jacket. "Miss Carsen," he reiterated. Again, I played deaf. "Everleigh," he nearly shouted with exasperation. I considered the ramifications of ignoring him and sprinting for the exit until two simultaneous obstructions stopped me. First, Hunter stepped directly in front of me, effectively blocking my getaway. Second, while winding the scarf around my neck, I was unaware the end had caught in the sleeve of my jacket as I effectively managed to strangle myself. Every effort to free the scarf only tightened my noose. The only redeeming aspect of this nightmare—if my escape failed, I could kill myself and be saved from further indignity.

Hunter carefully placed his hand over mine, and stilled the jerking motion that further deprived me of oxygen. He extended one finger, silently requesting a moment as he studied my predicament. After a series of calculated maneuvers, he draped the scarf loosely around my neck; how he managed to free me without dissolving into laughter remained a mystery.

"There we go. The oxygen deprivation must have impaired your hearing, explaining why you didn't stop sooner."

"Thank you. I have to get going now," I said, intending to step around him.

He neatly repositioned himself to block my flight. "I just need a moment of your time. I did save your life, you owe me."

"Calling in your favor for saving my life so soon? Fine, what do you need?" I tried to sound unaffected.

"Why thank you, Miss Carsen. I greatly appreciate your sacrifice," his tone lacked the acid his sarcasm should generate. "I wanted to tell you I identified the song you referenced yesterday. I listened to hours of Sara Bareilles' music to locate it. She is remarkably talented, don't you agree?" he asked conversationally. I hesitantly nodded my agreement. "I wanted to thank you for your compliment; I was touched that you felt I exemplified the song so completely that you were convinced it was written for me."

"What song would that be?" I hedged, certain his ego had guided him to the wrong song.

"Not Alone," he paused, "of course. The part about him not having to fight for her. Very touching."

"That wasn't the song I was referencing. I'm not even familiar with it."

"*Really?*" He drew out the word dramatically. "Then to which song were you referring?" He grinned like a cat who ate the canary.

The manipulative, conniving, scheming snake. He knew precisely what I had implied yesterday, having decrypted my slur. How dare he pretend I paid him a compliment? He was undermining my moment of greatness.

"You..." I trailed off desperate for words to reflect the magnitude of my anger. I looked him dead in the eyes and started again. "Sir, you are no gentleman."

With that parting gem, courtesy of Scarlett O'Hara from 'Gone with the Wind,' I strode to the exit, my shoulders back and head held high.

As I reached the door, he called to me, "And you, Miss, are no lady."

Shoulders sagged and my head bowed, I left defeated. He had done it again. Twice in as many days, that blasted man had circumvented my inspired attacks. What man can quote a scene from the 1939 film classic? That does not happen in real life, hell, it doesn't even happen in books. I halted hastily in the middle of the parking lot. Of course—how obtuse I have been—it was as obvious as a hooker at a debutant ball—Hunter. Was. Gay. It explained his extraordinary looks, for no straight man looks that good—it's God's joke at women's expense. It explained his dislike of women, at least this woman. It explained his willingness to sit and listen to emotive music and contemplate the lyrical significance. Most importantly, it was the only plausible explanation for him quoting Rhett Butler, the dashing yet scandalous civil war hero from the gold standard of chick-flicks.

A horn blared pulling me from my revelation, and I realized I was a statue in the middle of the parking lot. With an apologetic wave to the inconvenienced driver, I proceeded to my car. The mystery was solved to my relief. While there was no excuse for his rude behavior, I better understood Hunter. It wasn't personal, just a couple of body parts I possessed that were not his preference. I smiled with indulgent understanding. Actually, he was amusing in a Machiavellian kind of way, entertaining though sharp and judgmental. Despite his character flaws, if Hunter was a woman, I would befriend her. As a straight man, he unsettled me and was patronizing. However, as a gay man...what girl doesn't want a brooding, snarky, beautiful, gay best friend?

I had yet to consider the possibilities of his friendship as it pertained to my dating pool. Gay or straight, hot guys were friends with hot guys—birds of a feather. Hunter was my ticket to a new selection of drop-dead sexy fresh meat.

Crystal must have secretly hoped to convert him to team hetero. No wonder Hunter didn't reciprocate her advances. He didn't reject her outright to protect her pride, far more empathetic than I had given him credit.

I couldn't wait to tell Sam about my epiphany. She would be equally excited to expand our duo to a trio. As I drove to work, I turned on Lady Gaga's "Born This Way" and sang along enthusiastically.

⁕ ⁕ ⁕

After work, I headed home and found Sam sitting on the sofa reading a textbook.

"Hi, girlie. How was work?" Sam asked, looking up from her text.

"Great. I had an enlightening day." I geared up to share my revelation with Sam.

"I want to hear all about it, but before you share the details, I need a favor. I have been reading this calculus textbook for the last four hours. I'm in desperate need of fun before I turn into an automaton. Will you come to The Stop with me tonight?" The Bus Stop, commonly referred to as The Stop, was our favorite local bar.

"Sam, it's only the first week of classes, not even a full week, how can you possibly be turning into a robot already?" I didn't want to go out after working an eight-hour shift.

"You read one page of 'Theorems of Calculus' and you will understand the danger. Just a couple of drinks. Neither of us have class tomorrow," Sam pleaded.

"Okay, let's get dressed and head out. Are we wearing pants or dresses? Subtle or flashy?"

Sam grinned at my quick change of tune. "Pants, it's freezing outside. Understated sexy is the theme for clothing, hair, and make-up. Heels are required, there is no snow on the ground, so don't even bother trying to come up with an excuse. Now, scoot!"

After I showered, styled my hair, and applied my make-up, I slid into a vintage pair of black cigarette pants and a pin-tucked tuxedo shirt. I added a wide patent leather cincher belt, gold cuff bracelet, and a string of pearls. I completed the outfit with my black patent leather stilettos. Finished, I glance in the full-length mirror, pleased with the results.

Sam met me near the door appraising my wardrobe selection, "Well done. I have taught you well, young Jedi."

I shook my head at her Star Wars film reference. "Shall we?"

The Stop was the most popular bar in the area for the over twenty-one crowd, servicing mostly university students and young professionals. Designed as a pub, the exposed brick walls and wood floors established an atmosphere of relaxed sophistication. A small stage where local artists performed and a separate game room (including pool, foosball, and shuffleboard tables) exemplified the bar's laid-back recreational appeal. The Stop defied every cliché by strictly carding at the door, requiring valid identification verified by scanner. An additional benefit, the lack of underage girls deterred slime balls who sought inexperienced, easily persuaded, and less self-possessed targets.

We proceeded directly to the bar to find warmth of the liquid variety. I was surprised to hear piped music, as Thursdays promised live performers until midnight. The atmosphere was subdued despite the crowd, as if the music was dictating the temperament of the patrons.

We secured two stools at the long mahogany bar and spied our favorite bartender, Griffin, approaching.

"Hello lovely ladies. Good to see you both, it's been a couple of weeks. What can I get you?"

"We'll both have pomegranate mojitos, thanks," Sam ordered with a flirty smile.

He returned with our cocktails, smiling at Sam as he set our drinks before us. Sam extended a twenty but he waved it off.

"These are on the house, a welcome home drink. Besides, they may prove to be medicinal in a few minutes. I don't feel right charging you to lessen your prospective suffering."

"Thanks?" Sam and I replied in unison, both lost after his confusing statement. The Stop never gives free drinks. Never.

We clinked our glasses before enjoying our first sip. From the corner of my eye, I noticed Griffin, who had served us drinks minutes ago, mounting the stage. Ah, medicinal—I get it. He must be the live music for the evening. He didn't have much faith in his abilities if he believed his performance would necessitate alcohol to be tolerable.

I had seen Griffin countless times during my tenure at Hensley, both working at the bar and on campus. Neither Sam nor I had spoken with him beyond polite acknowledgements, but he always bestowed a smile or chin lift when he saw us. Despite our previous interactions, I felt I was seeing him for the first time. He was at least six feet four and strong, not artificial like a bodybuilder, but naturally muscled. An image of him dressed as the superhero Thor sprung to mind, which I instantly resolved not to share, unsure if he would see it as the compliment I intended. His wavy blonde hair glowed like a halo in the spotlight adding an ethereal quality. His facial features were decidedly Nordic with a square face and jaw, light eyes, high cheekbones, and a wide mouth with full lips. He could easily pass for a Viking, minus the raping and pillaging.

"Hi everyone, I'm Griffin Evensen. The artist scheduled to perform was a no show," he paused to allow the crowd to 'boo' their disapproval of the flakey musician, "so you're stuck with me. Don't worry, I'll restrict myself to covers, you won't have to suffer any clumsy originals. The silver lining is the set is only forty minutes, and the bar will remain open."

He smiled self-deprecatingly. He was charming, whether he sang in key or not, his introduction had earned him a fan. After positioning the acoustic guitar, he settled against a stool, trying to appear relaxed and failing miserably. The guitar seemed tiny against his vast body, similar to an average-sized man playing a ukulele. His entertainment score rose further as I couldn't fathom how he would finger the frets with his mammoth hands. He cleared his throat nervously before strumming the opening cords of "I'm Yours" by Jason Mraz. He was a masterful guitar player, just as good as the original track. It was the perfect opening song, inspiring Sam and me to bop and sing along.

His voice was fantastic, complimenting the song, and he was perfectly in tune, a pet peeve of mine. As his set unfurled his confidence rose, allowing him to relax and lose himself in the music. His set planning was clever—he transitioned from fun songs to comforting songs that offered greater depth of meaning, and I was captivated. After the final chords rang out, the trance holding everyone silent broke, the cheers and applause were nearly deafening. Sam and I whistled our approval as loudly as we could manage, trying to voice our praise above the roar of the crowd.

"Wow!" Sam whispered reverently. "He was amazing, I never would have expected that voice to come out of his body. And his set was brilliant! We should make a playlist with all those songs."

I agreed, and we texted ourselves the set list to download tomorrow.

"You still have to tell me about your enlightened day," Sam made air quotes around the word enlightened. "Spill it."

Sam listened intently as I recounted my run in with Hunter in painstaking detail. She snorted, unsympathetic to my plight of tolerating Hunter in another class. She believed fate was having a laugh at my expense and was smug when I revealed my presumptions about Hunter's intelligence were proved false. I edited out my near strangulation by scarf, determined to retain a small shred of dignity.

"...enlightenment struck on the way to my car—Hunter is gay!"

Sam was unconvinced. "Are you sure? That wasn't the vibe I picked up; my gaydar needle didn't even twitch."

"I'm positive," I stressed, then proceeded to share my observations as evidence. Yes, I was stereotyping terribly, not all gay men could be identified by looks, behavior, or attitude, and he didn't tick many of the points on my pigeonholed checklist. It was necessary to examine the nuances of Hunter to support my conclusion.

"You know what this means, don't you?" Sam stared at me blankly, clueless to the source of my excitement. "He is going to be our third Musketeer! It will be perfect."

"Insta-friend? I'm not sure, Ev. I see the draw for us. But what's in it for him? You've been rather insulting where he is concerned. He may not be receptive to your sudden attempts at camaraderie."

"He was rude to me first!" I nearly shrieked in defense. "Plus, I think he was enjoying the verbal warfare. It's a game now—albeit one he keeps winning—but I'll get points on the board soon. How could he not want to befriend us? Beautiful, smart, witty, fun, and loyal; he won't be able to resist."

"Should we devise an induction ceremony for him?" she mocked my excitement. After visible consideration she continued, "There would be benefits to finally having a gay bestie. Think of the pointers and insight he could provide on blowjob techniques alone. With his input, I could be legendary; no man would be beyond my reach. Do you know how many fights with future boyfriends my oral finesse could prevent? I'd even be able to persuade a man to see a romantic comedy with me *after* he was getting some." She gasped, clapping her hands excitedly, "Can you fathom how many pieces of jewelry this sexpertise would coax from my future husband?" These realizations had earned her full support of my nomination.

"Sam, too much information. Filter, please," I scolded, but smiled inwardly at her shared eagerness.

"Which part?"

"All of it."

Sam fully embraced Hunter as our soon-to-be third, even enumerating the advantages if he were here with us. As we danced she added, "It would definitely help to repel the riffraff two girls dancing together attracts."

As if on cue, a cute boy appeared behind Sam. She looked into my eyes for a cue—catch or release? I subtly pushed her shoulder causing her to lean into cute boy's chest, which was all the encouragement Sam needed. Spinning around she began to dance—or more accurately grind—with him and he offered no complaints.

I continued to dance adjacent to them, providing space but still indicating I was not alone trolling for men. I felt a body press against me from behind as hands gripped my hips. I turned my head to admonish the unsolicited advance and found Lincoln grinning widely, much to my relief. Linc and I had become friends freshman year and often danced together when we were out. It was innocent fun with no genuine hunger between us.

The night ended with my promise to meet Linc for lunch the next week, and Robbie—Sam's cute boy—attaining her number.

Chapter Four

"When we honestly ask ourselves which
person in our lives means the most to us, we
often find that it's those who, instead of giving
advice, solutions, or cures, have chosen rather
to share our pain and touch our wounds with
a warm and tender hand." -Henri Nouwen

I woke Friday morning at 11:00, a luxury for me, and found
Sam at the kitchen table eating breakfast.

"Coffee's in the pot, Eggo's in the toaster," she offered
succinctly.

I grunted before continuing to the kitchen to fill a mug with
my first cup of the day. I carried my coffee and waffles to the
table, almost ready to test my language skills, but not
quite. Sam recognized the signs and resumed her chatter.

"Robbie texted me this morning."

I raised one eyebrow to communicate my surprise and
approval.

"He invited me to dinner tonight. I don't have to work, so
technically I'm free. Do I seem too available if I say yes?"

I raised both eyebrows to communicate disapproval.

"Yeah, yeah, no games. If I like him and I want to go, I
should accept. He did text me within nine hours of receiving

my number," Sam sighed, "Okay, I'll do it. You always give the best advice."

I smiled wryly, knowing I had contributed little to her decision. Having consumed sufficient coffee, I was finally ready to speak. "Glad to help. He seemed nice enough and was cute. Go and enjoy yourself, but be careful, there are crazies on the loose."

I tried to joke, but we both had exercised caution when dating the past year. Prudence was a hindrance to casual dating. During my first two collegiate years I dated liberally, accepting most invitations. I generally liked people, and enjoyed a casual dinner while becoming acquainted; I was no hussy, though I did enjoy the attention of the opposite sex. When the attacks began, caution dictated I select my dates more discriminately. As the violence persisted, many suspected the perpetrator was a Hensley student, forcing me to exercise additional caution. With no suspects, I feared the possibility of finding myself on a first date with a perp. Consequently, I spent more time dancing with friends, such as Linc, than any potential suitor over the past year. One more reason to despise the lowlife—he was squelching my romantic pursuits,

"I'll text him now to accept," Sam announced animatedly.

Thinking of our recently established first date safety protocol, I said, "Remember to text me every few hours to check-in. I'll expect you home by midnight if I don't hear otherwise. Please don't forget, I don't want to contact the police for no reason. I read an article in Newsdaily that stated the police were inundated with missing person reports. The violence increased paranoia and spurred a ton of false alarms."

"Yes, mom," Sam chided me for my parental tone.

I arrived at work, ready to conquer the day. Higher Yearning was a staple in the community, located on one of the main thoroughfares in the central shopping area of Suffolk County. The middle to upper-class residential neighborhoods surrounding the shop provided ample clientele. A light brick exterior with large glass windows painted an inviting

picture. The marquee, anchored above a black and grey
striped awning, was mammoth and beveled with notched
corners in espresso colored wood. The letters were scripted in
a quirky font and inlaid silver. Between the word 'Higher' and
'Yearning' was a gold inlaid carving of a book resting beneath
a coffee mug with wisps of steam rising up.

Inside the shop, walls of exposed brick were dressed with
black and white photos of local landmarks framed in
black. Crystal chandeliers hung from the ceiling and chic wall
sconces provided ambient lighting. The seating area was
spacious with a mixture of red velvet couches, modern
wingback chairs in a gray damask, and espresso wood bistro
sets, creating separate conversation areas that could be easily
re-arranged. The wall behind the service counter was painted
red to match the couches, serving as a dramatic backdrop for
the multi-level glass showcase.

"Hi Marty, I'm here," I greeted my boss.

"Thank God. The paper order arrived today but still needs
to be checked and stored. The new girl called out...again. The
bakery order needs to be placed for next week, and I still need
you to go through the online catalogue of beans to select the
special next month." Marty always seemed frazzled, but today
she was extra-tweaked.

"No problem, Marty. I will get it all accomplished."

Over the past three years my responsibilities at Higher
Yearning consistently increased. I managed the staff,
scheduling, and supplies, while also keeping abreast of
competition in the area and new trends. Marty eagerly
relinquished any task for which I was willing to assume
responsibility. She was a wonderful woman, but she was burnt
out, after operating the successful business for twenty
years. With an empty nest, Marty wanted to retire with her
husband, allowing them to fulfill their dreams of traveling while
young and fit.

Timing is everything in life. I came into Marty's life when
she began to contemplate her future retirement. Marty came
into my life when I was discerning a career path and how to

journey from 'wanting' to 'doing.' Voilà—two people with symbiotic needs and aspirations. I loved coffee the way a sommelier loved wine, the way Bill Clinton loved an intern; I knew I wanted my own business, where the fruits of my labor benefited me directly. Once I met Marty, I realized that my desire to own a business and my love for coffee could be combined to forge my profession.

Having accomplished my chores, I checked in up front to ensure all was under control, releasing the barista for her break. I poured myself a dark roast and enjoyed a few sips before ducking below the counter to take inventory of the flavored syrups. The chime alerted me to an incoming customer as I hurried to finish my count. As I popped up from my squat and greeted the unseen patron standing before me. Once recognition dawned, I froze...again.

Hunter stood before me in all his masculine glory. His hair was windblown, effortlessly sexy, begging me to tame the errant locks with my fingers. His aquamarine eyes absorbed the overhead lighting and reflected at me with laser precision. What was he doing here? I was prepared to snap at him when I remembered my intention to befriend him. I graced him with a wide genuine smile and started over.

"Hello Hunter, what a pleasant surprise. What can I get you? Any beverage you want, it's on me."

Hunter was dumbstruck, equally shocked to find me behind the counter as by my radical change in temperament. He studied me for several moments, assessing my sincerity, but not reaching a conclusion. I stifled a snort when he tilted his head and shifted slightly as if a new angle might bring the situation into focus.

"Hi Everleigh, it's nice to see you, too. I'll have a large black coffee." His apprehension pronounced, unsure if I was escalating our game to another level.

"Sure thing. What type did you want? Is it to stay or to go?" I questioned in my sweetest voice.

"Just black, no sweetener or milk. To stay," he said with growing concern on his face.

"No problem, but what *type* of coffee? Columbian, Brazilian Santos, Papua New Guinea, Ethiopian Yirgacheffe, Costa Rican Tarrazu? The menu is on the wall if you want to review all the options. Oh, we have an amazing Kona special this month, it's a bit pricy but we all need to indulge once in a while," I smile encouragingly.

"Are you trying to mess with me again?" he accused cynically.

"What? Absolutely not. I just want to make sure I pour your preferred bean. I can usually guess a customer's preference, but you're tough to predict. There's more to you than meets the eye, something deeper beneath the surface."

I hoped he comprehended my acknowledgment of his secret and that it made no difference to me.

"Beneath the surface, huh?" He suddenly looked incredibly uncomfortable. "I'm not familiar with most of the coffees you just listed. I'll stick to Columbian, it's the only one I recognize."

His apologetic tone was familiar; first-timers were unprepared for our vast selection. Usually I poured medium-bodied Columbian when I spotted the overwhelmed expression.

"Coming right up."

He watched my every move cautiously, and I became disconcerted by the attention. "You can take a seat. I'll bring it over in a minute."

"That's okay, I'll wait for you to finish," he replied, reluctant to leave me unattended with his beverage.

Was he afraid I was going to poison him? Did he not notice how nice I was being?

"Hunter, I'm not going to poison you. This is my place of work, it would be unprofessional and bad for business. Furthermore, I have a feeling we are going to become good friends; poisoning you may put a damper on that budding friendship."

"Thank God, if it weren't for the sarcasm I would've been concerned you had been body snatched by aliens." He offered me one of his dazzling smiles, "So we are going to be good friends? Why the change of heart? I thought your opinions of me were resolutely in enemy territory."

"Absolutely we will be friends; in fact I need to officially introduce you to my best friend, Sam, who was at the self-defense seminar. You'll love her."

"I remember. She seems like a nice girl—very pretty—but I'm not interested in a relationship with her if you're playing matchmaker."

He thought he had identified the motive for my change in disposition, and I rolled my eyes at him.

"You are ridiculous. I'm not trying to set you up with Sam, you're not attracted to her, it would make no sense."

"Okay," he was lost after I denied his theory. "I didn't want ambiguity or assumptions to cause disappointment," he explained, unconvinced I was on the level.

"Stop the conspiracy theories, there's no hidden scheme for you to ferret out. You're new to Hensley and might enjoy the company of new friends. I am only inviting you to hang out for that purpose—got it?" He nodded his lips quirking up in an involuntary smile at my no-nonsense tone. "Maybe we could go shopping next week? Oh, and you have to come dancing next Saturday at The Stop. I need to check out your moves before I officially approve your application."

"Shopping?" He looked bemused. He must really need this coffee to revive him. "I'm not sure if I can fit it in this week; maybe another time. I can probably manage to meet you at The Stop next weekend for a bit, although I wasn't aware I had applied for a position. What position would that be by the way?" He raised his eyebrows questioningly.

"Your acceptance as my back-up dance partner. It's a very prestigious position, I assure you."

"I'm sure it is," he responded with an unidentifiable expression on his face. "I look forward to auditioning," he smirked enigmatically.

I handed him the coffee, trying to determine if I had just been warned of a coming dance floor catastrophe. He accepted the mug with a dazzling smile before making his way to a table.

I monitored him from the corner of my eye as I assisted other customers. I wanted to join him and engage in further conversation, but was thwarted by pesky patrons. I was refilling the bean jars when Hunter returned with his mug, earning himself bonus points.

"Thanks for the coffee, Everleigh, it was delicious. I'll see you in Business Strategy on Monday."

"Yep, see you there. Have a great weekend, Hunter!"

He returned my smile and left.

Phase one of 'charm new friend' was a success. I redefined the tone of communication, illustrated my kindness and generosity, and most importantly, scheduled a playdate for the following weekend. I was proud of myself. He was resistant at first—not trusting my transformation—but he warmed significantly after accepting I didn't intend to kill him.

I checked my phone to confirm I received Sam's first text— "All's well." Perfect.

I was exhausted by the time I finished my shift. My co-worker, Regan, had counted out the till, but her numbers didn't match the sales receipts, never a good thing. I let her leave, and carefully recounted, finding the correct amount was in the drawer—a twenty had found its way into the tens, which Regan hadn't noticed. After finishing the nightly reports and dropping the money in the safe, I set the alarm and locked up.

I walked to my car, which I always parked towards the back of the lot leaving the closer spots for customers, when I felt an unsettling tingle along my spine. I paused and looked around. The lot was deserted, but I felt like I was being watched. I increased my pace, hurrying to my car, but the feeling of unease was growing and I fought to contain my rising panic. It was all my imagination, paranoia. No one was watching me. I fumbled through my bag, trying to locate my car keys as expeditiously as possible. Where the hell were they? I was breathing rapidly, my fear reached a level that caused a physical response. Please, please dear God, help me find my keys. My fingertips connected with the keys in the bottom corner of my purse as a hand grabbed my shoulder.

"Ahhhhh!" I shrieked at a decibel I had never before reached.

The hand released me instantly. "Ev, holy shit, calm down. It's just me, Linc."

I recognized the familiar voice. He was safe, my friend, wasn't he? I spun around to face him, slamming my back painfully against my car door.

"Linc, what are you doing here?" accusation permeated my voice as my heart hammered in my chest.

"Ev?" He examined me carefully, confused by my tone. "Wow, you really are terrified. I'm not going to hurt you, how could you even think that?"

He took a step away, granting me space, making me feel safer, less confined. I looked in his eyes and realized I had hurt him with my suspicion. I was immediate flooded with guilt.

"I'm so sorry Lincoln, of course you would never hurt me. I'm on edge with all the attacks, and I felt someone watching me, I just panicked. Forgive me?"

"Sure, Ev. I understand," traces of disillusionment remained.

He couldn't possibly understand, no man could. It was impossible to explain what it was like to be a woman under the best of circumstances, the awareness of our vulnerability, the inherent wariness. And in these extraordinary circumstances—he could never fathom the effects of living every day under the threat of assault, the constant vigilance required for self-preservation, doubting every man we encountered whether stranger or friend. Even now, in the shadowy parking lot late at night, I could not fully relax and trust Linc; I couldn't fully withdraw my defenses and shook my head sadly.

"We're all paranoid right now, please don't take it personally. It's not you." I tried to smile convincingly, likely failing. "So, what brings you here?"

"I was driving by after a McDonalds run when I spotted your car in the lot I decided to pull in and eat here, make sure you made it to your car safely. I was going to knock on the door to let you know I was here, but I didn't want to scare you," he smiled ruefully. "Guess I failed in that regard."

"Text me next time to let me know you're lying in wait. You took ten years off my life tonight." I swatted his shoulder playfully, beginning to relax.

"Will do, sorry for scaring you. If it's any consolation, I may suffer permanent hearing loss. I am surprised the police haven't shown already with the volume of that scream."

"Thanks for checking on me, it was very sweet." I gave him an awkward one-arm hug. "I need to get home, I'm shot. We're going to be at The Stop this Saturday if you want to come by."

"Sounds good, maybe I will."

We said our goodbyes and I climbed in my car, immediately locking my doors. I was shaking most of the drive home, more from my adrenaline surge than the cold weather, as I tried to ebb my fear.

I exited the bathroom when I heard the front door open and Sam murmuring, presumably to Robbie. I ducked into my room to get dressed and provide privacy.

A few minutes later Sam yelled, "You can come out now." As I headed into the living room she continued, "How was your night?"

I didn't want to talk about my freak out with Linc. Even though Sam would understand, I was still embarrassed by my reaction.

I deflected, "Screw that, how was your night?"

"It was great. He picked me up on time and we had a romantic dinner at Bella Luna. He suggested a drink afterward, so we went to that trendy new martini bar."

"Thank you for the cliff notes version, now can I have the full story? Since when are you stingy with details? Usually I'm begging you to edit."

"I *really* like him, I don't want to jinx it. It was comfortable, almost familiar, but exciting too. We talked about everything—school, work, families, friends, how we envision the future. It was a perfect first date. I even told him about my crazy family and he didn't run for the hills."

"Sam that's fantastic. How was the goodnight?" I wagged my eyebrows suggestively.

"Amazing! He kissed me soft at first, and then got down to business. If his tongue technique was any indication, I will be a fantastically happy girl in the foreseeable future."

"And there is the Sam I've come to expect and cringe from. Overshare!" I shuddered for effect. "Play devil's advocate, what flaws did you find?"

"None really. He is in a fraternity—Kappa Sigma Tau—if you consider that a flaw."

"It's not a ringing endorsement, but it doesn't bar him from competing. Isn't that the frat with more money than sense?"

"Yeah, all of the members are legacy and loaded—well, their parents are at least. They have a reputation for crazy parties and over-the-top pranks, but Robbie swears most of them are good guys."

"At least Robbie is comfortable with affluence. He won't be scared off by your parents if he makes it to that round."

I acknowledged the commonality Sam shared with Robbie, which she had tried to gloss over for my benefit. Sam was sensitive about discussing her family's fortune. An unnecessary concern on her part, but thoughtful nonetheless.

"I invited Robbie to come dancing with us next Saturday." Sam sounded excited.

"Speaking of next Saturday, I invited Hunter to join us." I proceeded to recount his visit and we deemed my mission a resounding success.

Chapter Five

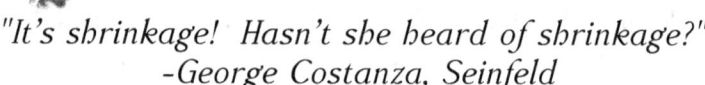

"It's shrinkage! Hasn't she heard of shrinkage?"
-George Costanza, Seinfeld

Monday morning dawned with a thud, literally, as I fell out of bed in the midst of a dream I couldn't remember. I hadn't fallen out of bed since childhood, except for once—but, I was not the only one who fell out of the bed, and it was worth it. This time, all I had to show for my descent would be a bruised hip. After my obligatory cup of coffee, I dressed in dark jeans, navy sequined tank, and my soft cashmere navy cardigan. I threaded a red leather belt through my pants and slipped my feet inside red quilted ballet flats.

I arrived on campus early, killing time in the atrium of the building when I saw Hunter approach. Did the man ever have a bad hair day? He was wearing dark jeans, a navy sweater, and red chucks. The wide hammered silver band on his middle finger reflected the sun, winking at me. I assessed him with disbelief. He made a small gesture with his hand greeting me. Shit! I'd been busted gawking.

I shook my head disapprovingly as he strode toward me.

"Are you spying on me, Mr. Charles?" I asked in my most haughty tone.

"Not in the strict sense of the word, Miss Carsen. Monitoring would be more accurate—for your safety, of course."

I brazenly perused him from top to toe, followed by a pointed glance at myself, "If you aren't spying then how did you manage to copy my attire with such precision? Do you also have plans to dye your hair blonde, too?"

He chuckled while taking note of our matching attire. "I see your point. I debated going blonde as well, to complete the facsimile, but I wasn't sure I had the skin tone to pull it off."

"I was going to invite you to join me for lunch, but clearly it's futile. Whatever would people think?"

"That we share the same chic fashion sense? You could run home and change your clothes before lunch, problem solved."

"Why don't you go home and change?"

"I look too good to deprive the masses," he declared full of self-derision.

"And I don't?" I returned imperiously.

"You, Miss Carsen, are equally alluring and will surely distract the student body."

"I don't think I want to play with you anymore, you always outfox me," I pretended to pout.

"Don't sulk; it doesn't complement your outfit. Besides, you would be bored to tears if I didn't present some challenge."

I conceded—he was spot-on. "It's an odd coincidence. We're wearing our gendered version of the same togs."

"Togs?"

"Clothes," I gestured in exasperation as he smirked. "What? I've been on a British literature kick lately. Stop judging me."

"Come on bibliophile, class is going to begin soon."

Afterwards, Hunter walked with me to the center of campus.

"Where are we meeting for lunch, assuming you're willing to be seen in public with me despite our coordinating attire?"

"If I must," I consented dramatically, "Let's meet at the buffet after class."

Spending an hour in Intro to Acting pretending to be circus animals had worked me into a feeding frenzy. Meg at Cup O'Joe addressed my first necessity and I made my way into the buffet to oblige my second. I scanned the dining area and located Hunter next to the windows. I made my way to the table dodging all forms of obstruction, stationary and otherwise. As I approached, Hunter rose to greet me, gallantly appropriating my tray to place it on the table. He dramatically pulled out my chair and assisted me as I sat. I appreciated gentility as much as the next girl, but the whole scene struck me as abnormal.

"Care to tell me what that was about?" I distrustfully queried.

"I was merely practicing proper etiquette." The twinkle in his eyes belied his innocent excuse.

"You were trying to call attention to our matching faux pas, weren't you?"

"I will neither confirm nor deny."

"Ass," I muttered beneath my breath.

"That is the second time you have called me an asshole," Hunter said sternly.

"I have never called you an asshole—to your face—I simply left a trail of breadcrumbs from which you could deduce my meaning."

"Ah ha. You finally admit that our song is 'Sweet As Hole'."

"I will neither confirm nor deny," I said, mocking his earlier statement.

"It was exceptionally ingenious of you."

"I know, right?"

I caught his smile and realized my mistake. He had tricked me, and I confessed the song I had insulted him with.

"Dammit, Hunter. How do you always outmaneuver me? They should have *you* interrogate suspected terrorists. You would trick them into revealing their evil plot every time."

"Nah, terrorism isn't my specialty." He winked before suddenly whistling, "That is some lunch you have there."

"I'm as hungry as the bear I just spent the last hour pretending to be. A salad was not going to tame my ravenous need. Besides, who am I trying to impress?"

"Not me, that's for sure," he answered quickly with synthetic sorrow.

"Here I thought you were a martial arts instructor. Are you moonlighting as a comedian?"

"Martial arts *is* my moonlighting gig," he paused as if weighing his words. "Where is Sam?"

"I'm not sure. She planned to join us." I searched the dining room and saw her at the cashier with Robbie beside her. "There she is, her new guy Robbie is with her. Don't ruin it for her by—just try not to be yourself for a little while."

"You are a cruel woman, Everleigh."

I waved to get Sam's attention. She gave me a huge smile as she approached and darted her eyes toward Robbie and then widened them to communicate her pleasure at the unexpected company.

"Hi Ev. Hunter this is my...Robbie. I mean, my friend Robbie."

Sam's complexion turned a shade of red I had never before seen. Interesting; Sam never feels embarrassment, even when it would be appropriate.

"Robbie asked me to lunch today, but since we already had plans, I invited him to join us."

"Nice to meet you Robbie," Hunter shook Robbie's hand, "and good to see you again, Sam. I'm glad you're here. I was just asking Everleigh if she felt I was wearing too much blue today. Your opinion would be invaluable."

Sam looked him over. "Looks good to me, it compliments your eyes."

"Are you sure? Everleigh had some objections. Let me stand up so you can consider the full picture."

Hunter rose, stepping back a few paces before slowly spinning around to provide a 360-degree view. I growled loud enough that Sam heard; she glanced in my direction trying to ascertain the source of my angst. Unable to determine the cause of my distress, she turned to offer Hunter the approval he sought, but instead her head whipped back in my direction. She paused taking inventory of me before bending over and ducking her head beneath our table. She returned topside with a look of amusement painted on her face.

Hunter laughed, loudly.

"Alright Zoolander," I said, referencing the over-the-top fictitious model, "you've had your fun, sit down and eat."

Hunter wiped crocodile tears from his eyes while returning to his seat.

"Have you two taken to coordinating your outfits in the morning?" Sam got in on the ribbing, "you haven't made the effort with me since fifth grade, Ev. Are you replacing me?"

"I fully intend to replace you after this betrayal, but Hunter failed his audition as your understudy," I seethed.

"Fantastic. Sam, it appears you now have an opening. I would like to apply, where should I direct my resume? How many references do you require?" Hunter taunted me further.

"Sorry man, I just got the job. Day late, dollar short," Robbie chimed in, joining the roast. "Sam, does this mean we have to start dressing identically, too?"

"Screw you all. I need to find new friends. And you Robbie, I was just starting to like you. You're on my list now—written in pen."

"Sorry Ev, I have to follow the majority, I'm not strong enough to stand on my own against the dominant party."

Despite my words to the contrary, I liked what I had seen of Robbie thus far. He didn't hesitate to join the banter and he was entertaining. He went out of his way to see Sam again before their next scheduled date and adapted to her plans. These were all good signs, Sam was happy and they seem well suited.

"Not to be a downer, but did you guys hear about the attack last night?" Sam redirected the conversation.

"No, I haven't heard anything around campus. What happened?" I asked, concerned another girl had been hurt.

"I overheard a couple of Beta Gamma Gamma girls talking about it in the bathroom. They said one of their sisters was attacked after their sorority meeting—they were really shaken up. Apparently, she was beaten brutally and...sodomized," Sam whispered the last word. "When she didn't come home last night, her roommate called the sorority house to check if she had slept there. A few sisters went to see if her car was in the lot and found her near the trees. She was a mess with rope burns on her wrists and ankles but there was no rope nearby. She's in the hospital, but when she regained consciousness, she couldn't identify the attacker. He came from behind her and put something over her head. The only thing he said was "This is what you want, isn't it?" Sam trailed off, shaken by the recounting.

I prayed for an easing of the victim's suffering and that she was surrounded by love and support. I couldn't imagine how I would go on if I experienced such horror, or worse, if the sadistic bastard harmed someone I cared about. I shuddered at the thought.

I looked around the table and saw Sam shared my thoughts. Robbie was discernibly unnerved, probably imagining the same as me. Hunter looked incensed. We sat silently until the screech of Hunter's chair pushing back against the floor tiles ended our rumination.

"Sorry, I have to go. I'll see you tomorrow, Everleigh. It was good to see you again Sam. Nice meeting you Robbie."

"That was abrupt," Sam said to no one in particular, once Hunter had departed.

"Tragedy impacts everyone differently. Maybe he knows someone who suffered similarly. Did you notice how angry he was when you told us what happened?"

It was the first time I had ever defended Hunter instead of assuming the worst of him.

"I better get going too. I have a ton of reading to catch up on." Robbie leaned over to give Sam a distracted kiss on the cheek before disappearing with less tension than Hunter, but still troubled.

"I sure know how to clear a room," Sam tried to lighten the mood, but it was a lost cause. We were both disturbed by the grim news as we ate our lunch in silence.

Tuesday morning I awoke before my alarm, feeling rested. I poured my morning caffeine fix and decided to relax in front of the TV before getting ready. I was preparing to change channels when a picture of Hensley flashed on the screen, and morbid curiosity got the better of me, so I didn't turn it off. The anchorman reported the attack Sam relayed yesterday, including the fact that this was the fifteenth assault in sixteen months and the perpetrator was still at large. Experts were speculating that more attacks might have occurred previously, but gone unreported. The police had no leads, witnesses, or suspects, and victims were unable to identify their attacker. Sources confirmed that sexual assault occurred during the last assault, but police found no DNA evidence. I turned off the television feeling oppressed by my sorrow for those injured at the hands of a deviant.

When I arrived at Hensley, I purchased coffee and settled on a padded bench along the wall, waiting for Hunter to arrive. If we matched today, an intervention would be added to the week's agenda. A few minutes later I spotted him headed my way.

"Would you believe I almost wore that exact same outfit today?"

"Yes, I would, it seems your style," I teased him, "it would have been an improvement over your current attire."

"It was a long night and a cold morning. I lacked the motivation for anything other than comfortable and warm," he shrugged confident in his ultra-casual appearance.

I nodded, familiar with the feeling. "I've had those days. If Sam didn't hide, cut up, or burn all of my comfy clothes, I may have opted for the same."

"She didn't burn your clothes," he remarked incredulously.

"She despises casualwear in public; it's her crusade. I can only confirm with certainty one pair of flannel pants, but I suspect others have followed in their wake. She fears throwing them out in the trash because she doesn't want to find me riffling through dumpsters. I can't blame her—for a perfectly worn pair of sweats, I probably would."

He laughed, undoubtedly assuming I was kidding. You know what they say about assuming—you make an ass out of you and I'm right. Maybe that was not the exact quote, but I preferred my version.

"Everything okay? You rushed out yesterday like you were on a mission."

"Yeah I did. Those girls should not have been spreading the gruesome details of their friend's suffering in public. I wish Sam hadn't repeated it either, it should be confidential. I had to call work, so it seemed like the right time to leave. Sorry if I was abrupt."

"No need for apology, I was just concerned. I understand your point about protecting the victims. I'm positive Sam's intention was innocent, but she just needed to share the story to relieve some of the burden of knowing. She'd never maliciously gossip—actually she would, and does—but not about anything so serious."

"I know, her compassion was more than evident. Don't feel you need to defend her to me," he smiled understanding my loyalty. "How much time did you spend fretting over my wellbeing yesterday? Did you pace the floor all night anxious, worried I was distraught and alone?"

"Egomaniac. I was worried initially, but then I forgot all about you."

"If that were true you wouldn't have remembered to ask this morning. Evidently my welfare was still on your mind, proof you care."

"Yes, I care—the same way I care about all my friends and even some strangers," I spoke to him as if explaining a terribly abstract concept.

I was a camp counselor one summer and mistakenly mentioned heaven in an off-handed remark to my young campers.

"Miss Ev, what is heaven?"

"Heaven is the place where your soul goes when you aren't here anymore."

"Why wouldn't we be here anymore?"

Obviously, I was not tackling death with a four year old, so I deflected, "I don't know, but that is a really long time from now, so don't worry about it."

"What's a soul?" the curious little bugger continued.

"A soul is the essence that makes you who you are. It exists forever."

"What's essence?" Okay, I had it coming for that poor word choice.

"Essence is the spirit inside your body that thinks and feels emotions like love."

He looked down at his stomach before asking, "Where is it inside me? Can it fall out?"

At this point, I threw in the towel. I had not even entered college yet, and when I finally did and took a Philosophy class, I struggled for the B- I received. That bloody B- has been a blight on my cumulative grade point average ever since. Searching for rescue from the conversational black hole this boy had become, I threw a Hail Mary pass.

"Look, Miss Jessie is giving candy to her campers. Why don't you go ask her for a piece?"

Jessica didn't forgive me for a week once mutiny broke out amongst her kids when she was accused of not sharing candy. "Some strangers? Why not all strangers? What strangers do you not care about? Are you harboring anti-tea drinker sentiments?" Oh no, it was happening again, and I had no make-believe candy to divert this man-child. I had to stop this, or he would warp my mind until I couldn't find my own nose. I gathered as much feigned excitement as I could.

"Oh, Oh, Oh, Hunter look! Isn't that Chuck Norris, the famous martial arts guy?"

He knew I was lying, but the remote possibility got the better of him. He turned in the direction I was pointing as I ran for the restroom.

"Not cool, Ev. Not cool at all," Hunter shouted at my retreating back. "You shouldn't get a man all worked up like that and then take it away. That makes you a co—" he trailed off as if he surprised himself and then resumed, "That makes you a tease, Miss Carsen."

He regained the upper hand in our verbal sparring while I was making my escape. He was too quick, too unruffled. This was getting out of control, in other words—it was getting fun. I reflected on the source of my failures while in the restroom. I had to stop providing opportunity for him to retort; I had to time my verbal blows more precisely. If I left myself open, he would get me every time. A plan developed in my mind that it was now time to execute.

When I walked into class, Hunter was already seated and looking smug. No problem, let him enjoy that victory. It would distract him from my impending evil scheme.

"Do you forgive me Ev? I don't want hostility to get in the way of our verbal warfare."

"Not yet, Mr. Charles, maybe after class."

Dr. Kull entered the room and promptly began his lecture on the importance of ethical business practices to the longevity of a corporation. I took copious notes on *my precious* and absorbed as much as I could. At the end of class, Dr. Kull asked if there were any questions on the lecture, and I raised my hand.

"Dr. Kull, just a quick question. I was debating with Mr. Charles before class regarding the matter of malleable ethics."

"Interesting, go ahead, Miss Carsen," Dr. Kull permitted.

"I understood that ethical business practices, such as discrimination against applicants, were malleable in specific cases. I cited the entertainment industry as an example of times when it was ethically acceptable for a casting director to hire based on gender, ethnicity, and aesthetics. Hunter strongly disagreed. Using my example he stated that, as governed by the Federal Equal Employment Opportunity, EEO laws, the entertainment industry should be held accountable for discrimination in hiring. He claimed a casting agent would violate ethical business practices and could be found discriminatory for rejecting an actor for exclusively aesthetic reasons. Hunter proposed a man auditioning for the lead male role in a pornographic movie who was rejected due to his inferior penis size. Hunter believes this should be considered discrimination under the EEO. He said that as long as the man had a penis and was able to engage in sexual intercourse on camera, the size of his member should not be relevant. He claimed that by systematically rejecting men with smaller penises, the casting agent was violating EEO and there was a substantial potential for a class action suit accordingly. Furthermore, the production was encouraging discriminatory behaviors by altering the perception of women as it pertains to average penis size and the correlation between size and functionality. He was quite adamant about it, actually, and I was wondering if you could settle our debate."

I heard Hunter choke behind me. Priceless. Dr. Kull cleared his throat, collecting his thoughts.

"You and Mr. Charles have certainly presented an interesting case study. I believe you're correct Miss Carsen, the casting agent in question could claim they are selling a fantasy in their films and as such, the size of an actor's penis would be pertinent. Laws and their interpretation do change. It's possible if such a case were to come before federal court, a discrimination judgment could occur. Although, I believe such a ruling is unlikely. Thank you both for your informative participation. See you all on Thursday."

As I walked out of the room, I caught Dr. Kull pat Hunter's shoulder sympathetically. I stifled a giggle and picked up my pace, unsure if my personal safety was in jeopardy. My plan seemed brilliant during its conception and executed beautifully. However, I didn't factor in the sacred relationship between a man and his penis. Inferring that a man's penis size was subpar was tantamount to...well, I do not actually think there is anything worse for a man. I increased my pace to a jog hoping to make a clean getaway, and provide the opportunity for him to cool off before finding the humor in my efforts.

Hunter was suddenly beside me. I was positive he could outrun me, even with my adrenaline pumping, so I slowed to a walk. I decided to speak first to control the tenor of the conversation.

"I forgive you now," I smiled at him as if all was well.

"You do? How magnanimous of you."

I could not read him. Should I make a run for it—on the off chance he tripped over an untied shoelace—providing me the possibility to live another day? I threw caution to the wind.

"Do you forgive me?" I asked meekly.

"There is nothing to forgive."

Say what? Did I hear him correctly? Was he launching an immediate counter-attack?

"You do?" I heard the uncertainty and hope in my voice.

"I do, you were inspired. You trounced me thoroughly and left no quarter for redirection. I bow to your genius," he then bowed to me. "You're the undisputed victor of this battle."

"No hard feelings?" My hopes were rising.

"None at all. I almost swallowed my tongue, but it was worth it. I'm truly impressed, my worthy adversary. I can only respect your ability." He bestowed his captivating smile, which I knew was sincere.

That went better than expected, leaving me confident. "Can I ask you one question?" I ventured. If I didn't ask, it would fester in the back of my mind.

"Shoot."

"It's my understanding that men are sensitive about the size of their equipment. I thought it was unpardonable to insult their manhood." I looked at him to verify my long-held belief.

"That's true," he gestured for me to continue.

"Then why aren't you livid?"

"Because it's only a crime punishable by death if it's true." He raised one eyebrow at me to emphasize his point. "Have a great day, Everleigh."

He sauntered away, leaving me with only one conclusion. He did it again, it should not have been possible! There was no way to recover from the blow I had landed in class, yet he did it. I now have an image of Hunter in my head I will never be able to rid myself of—not that I necessarily want to be rid of it. It was too depressing to dwell on the reality he was only interested in utilizing his impressive appendage as part of a matched set. Thank goodness it was sub-zero or I would have no excuse for my flushed cheeks. Oh well, a girl can dream...vividly.

Chapter Six

*"You have people come into your life shockingly
and surprisingly. You have losses that you never
thought you'd experience. You have rejection
and you have to learn how to deal with that and
how to get up the next day and go on with it."*
-Taylor Swift

It was two hours until close when he walked in. Against my
will, my eyes traveled to his crotch, I hoped that reaction would
not become a permanent affliction. He was clean-shaven,
which was a first. I had a working theory he shaved at night to
ensure he had that sexy stubble all day.

I was about to call out my greeting when I noticed he was
not alone. Crystal came into view shortly after Hunter cleared
the door. She was beautiful in an obvious way—if you're into
that whole perfection thing. She was in her mid-twenties, but
carried herself with the presence of a woman more
established. She wore brown pants that could have been
painted on, and a cream cropped leather jacket was expertly
fitted over a matching turtleneck. Her high-heeled
vanilla/beige snakeskin ankle boots were to die for. Sam would
have pilfered them, regardless of size. Her hair and
complexion were flawless. How she managed to look elegant
and overtly sexy in equal measure was beyond me.

Hunter gave no indication that he noticed me. As they approached the counter, a tingle of apprehension ascended my spine. Why had Hunter not said hello? He knew I worked at Higher Yearning, logic dictated he would look to see if I was here when he entered and greet me accordingly. We had become friends after all; perhaps he was more upset over my stunt today than he led me to believe.

"Hello. I would like a cappuccino with skim milk and a glass of water," Crystal requested politely.

"Hello Hunter, what can I get for you—Columbian black?"

"Yes, that would be great," he responded impersonally.

"To stay or to go?" I directed my question at Hunter, hoping for a reaction.

"To stay, please," Crystal instead responded.

I began to prepare Crystal's cappuccino in one of Higher Yearning's trademark red mugs while surreptitiously listening to their conversation.

"Have you been here before? I've wanted to try their coffee since we began collaborating with the University. Thanks for agreeing to join me."

"I've only been here once before. It's really no trouble," Hunter replied nonchalantly.

"I wish we had time to grab dinner first. Maybe next time?"

"Maybe," he offered noncommittally.

"I know a great Thai restaurant not far from Hensley. They have the best panang curry I've found on the island."

"Sounds good."

She was a dog with a bone, who just wouldn't let it go. Was it not obvious he didn't want to date her? Evidently, she was so unaccustomed to rejection she missed his signals. Short of declaring his sexual preference outright, what more could he say and still maintain politesse? I finished Crystal's cappuccino and poured Hunter's Columbian before presenting them with their drinks.

"I've met you before, haven't I? You look so familiar." Crystal scrutinized me trying to place where we had met.

"Yes, I was at the self-defense seminar last week. You're Crystal, right?"

"Right!" She seemed excited to have solved the mystery, "I remember you now." She paused realizing I had been invited to leave the session.

"You had to leave early last week. I hope you can make it tomorrow."

She kindly overlooked the fact that I had been abruptly kicked out by her companion. It appeared she genuinely wanted me to return. Shoot, I couldn't call her a bitch in my mind if she was going to be nice.

"I'm not sure if I will make it tomorrow," I offered no further justification.

"You have to. Hunter, tell her she has to come tomorrow." Crystal grabbed hold of Hunter's arm beseechingly.

"Miss Carsen is welcome to return to class tomorrow, provided she can do so with the appropriate mindset, and promises not to disrupt the instruction again."

Were we reverting to his original state of being? We had moved passed this, and built a friendship. We even had our thing— bantering and trumping each other. Now he wanted to pretend I was a random acquaintance and resume disparaging me? You can't discuss your third leg with a person, then pretend they are a stranger.

Crystal and Hunter relaxed into a pair of wingback chairs near the front window. Their hushed conversation couldn't be overheard, effectively thwarting my snooping. Occasionally, Crystal would giggle while reaching her hand to touch Hunter with deliberate innocence.

I was fit to be tied by the time they rose and headed out the door. Hunter exited without even a nod while Crystal sent me a small wave with her hope to see me tomorrow. Fat chance! Crystal had proven herself amiable today. She was compassionate and encouraging, graciously "forgetting" her first impression of me. I wasn't about to invite her to be our new third Musketeer, but she had gained my respect.

On the other hand, Hunter had lost my esteem. I was officially revoking his Musketeer status, he would have to turn in his feathered hat and rapier. He could take his bipolar disposition elsewhere, because I was all stocked up on crazy.

After work I headed home, needing to share my exasperation.

"You will not believe what happened today," I declared.

"Uh-oh. It's never a good story with that lead in. Talk to me."

"I fired Hunter."

"I didn't know he was working at Higher Yearning," Sam said, clearly lost.

"I mean I fired him as our third. I have severed all contact, he is dead to me."

I paused, assessing where to begin; the day had been a rollercoaster. Revisiting Hunter's trouser anaconda would be too diverting—especially for Sam—so I omitted that revelation. I outlined the events of the day and ended with my final complaint.

"...and he left his dirty mugs on the table."

"That's really weird. He was so nice at lunch yesterday. He fit in well and I thought you two had moved past all the drama," Sam lamented.

"Right! You can't move past an incident and then bring it back up at a later date as if there had never been a resolution. He doesn't have that right, he's not a woman. We own that privilege exclusively. Possession of a penis bars him from reopening closed cases." I released a sigh heavy with disappointment as I slumped on the couch.

"I admit I was disruptive last week. I feel bad for joking in the face of such ghastliness. I can't fathom why he pulled the one-eighty. Why does it even bother me?"

"He was growing on you and now he's callously discarded you with no warning. You don't let many people in, Ev. You have tons of casual friends and you date liberally, but you're exceptionally selective in who you share yourself with. You were beginning to let him into your life—provided he survived the gauntlet you were throwing down—which is huge for you. I won't give you a hard time for guarding yourself because you're not an emotional hermit. Just don't let this bad experience turn you into one."

"When did you become so sage?"

"The truth, it is, I speak." Sam answered with a surprisingly good impersonation of Yoda.

Sam had an infatuation with the actor Hayden Christensen, which resulted in her watching all of the Star Wars movies on an endless loop for a solid year. I never saw the appeal, but to each her own.

"You still have to come with me tomorrow morning," Sam threatened.

"I most certainly do not. Did you not hear my story?"

"You promised you would do this with me. I don't want to go alone," Sam whined.

"Circumstances have changed. There must be an escape clause for asshole senseis."

"Firstly, it was an ironclad contract—no loopholes. Second, you still have to see him four days a week in class. What's the difference?"

"The difference is that he is the authoritarian at the self-defense seminar. In class he is my equal and no interaction is required."

"Don't you want to confront him when it's your choice to be present and illustrate how unaffected you are by his callous disregard?"

She did have a point there. If I chose to participate, I could show him how little his dismissal meant to me. Still, was it worth risking additional censure? I would have to exhibit my best behavior and be a model student, which was not an appealing prospect. The effort to curb my sarcasm was not worth proving he didn't influence me.

"You almost agreed," Sam remarked to herself.

"I don't want to be forced to behave myself under threat of public castigation. It's not worth it."

"I didn't want to bring it to this level, but you leave me no choice," Sam prefaced, "Are you familiar with the logistics of self-defense training? The instructor demonstrates the techniques and you repeat. After this, the instructor dons a full body suit and you practice all of the skills you just learned in a combative atmosphere to ensure your muscle memory and mind are prepared to defend if necessary. It was a little scary, but a lot of fun."

"I can see the logic," I replied, having no idea where she was going with her latest bid to persuade me.

Sam paused to ensure she had my full attention. "If you participate in the class and are a good little girl during the lecture, you will get a sanctioned opportunity to unleash on Hunter. In fact, in order to comply fully with the seminar you would be expected to put forth your best effort to beat the arrogance out of him."

Forget Marilyn vos Savant, the woman with the highest recorded IQ currently living, to me Sam was the genius.

"This, my calculating friend, is going to be fun."

When my alarm sounded Wednesday morning at 6:30, I crawled from bed with as much enthusiasm as I could muster prior to my consumption of coffee. Today was special. I was going to kick the patronization out of Hunter Charles. I dressed quickly, eager for class.

"Sam, I'm heading out. I'll meet you there," I hollered on my way out the door.

When I arrived, Crystal spotted me and offered her welcome.

"Everleigh, I'm so glad you decided to return. You seemed reluctant yesterday."

"I promised my roommate I would participate in the seminar, and she wouldn't let me break my word."

"I'm glad. Every woman should have the knowledge and basic skills to protect herself." Crystal returned to the front of the room to finish her preparations.

Hunter arrived shortly thereafter, walking by without a glance. I looked to Sam ensuring she noticed the snub. She rolled her eyes in response to his cold shoulder.

Crystal called the class to order and I resolved to pay attention and act appropriately.

"Hello again ladies. It appears everyone has returned for our second session, which thrills me." Crystal proceeded to disperse more safety measures than I could absorb. Thankfully, she had provided a packet containing most of the information she was covering. I highlighted the information I found most pertinent as she reviewed each.

"When in public, pay attention to what is going on around you. Don't talk on your phone or listen to music in a public place."

"Always have your keys in hand when approaching your home or car. Do not unlock your vehicle until you're within arm's reach."

"Position your body so that it would be difficult to approach you from behind without your knowledge. At a party, keep your back to the wall. When unlocking your car, angle your body so your back is toward the car."

"If threatened, appear confident and strong. Perpetrators can be discouraged if the prey looks like it will be too challenging. This is not a hard and fast rule, but submissiveness is rarely a deterrent."

"Everyday items can be used as self-defense weapons. If forced to engage, be resourceful—a rock, hair-spray, pen or pencil, and umbrella have all been used as successful defense tools."

"If you fear you are about to be raped try to vomit, urinate, defecate, spit, anything to detract from your appeal. This will not always be a deterrent, but it has been proven to work. If he provides access to his exposed groin, grab his scrotum, twist, and pull down quickly with all of your strength. This can effectively castrate your attacker."

When Crystal finished, Hunter stepped forward and I suppressed all feelings churning within to focus on the task at hand.

"Crystal has done a wonderful job coaching you on awareness and prevention. I hope that these strategies will be enough to protect you from a predator, rendering everything you learn from me superfluous. Unfortunately that's not always the case; my goal is to prepare you should Crystal's techniques not be sufficient."

"The goal is always to avoid physical confrontation. I don't care if you're an eighth-degree black belt, do not engage unless it is your last resort. The best preventative measure is always escape. You must never allow your attacker to take you to another location."

"Everyone stand up and spread out. We are going to continue learning physical self-defense techniques. If you must engage, your intent is not to punish but to provide yourself the opportunity to run. With that said, if you must defend yourself, commit to it, and do not hold back. In a survival situation nothing is off-limits, there is no such thing as a cheap shot."

"Many of the defense techniques I'm going to demonstrate today derive from Krav Maga, the Israeli national martial art, which is dedicated to no-holds-barred incapacitation for the purpose of street survival. If you wish to continue studying martial arts for the purpose of self-defense, I would strongly suggest Krav Maga. I could suggest a school for you, if needed," Hunter chuckled at his own joke.

Hunter spent time showing us how to break arm holds, which we practiced with partners. He demonstrated various self-defense moves, which we practiced solo before trying the skills against weight bags.

"Let's recap while Crystal and I suit up. Your elbow is the strongest point on your body, use it. If you end up on the ground, use your legs to kick free from your attacker. Go for his weakest points: eyes, nose, ears, throat, groin, and knees. You can also use your head for a forward or backward head-butt. It may sting you, but it will stun him."

Hunter and Crystal attired themselves in protective suits and headgear, which were padded to protect from serious injury to them or us. They were both covered from head to toe, enabling us to practice all the techniques on a willing partner without fear of injury. I examined their padded forms. Damn it—Hunter even looked good dressed like a marshmallow!

When it was my turn to face him, I was ready. My anger had waned during the lecture, until it was only an ember. As I stood before him, he addressed me as "Miss Carsen" in the same impersonal tone he used for everyone else—the fire of my rage flared. I put the full force of my anger into every punch, elbow, gouge, strike, foot stomp, and kick. The entirety of my betrayal culminated in a fierce knee to the groin, which caused Hunter to grunt. He may have been protected, but the force of my blow still registered; I couldn't help but feel satisfied.

After the seminar, I showered and changed in the locker room before heading to class. I walked in and took my seat, never looking at Hunter although I could feel his presence behind me.

When class ended, I gathered my belongings and departed. I only made it twenty feet before Hunter caught up with me.

"Hey ultimate fighting champion, what's the rush?" he asked while easily matching my brisk pace.

I looked at him as if he was insane, which I was beginning to believe he was. He had all of the signs of dissociative identity disorder as per my Psychology 101 class. I focused ahead of me without a word in response.

"Ah, the tried and true silent treatment. My sisters were black belts in the art. Shall I interpret your muteness as a sign of your displeasure?"

Did he just say displeasure? As if he borrowed my pen and neglected to return it. He was stark raving mad, there may be grounds to institutionalize him. I continued my campaign to ignore him. I had pledged he was dead to me—unless I was presented the opportunity to rough him up again in which case he could be reanimated—I intended to stick to my pledge.

"I bet I could make you talk."

Hunter was trying to restart our games as if nothing had changed. I wouldn't be duped this time.

"Were you disappointed I didn't chat with you at Higher Yearning?"

Didn't *chat?* He had to be joking. The man pretended I was the amazing invisible barista. I greet the checkout girl at my grocery store and I don't even know her name, it's basic common decency.

"Just let me explain."

I turned to him, about to unleash my anger, before realizing it would expose how much he had hurt me. I caught myself, instead giving him a scathing look and continued walking.

"Everleigh, please," he pleaded, grabbing my wrist and pulled me to a stop.

I looked at him contemptuously then down to where his hand had locked onto my wrist, which he immediately released and allowed me to walk away.

I joined Sam and Robbie for lunch at the Hensley Union Café and conveyed that the situation with Hunter had deteriorated. After we finished our meals, several of Robbie's fraternity brothers came to our table. They were attractive, clean cut, and reeked of wealth. Robbie seemed hesitant to introduce us, but he put his arm around Sam—claiming her—which made his reluctance forgivable. Taking matters into my own hands, I introduced Sam and myself to the three brothers. Their words were urbane, but their lascivious appraisal was off putting. Heath, the obvious ringleader, invited us to a frat party Saturday. Robbie declined and stated we already had a commitment, but Heath suggested we stop by after. I stepped in to decline, citing my need to work the next day, and Robbie's appreciation for the assist was evident. I didn't believe he was ashamed of us—he had readily claimed Sam—but I suspected Robbie was preventing Sam from seeing him in 'frat mode' for fear she would be repelled, which was both insightful and correct. Heath finally accepted our decline and said we were welcome anytime before departing.

"That was special. How can you be friends with those turds?" I had to ask Robbie.

He groaned pitifully. "I know. I hate the fraternity lifestyle, but I don't have a choice. The last six generations of males in my family have attended Hensley and been members of Kappa Sigma Tau. I avoided pledging my freshman year, claiming to be overwhelmed by my studies, but sophomore year my dad applied the pressure. He said if he paid for my education, the least I could do was honor the family tradition. The threat wasn't exactly veiled. I participate minimally to retain my membership, but it's not my scene. Most of the brothers are good guys, but all of them are pompous and overindulged." Robbie sounded defeated.

Sam kissed his cheek, offering what consolation she could since she related to the potent mix of family and prosperity. I sent him a sympathetic smile before excusing myself to return home to study, providing them time alone.

Chapter Seven

*"Forgiveness is the economy of the heart...
Forgiveness saves the expense of anger, the cost
of hatred, the waste of spirits."* -Hannah More

I dressed carefully the next morning as if coating myself in armor. I was sending a message with my shredded boyfriend jeans, military jacket, and black combat boots. I wanted a physical representation of my strength, to show Hunter I would not be persuaded by pleas or excuses. My hair was pin straight parted down the middle and my make-up was ferocious. I was a warrior, ready for silent battle.

Like any good warrior, I had a plan. I timed my arrival to Business Ethics seconds before class began. Avoidance was a valid defense tactic, I had learned; after class, employing the same avoidance tactic, I cornered the professor for clarification on a reading assignment, allowing enough time for the room to empty before my exit. I was cautiously optimistic that Hunter would not bother to wait around. Optimism can bite me.

When I exited the classroom, he was leaning against the wall facing me. He embodied James Dean down to the fitted denim, white tee, and leather jacket—the only thing missing was the token cigarette. He inspected me from head to toe and smirked, as if knowing my intent.

I walked past him as if he wasn't there, but he fell in step with me and I felt him prepare to engage.

"Are you ready to forgive me yet?"

I kept walking.

"Haven't we reached the statute of limitations for your enmity yet?" he tried to coax a laugh.

One foot in front of the other, I paid no attention to his ramblings.

"I believe it's your turn to forgive me."

I continued to employ my selective hearing.

"Have you considered how this hostility will affect the children? Think of little Sam and Robbie."

Okay, that one was somewhat funny, but I gave nothing away.

"Do you know if you asked my mother to choose one word to describe me what she would say?"

Douchebag? No, his mom probably doesn't curse.

"Persevering, tenacious, persistent, unrelenting, and indomitable. That was more than one word, but mom is verbose."

Did this guy have a pocket thesaurus?

"I won't accept your refusal to forgive me. You would save yourself countless headaches and time if you caved now. I'm prepared to switch to guerilla warfare."

Was he threatening me now? I was not sure I wanted to know what his version of guerilla warfare entailed. He was intelligent and perceptive. Would he ransom *my precious*? Steal the spark plugs from Papa Smurf? Hide the coffee machine? No, even he would not sink that low. Besides, all of these acts would require breaking the law. He wouldn't break the law, would he?

"Last chance," he warned ominously.

I am woman enough to admit I was intimidated. Hunter wouldn't physically harm me, but numerous items I depend upon to get through the day could be at risk. Stop! I must be strong. Cloaked in armor, I was prepared for combat. Bring it on Mr. Charles!

And then he did it. I never saw it coming, could have never anticipated his attack. I was unprepared for its horror, the effects of which would stay with me for a long time to come. Hunter did the unthinkable...he began to sing...

"This is the song that never ends
It just goes on and on my friends
Some people started singing it not knowing what it was
And they'll continue singing it forever just because
This is the song that never ends..."

I tuned him out but his poisonous seed had taken root. As I strode away, I could hear him continuing the refrain over and over. It carried on the wind as if haunting me. My only consolation was that he, too, would now have the infernal song stuck in his head. When I reached my car, I turned the radio on and sang along, certain it would remedy my condition.

After the longest work shift of my life, the incessant song was still playing in my head on repeat. I had to admit his method, though shockingly juvenile, was staggeringly effective.

By the time I arrived home, my mood was dark and violent. If Hunter had been near, I would have inflicted bodily harm so severe that if he ever attempted to sing the unceasing song again he would have to do so several octaves higher.

Sam read my black mood while perched on the loveseat. She held out her arms in the universal gesture for a hug. I shook my head vigorously, not wanting comfort.

"What happened? Was it Hunter again?"

I nodded, not able to speak without shrieking in outrage.

"What did he do?" I shook my head again ominously. "Tell me. You can't keep it bottled up inside."

"Sam, you don't want me to share this with you. Trust me."

"It can't be that bad."

"You'll regret it, and then be mad at me for subjecting you to my suffering. You may kill Hunter and I have no desire to visit you in Riker's Penitentiary."

"Now you're just being melodramatic."

Melodramatic? She was picking the wrong time to be stubborn. "Fine! Just remember you asked for it! Hunter stalked me after class. He tried to persuade me to forgive him. I persisted with my silent crusade—"

Sam interrupted, "Maybe you should forgive the poor guy. He seems genuinely sorry and you do like him. We all make mistakes. He could have had a reason you haven't thought of."

"Sam, this is your last warning. Drop it."

"Just tell me already," she shouted in her impatience.

She asked for it, so I unleashed the insidious song.

Sam stopped me, "Enough, enough! I'll admit, it was devious, but is it really that bad? Might your hurt feelings from yesterday's slight be causing you to overreact?"

"I've been living with this curse for eleven hours. Talk to me in the morning and we'll see if you still think I'm overreacting." I sighed, defeated. "I'm going to bed, I'll see you in the morning. Thank you for caring enough to want to share my pain."

"Goodnight, drama queen," Sam called to me.

I would not leave that cheap shot unanswered. "By the way Sam, in my head the voice singing, is Lamb Chop."

I left her with that thought, planting my own vicious seed. Now Sam would hear the irritatingly affected nasal voice of the lamb puppet singing the interminable song. When it came to retaliation, Hunter had taught me well.

When I finally awoke Friday morning, it was afternoon. It had taken hours to fall asleep the night before due to the damn song cycling through my head. I ran into the kitchen to grab my coffee, but was horrified to find the machine was off. No coffee? Shit! As I walked out of the kitchen, Sam eyed me accusingly from the table.

"I unplugged it as punishment for inflicting that song on me. I didn't fall asleep until after 3:00," she admitted resentfully.

"Hey, I warned you repeatedly. If you want to be mad and exact revenge, look for Hunter."

"Make no mistake, he will get his. This is awful. How do you make it stop?"

"I still haven't found a cure. If you find one let me know." I paused to study her, "Are we good?"

"Yep, I already got my payback with the coffee pot. You being deprived of a cup before work has evened the score. Have a good day!"

By Saturday morning, my nerves were frazzled. I had endured two nights with minimal sleep due to Hunter's devil song. Every time I would get a reprieve, something would remind me of Hunter and the torment would begin again. Sam, luckily, had been able to shake the earworm with Robbie's help. I was desperate enough to consider a one-night stand to find relief.

Over coffee, Sam reminded me of our plans to go dancing with Robbie at The Stop.

"Sam, don't make me go. I'm grumpy. Hunter was supposed to come when we made the plans. Now I'll be a third-wheel," I whined. I didn't want to enjoy myself—I wanted to sulk.

"You make a commitment and you're going to keep it. It will help you out of the doldrums. I could have Robbie bring a friend for you."

"No thank you. I don't want to spend the night with one of Robbie's frat brothers."

"Of course not. Robbie does have other friends, you know."

"I don't need you to set-up a playdate. I'll text Lincoln to see if he is going tonight."

"That is a good idea. You two always have fun when you dance together. He is a harmless diversion, precisely what you need."

I wasn't sure if Linc would respond after my reaction when I last saw him. My phone alerted me to the incoming text, and I smiled my relief when I read his response.

"Linc said he was planning to go tonight and he'll see us there."

When I arrived home, Sam greeted me at the door—head full of rollers—and pushed me toward the bathroom.

"Shower quick, we only have one hour to whip ourselves into Goddesses of Athenian proportions."

"I'm glad to hear we aren't aiming too high," I deadpanned.

Sam executed a masterful upside down French braid that ended in a messy knot at the top of my head. The style was alluring and exposed my neck advantageously. In the back of my closet, I found the perfect sleeveless, mock neck dress with a keyhole back. It was made from black lace, and hugged my every curve. I accessorized with delicate gold chandelier earrings, and an assortment of gold and black lacquer bangles in various widths and patterns. I heard Robbie and Sam in the living room and hurried out.

"Hi Robbie," I greeted distractedly.

He was dressed in dark wash jeans and a light blue shirt. He was handsome and more relaxed than I had ever seen him. His eyes were glued to Sam, drinking her in. Sam rushed us out to Robbie's Range Rover, and after showing our IDs at The Stop, we headed for the bar. I scanned the crowd and spotted Linc waving as he approached. I introduced Robbie to Lincoln as we finished our drinks. Liquor ingested, we headed to the dance floor.

The music was fantastic, beats and rhythms perfect to lose myself and move. The four of us danced together for an hour before I was dying of thirst and excused myself to get a drink. Linc left to talk with friends, but promised to find me later. Returning to the bar, I positioned myself for maximum visibility. Griffin finished with his customer and came directly to me.

"What can I get you, pretty lady?"

"I'll have a belladonna and a water, please."

"Is that Sam's boyfriend?" he asked while mixing my drink.

"It's still new, but I would say yes." I smirked inwardly, realizing Griffin's crush. Too late buddy—you snooze, you lose. Griffin nodded, understanding he had missed his opportunity.

"By the way, I wanted to tell you how incredible you were the other night." Griffin looked at me with confusion, clueless to what I was referring. "When you performed. You were amazing and the set list was killer. Sam and I both created a playlist of the songs you sang."

"Thanks, it was no big deal; we were in a bind so I had to help out. It was better than my stand up, but not much," he shared self-deprecatingly.

"You don't perform often? You played like a pro and your voice is astounding."

"I perform occasionally but never here, that was a first. I have to go, they're three deep. Sorry." He left me with an apologetic smile and without payment.

I finished my drink and guzzled water in an unladylike fashion. Thirst quenched, I rejoined Sam and Robbie on the dance floor. Robbie's moves were typical—not bad, but not impressive. Sam seemed to enjoy his style as she ground her butt into his groin—someone was getting lucky tonight. I added a little space between Sam and I, to provide the illusion of privacy as their dancing grew more heated.

I felt a body behind me and figured Linc had returned. When an arm wrapped around my waist and I saw the ring, I knew it was not Linc. I spun to face the owner of the encroaching arm, and the moment I met his phosphorescent eyes it started—Lamb Chop was singing over the music in the bar.

I groaned pitifully.

"Something wrong?" Hunter inquired, leaning in close to my ear.

"You're a freakin' trigger. What are you doing here?" I asked with antagonism.

"You invited me," he offered amicably.

"That was before."

"Before what?"

"Before you planted the Trojan horse in my head. I haven't slept in days."

"Poor baby. I did caution you that withholding your forgiveness would be unpleasant."

"There is unpleasant and then there is fire ants crawling through your brain, your little stunt was the latter. I feel like I have an incurable disease."

"If you promise to forgive me, I'll make it stop," he whispered, his lips grazing my ear. I shivered, an irrepressible response to his proximity and touch.

"You promise?" I didn't trust him as far as I could throw him.

"Yes, I promise. I have never lied to you Everleigh. Never."

"You have a deal. Cure me and you are forgiven."

"Not just forgiven—I want to be friends again." He upped the ante. Hustler.

"I'm promising forgiveness. I will give you the *opportunity* to regain my friendship but it's up to you to earn it," I counter offered.

"Good enough. Follow me."

"Where are we going?"

"Away from the masses," he explained vaguely.

Following him, I finally had an opportunity to assess his assets. Sweet baby Jesus! The man's derriere could bring a woman to tears. He was wearing fitted black dress pants that lovingly caressed every curve. Hard muscular globes met my unwavering gaze. We must have reached our destination because he stopped walking. I, however, didn't notice while struggling to contain my desire to fondle Hunter's posterior. Instead of halting gracefully, I crashed into him, and Hunter pivoted to catch me before I teetered over.

"You, miss, are a menace. First, you try to castrate me in class, now you try to take me down and thrash me. Violence is not the answer, Everleigh," he teased while ensuring I had regained my balance.

"Hey, I was behaving myself as you commanded. I dedicated myself fully to the lesson."

"What about just now? You weren't trying to knock me over?"

I decided that providing an honest answer about the cause of the collision wasn't in my best interest. I needed to take evasive action.

"Okay Doc, where is this cure you promised me? No more stalling."

"Scientists have conducted studies on how to get rid of a song that's stuck in your head. Do you know what they found the best cure to be?"

"If I did I would not still be suffering."

"Anagrams," he provided simply.

"The word games? My mom used to do those with me when I was younger. You just have to rearrange the letters to find the words, right?"

"Exactly! Scientists found anagrams could force the intrusive music out of your working memory allowing the song to be replaced with other more amenable thoughts. If you're cognitively engaged it limits involuntary memory retrieval."

"Thanks for the neurology lesson but that doesn't help me at the moment, unless you have a book of anagrams in your back pocket." I was frustrated to have a solution finally without the means to implement it.

"In fact, I do. I brought a few anagrams with me tonight to fix what I broke."

"Hand 'em over," I said desperately.

Hunter pulled a paper and pen from his pocket and handed it to me. I unfolded the document where a few anagrams were printed. He turned to offer me his back as I studied the lines:

rm ehscalr si roysr .
ot egovfir si nivedi .
turnhe sisems ish nrdeif .
anc eh vaeh ortahen hnceca ?

I work on each one individually, word by word, writing my answer in pen beneath the original line:

rm ehscalr si roysr .
Mr Charles is sorry.

Okay, I have to give him credit for creativity. As far as apologies go, this was impressive. Effort and advanced planning were required. I proceeded to the remaining lines.

ot egovfir si nivedi .
To forgive is divine.

turnhe sisems ish nrdeif .
Hunter misses his friend.

anc eh vaeh ortahen hnceca ?
Can he have another chance?

If I had not promised to do so, I would have forgiven him anyway. After solving the last line, I wrote my answer on the bottom of the page:

sye !

I handed the paper back to Hunter with the pen. He read it and laughed while pulling me in for a hug. I wrapped my arms loosely around his neck in return. He placed his mouth against my ear again, and goosebumps rose on my arms.

"Thank you, I'm truly sorry. I wanted to remain professional during class, and Crystal is a work colleague. I could have handled it better. Please forgive me," he whispered contritely.

I slid my right arm from his neck, placing my hand on the back of his head, and pulled his ear closer to my lips.

"You're forgiven. I understand your intent and can respect it, but don't treat me as if I'm disposable again. There is a middle ground between friends and strangers that is not hurtful. Try to stay in that zone," I softly shared with more openness than I had planned. "Thank you for my anagrams, they were incredibly thoughtful."

He squeezed me to him. "I will, and you're welcome. I'm not fond of silent Everleigh. It was against the laws of nature," he joked as he released me from our embrace. "Come on, let's go dance."

I followed him back to the dance floor where Sam and Robbie were simulating intercourse. Hunter and I looked at them, at each other, and back to them—then we laughed.

We danced together, watching one another as we found our groove. I expected Hunter to be a good dancer since he was conscious of movement from lifelong study of martial arts and he was confident. What I didn't expect was Hunter to be seduction personified on the dance floor. His movements were fluid and controlled, no over-the-top gestures or gyrations. He moved naturally from his core, his legs, arms, and neck working together to embody the music; it was beautiful and sensual. Hunter worked his abs and hips with mesmerizing expertise causing the women around us to watch appreciatively—I was waiting for someone to slip money in his waistband. He continually positioned himself between me and everyone else, guarding my personal space, protecting and allowing me to focus on having a good time.

After a couple of songs, we established a rhythm and got lost in the music. He placed his hands on my hips guiding me closer, rolling his hips to meet mine as I followed. We danced as one, slithering and sliding—it was give and take, push and pull. He positioned his right thigh between my legs and we rocked lower, bending our knees while pressing against one another. He used his left hand to grab mine and raised his arm, gently guiding me with one hand on my hip, causing me to twirl until my back was securely against his front. He lowered his arm, still holding my hand across my body and gripped my hip. I wound my free arm around his back and hooked my finger through his belt loop. Following the waving motion of his core with my own, I drowned in sensations. He rolled his hips and I pressed my rump harder against his groin to maintain contact as we moved.

Oscar Wilde said, "Dancing is a vertical expression of a horizontal desire." I know Hunter was not expressing his desire to get me horizontally, but he was certainly ratcheting up mine for him. When his hand drifted from my hip up to my ribcage, I knew it was time to take a break before I embarrassed myself by doing something stupid and uninvited.

I looked over my shoulder to catch his eye and our gazes locked. We stared at each other as we moved under a spell. Everything else fell away except for the sensation of his body against mine moving sinuously, tempting me. I leaned my head in, closing the gap between our faces. We were inches apart and I was seconds from making a fool of myself—saving me from myself, Hunter tilted his head to the left and suggested we get a drink. I nodded my agreement and followed, allowing him to clear a path as I traveled in his wake.

I requested water, there was no way I was adding alcohol to the hormones ravaging me. As he turned to order our drinks, Lincoln returned.

"Hey hot mamma. You looked good out there."

"Thanks Linc. Where have you been? How's your semester going?"

"Just catching up with friends." He gestured to the opposite side of the bar where a group of students had gathered. "I have an easy semester, which is a nice way to end my college years."

"Aren't you going to grad school?" I recalled him telling me he planned to get his masters in economics.

"Yeah, don't remind me. I choose to pretend I'm done with school after this—at least until after graduation." Linc laughed.

"I hear you. I was debating a master's of business administration, but with my additional responsibilities at Higher Yearning following graduation, I'm not sure if I can manage both. I'm going to take a year to decide."

"Good idea. By the way, you still owe me a lunch. Text me when you know which day you're free this week."

As Linc razzed me about our missed lunch date, Hunter turned back from the bar and extended my water, sliding his free arm around my waist—the universal male sign of claiming his property. Linc abruptly said goodnight, placing a friendly kiss on my cheek, which I returned. Hunter pulled me further into his side in response. Linc raised an eyebrow to me but said nothing more.

"What was that?" I questioned Hunter, confused by his possessiveness.

"Nothing. I wasn't sure if his attentions were welcomed, I was acting as a barrier. You need to be careful; this is a breeding ground for predators."

"That's Lincoln, my friend for the last four years, you dolt. He is also usually my dance partner when I'm not on a date. Don't try and intimidate him," I scolded.

"Sorry, I misunderstood. It sounded like he was pressuring you for a date. He mentioned you blew him off and I didn't know if you had done so purposefully. I was trying to protect you."

"Thanks for your concern but I don't need to be protected from Linc. He's a good friend, that's all."

"Is he straight?"

"Yes."

"He may respect that you aren't interested in more than friendship but that doesn't mean he wouldn't be interested in more if you were willing," he shared sagely.

"No way, Linc is not interested in me like that."

"You're too smart to believe that. I saw how that boy was looking at you and his reaction when I put my arm around you. He wants you."

"You're way off base."

"Everleigh, you're a stunning, sultry, sensuous woman; there isn't a man in this room who doesn't desire you—who wouldn't bring you home at the slightest indication of your interest."

"You mean there isn't a straight man in this room that doesn't desire me."

"Of course. I thought that was assumed."

"I believe you're overstating my appeal but thank you, nonetheless." I wanted to change the topic from desire because I was feeling it like a battering ram. It was depressing that the object of my yearning was not attainable.

"Everleigh, you need to be inordinately careful. Listen to everything Crystal said at the seminar and take it to heart. I'm not an alarmist; this is a uniquely dangerous time to be at Hensley. The police still haven't apprehended the assailant. It could be anyone—stranger, student, or teacher. It could be someone you have been friends with for years or dated in the past. You can't assume anyone is safe."

"I know, I know. I'm already paranoid without you adding to my worries. You know, I nearly had a heart attack the other night when Linc surprised me as I was leaving work. I practically accused him of intending me harm. I was afraid of Linc, someone I've been friends with for almost four years. I'm lucky he was even talking to me tonight after the way I reacted."

Hunter's emotions were shuttered as he asked, "Why was he there, Ev? Were you alone?"

I sighed, embarrassed once again. "Yes, I was alone. He was coming to make sure I was safe, and I freaked out and screamed like a banshee, a paranoid nutjob."

"Does he meet you after work often?"

"No, it was the first time, I felt someone watching me, and when he came up behind me..."

"I'm not comfortable with what you're telling me. His sudden change in behavior, your instinctive fear. Don't give him your unguarded trust. Don't allow yourself to be in a position where you're alone with him."

"Hunter, you're overreacting. Linc is safe, he's a friend."

"No one is safe right now. You can't trust anyone. And no more leaving work alone at night," he ordered, clearly accustom to having his dictates followed.

"How do I know you aren't the bad guy?" I asked, trying to lighten the mood.

"The only person you're indisputably safe with is me. I promised you, Everleigh. I have and will never lie to you—you can depend on it, if nothing else." Hunter stared into my eyes, willing me to see his earnestness, then he smiled.

"And you can definitely include Sam on the safe list. She does not have the body mass to overpower most fifth graders."

"Thank you Hunter. I will be cautious, I promise," I vowed to him. "I should find Sam and save her from getting arrested for public indecency."

He chuckled, knowing I was right.

When we were all ready to leave, Sam and I had a silent conversation that confirmed Hunter and I had made amends. She mutely asked if Robbie could sleep over, to which I consented. Robbie seemed trustworthy, but after my conversation with Hunter, I decided to forgo my usual headphones to tune out the headboard thumping. I wanted to ensure I could hear if Sam cried for help. I also decided to lock my bedroom door and keep my cell near the bed.

Hunter walked with us to Robbie's car and gave me a bear hug, lifting my feet off the ground before carefully setting me back down. Before he released me, he whispered in my ear, "Remember your promise to be cautious."

After offering his goodbye, he turned to leave. After several steps, he returned and caught my arm as I was climbing in the backseat.

"Where's your phone?"

I pulled it out of my clutch and handed it to him.

"I want to give you my phone number in case you're ever in trouble or if you just need a friend."

"You two seem to have made up nicely," Sam said from the front, after I climbed into the backseat. I could hear the smirk in her voice.

"Yeah, he apologized and explained. I forgave him with a stern warning not to let it happen again."

"Yes, I noticed how stern you were on the dance floor. I needed a drink to cool off after watching you two."

"Oh, you're one to talk. You and Robbie were in jeopardy of arrest for public indecency on the floor."

"Robbie and I were hot, I'll give you that, but you and Hunter set the building on fire. Anyone standing in a five foot radius had spontaneous orgasms by proxy."

Robbie made a choking sound; I guess he had not heard Sam unfiltered before now.

"Don't be ridiculous, we were just dancing. There were other people being far more explicit than us."

It was true. Many couples flaunted their sexuality on the dance floor. Women bending over while men stood behind them, pumping their hips forward and back. I'm still unconvinced actual copulation wasn't occurring in some cases.

"Yes, others may have been more explicit, but your chemistry was scorching."

"We may have friendly chemistry but not sexual chemistry. Hunter doesn't..." I trailed off not feeling comfortable outing Hunter to Robbie.

Sam understood and dropped it. She had seen me through every crush, boyfriend, and lover I ever had. She probably recognized how close I had come to proving myself an unadulterated imbecile by kissing Hunter.

"Sorry Ev, Sam is right," Robbie joined in.

"You have to say that. It's your obligation to agree with Sam during the preliminary courtship phase."

"True as that may be, she is right. I would still agree even if I wasn't her boyfriend."

"You're my boyfriend?" Sam asked, sounding surprised and pleased.

"Of course I am," Robbie confirmed, before doubting himself. "Aren't I?"

"Of course you are," Sam made it official.

I remained quiet, letting them have their moment. They gazed into each other's eyes at the stop light. It was sweet, but it was making me mildly queasy and envious. I missed that part of early relationships. I hadn't had a serious relationship since Drew, sophomore year. There was no dramatic scene, it just fizzled out as our lives and schedules lead us in different directions. He was nice and I cared about him, but it never went deeper. We ended as casual friends with no awkward residual effects from our parting. Each semester we would find time to share a cup of coffee and catch up. Drew was a good guy, just not the guy for me.

I was ready to meet someone new, someone to share my life with, warts and all. I just hadn't met the right man. I needed someone intelligent, motivated, funny, caring, strong, tolerant—because let's face it, I was no picnic. Someone who could stand up to me when I was wrong, would admit when he was, and would stand beside me when needed. Of course, I had to be attracted to him and it would not hurt if he could 'wow' me with his mattress prowess. I realized it was a tall order—I didn't want to settle and regret time spent with the wrong man—instead I was waiting patiently. In the meantime I casually dated several nice guys, occasionally enjoying one all night. If I could find a guy like Hunter—a hetero-Hunter—with his characteristics and our chemistry, who could love my brand of crazy, and looked like him—that would be a winning combination.

Chapter Eight

*"The one who can't restrain their anger will
wish undone, what their temper and irritation
prompted them to do." -Horace*

My truce with Hunter held strong after our reunion at The
Stop. We resumed our repartee and friendship, which was a
welcomed return. I was careful to respect Hunter's need for
professionalism during the sessions and he refrained from
treating me like a leper. My days were far more interesting with
Hunter in my life. He had become a part of my daily routine,
an expected component to my happiness. I could hardly
remember what it was like before he shoved his way in.

Valentine's Day arrived the next week and Sam was
excited. It was the first time she had a serious boyfriend during
the holiday since freshman year. Robbie went overboard with
flowers, chocolates, stuffed animals, and a lavish dinner
followed by an evening at the best hotel in the area. He gave
her a beautiful pair of diamond and ruby earrings, which Sam
adored. My day was not a romantic celebration, but at least I
wasn't alone. I worked the night shift, allowing those with
significant others to enjoy a night of romance. Hunter showed
up at closing with a single yellow rose and a bottle of wine. We
locked the doors and he helped me finish cleaning up. Hunter
and I sat for hours sipping wine and chatting about nothing and

everything. He walked me to my car at the end of the night and gave me a warm hug. Having a friend to spend the night with took the sting out of my single status during the most romantic day of the year.

Hunter became a regular part of our crew. Over the next two weeks we fell into a routine. Mondays and Wednesdays we would all meet for lunch on-campus. Thursday nights we would usually grab dinner before enjoying performers at The Stop. Fridays were christened Sam and Robbie's date night. I would meet up with other friends to enjoy a movie or drinks. Saturdays, Hunter would come to Higher Yearning at closing and we would hangout. Sundays, were reserved for homework and girlie time—chick-flicks, painting nails, junk food binges, or shopping.

Sam and Robbie's relationship was progressing well. I got to know Robbie during our dinners and lunches, he was a good guy who treated Sam well and appreciated the person she was. Sam was comfortable being herself around Robbie and enjoyed his company. During one of our Sunday chats, Sam confided that she was falling for him. She was not ready to say the words, but I felt it was imminent. I could see a future for the two of them, maybe even marriage. Sam's family was sure to approve given the stature of Robbie's familial connections, which was not a requirement for Sam but it would make her life easier.

Life was good, except the attacks on Hensley's female population continued on a weekly basis. A distinct pattern was emerging; assaults usually occurred over the weekend and news coverage would begin Monday morning. The atmosphere on campus was deteriorating as the number of victims increased. Details leaked through the campus grapevine were tremendously disturbing. The modus operandi was consistent with the attack on the Beta Gamma Gamma sister, but with every incident the severity of the assaults escalated, if rumors were to be believed. Hensley administrators issued warnings for all female students to practice circumspection and requested vigilance from all students, encouraging us to report suspicious circumstances to campus security. Reporters indicated the police were struggling to identify the assailant due to a lack of DNA evidence and conflicting physical evidence at the crime scenes. The community was crying for further intervention from the Federal Bureau of Investigations, but FBI assistance was reportedly restricted to consultations with their behavioral science unit.

Robbie and Sam went skiing in Vermont at his family's chalet during Spring break, while I worked extra shifts and enjoyed my class-free week; Hunter kept me company when available, and the week sped by. When Sam returned she told me Robbie had dropped the "L-bomb" and she had returned it. They stopped for lunch with his family on the way home and then shared dinner with Sam's family that same evening. The family meet-and-greets went well, which was another obstacle overcome. She confessed to envisioning herself marrying him one day.

We broke tradition the first Saturday of March when Kappa Sigma Tau hosted its annual house party, a requirement for all brothers to attend. It wasn't clear what distinguished this fraternity party from the many others they held, but Robbie insisted there was no way for him to skip it. He invited Sam and me, but his lack of enthusiasm was obvious. Robbie did his best to avoid his frat brothers, but when forced to interact with them in our presence, he tried to shield Sam and I from their attention. I assumed he still feared Sam would lose interest if she saw him in that environment. Determined to reassure him, Sam decided to attend and I agreed to join when Hunter committed to tag along. Robbie was blatantly relieved Hunter would be present to shelter Sam and me from unwanted drunken advances—Kappa brothers were notorious playboys.

As we entered the house it was clear Sam and I would be winning an award for the most modest attire. I felt Amish compared to the girls walking around, most of whom had just seen their eighteenth birthday. Hunter grunted his disgust as Robbie led us through the house. Once we had settled into a remote corner, Robbie excused himself to make his attendance known. Hunter opened two beers and distributed them to us.

"Don't drink anything other than the beers I brought and only if one of us opens it. If you put it down, don't drink it. You have three each, so make them last for however long we are trapped in this God forsaken shithole," Hunter ordered with non-negotiable authority.

"You don't want any?" I asked, understanding his concerns regarding our safety. It explained why he brought a blueberry microbrew that would likely never be found at a frat party—it would be easy for us to identify and protect. It was not lost on me that he brought a limited quantity to ensure our sobriety. He needn't worry, there was no way I would risk intoxication in this environment.

"No, I'm not drinking tonight. Besides, that beer is too fruity for me, but I thought you would enjoy it. I know you don't like real beer. I would have brought a pot of coffee if I'd had an easy way to ensure it couldn't be tampered with."

"Are you our guard dog for the evening, Mr. Charles?" I asked with mock innocence.

"Yes, tonight I'm your pit bull."

"Sam, should I scratch him behind the ears?"

"I don't know, Ev, he might try to hump your leg."

We both laughed while Hunter shook his head at our antics. I wouldn't object if Hunter humped me, but it seemed best to keep that inclination to myself.

After three hours, we had only seen Robbie a handful of times and only for a few minutes. Tired of entertaining ourselves in the foul environment, we were done. Hunter volunteered to take us home, which Sam and I gratefully accepted. We went in search of Robbie with Sam leading the way, trailed closely by Hunter and I followed in the rear practically glued to his back. We located Robbie manning the keg on the back deck—he looked downtrodden, sober, and freezing. Seeing our approach, he asked another brother to operate the keg and came to greet us.

"Sorry, baby. I have been assigned to one crappy task after another," Robbie grumbled.

"Don't worry, babe. We all understand, but we're going to head out. Ev has work tomorrow, and I'm spent," Sam assuaged.

"Let me walk you out," Robbie said, taking Sam's hand and headed to the front door.

We were about ten feet from freedom when Heath intercepted Robbie.

"Hey man, you can't leave; you're on keg out back," Heath decreed.

"I'm not leaving, Heath, I'm just walking Sam out. She's heading home, I'll be back in five minutes."

Heath finally noticed the rest of us. Sizing up Hunter, he resolved to make nice—a wise decision on his part. Heath was tall and built; six feet one with muscles I suspected had been enhanced by unnatural means; he was undoubtedly accustomed to being the toughest guy in the room. Hunter was taller by an inch and cloaked in muscles earned through physical discipline instead of chemical enhancement. Heath still had traces of youth in face where Hunter was a man, a robust powerful man with a commanding presence. It was the air of unyielding strength emanating from Hunter that likely persuaded Heath to back down.

"Hey man, I'm Heath Varbeck."

Heath extended a hand to Hunter, which he accepted without enthusiasm.

"You should stay and hang out, the party is just getting started. We have the select liquor downstairs—I can hook you up."

"No, the girls are ready to get home," Hunter replied adamantly.

Heath changed tactics, addressing Sam. "You aren't going to leave your boy here all by himself, surrounded by beautiful, willing women, are you?"

"There's no point in staying. I have barely seen Robbie tonight because he had to serve the rest of you. Besides, I trust him."

"A confident woman, naïve perhaps but confident. Ignorance is bliss or so they say," Heath condescended.

"What about you, lovely? Are you leaving with these lightweights, too?" Heath turned his attentions to me. This was a miscalculation on his part because I was out of patience.

Spurning him, I stalked toward the door, inciting Heath who grabbed hold of my wrist firmly. My arm was extended behind me at an awkward angle, trapped in his uncomfortably tight grasp, and forcing me to pivot in his direction to lessen the tension on my shoulder.

"I was talking to you," Heath hissed at me.

I was about to offer a cutting reply demanding he release me, when the energy around us crackled dangerously.

"I strongly suggest you release her now," Hunter addressed Heath, his tone even and devoid of any emotion. His stance appeared casual, but I noticed the subtle adjustments made in preparation—Hunter had taken a fighter's stance. His threat was restrained, but the effect was unnerving. Hunter was fearsome without having to be blatant.

Heath tried to mask his apprehension, but traces were visible beneath his mask of bravado. He viciously crushed my wrist in his meaty grasp—reprisal for Hunter's audacity—before relinquishing me.

"Are you alright?" Hunter asked me quietly with concern, never removing his eyes from Heath.

"Let's just go. Now."

I didn't intend to tell him my wrist was killing me and would likely be covered in bruises tomorrow, it would only escalate the confrontation. Hunter had a tight rein on his fury, but his restraint was at its breaking point. If I told him Heath had hurt me, Hunter would go nuclear.

Heath turned to leave, only to find his path obstructed by Hunter.

"If you ever lay your uninvited hands on a woman again, you will regret it." Hunter snarled. "And if you ever—*ever*—so much as look at Everleigh, I will destroy you...fuck the consequences."

Leaving Heath with his oath, Hunter gently wrapped his arm around my shoulder and guided me out of the house with Sam and Robbie trailing.

"I'm so sor—" Robbie began, but Hunter cut him off.

"Don't!" Hunter took a calming breath, "please, just say goodnight to Sam so I can get the girls home."

"I'm so sorry, Sam, this is why I try to avoid the frat. Heath is an ass when he doesn't get his way," Robbie sounded defeated.

"Robbie, I know you're a reluctant participant. Nevertheless, I can't believe you would forsake your integrity to be part of any organization that would include Heath, regardless of the pressure from your family. Just..." Sam shook her head, not wanting to punish Robbie when he was already punishing himself, "just call me tomorrow." Sam kissed him on the cheek and walked away.

"I'm sorry Ev," Robbie added as an afterthought.

I nodded my acceptance and we all walked away, leaving Robbie in the den of debauchery. We were lost in thought while walking to Hunter's black Yukon. Hunter opened our doors and Sam climbed in the back while I climbed in the front. Once Hunter had started the car, he turned on the overhead light and gently lifted my wrist to examine it.

"Damn it," he seethed, "your wrist is going to be covered in bruises. Why didn't you tell me? It must be throbbing."

"I knew it would lead to a fight, and I just wanted to go home and forget about this whole disaster."

"You need to ice your wrist when you get home. It will help to minimize the swelling and bruises."

Hunter drew several calming breaths. "It's taking every ounce of self-discipline I've learned over twenty years of training to keep myself in this car."

"Why didn't you kick his ass? That son of a bitch put his hands on her!" Sam ranted at Hunter. She wasn't mad at him—she was livid that Heath accosted me and disenchanted Robbie stayed behind.

"I was there, Sam, I know exactly what he did. It would've been satisfying in the moment—more gratifying that you can imagine—but tomorrow when the police came knocking on my door, I would have had a lot to answer for. I have been taught for years that martial arts provides the ability to fight, but with ability comes responsibility. I believe in only using my skills to defend and protect when all other options are exhausted. Negotiation, diplomacy, even walking away is more honorable and requires more strength of character than using force."

"But he was hurting her!" Sam argued, unsatisfied with the answer.

"I didn't know he was hurting her at the time, I thought he was just restraining her. Everleigh didn't share that pertinent piece of information with me. The situation was riding the razor's edge between non-confrontational resolution and violence. I erred on the side of caution and Heath backed down; I made the right decision." Hunter sounded as if he was trying to convince himself more than Sam.

"Well I'm glad your honor is intact, even if Ev's wrist isn't," Sam sniped viciously. It was a hit below the belt as far as I was concerned.

"Sam, enough. I'm fine, let it go," I cajoled, "Hunter, thank you for intervening and defending me. I was relieved you kept the situation calm and stable. You're right; a brawl would have only caused a volatile situation to deteriorate further." I placed my hand on his arm to reassure him that his course of action was my preference as well.

"I promised that I would protect you. The best way to do that was diffuse the situation and remove you both from danger." He sounded more comfortable with his decision this time, which reassured me.

"How could he have stayed there?" Sam asked resentfully, thinking of Robbie.

"Don't be too hard on him, Sam. He's probably afraid of retaliation. Fear is oppressive, often preventing good people from acting righteously," Hunter suggested. "Give Robbie the opportunity to apologize and explain."

"How can he justify his choice? I'm hesitant to commit myself to someone who stands by idly like Robbie did. He stayed, which is tantamount to condoning Heath's conduct."

When we pulled into our complex, I directed Hunter to our building and we all walked inside to our apartment door.

"Do you want to come in?" I invited Hunter.

"I shouldn't. It has been a long night and you have work tomorrow."

"Night Hunter, thanks for your help. I apologize for being a bitch, you handled the Heath thing admirably," Sam apologized for her misplaced anger.

"No apology needed."

Hunter pulled Sam into a one-armed hug. I turned to Hunter, placing my hand on his chest.

"Thank you again. I meant what I said in the car, you did the right thing tonight."

He was still stewing, so I tried to lighten the mood.

"I'm only disappointed you intervened before I got to practice my bad-ass moves. I was ready to palm strike under his chin and hook my fingers into an eye gouge."

Hunter chuckled at my bloodlust. "You remember your number one goal during a confrontation, don't you?"

"Kick him in the nuts?" I teased. "Run, I haven't forgotten. However, had he not released me I would have been forced to 'create' my opportunity." I winked saucily.

"You little minx."

He pulled me against his body engulfing me in his arms.

"I'm glad you're feeling better. Ice your wrist, hopefully it won't bother you at work tomorrow. Goodnight."

He placed a kiss on the top of my head before releasing me.

As I entered the apartment, Sam was standing next to the kitchen table reading her phone.

"Robbie texted me ten times in the last thirty minutes. What should I do?"

"You should forgive him, but be honest about your concerns. Tell him you were disappointed he didn't address his frat buddy's behavior and diffuse the situation. Let him know that you were hurt when he chose to stay. If he can handle the truth and apologize, you two should be fine." Sam was nodding along with me. "School will be over in two months and the frat will be out of his life...out of your life. You can't be irritated with him for being afraid of Heath, that guy is huge. Hunter has twenty years of martial arts training to give him confidence against a bully like Heath. It isn't fair to hold Robbie to the same standard. Give him a chance to make this right if you still want a future with him."

"You're right." Sam sighed tiredly, "I'll text Robbie back and let him know I want to talk tomorrow."

"Good plan."

I grabbed an ice pack out of the freezer before heading to bed, ready to put the evening behind me.

During the last self-defense class, Hunter extended an invitation for all of us to continue our training at any of the Higosha Dojos. We could join their Krav Maga classes at no cost for as long as the attacks persisted. He also generously offered a fifty-percent discount in any future classes. It was an impressive gesture by Hunter and his family, proof of their commitment to our safety. Though Sam was glad that she had participated in the seminar, she didn't want to continue studying martial arts. I, on the other hand, had grown to love the training. It was great exercise and I felt more confident knowing basic defense skills. I was seriously considering taking the Krav Maga class on Monday nights.

Hunter and I grew closer over the next six weeks. Next to Sam, he was the person I confided in the most, I had come to count on him as a part of my daily life. When I told him about losing my mom, he asked about my father and I told him I never met him. When I was a senior, my mom told the truth and let me make the decision if I ever wanted to find him.

Mom had been dating my father for almost a year when she discovered she was pregnant. When she informed him, he freaked and told her she had to have an abortion. My mom refused to abort me, much to his dismay. He finally admitted he was married with no intentions of leaving his wife—mom was just a "pleasant diversion." She was shocked and furious; she would never knowingly enter a relationship with an attached man. He swore that if my mom decided to keep me, he would never offer assistance, monetary or otherwise. Mom stopped seeing him, but after I was born, she contacted him for support. He refused to help and when she threatened to take him to court, he countered by threatening to fight her for full custody and said she would never see me again once he won. My mom had no money, family, or resources to fund a legal battle. Frightened he would follow through on his threats, she never pursued support. She told me his name, but I never intended to find him—I want to know him even less than he wanted to know me.

In turn, Hunter told me about his parents and siblings. He shared the influence his father and martial arts had on his life. His respect for his father and closeness to his family were a defining part of who he was. He told me stories about his semester abroad in Japan, where he felt like Andre the Giant, but it shaped his views of the world and his appreciation for cultural differences. When he shared about losing his best friend in a drunk driving accident, my heart broke.

Hunter and I shared our favorites—movies, food, and literature. The best were our most embarrassing moments. For me—the first time I had sex in high school and I refused to take off my underwear. For Hunter—wetting his pants in front of his family and friends during a karate tournament where he failed to block an illegal kick to the bladder. His was much worse and it made me feel better. Although, he did ask me to explain why I refused to remove my panties, which I couldn't explain to this day. I hypothesized I was too nervous and having them on made me feel safe.

We shared stupid moments from our day and random thoughts when they popped into our heads. We continued our banter with a vengeance, and I still had not managed to get the last word—but I was getting closer to a win, or so I hoped.

I asked Hunter why he was single, if there was some pitiful sob story of heartbreak he was withholding. He denied any tragedy, but said he was at a place in his life where the type of committed relationship he wanted would not be possible; it was vague but I let him get away with it. He lobbed the question back at me, and I said I had yet to meet a man I wanted, who wanted me, and whom I could envision spending the rest of my life with—without the desire to smother him with a pillow while he slept.

Hunter's hugs wiped away my bad days, and when he kissed my head I felt treasured. In a perfect world Hunter would share my sexual attraction and we would have an epic romance, but reality didn't follow the plot of romantic comedies. I accepted the best friend alternative with gratitude for the grace it was.

Chapter Nine

"Assumptions are the termites of relationships."
-Henry Winkler

I decided to join the Krav Maga class at Higosha Dojo on Monday nights, and met with Hanshi Rosati, who graciously welcomed me. He was already aware that the Charles family offered classes to the seminar participants, which saved me from the awkward "this is supposed to be free" conversation.

I quickly fell in love with Krav Maga—the class was fast-paced, providing a cardio workout mixed with the defense training. The power and form of my punches, elbows, kicks, and knees had improved greatly after only two classes. By my third class, Sensei Alex said I was ready to practice with a fellow student. He requested Josh, one of the more advanced students, to partner with me, to my delight. Josh was the most proficient student in the class, in his late-twenties, and stood six feet tall with a beautifully sculpted body, and rich chocolate brown eyes that conveyed warmth. His medium brown hair was cut short in a style that suited him.

Krav Maga involved close holds and maneuvers that resembled wrestling, and we often found ourselves twisted together, frequently the result of a misstep on my part. Being sweaty and tangled with a stranger could become extremely uncomfortable, but Josh put me at ease. He was patient as we practiced and helped correct my errors without superiority. In one of my more humiliating moments, I got to know Josh intimately—we were working on a skill where Josh grabbed me from behind with his arm wrapped around my neck. I planted my feet shoulder width apart, grabbed his forearm with both hands, leaned forward, and used momentum to flip him over my shoulder, which resulted in him landing on his butt with his back against my shins. Everything went as planned. Unfortunately, I forgot to release his arm and, as my momentum continued, I fell head first over his shoulder, landing with my face in his lap and my hips resting on his shoulder. The force of my landing pushed his upper body back to the mat in a clothed approximation of the classic 69 position. As if this was not bad enough, I managed to knock the wind out of us both. Little Josh—respectably sized Josh to be more accurate—began to stir before I did. I'm not sure who was more embarrassed, but I could not hold Josh's response against him. It was an involuntary reaction to the position, a position that was completely my fault. I rolled off and stood as casually as possible, extending my arm to assist him to his feet. When he grabbed my hand, our eyes met and we both lost it. We were laughing so hard we fell back to the floor, side-by-side. Wiping my eyes, I turned my head to Josh.

"Sorry, I guess you weren't ready for the advanced maneuver. Don't worry, you'll catch on eventually."

Josh's deep laugh filled the dojo. "You should have warned me you were masquerading as a beginner," Josh continued my joke with a smile. "I believe it's customary to buy you dinner now."

"You should, after the way you manhandled me," I said with mock seriousness.

"I'm fairly certain you were the one doing the manhandling." Josh winked. "Nonetheless, I reaped the benefits, so I owe you. How about dinner this weekend?"

"I'm free Saturday."

"It's a date. Would you like me to pick you up?"

"Please don't take this the wrong way, but no. I would prefer to meet you at—" I paused giving him a chance to fill in the blank.

"I applaud your caution. Will 9:00 pm at Chez Madeline work for you?"

"Chez Madeline sounds wonderful, I have always wanted to eat there."

When class finished we exchanged numbers and goodbyes with a promise to see each other on Saturday. When I arrived home, Robbie and Sam were cuddled on the couch. I shared the story of my lap dive, despite my embarrassment; it was too funny not to share. When Sam and Robbie finally stopped laughing, I also relayed the news about my date.

"Finally. I was going to post a profile on one of those dating sites if you didn't get back in the game soon. It has been over two months since you've accepted a date."

I worried she would make the connection to the beginning of my friendship with Hunter, which would require an explanation I had no intention of providing.

"Thanks for the vote of confidence Sam. I've been busy with school and work. Plus, with the attacks persisting on a weekly basis, I don't feel comfortable accepting dates from guys I don't know."

"You have a valid point. Josh sounds great, maybe he is the one."

Why was it every time a friend found love they tried to recruit you to Team Amour? Was it the appeal of double dating? The phenomena always baffled me.

"It's just a date, Sam. Let's not put the cart before the horse. Josh is great and hot, but it's a little early to pledge undying love."

Robbie decided to join the conversation, "What's Hunter going to say?"

"Be cautious and text him when I get home would be my guess."

I shrugged, confused by Robbie's question, but he stared at me as if I had grown a second head. "What?" I was fairly certain I had not grown any additional appendages in the past thirty seconds.

"Ev, Hunter is not going to be happy about you dating this Josh guy," Robbie answered as if I was dense.

"Why would he care?"

"Because he is your *un*-boyfriend. The two of you are a couple in every way but name."

"Uh, no we aren't."

It was at this point I remembered that I had never clued Robbie into Hunter's sexual preference. I wanted to shout that Hunter and I were missing another key component of a romantic relationship, a component I could not live without for the rest of my life.

Instead I said, "He is one of my best friends—nothing more. You're reading it wrong."

Robbie would not drop it, "A man does not spend that much time with a woman if he's not interested—even if they are friends."

"I'm not worried about it. I can guarantee he won't be bothered that I'm dating Josh. I think Hunter would actually like Josh. If he had been at Krav today he would have laughed till he wet himself."

I thought Robbie's eyes were going to pop out of his head. Picturing the scene, Robbie clearly imagined a different reaction than I had predicted.

"If you say so," he finally said, doubtfully.

Since Hunter had never seen fit to confide in Robbie, I didn't feel right outing him even if it would eliminate his persistence. I shrugged again, not wanting to repeat myself.

"Really baby, Ev is right. I understand your confusion, but you have to trust me, it isn't like that between them."

Sam tried to help me out, understanding my predicament. Robbie shook his head as if we were both nuts but let the subject drop.

I wished them both goodnight and took a shower before climbing into bed. I went to sleep smiling to myself; it was the first time I had been this excited for a date in years.

Sam and Robbie were unable to attend our weekly Thursday night trip to The Stop, but Hunter and I decided to go, not wanting to break tradition. I had not seen much of him this week as his parents were visiting from Connecticut. We ordered drinks from Griffin and settled into a table with a good view of the stage.

"How was your family time?"

"It was great. My mom kept a constant stream of food in front of me; it's the Italian in her. I visited a couple of dojos with dad. He taught a class which I joined; it was like old times. I even went to the one near campus where you're taking Krav. I mentioned you and Hanshi Rosati said you were doing exceptionally well for a beginner."

"Hanshi was wonderful when I met with him. Don't rat him out, but he even gave me my uniform for free. You should also tell your dad Sensei Alex is a keeper. I partnered with him the first two classes so he could help me catch up with the other students. He said my previous martial arts instructor was a hack," I teased.

"A hack, you say? Alex is talented, but I could still beat him into next week."

"That's the first time I've heard you be conceited about your martial arts skills."

Hunter averted his eyes, unsure how to respond to my observation. He was usually humble about his abilities; it was a departure from character. I think I had shamed him by pointing it out so I decided to change the subject and alleviate his discomfort by sharing my embarrassing moment of the week.

"Speaking of class. I had one of my finer moments this week."

"Oh really, do tell."

"I don't know, it's humiliating. You have to promise not to laugh at me."

"I can't promise when I don't know what you're going to say. If I make such a promise, I may not be able to keep it knowing the situations you manage to get yourself into. What did you do, kick Sensei in the balls? Did the weight bag knock you out? Wait I know—you were so sweaty when attempting a roundhouse kick you fell on your butt instead?"

Hunter laughed imagining my many possible snafus.

"I'm glad you're enjoying yourself at my expense. I wish it were one of those, my catastrophe was worse."

"Now you have to tell me."

"Not unless you tell me something humiliating first." I refused to suffer alone.

"Does it have to be martial-arts related?"

"Nope. I'm open to anything that caused you to go full-blown tomato red, provided you were over the age of twenty-one when it occurred."

"That bad, huh? Okay, give me a minute to think."

We both sipped our drinks while Hunter pondered.

"I got one. Senior year at Columbia I had to take French 101 to fulfill my language credit. I had to pass in order to graduate and I have a mental block where French is involved. Fifty-percent of our grade was based on an oral presentation at the end of the semester. I slaved over this thing for weeks. So, standing before the professor and twenty classmates, I began my presentation. My assigned topic was how I prepare for school each day. I described my morning routine, in my poor interpretation of French, intending to explain that I shave in the shower, but I knew something had gone terribly wrong when half the class began laughing and even the professor was covering her mouth to hide hysterics. After class, I asked the professor what I had said incorrectly, and she suggested I ask the teacher's assistant. I caught him on his way out, and asked him what the hell I had said. The guy laughed in my face before cluing me in that I had told the whole class I stroke myself in the shower every morning because it left less of a mess than when I do it in the sink. The TA was a male, which I can only presume is why the professor sent me to him."

I succumbed to the comicality. I was caught between the hilarity of Hunter's epic blunder, and the visual he conjured of stroking himself. It didn't help that he had previously alluded to the fact that he was enormously gifted. I simultaneously turned beat red and choked on my own saliva, as tears poured from my eyes. It was too much, never before had laughter and arousal been so closely tied. When I finally composed myself, Hunter gave me a rueful look.

"For what it's worth, I passed the class with a B-, but in the interest of full disclosure, I suspect it was a pity grade. I didn't deserve more than a C."

That started me laughing all over again.

"I want you to know that you have given me carte blanch to laugh in your face."

"Fair enough, it was worth it. It may be a tie for the mortification trophy this evening."

I proceeded to explain my faux pas with Josh. Hunter laughed to the point of convulsions when I painted the picture of my literal nosedive. His merriment came to an abrupt halt when I described Josh's involuntary reaction to my provocative position, which surprised me as I thought it was the cherry on top of my undignified sundae.

"He did what?" Hunter asked quietly, too quietly.

"Little Josh rose to greet me." His stare was unnerving. "What? I thought you would have laughed yourself to the floor by now."

"Did you tell Sensei what that pervert did to you?"

"Did to *me*? I'm the one who took the kamikaze trip into his groin. He had no control over his reaction."

Hunter was furious, "Of course he did. All men over the age of eighteen have learned how to control their arousal at inappropriate or inconvenient times. Do you think I haven't needed to tame nature when it would have been preferable and far more enjoyable to let my instincts lead me? It's certainly not easy or convenient, but it's what any decent guy does."

"I'm sorry if Josh doesn't have your stellar control; it's not like he had any forewarning, I caught him off guard. Maybe he found me so irresistible that my effect couldn't be denied."

I jested to smooth Hunter's ruffled feathers, which proved to be a wrong move.

"You're convinced Josh is more attracted to you than other men who bothered to exert control of themselves because he didn't show you that respect? Are you kidding me? You're out of your damn mind! What you're saying has no basis in logic, the man disrespected and groped you." Hunter was past furious, having moved on to postal.

"He didn't grope me! You're completely overreacting. I guess I shouldn't bother telling you that the silver lining to my humiliation was I got a date out of the catastrophe."

It seems I waved a red flag in front of the bull. Hunter was still as a statue, resuming his whispered tone.

"Wait, I must have misunderstood you. I thought I heard you say you're going out with this miscreant."

"Yes, we're going out on Saturday. He felt obligated to buy me dinner after what happened."

Hunter stared at me wide-eyed, unblinking for what felt like an eternity.

"What were you thinking?"

It sounded like the question was directed more to himself than me, but I decided to answer. I knew I was adding jet fuel to an inferno, but I was so annoyed with him at that point I didn't care.

"I was thinking he's cute, funny, nice, and made an uncomfortable situation bearable. I haven't been on a date in over two months. I'm sexually frustrated, dammit."

"You're going to fuck *him*?" Hunter roared.

"I don't know, maybe. Not on a first date, of course, but if we have a good time, after a few dates, it's a possibility. What do you expect? I'm human and I haven't taken a vow of celibacy—BOB, the vibrator, can only be my battery operated boyfriend for so long."

Hunter stood up so fast our drinks toppled over. He began to pace in front of our table, visibly agitated as I sat stupefied. "Is this an overprotective big brother thing? You're about to have an epileptic fit because I'm going on a date with a nice guy who is aroused by me, and I *may* sleep with him in the future. What is the big deal?"

"I am *not* your brother!" He snapped, and then muttered to himself, "'What's the big deal' she asks me." He resumed his pacing, trying to regain his composure but failing miserably. "I can't have this conversation with you right now. I can't—" he trailed off, thought unshared. "There is nothing I can say that will stop you. I just can't, I have to go."

With those parting words, he stormed from the bar without a backward glance.

I stared at the empty space he left for several minutes before I remembered the drinks, which began to drip into my lap. I scanned the table for napkins but found none. Thankfully, Griffin materialized with a rag and a glass of water.

"Here you go," he handed me the water before cleaning the table. I raised a doubtful eyebrow at the water. Griffin read my reticence and explained, "It's two-fold. First, I'm not sure how much of the drink you consumed before you took to wearing it and, while I'm sure you would love to get out of here, I can't let you leave until I'm positive you're sober. Second, it just gives you something to do...you look a bit staggered."

I nodded and sipped the water, realizing he was right. I needed something to do with my hands other than punch the wall beside me.

"How about I keep you company for a little while until I'm sure you're good to drive. The bar is slow so Jeff will be fine on his own," Griffin offered kindly.

"Sure, that sounds like a plan."

"You want to tell me what happened?" Griffin asked carefully, as if afraid I may burst into tears.

"To be honest, I have no clue."

"Give it a shot. Maybe I can help you sort it out."

So I told him everything, beginning with my lap dive and ending with Hunter's apoplexy over my date. Griffin never interrupted me, but nodded at key points as if it all made perfect sense. I was glad someone seemed to know what was going on.

When I finished I sighed with exasperation, "I don't know what his problem is."

"You don't?" Griffin asked me with surprise.

"No clue. It seems like every once in a while he does something so out of character, I feel like I don't even know him." Again, Griffin nodded as if it all made perfect sense. "Well?"

"He wants you," Griffin stated simply, as if that explained everything I had told him.

"He has me, we're best friends, and we see each other almost every day."

"No, he *wants* you, as in—he wants you in his bed, on his arm, and in his life. He wants you to be his."

Not this again, it was a repeat of my conversation with Robbie. The only difference is Hunter had just lost a little bit of my loyalty with his inexplicable temper tantrum, and I was feeling less inclined to protect his bedmate preferences.

"No he doesn't," I returned vehemently.

"Yes, he does," he shot back at me with equal vehemence. Was Griffin reading from Robbie's script?

"I assure you, he does not."

"And why, pray tell, is that?"

"Because he's gay," I finally let the secret out, and felt instant relief.

"Gay? Hunter? No, Ev, that guy is not gay. Trust me."

Griffin sounded so sure, he almost convinced me.

"No, he is. Not all gay men fit into some contrived mold."

"True, nevertheless that man is most definitely *not* gay. He prefers women, and the woman he wants—desperately—is you."

"That makes no sense, Griff...can I call you Griff? He's my best friend. We have been hanging out nearly every day for over two months. If he wanted me, he could have made a move at any time."

"I don't know why he hasn't tried to close the deal, but he definitely wants you. I see you both here on Thursdays. He watches you like a hawk, follows your every move. The way he looks at you when he doesn't think anyone is watching is filled with longing. I'll admit I was surprised nothing had transpired yet. I figured you weren't into him, and he was taking what he could get. Do you want him?"

I pretended to think about my answer when every cell in my body screamed "hell yes!"

"Yes, I'm attracted to him," I answered casually.

Griffin chuckled, "I see how you watch him when he isn't looking, Ev. I see the same desperate longing in your eyes. Did he actually tell you he was gay?"

"No, it was the sum of several observations that led to my conclusion."

"Now who's stereotyping?" Griffin repeated my reprimand.

"I'm so confused."

"My best guess is he wants you, but he doesn't *want* to want you."

Well, that was disheartening. How could I have thought he was gay? I'm not a stupid woman, but the answer was simple—his being gay was more palatable than whatever reason he had for not wanting to date me. Besides, if he was gay I could still be friends with him despite my attraction.

Why would he reject the prospect of a relationship with me? Even Robbie called him my *un*-boyfriend. We had a meaningful relationship, one that omitted romance or sex, but was completely fulfilling in every other way. Was that it, did he not find me stimulating? No, Griffin said he had seen Hunter's desire for me and I sensed it on occasion. When we danced...when I almost kissed him.

If he sought my friendship and was enticed by me, why would he not date me? Perhaps he saw no romantic future between us; I could envision him choosing amity in lieu of a fling. Unfortunately, my appraisal of our romantic potential differed drastically. I believed in our potential, an enduring devotion. What convinced Hunter we were unsuitable? Should I ask him? No, that was too pathetic. If he had resolved not to pursue such intimacy, I wouldn't demand justification with the intent to persuade him otherwise. I would continue to want what he refused to give, over time becoming resentful, which would inevitably suffocate our friendship. Crestfallen, I admitted our friendship was doomed. I couldn't stifle my now acknowledged longing, and I couldn't engender his affection. The only consolation, our condemned relationship and my steadfast yearnings presented a salacious opportunity. If I couldn't have Hunter for life and I was destined to lose him as my best friend, then I could enjoy his company for a time to our mutual benefit. I did tell him I was sexually frustrated.

There was my new game plan. I would seduce Hunter—partake of some delicious, sweaty, guilt free romps, and then we would part ways amicably. I would be devastated but that was inevitable now. If I was destined for heartbreak, I might as well enjoy the ride getting there. Buoyed by my decision, I started to feel a bit better and smiled to myself. Hunter and I had always enjoyed the game of tormenting one another. That game just got a whole lot more interesting, and I planned to play dirty.

"Uh-oh, I know that smile. I have seen it on women's faces before." Griffin broke through my scheming.

"And what smile would that be?" I questioned innocently.

"It's the smile that foreshadows a man's demise. What are you planning, lady?"

"No demise, my plans will be enjoyed by all. No need to fret. I will tell you...none of them are particularly lady-like."

Griffin groaned, "I've created a monster!"

"Don't worry about Hunter. If he doesn't want my advances he is perfectly capable of protecting himself."

"So you're going to try and persuade him to make his move, finally?"

"Not the way you mean. I'm going to seduce him without pursuing a romantic attachment."

"I never said he only wanted a sexual liaison. I said he wanted you to be his. If you want the same, you should talk to him."

"Even if he did want a serious relationship with me, he doesn't *want* to want it. I have no idea why and it doesn't really matter, I'm not going to be able to change his mind. Only he can do that, and if it hasn't happened by now, it's not going to."

"Not everything in life is so cut and dry, Ev. You should talk to him. Just tell him what you want, what you're willing to accept, and let him do the same. You could be sacrificing the possibility for something amazing and permanent for something pleasurable but temporary."

"You know, Griff, you're one smart cookie. Did you learn this wisdom in bartending school or the school of hard knocks?"

Griffin laughed at my quip. "A little while bartending, a lot of hard knocks, and a whole lot at Hensley."

"Hensley?"

"I'm a finishing up my Ph.D. in Clinical Psych. The main area of focus for my dissertation is human behavioral choices and the thought processes that determine them. For example, two people can experience the exact same event, such as a plane crash. They can both walk away unharmed with no losses, but how each processes and reacts to the experience shapes their future thought processes, behaviors, and choices."

"My, my—aren't you the closet geek? I never would have known."

"Don't blow my cover. It's taken a long time to cultivate my bartender mystique."

"I like you Griffin, you're a good man. Thanks for listening and for the advice. I will talk to Hunter." I squeezed his hand to emphasize my appreciation. "If there is ever anything I can do for you, just let me know."

"Actually, to prevent my own hypocrisy, I have to ask—is Sam still dating that guy?"

"Yeah she is, sorry. It's serious too, I wouldn't hold your breath for her."

It may not be what he wanted to hear, but he would appreciate my directness.

He nodded. "Then I'll ask a favor of you—if the situation ever changes, give me a heads up. You know where to find me."

"I promise I will."

"Okay, you're officially cleared to drive now."

"You're confident I'm sober?" I laughed.

"You were always sober; you had less than half of your drink before the spill. You needed to talk, which meant I needed to detain you and provide the opportunity."

"Sneaky, sneaky man."

Griffin grinned and walked me out to my car before giving me a brief hug.

"Goodnight, Ev, and good luck."

I drove home, my feelings assuaged by the many revelations of the evening. I had a clear mission for which I needed to develop my strategy. Operation 'Bring Hunter to his knees' was green lighted. This was going to be fun.

Chapter Ten

"Most virtue is a demand for greater seduction."
-Natalie Clifford Barney

The following day, I brought Sam up to speed on all that had transpired the night before, only editing my promise to Griffin regarding Sam. I didn't want Sam to feel uncomfortable when we went to The Stop, knowing Griff was pining for her. Sam didn't seem as shocked by Hunter's actions and my revelation as I anticipated. When I finished, I looked at her expectantly.

"I was afraid this would happen," Sam began.

"What does that mean?"

"Ev, for someone who is incredibly perceptive, you have a major blind spot when it comes to Hunter."

I wanted to argue, but she was right. I was sightless when it came to Hunter. My desperation to keep him necessitated impaired vision. I couldn't imagine my life without him; hence, I rejected any proof that would force me to acknowledge the possibility of romantic entanglement. I could accept his refusal when there was a cause that had nothing to do with me.

"How long have you known?" I asked Sam.

"Known what? I knew you wanted him from the first day, after your Business Strategies class. When you told me about your verbal sparring I saw he captured your attention, otherwise you would have rebuffed him without another thought."

"When did you know he was straight?"

"The first time you told me he was gay; I had yet to meet him outside of the confines of the self-defense seminar. You had more interaction with him in an informal setting, so I trusted your judgment. But after our first lunch, I had my suspicions. He watched you too attentively to be platonic. I considered saying something then, but your banter was captivating, a well-choreographed dance. You each had a unique understanding of the other and how far you could push. You hadn't even known each other a week and you already had your own inside jokes. You were unguarded with him, at ease and open. I considered telling you, but I didn't want the distraction of lust to interfere. Then he pulled the cold-shoulder routine, and I doubted myself. I was afraid he was playing games, liking the chase, so I dropped it."

I nodded my understanding. "But after the dancing, I had no doubt. I wasn't overstating when I described your chemistry as scorching. You were so in tune to each other, completely oblivious to the world around you. I saw you almost kiss and he wanted it as much as you did. I don't know what caused him to break away, but I have no doubts he wanted it too. I debated the virtues of telling you a hundred times, but you had grown so close, I didn't want to take that away from you. You were content, the happiest I've ever seen you, wrapped in ignorance."

"I came to the same conclusion last night. The only way to keep Hunter indefinitely was for me to remain unaware. That's no longer a possibility, our friendship has an expiration date. There's no way for me to repress my desire for more, which will worsen the more we are together. Friendship can't exist when one party wants more. My discontent will poison the relationship with bitterness, or I will force space because of the ache of denial."

I could already feel the fissures beginning in my heart. "How am I supposed to survive losing one of my best friends? I wish you had a super power to wipe my memory of last night. If I had never taken that stupid Krav Maga class none of this would have happened," I complained.

"It would have happened eventually. If not Josh, it would have been another guy. I do think Hunter's jealously is telling. Are you sure there is no chance?"

"It's been over two months. We see each other every day. Apparently, I have been broadcasting ready, willing, and able signals to anyone within a fifty-mile radius. If he were interested, he would have taken the initiative. Whatever his reasons, he has resolved not to pursue more than friendship. I'm not going to beg."

"I still think you should talk to him and make sure there's no chance."

"I will, I promised Griffin the same."

"Shall I assume you are planning on tasting the forbidden fruit before the vine shrivels and dies?" Sam smirked, reaching the same conclusion I had last night.

"You know me too well."

"I sense a trip to the salon for a Brazilian in your future," Sam laughed.

Actually, it wasn't a terrible idea. Sam had been singing the praises of a Brazilian wax for years, claiming men were driven wild by the results. I held firm in my ability to groom my nether region on my own. However, Hunter was exceptional, I had no doubt it would be the hottest sexy time I ever had. He may just warrant extra special efforts.

"Can I get the name of the salon?"

"I bet Hunter is an ace in the sack."

"If I had any doubts, which I didn't, after dancing with him they would have been laid to rest. His hip action was unparalleled. Plus, he already admitted he was packing heavy artillery," finally sharing that juicy tidbit.

"Then there is only one thing for you to do."

"And that would be?"

"Ride 'em cowgirl!"

As I arrived home from work Friday night, I noticed a figure lingering in the shadows near the entrance to my building. I strained to identify the silhouette, but it was indistinguishable from a distance. I was certain it was a man based on his size. Each building housed four apartments, so he could be visiting another tenant.

As I approached, I felt my heart rate accelerate and my breathing coming more rapidly. I surveyed my surroundings, but no one was around this time of night. Shit! I had no easily accessible tools to defend myself, and I was too close to run for safety successfully. I considered screaming to attract attention, but shelved the intent not wanting an audience when it was proven I was once again being paranoid.

I strode to the door exuding a confidence I didn't feel, hoping my concern was unfounded. I was mere feet from the door when a body stepped in front of me, blocking my path. I drew a deep breath, prepared to scream for my life.

"Hello, Ev. It's good to see you."

I was startled and the scream died in my throat. "Drew? Is that you?"

I stepped back and took stock. Yes, it was Drew. I was moderately relieved, but unwilling to relinquish my caution fully.

"What are you doing loitering outside my building at eleven?"

He smiled bashfully, "Sorry if I scared you. You've been on my mind lately, and when I was driving by, my car just pulled in of its own accord."

"Oh, it's nice to see you, of course, you just surprised me." I remained out of arms reach, just in case. Drew and I had dated for nine months, and he always treated me well. We ended amicably and still saw each other socially on occasion. I had no justifiable reason to doubt his intentions, but Hunter's cautions could not be ignored.

"I knocked on your door, but no one answered. I knew you would be home soon if coming from work, so I decided to hang out for a bit to see if I could catch you," he explained reasonably.

"It's great to see you. I have been meaning to call so we could grab coffee and catch up. How have you been?"

It was awkward having this conversation outside in the cold, but I didn't feel comfortable inviting him in knowing Sam was on a date with Robbie.

"Good, good. I've wanted to talk to you for a while now, do you mind if I come in?"

"Now's not a great time, Sam is inside with her new boyfriend, she probably wouldn't appreciate my bringing a guest if she didn't answer the door when you knocked."

"Ah, I understand. This wasn't how I envisioned our conversation, but...I miss you Ev, I want you back. I have always thought of you as the one that got away," Drew said intensely.

At any other time in my life his last statement would have been romantic, but the attacks at Hensley cast a sinister filter on his words. My skin crawled with unease.

"Drew, I'm flattered, really, but we gave it our best shot and it didn't work out. I am glad to still call you my friend, but I can't see us ever being more."

Drew pulled his fingers through his hair in frustration. "Don't you remember how happy we were together, how much fun we had? I know I was wrong to let you go, you slipped through my fingers while I was distracted by school and life. It was a mistake. I know we were meant to be together, Ev. You have to feel it, too."

"I'm sorry, but I don't. Yes, we had fun, our relationship was good while it lasted, but we wouldn't have both been so easily distracted if we were meant for one another. Please, don't ruin the memory of what we shared now. I'm not the right woman for you."

"But you are, I can't stop thinking about you. Every woman I have been with since pales in comparison. I even imagine it's you when I'm inside of someone else."

Warning lights were flashing—danger! Not only *way* too much information, but it was also creepy beyond measure. I needed to get inside and away from him with all haste.

"Drew, I'm seeing someone. I'm not available, I can't be with you," I stated resolutely.

"You are? Who is he? Is it serious?" He was visibly unsettled by the news.

"I am and it is. I'm sorry, but we aren't going to happen. Please try to accept it and I wish you the best. I need to head in now, I'm freezing. Goodnight."

I reached for the door and looked back over my shoulder, "And goodbye."

He didn't move as I entered the building and ran to my apartment, quickly entering and locking the door. Once safely inside I texted Sam to make sure Robbie would escort her to the door in case Drew remained outside. What once would have been a fairly common, albeit uncomfortable, conversation with an ex, now felt ominous. I was shaken by the exchange, unsure if I was overreacting. I checked the door again and verified all the windows were locked before going to bed. It took a long time for me to relax enough to fall asleep, and when I did, my dreams were dark and foreboding.

Still unsettled after my run-in with Drew, I reconsidered my date with Josh. Dating suddenly felt like a very risky endeavor. I eventually decided to proceed as planned; Josh was a nice guy and we would be in public the entire time. If I gave him the opportunity, and toned down my newly acquired suspicious nature, maybe it would turn into something, although it was unlikely given my desire for Hunter. If nothing else, the date would keep the flames of Hunter's jealousy stoked, which would make my seduction far easier. Turning anger to passion was far easier than turning amity to desire. I would subtly lay the groundwork this week, and then lure Hunter into my carnal web with sultry dancing next Saturday. If the plan was a success, I would be a thoroughly satisfied woman the following morning.

Despite my carnal plans for Hunter, I was committed to giving Josh a chance on our date. I knew Hunter and I had no future by his design. Why not open myself up to alternative opportunities? I resolved to keep things casual with Josh for as long as I was pursuing relations with Hunter. I didn't want to mislead anyone. I was already walking the tightrope of respectability dating Josh while intending to screw Hunter; I wasn't going to take the plunge into Tramp Town. I could proceed with a clear conscience as long as I didn't make any commitments. I wasn't concerned for Hunter, he knew about Josh and was not interested in commitments.

With my parameters in place, I prepared for my date. Chez Madeline was one of the nicest restaurants in the area, giving me an opportunity to dress with more elegance than usual. I selected a sleeveless aubergine bandage dress with a pair of strappy silver stilettos. I added a smoky gray pashmina for warmth before heading out with my keys in hand.

I was thankful that Chez Madeline offered self-parking in addition to valet, as I didn't relish the idea of having to drive my old Honda to a valet stand. It was shallow, I know, but Papa Smurf would stick out like a sore thumb among the Mercedes and BMWs.

Josh waited for me just inside the restaurant, stepping out to take my arm as I approached. He wore a beautiful black Armani suit paired with a slate gray shirt and eggplant silk tie. I realized our outfits complimented each other and was senselessly pleased. Josh assisted with my coat before handing it to the coat check. He slid the claim tag into his inner suit pocket, the gesture of care not lost on me.

"Good evening, Ev. You look stunning." He took a minute to appraise me approvingly, "And I thought you looked good in your Krav uniform."

"You look rather dapper tonight yourself."

"Did you want me to hold on to your valet ticket?"

"No thank you. I don't have one."

He gave me a questioning look.

"I was afraid the valet would be tempted to steal my car. I prevented a crime by parking myself."

Josh surmised reasoning and laughed. "I drove a '93 Chevy Caprice in college. It can't be that bad."

"No, not quite that bad. It's an old Accord, but at least the model is still in production," which earned a chuckle from Josh.

"Shall we?" He extended his arm to me again.

"We shall."

When the server arrived, we both requested a glass of Sauvignon Blanc to accompany dinner. Josh ordered the Grande Tasting for two, for which Madeline's was famous. He declined the wine pairing as we were both driving. The meal was opulent: Pine Island Oysters on the half-shell, braised sea bream, arctic char, seared foie gras, duck leg confit, roasted lamb, artisan cheese board, and a trio of sorbets. For dessert, we were served a ginger almond tarte, the house specialty.

The company rivaled the meal. Josh and I discussed our lives, family, friends—excluding Hunter— and plans for the future. The conversation flowed naturally and was entertaining. Josh was an exemplary date. By the time we finished our dessert and coffee, I was stuffed. I quickly regretted my body hugging dress, which would be far less complimentary after my overindulgence.

Josh claimed my coat and assisted me into it before escorting me to my car. I thanked him for a lovely dinner and great company. Seizing the opportunity, he invited me out the following Saturday. I had to decline as I had plans, part of my Hunter seduction scheme. I felt a moment's guilt before remembering I was only dating Josh casually, no promises made. He requested a date the following Saturday, and I happily consented. Josh gently cupped my cheek with his warm hand and leaned in, placing a gentle kiss on my lips. It was too chilly to linger outside, so he took the keys from my hand, unlocked and opened my door. After assisting me, Josh closed my door gallantly and waved goodbye. As I drove home, I relived my evening—this was my most "adult" date on record. Josh was charming and chivalrous. He listened, appreciated my humor, and was supportive of my goals. I was attracted to him—not the all-consuming magnetism I felt with Hunter—but Josh did incite desire. He was available and enticed, which Josh made clear without pressure. He was precisely what I needed, it would be premature to predict if we had a future, but I was enthusiastic about the prospect. Unwelcomely a thought arose—the only way the night could have been better was if I had been with Hunter.

After work on Sunday, Sam and I went to the diner and plotted my course of action for plan 'Ride 'em, Cowgirl.' I theorized this would be a long-term initiative, therefore I should begin subtly and build the offensive over time. It would serve to weaken his resolve and allow a less awkward transition from a non-physical to carnal relationship.

I arrived at school on Monday thirty minutes before class started, which was when Hunter and I usually met. I had not heard from him since his outburst, leaving me unsure if he would appear. I shrewdly left an extra button on my shirt undone and added a long necklace to accentuate my cleavage. I decided not to bring up my date unless Hunter broached the topic, and then only provide minimal details. His jealously was a good sign, but I didn't want to exacerbate it causing a fight. Hunter's awareness that another man desired me, and my reciprocal interest, was sufficient.

Hunter was waiting for me holding two cups of coffee. When he handed me my cup, I saw he had written on the top, "I'm sorry!" I set my cup on a table before taking his and doing the same. He looked at me curiously, unsure of my intent, but I ignored his apprehension and proceeded to wrap my arms around his waist. He quickly wound his arms around mine in return, holding me close.

"I *am* sorry, I was completely out of line. I shouldn't have vented my frustration on you, and I never meant to disrespect you. I was miserable this weekend knowing I had upset you and not being able to talk to you. I need you in my life, Everleigh. You have become so important to me—I can't stand the thought of losing you because I can't control my infantile temper. It's no excuse but—I worry about you."

I pulled my arms from around his waist and encircled his neck, playing with his hair. This was more intimate than I had ever been, and I saw the surprise in his eyes before he quickly hid it. He tightened his hold on me infinitesimally.

"You can't lose me to some other guy, Hunter." This was true in the strictest sense, he could only lose me if he didn't want me. "You're just as essential to me. I don't know what I would do if I didn't have you."

I laid my head on his chest, needing the comfort. I knew my time with Hunter was limited unless he decided to pursue a new type of relationship with me.

"I missed you all weekend, and I was nervous you wouldn't show up today. I don't want to fight with you. I wasn't trying to bait you, honestly. It never occurred to me you would be bothered if I dated someone. Why did it bother you?"

I reluctantly ventured into the dreaded conversation, but I had promised Griffin and Sam I would verify my conclusions before officially commencing plan 'Ride 'em, Cowgirl.'

"Like I said, I was scared of losing you. I haven't had any competition for your attention before now, and I didn't like the idea of sharing my friend."

Okay, he used the F-word, not a good sign, but not conclusive.

"Hunter, are you gay?"

"What?" he sputtered in shock, "no, I'm definitely not gay. Not that I have any problem with it—love is love—but I'm attracted to women. Why would you even think that?"

"I've thought you were gay since you quoted 'Gone with the Wind'. It wasn't until Thursday that I started to have doubts. You seemed so jealous; I thought you might have been upset that someone else was getting a slice of cake that you wanted."

"You thought I was gay this entire time? That explains why you suddenly switched gears from enemy combatant to wingman. It explains a lot actually." He paused as if reevaluating the world as he knew it. "For the record, I have a mom and sister who are obsessed with the movie. I've seen or overheard it a thousand times. I could probably quote the entire script verbatim."

"That explains that." I determinedly pressed onward, "Were you jealous Hunter? Were you worried another little boy was going to play with the toy you wanted? You've never indicated you were attracted to me."

Hunter shook his head. "Everleigh, I can't believe you even have to ask. You are overwhelmingly beautiful, inside and out. If we weren't friends you would have been under me that first week."

"Confident much?"

"Am I wrong?"

"I plead the fifth." I decided to push a little further since he was being forthcoming, "So you were jealous?"

He released a breath, heavy with frustration. "Yes, I was jealous; insanely, irrationally jealous. Does that make you happy?"

"Of course," I cheekily replied. Hunter shook his head at me chuckling.

"It's true, I don't like the idea of sharing your attention, but I also didn't like the idea of another man getting a taste of what I can't have."

And there it was, the confirmation I was dreading. I wanted to abort the entire conversation, but I recommitted myself to seeing it through.

"Why can't you have me? You know I'm attracted to you, too."

I pressed myself against him reinforcing my point. Hunter groaned in response.

"Everleigh, if we had sex it would be incredible, no doubt, but then what? I'm not at a place in my life where I can offer you anything more than friendship or sex...as much as I may want to. After we sated our lust, things would get complicated. I can barely deal with you dating now; if we slept together, it would drive me mad. We would have no claims on one another, but expectations would still arise. Our friendship would never survive, and I refuse to lose you. In the future, when I can, I would like to revisit this conversation, but for now, I need to keep things platonic."

Oh, it was so much worse than I thought. I was the cliché, Plan B. The friend kept on the backburner in case something better doesn't present itself. How long was he hoping I would wait—a year, five, ten? I took a deep breath to cool my temper and my injured pride. I had asked the question, I couldn't fault him for his honesty, even if the truth was the last thing I wanted to hear.

"I can't be your Plan B, Hunter. I won't sit around alone and celibate, waiting for the day you conclude there are no superior options. If that is what you're hoping for, I can't give it to you."

"You are *not* my Plan B" Hunter belted out, "that wasn't what I meant. Now is just not the right time. I'm not stalling you to sow my oats. It's nothing like that. I just can't..." Hunter growled his frustration. "I can't explain it any better than I already have. I'm not asking you to wait for me to sort out my shit. I'm asking you to be my best friend. I don't want to change anything; I don't want to lose you." His despair was so evident I almost felt sorry for him. Almost. "I wish you hadn't broached the topic now. I understand I invited it with my reaction, but, damn it...I just don't want things to change."

"It's okay. I'm glad you told me the truth. I hear you and I understand, really I do. Yes, we can put this conversation behind us and still be friends. I can't promise things will not change, people and relationships evolve all the time, but I don't want to lose you either. If I could, I would do everything in my power to prevent it."

Unfortunately, the end of our friendship was inevitable. I had a moment of clarity during our conversation, finally admitting I wanted Hunter. I wanted him forever, above all others. I loved him as my best friend, but I finally accepted that I was also in love with him, and he just told me he could not give me what I wanted most—his love in return. There was nothing to be done about it, no case to be made, because if my heart was going to shatter either way, I would take whatever moments I could hoard and create some steamy memories to keep me warm during the lonely nights to come. Maybe Sam was right months ago—Hunter could be the fantasy I turned to in twenty years when I needed erotic inspiration. The only certainty was I would never regret nights spent with Hunter once he was gone.

"Thank God. I wish things were different, that I was able to give you more. I just can't, not right now. I won't ask you to wait an indefinite period of time, it's not fair to you. I promise to be your best friend and support you, no more irrational outbursts." He hugged me tighter and kissed the top of my head before whispering in my ear, "I wish I could tell you how much you mean to me, but words would never be enough."

Hunter released me from our hug and looked around, "Time to go."

Conversation completed, emotions poured out, it was over. I kept my word to Griffin and Sam. I'm not sure if I was glad to have done so, but at least I could move forward.

Hunter picked up our coffees, handed me mine, and then took my hand in his, leading me to our class.

After Intro to Acting, we all met for lunch at Westside BBQ. When I sat down Sam lifted an eyebrow, to which I responded with a small shake of my head and a frown. Sam returned my frown before shrugging, then lifted her arm up rodeo style and said aloud, "Ride 'em, cowgirl!"

Robbie and Hunter both looked at her as if she had lost her marbles, but I just laughed and laughed. If I couldn't cry, then I was going to laugh until the hurt stopped.

As the weeks passed we kept to our usual routine. I saw Josh at Krav Maga where he partnered me again, free of mishaps. He took me for a cup of coffee afterwards and we had a nice time; it was benign and pleasant. I was having trouble mustering the same level of attraction I had for him on our date. I was not ready to throw in the towel yet, but I was less optimistic. Josh was wonderful, but was dim when cast in Hunter's shadow.

Hunter and I were back to normal—both pretending our conversation had not happened. The only difference now was I made a concerted effort to touch him frequently, stand closer, hug longer, and press my body into his. What surprised me was Hunter responded to my mild advances in kind. He held my hand when he could find a justification, put his arm around me constantly, and occasionally slapped my butt playfully. He even began to kiss my forehead hello and goodbye, as if the top of my head was no longer good enough and he had to inch closer to my lips.

Sam was trying to convince me it was time to step up the seduction, but I was not ready. I was enjoying the new intimacy in our friendship, and I didn't want to lose it too soon by escalating my sexual advances. Each day I pushed a boundary slightly further and, thus far Hunter's response was favorable and reciprocal. We were all going dancing on Saturday, further progress would be achieved when we danced, I was certain. There was no reason to artificially engineer something that would occur naturally.

I know Sam didn't understand. She had the man of her dreams and she knew she could keep him. She could enjoy him fully without the need to curb her instincts and desires. I was happy for her, thrilled even, but it was hard not to covet her liberties.

Every day that passed was one less day I would have with Hunter. The further our relationship progressed, the closer we came to acting on our desires, the closer the end was. It was bittersweet. I cherished every little touch, every moment we spent together, because they were finite. I loved a man who could not fully return my love, not in the way I wanted. Every day the pain deepened and another crack was chiseled in my heart, as the impending loss loomed. I tried not to focus on the grief that was to come, and instead lived in the moment. After all, these moments were all that would remain when he was gone.

Chapter Eleven

"*Through this experience we have been warned
—learn everything, don't forget anything!*"
-Karl Liebknecht

Saturday night finally arrived and I was ready. I dressed how I felt: lustful, covetous, hungry, and carnal. I wore a tiny red dress, which was shorter than any I had ever worn. It was a deep red, one shoulder, fit-and-flare with a black satin band defining my waist. No other adornments were necessary. The color spoke volumes and the overall effect was tantalizing when paired with black snakeskin heels.

Hunter and Robbie met us outside The Stop; if my goal was to capture Hunter's attention—mission accomplished. Had he been animated, his jaw would have dropped, tongue unrolled from his mouth pooling on the floor, and horns would have sounded '*ah-ooh-gah, ah-ooh-gah!*' He strode up and pulled me against him, impulsively kissing my bare shoulder near the base of my neck, an unexpected and welcomed greeting.

"Woman, what are you trying to do to me? Holy shit! You can't leave my side tonight."

He pulled me tightly against him and I could feel a hard ridge against my hip—my, oh my. I was lost in the moment until I felt a series of vibrations against my pelvis.

"A little lower and that could be effective," I taunted.

"You're evil," he muttered as he pulled his cell from his pocket and checked the screen. "You have to be kidding me, I'm sorry, I have to take this. I'll be right back."

When I turned to face Sam, she was gloating, words unnecessary.

"I'm staying at Robbie's tonight," she casually advised. I nodded.

Clearly unsatisfied I had not risen to her bait, she continued, "You know, in case you feel the need to rearrange your bedroom furniture tonight. You have been talking about moving your bed. Maybe Hunter could help you. He seems *up* for the challenge."

I rolled my eyes, not dignifying her comment with a response.

"Are they finally going to do it tonight? Thank God," Robbie teased.

"Not you too. Sam can get away with it; you're risking reprisal," I cautioned him.

Hunter returned, ending their fun. "I have to go, work emergency and I'm the closest. I'm so sorry," he told us collectively before reaching for my hand and pulling me a few feet away.

"You're heart-stopping in that dress. If there was any way I could get out of this, I would."

He pulled me into a tight embrace and lifted me off my feet. He kissed my forehead before slowly sliding me down his body.

"Be careful tonight. Stay with Robbie and Sam, please."

"I will. Go fix your problem, and if you get done early enough come back," ...'to me', I wanted to add.

"It doesn't look promising, but if I can I will. Text me when you get home so I know you're safe, and make sure your doors are locked."

"I promise."

He gave me another squeeze followed by a kiss on the top of my head before releasing me reluctantly.

"Take care of my girl tonight," he commanded to Sam and Robbie with a departing wave.

I rejoined my friends, disappointed that Hunter had to leave. At least he'd seen me dressed up and liked what he saw. Remembering his approval, I smiled—definitely worth the effort.

"His girl?" Sam smirked.

"Your guess is as good as mine," I shared in her surprise.

Once inside we shared a round of shots before heading to the dance floor. After several songs Linc joined us, I was thrilled things had returned to normal between us. We danced for over an hour before he received a call and left to meet friends at another club. What was with me tonight? All my dance partners were being called away. I spotted Sam and Robbie a few feet away where they were intently practicing for their endeavors later in the evening. Deciding to give them alone time, I waved to Sam, pointing to the bar to indicate where they could find me later. She nodded her understanding and went back to checking Robbie for cavities.

I found a stool at the far end of the bar next to the wall, which provided a little breathing room from the crush. Griffin waved the universal sign for 'just a minute.' True to his word, he was standing in front of me shortly thereafter.

"What is up, pretty lady? Where's the rest of your crew?"

"Sam and Robbie are dancing. I lost Hunter to a work crisis before he even made it inside. Then I lost Linc to another club; apparently my man repellent is working. I was ready for a break, so I figured I would set up shop here and people watch."

"Good plan. Do you want a drink?"

"A mojito and a water, thanks."

When Griff returned with my drink, I took a sip and hummed my approval.

"Everything worked out with Hunter?"

"Eh, sort of. I did talk to him, as I promised, and I was right. He *wants* me but he doesn't want me. He could only offer me friendship."

"Are you okay with that option?"

"Do I have a choice? I think it's too late for a lifelong friendship. I have alternative plans."

Griffin shook his head and laughed at me.

"Don't tell me, let me guess—you've realized you're in love with him but you can't have him. It's an impossibility to remain best friends with someone you're in love with, so you're throwing caution to the wind and luring him into bed to enjoy your wares, before running in self-preservation."

Damn, he was accurate and succinct.

"That's it in a nutshell. You're good at this."

"I know," he smiled at my compliment, "it's easier to have perspective when you aren't emotionally involved. Okay, back to the masses. I will come check on you later. Holler if you need me."

"Will do."

I spent the next half hour watching couples fight, girlfriends dance drunk, and guys strikeout. It was as entertaining as any reality show. Any more spray tans and we would be entering 'Jersey Shore' territory. I was beginning to get restless when a steel arm banded around me, pulling me back against an unforgiving body, nearly causing me to fall off my stool.

"Hey," I yelped while trying to right myself.

"Where's your guard dog tonight, princess?" he whispered in my ear while pulling me against him painfully.

I was at an unfavorable angle and his arm locked me against him, restraining me diagonally from below my left breast to right shoulder. My left arm was trapped, unusable. I had hooked my feet around the legs of the stool to prevent from falling, but this left me without the use of my legs and at his mercy. I scanned the area to see if anyone would intervene, but no one had noticed.

Looking over my shoulder, I verified it was Heath who had imprisoned me. I used my right elbow to jab him in the ribs, but couldn't generate enough force behind the blow to make any meaningful impact.

He laughed at my efforts. "You'll have to do better than that, kitten, but make it count because I'll give it back to you two-fold."

"Let me go or I'll be at the fourth precinct filing a complaint before your daddy can speed dial the family lawyer."

"I'll just tell them you're retaliating because I shot down your sexual advances. Who do you think the police will believe—a poor girl dressed like a hooker or the respected son of a prominent executive? Any skeletons in your closet will be on the nightly news before you can say boohoo."

"You pompous prick," I shouted, "You can't get a woman to consent willingly so you try to force her compliance? You know what the problem is, don't you? Those Facebook pictures of your microscopic dick are enough to chase women away, even if your disposition isn't."

My plan was to keep him talking by spouting concocted yet plausible accusations until I could get help. I was screaming, but the music was so loud I was muted to all except those right next to me. The people to my right had turned their backs, purposefully missing the confrontation, and Heath's friends were blocking the rest of the club's view.

"You fucking bitch!" Heath's hand left my shoulder, about to grab my neck when something, or rather someone, flew over the bar.

I didn't see, but heard a fist connect with Heath's face causing him to stumble back, as Griffin's voice screamed for the bouncers. I tumbled back without Heath bracing me, but the other bartender grabbed my hand from across the bar steadying me.

"If you ever step foot inside my bar again it will be the last time you have use of any extremities. Don't you ever lay your hand on a woman, you pathetic piece of trash!" Griffin roared ferociously.

Two bouncers made their way through the crowd and dragged Heath out of the bar with his friends in tow. Griffin approached me, slowly placing a hand on my shoulder and scanning for injuries.

"Are you okay, Ev? I'm sorry I didn't get here sooner. I didn't see what was happening until you started screaming. Did he hurt you?"

"I'm fine Griff, just a little shaken up. That's the second time he grabbed me, I have no idea what his problem is."

"His problem is he's a fucking narcissistic sociopath."

"Is that your professional opinion?" I joked to ease the tension gripping Griffin's entire body.

"Actually, it is. I can't believe he put his hands on you before this. You need to call the cops and file a complaint," he counseled insistently.

"What's the point? I'm not going to have any marks to substantiate my claim. All you saw conclusively is that he had his arm around me awkwardly. It will be a 'he said/she said' complaint. Best-case scenario will give him a slap on the wrists, but I don't think daddy's lawyers would even let it get that far. He's not worth wasting my time."

"You're making a mistake, Ev. You're minimizing what he did because you don't want to deal with the consequences of reporting him. I understand, but it's the wrong decision. He's a classic bully, those types of personalities will continue to push until someone pushes back. He most likely had his father to clean up any trouble he found in the past, but with enough complaints on record the next district attorney may not be willing to turn a blind eye to his aggressive behavior."

"You're blowing this out of proportion, Griff. He's a spoiled, egotistical jackass with major roid-rage, but I don't think he is a real danger to me. I pricked his pride."

"It's your call, but I still think I should get the cops here."

"No," I declared firmly with no room for negotiation or persuasion.

Griffin sighed dramatically, "Fine." I could tell he was frustrated. He suddenly spun to the trio standing to my right. "And you three...get the hell out. You stood there and pretended to be deaf and dumb when there was clearly a woman in trouble."

"Thank you Griff. I don't know what else to say." I climbed off the stool and hugged him.

"What is going on over here? You getting snuggly with Griffin?" Sam came up beside us sounding confused.

I gave her a brief rundown of what had occurred; subsequently Sam...lost her mind. She let fly a string of curses that would have made the most hardened 'Sons of Anarchy' biker blush, in combinations I was certain had never before been conceived before. She threatened every part of Heath's person ending with a threat to castrate him and shove his balls so far down his throat that he would have breasts. She raged while pulling her earrings from her ears and slipping off her shoes, threatening to find him at the frat house or wherever he may be. She was so out of control that Robbie could not contain her, despite his best efforts. Griffin, giving up on Robbie's ability to take care of Sam, swept her up bridal style, and carried her out the back door of the bar. Once outside he began to whisper to her. He soothed and implored her to calm down while holding her securely against himself to prevent either of them from being injured. Finally, she was mollified after Griffin swore he had delivered several shots guaranteeing Heath wouldn't be able to breathe comfortably for days. Having finally regained her composure, Sam noticed she was in Griffin's arms and Robbie was standing to the side impotently. Suddenly she was as red as my dress.

"I think I'm done, you can put me down," she demurred. "Thank you."

Griffin reluctantly began to lower her to the ground when he noticed her bare feet.

"Where are your shoes?"

"Umm, I'm not sure. I have one, I think I may have thrown the other."

Sam raised her hand demonstrating her lone shoe. If possible, she would have crawled under a rock and emerged after an indeterminate period of time, such was her mortification.

"Don't worry, we'll find it when the bar closes. You can pick it up tomorrow," Griff offered as if hurling her shoe across a bar was the most mundane act in the world. Maybe it was more common than I realized. "I'll just carry you to your car."

"No," Sam nearly shouted, "I mean, that isn't necessary. Thank you."

"Samantha, I'm not putting you down on the dirty ground barefoot. It's not a problem; you weigh less than my ten year old niece," he endeavored to ease her discomfort.

I knew Griffin was enjoying these few moments holding Sam in his arms and, after his rescue I was inclined to enable him.

"Robbie, why don't you take Sam's keys and pull her car around? I can drive us home," I suggested.

"Okay, I can do that. Where is your purse, babe?" Robbie asked Sam mildly. I'll never know what the trigger was, but Sam lost her mind again. This time, Robbie bore the brunt of her wrath.

"Don't you dare call me 'babe.' It was your motherfucking friend that touched Ev, again. This is the second time that he laid his hands on her, Robbie. What are you going to do about it, huh?" Sam was gesturing wildly but Griffin kept a secure hold on her, not interfering, but ensuring her safety.

"Why are you blaming me? I was not even there this time. Heath is not my friend, you know that. He is the president of Kappa Sigma Tau so I have to interact with him, but that is all. I don't know what you want me to do."

Robbie was hurt by Sam's censure. I could understand how he must feel, but he was missing her point entirely.

"What I want you to do is not associate with a fraternity who would choose a felon-in-waiting as their president. I want you to be a man, stand up to your father, and quit the damn frat because it's the right thing to do. I want you to recognize that my best friend, who also happens to be your friend, has been hurt by your *brother* twice. Twice! What is it going to take before you separate yourself from him completely? Grow a fucking pair! If you won't do it for your own self-respect then do it out of respect for me!"

"Sam, there are four weeks left of school. There is only one mandatory frat event remaining. What would be the point of quitting now when I suffered for three years to keep the peace with my dad and have the benefit of the networking frat alumni provides after graduation? I agree Heath is a worthless piece of crap, but if I quit now he wins. I need to stick this out. When you calm down you will see my perspective. I'll go get the car."

Robbie walked away, ending the conversation before it could spiral any further out of his control.

"It has nothing to do with sticking it out; he just wants to take the path of least resistance," Sam said to herself.

"Cut him a little slack, Sam. We are all emotional right now, and he is in a tough position. He does have a point about school almost being over. Don't give him the ultimatum to choose between you and the frat unless you seriously mean it. Sleep on it before you make any rash decisions," I encouraged.

"I don't know," Sam sounded exhausted, "what do you think Griffin? You seem like a smart guy."

"It's probably best if I keep my opinion to myself on the matter," Griffin answered diplomatically.

"Come on, don't hold out on me. Give me your honest opinion."

"You can tell a lot about a person by those they associate with. In order to be a man you have to be willing to stand up for yourself and those you love. We are defined by the choices we make and must live with what they say about us," Griff paused thoughtfully before staring deeply into Sam's eyes. "I think if I had a woman like you, Sam...I would never make her feel second to anything for any reason. And as Ev's friend, I would never tolerate anyone harming her."

"Wow," Sam and I said in unison.

Griff shrugged, "You asked my opinion."

Sam turned to me, "Is he always like this?"

"Pretty much," I answered truthfully.

"Wow," Sam reiterated.

Unconsciously, she rested her head on Griffin's chest as Robbie pulled up in Sam's car and exited.

"Sorry, I didn't know where she parked."

He looked at Sam settled comfortably in Griffin's arms, his displeasure showing. Griffin read Robbie's discontent and moved to the car, gently placing Sam inside and closing the door, then turned back to Robbie.

"Sorry man. I didn't mean to step on your toes, but I had to get her out of the bar before she hurt herself or others. There aren't many benefits to being an oafish leviathan, but one of the few is I can easily subdue and maneuver people when necessary. I hope there are no hard feelings."

He pacified Robbie's injured pride at being unable to control Sam, deprecating himself to make it easier for both of them. I wanted to adopt him as my big brother and keep him forever. Seriously, if Sam was sticking with Robbie, which I was no longer certain I was in favor of, then I needed to find a special woman for Griffin.

"Yeah, I get it man," Robbie responded. "Hold on for a few minutes, Ev, I'll get my car and follow you home." Robbie walked away before I had a chance to assure him it was unnecessary.

"I want you to know Griff, I'm proud to call you my friend. You were incredibly brave to protect me tonight, and to open yourself up with such honesty to Sam. You're one special guy."

Griffin glanced behind me to assure himself Sam wasn't listening. "Ev, between us—Sam's right. The decisions Robbie made suggests a lack of conscience and weakness of character, the kind of defect that will not improve or change; he's not the one for her. I'm not letting my covetousness color my opinion on this, I swear. I only want her happiness, even if I have no significant part in it. Think about what she said and come to your own conclusions, but if you want my advice, she is destined for disappointment with him. She's too strong and principled for someone as biddable as he is."

"Griff, if I was not hopelessly in love with Hunter, I would marry you today."

"If my emotions weren't otherwise engaged," Griff's eyes drifted to Sam, "I'd accept your proposal—maybe. You're a bit of a handful."

I laughed, "And Sam's not?"

"She's small enough I can practically fit her in my palm. Totally manageable."

Robbie's headlights illuminated us, and I gave Griffin a fierce hug before departing.

When we arrived home I parked in front of our apartment while Robbie idled, watching us walk to the door without attempting to engage Sam. He knew her well; she would need time to cool off.

Once inside I remembered my promise to Hunter and sent him a text.

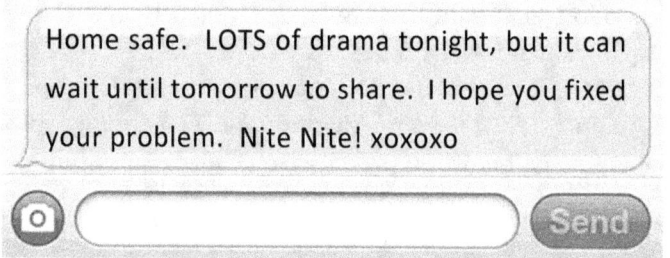

Home safe. LOTS of drama tonight, but it can wait until tomorrow to share. I hope you fixed your problem. Nite Nite! xoxoxo

After hitting send, I fell into a dreamless sleep.

I awoke Sunday morning feeling hung over from the emotional tempest the night before. I needed to get moving if I was going to be on time for work. A shower was necessary to wash away my raccoon eyes—never a good look for a lady. By the time I finished two cups of coffee, showered, and dressed, Sam was also awake and staring at the TV with rapt attention.

"Have you heard?" Sam asked me grimly.

"Heard what?"

Sam muted the news, "They found a body in the lake near Telly Quad last night."

I gasped at the shocking news.

Sam continued, "According to the news, the girl's identity has not been released, but it's confirmed that she was a student at Hensley. The police made a statement—they suspect the murder is linked to the attacks, but they will not officially acknowledge a connection until they receive the autopsy results. The detective said the death was not accidental, and police have requested assistance from the FBI. Hensley is going to be releasing a statement later today."

"This is awful. Who would do something so vile? Do you think it is the same person as the other attacks?"

"I was thinking about it. The murder must not have been premeditated if the police are linking it to the assaults. I wonder if the attacker lost control and beat her to death and then threw her in the lake to cover it up. If it was an ordinary drowning they wouldn't be so quick to make the connection," Sam speculated, the years of watching primetime crime shows were showing.

"There were probably indicators of the previous attacks too, like the rope marks the Gamma girls were talking about."

"That would make sense. The police are not releasing any more details while working with Hensley to identify her. My mom actually called to make sure I was alive after she saw the news this morning, that's why I'm up. Can you imagine? She asked me to consider withdrawing from Hensley. She also said she would pay for you to finish school anywhere you wanted next year."

"I can't Sam, I am a month from finishing. I made a commitment to Marty, and my future at Higher Yearning is dependent upon me being in the area. I will just have to be vigilant until the deviant is caught."

"I know. I feel the same, but I had to extend her offer."

"I hate to leave now, but I have to get to work."

Throughout the day, I received texts from friends checking in. Everyone was scared and needed to confirm their friends' wellbeing. Linc texted me to call if I needed to go anywhere after dark and he would accompany me. Josh sent a text to see if I was okay and if I needed anything, which was especially sweet. Even friends from high school were texting me when hearing about the news. Hunter texted me to check in mid-day.

You okay?

Yeah!

Just a bit scared after the news.

Do you need me to come by?

No, I'm fine. Sam and I have girl time tonight. She has a lot to figure out after last night.

My phone rang. I looked at the screen to find it was Hunter. I told Regan, who was covering the front, I was going to take a call and to holler if she needed me before answering.

"What happened last night?" Hunter greeted me.

"Hello to you, too. Last night was nuts, although it seems inconsequential in light of this morning's news. I presume you heard."

"Yeah, I heard. I didn't text earlier because I knew you were safe. I wanted to talk with you and Sam about additional safety measures. I don't want either of you going out alone after dark."

"Hunter, that's impossible. We can't have escorts everywhere we go. We will be careful, text each other whenever we arrive and leave a destination, and not go out alone."

He sighed his frustration, "Ev, this is critical. There have been twenty-three attacks and now a girl is dead. If the death is linked, as the police are indicating, that shows an escalation in violence. I have a feeling it's a Hensley student since all the victims attended Hensley. It could be anyone, you have to be more than cautious; you need to be paranoid until they catch this scum. I couldn't live with myself if something happened to you."

"I know, I'll be careful. I won't trust anyone other than my 'safe list', which consists of you and Sam. Oh, and I've officially added Griffin as of last night."

"Griffin? What exactly happened last night?" Hunter sounded serious.

Remembering his reaction the first time Heath touched me, I regretted my allusion. With the tension from the murder, Hunter was already on edge. I decided it was best to evade his question to save him the unnecessary stress.

"It was really nothing. Not even worth discussing. I'm sure you have a ton to do, I'll let you go."

"Everleigh, I'm not going to ask you again. You can tell me now or I can drive to Higher Yearning and extract the information in person." I knew he would make good on the threat. "As a side note, trying to divert my attention only confirms it isn't something trivial."

"There was a situation at the bar last night, but Griffin handled it. Then he carried Sam out and we all went home." It was the truth, in its most rudimentary form.

"Is Sam okay? Was she hurt?"

"Sam is fine, he didn't touch her. She lost her temper, so Griffin had to carry her out back to ensure she didn't hurt herself."

"Wait, you lost me. Where was Robbie?" Hunter was perplexed, "What set Sam off?"

"Robbie was there, but he couldn't calm or restrain her, so Griffin just scooped her up while Robbie trailed behind. Actually, now that I think about it, it's quite funny. Griff has a huge crush on Sam, so I think he enjoyed the duty."

"Yeah, I know Griffin has a thing for Sam. He has as long as I've known him."

"Wait you knew? Why didn't you say anything?"

"A man is entitled to his secret desires, especially when the object of said desire is unavailable. Besides, it's nearly impossible to miss; he looks at her as if she's the last glass of water in the Sahara desert."

"Well, Sam's not clueless anymore. She definitely noticed Griff last night, and he essentially declared his interest."

"Good for Griffin," Hunter mused, "he's a respectable guy, better suited for Sam than Robbie is in many ways. You never told me what set Sam off."

I hoped I had distracted him, but there was no getting out of it. Hunter was a dog with a bone.

"It was nothing, some guy grabbed me, and Griff stopped him."

"What?" Hunter shouted causing me to pull the phone further from my ear, "and you thought to gloss over that fact? No wonder Sam went off the deep end. Are you okay?"

"I'm fine. Griffin jumped over the bar and pulled him off me before it escalated. I'm not hurt." Except for the bruise on my rib cage, which it didn't seem wise to mention.

"What aren't you telling me?" aggravation colored his tone. Relenting, I described what had ensued, except who my assailant was and his commentary.

"Are you fucking kidding me? You made it sound like some guy grabbed your arm. He assaulted you and intended to choke you. Why the hell did Griffin not call the cops? I'm taking you down to the station."

"No," I said firmly, "Griff wanted to call the cops but I wouldn't let him. It was a 'he said/she said' situation and nothing would have come of it, I didn't want to spend my night at a police station. It's over."

"Who was it, Everleigh? Was it Linc? I told you he wanted you. He seemed harmless, but after he showed up at Higher Yearning that night, I'm not so sure."

I cut Hunter off immediately, pissed he was once again disparaging Lincoln, casting him as a villain. "It was not Linc. I told you Lincoln is my friend and a decent guy. It was Heath, you moron."

Silence.

"What did you just say?" Hunter asked in an ominous whisper.

"It was Heath," I answered quietly, defeated.

"And you didn't think that was important to mention? This is the second time that bastard laid his hands on you. Fucking-son-of-a-bitch-motherfucker!" I could not help but think that was a lot of inbreeding. "I should have killed him the first time. I knew there was something wrong with him. Fuck!"

Following Sam's example, Hunter proceeded to lose his flippin' mind. He rarely cursed, but they were flying from his lips like bullets from a machine gun. I was beyond appreciative he was not at The Stop to witness what happened, otherwise Heath would most likely be in the morgue. Hunter's ironclad control had shattered.

"You didn't call the cops? This is the second time, Everleigh. He grabbed you and threatened you in public. This is serious. You may have sufficient grounds for a restraining order." Hunter was regaining control, planning a course of action.

"I can't imagine why I thought you would overreact," I said heavy with sarcasm.

"I'm not overreacting. I wish I had known this last night, I would have found a way to come to you. I wish I had been there to protect you, but I'm glad Griffin took care of the situation, and it sounds like he did a good job of it." Hunter sighed, "I wish I could hold you right now. I need to feel you in my arms and know you're safe."

"I'm safe, Hunter. It was a little scary, but I kept my cool and everything turned out alright."

Hunter grunted his disapproval of my assessment, but said nothing more.

"I have to go make some phone calls for work. Please reconsider filing a report. You have Griffin as a witness."

"I'll think about it," I lied.

"Thank you for finally telling me. I don't want you to keep secrets from me. There is nothing you can't tell me, Everleigh."

"I know, thank you for your concern. I know you worry. I promise I will be on high-alert, and if I see Heath I will head the opposite direction."

"Thank you. I'll check in with you later."

I ended the call and shook off my disquiet. I had to finish my shift, and then help Sam sort herself out.

Chapter Twelve

"Men, we don't need you to be a knight in shining armor. We just need you to be a little bit brave, just a little bit." -Virginia Madsen

As I drove home from Higher Yearning, I brainstormed what advice I should give Sam. I knew we would discuss the events of last night, including Robbie's situation, but I didn't know what to tell her. I liked Robbie, he and Sam were good together, complimentary. Yes, he was passive, but not everyone could be Mr. Alpha Male like Hunter and Griffin. Sam was happy, with the exception of Robbie's association with Kappa Sigma Tau, which would be ending shortly. Sam deserved to be loved and cherished, and Robbie gave her that, but so could many others. Griffin was certainly willing. Was Robbie the right partner for Sam? They shared common interests, knew the same circle of people, experienced similar upbringings, and understood the effects of obscene wealth. All the puzzle pieces were in place—so what was my hesitation?

I wouldn't even be questioning my judgment if both Griffin and Hunter had not opened their big mouths, letting their doubts pervade my mind. I trusted them both and they concurred Robbie was not the right guy for her long-term. So what do I tell Sam? I didn't know the right answer and it was a decision only she could make. I resolved to help her think through all angles and support her decision.

When I walked into the apartment, an aromatic feast for the senses greeted me. Sam had been playing chef, which meant she had also been pondering the Robbie situation.

"I'm home!" I called into the kitchen.

"Perfect timing, dinner is ready. Drop your stuff and sit down."

"I smell you've been thinking things over," I joked as I settled into my usual seat.

"Yes, I've been considering options while preparing a veritable feast: orange fennel salad; lobster risotto with asparagus and roasted tomatoes; chicken breasts stuffed with mushrooms, mozzarella, spinach and onions; and broccoli rabe in garlic. I also made Tiramisu for dessert."

"Wow. You should be conflicted more often if I'm going to benefit with this type of dinner."

Sam returned with our salads accompanied by fresh semolina bread from the bakery.

"Did everyone and their mother check on you today?" Sam asked laughing.

"Right? It was nuts. People I haven't heard from in months were suddenly 'touching base.' Most were concerned, but I suspect some were fishing for details as if the cops are consulting me." I shook my head at people's need for gruesome details. "I spoke with Hunter and told him what happened last night."

"How did he take it?"

"About as well as you did. I don't think he threw a shoe, but I may have heard glass crashing against a wall."

"What did you expect? That boy loves you," Sam stated as if her comment was no more remarkable than an observation about the weather.

"As his best friend, yes, but that's not what you meant, is it?" I exhaled, "You know what he said. Don't raise my hopes for something that can never be."

"He said he didn't want a committed relationship at this point in his life, that's not unusual for a man under thirty. He never said he wasn't in love with you. I will admit those two statements are usually mutually exclusive, but in this case, I have no doubts he's in love with you."

"Stop, just stop. It's hard enough knowing that he wants me but doesn't want a relationship with me. I couldn't deal with knowing he is in love with me and still doesn't want me. When I'm with him it feels right, like coming home. We fit together. Sam, my heart is already breaking, please, don't sow false-hope—it will only increase my pain later. My heart can't take the devastation." I was close to tears, but I fought them back, "You know what they say—when someone tells you something about themselves you don't want to hear—believe them."

Sam gave me a sad look. I shook off my despair and redirected the conversation.

"Enough of my whining. What is going on with you?"

"I've decided to give Robbie another chance. I abhor Heath but Robbie was right, he will be out of our lives in a month and we will never have to think about him again. I wish Robbie could break from the Kappas, but I understand the pressure to pacify parents and the connections the frat provides will be helpful. He isn't choosing them over me, he's just invested so much effort already it would be wasteful to walk away now with nothing to show."

"Except his pride." I hastily continued, "I'm sorry Sam, you know I like Robbie and I will stand beside you no matter what you choose. My only fear is how easily he sacrifices conscience for his benefit. I know you love him and he loves you, I just want you to be sure."

"I understand your point, but I don't think he's forgoing his conscience. In my heart, I believe he is just scared. He would never let someone hurt me or anyone else if he could stop it. After the fact, choices become more complex. Right and wrong becomes less defined," Sam's defense of Robbie reaffirmed her decision. "I love him."

"Okay. If you have made your choice, then I'm on board."

We finished Sam's delicious dinner and my doubts about Robbie lingered, but Sam was discerning and I had to trust her instincts.

We spent the rest of the night watching chick flicks and painting our nails, trying to forget all the drama.

I arrived at school Monday morning and walked straight into Hunter's waiting arms. He held me close, rubbing my back with one hand and cupping the back of my head with his other. My arms wrapped around his waist in a vice grip as he rocked me gently, occasionally kissing my head while breathing me in. I burrowed into his chest and never wanted to come out, this was where I belonged. I soaked in the feel of Hunter for as long as possible.

"I missed you," I whispered

"I missed you too," Hunter replied with his cheek resting on the top of my head. "I almost came over last night to reassure myself you were okay."

"Why didn't you? You've never actually been inside our apartment."

"I knew you and Sam were rehashing; did she decide what she is going to do about Robbie?"

"She's standing by her man, giving him another chance." I shrugged. "I think she is making justifications for some of his character flaws, but no one is perfect. She loves him."

"He's not a bad guy. I just think she needs more than he can give her. She is so strong and protective. Robbie's...not."

"Maybe they complement each other that way. Balance out each other's strengths and weaknesses."

"Maybe," he didn't sound convinced but dropped it and released me.

As I stepped back and looked at him, I saw how weary and ramshackled he appeared.

"Rough night?"

"Rough couple of nights. I was worried about you, and I have a lot going on at work. I haven't slept much in the last few days. I'll catch up soon, I hope."

"Anything I can do?"

"Just take care of yourself and avoid Heath, along with your other admirers. That will help alleviate my worry."

"I will, but that's for my benefit, to keep me safe. Anything I can to help you?"

"Just be you, Everleigh. That's all I need."

He handed me the coffee and took my free hand, lifting it to his lips and kissing the top before leading us to class. Another first.

During class, Sam texted to cancel our standing lunch so she and Robbie could have time to talk. Hunter had a commitment too, so I texted Linc to see if he was free and we decided to meet. I was glad to fulfill my promised lunch date and we would be in a public place, which would appease Hunter, if I intended to tell him—which I didn't. Linc greeted me with a hug and a kiss on my cheek.

"Hey girlie! We finally do lunch."

"Better late than never, it's good to see you. How are you?"

"I'm well. Enduring the final weeks of my last semester of undergrad, like everyone. How about you?"

"I'm hanging in there. Feeling the stress of the murder along with every other woman on campus. I'm not sure if you men can appreciate how draining it's to be constantly on guard—feeling like you're perpetually in danger. To some extent women have to live with the worry in our consciousness at all times, but with the attacks, we have to be incessantly vigilant. It's grueling."

"I never really thought about it before, but you're right. I guess men take for granted that we don't have the same level of vulnerability."

I nodded my agreement with a mouthful of salad and, noticing my predicament, Linc carried the conversation.

"Did you find another dancing partner after I ditched you on Friday?" He laughed.

"You don't even want to know."

"Uh-oh. What happened?"

I gave him the rundown of Saturday night's events after his departure.

"Are you serious? I feel awful for leaving now."

I will never understand why men take responsibility for events they could have never predicted.

"Wait, isn't Heath that muscle head from Kappa?"

"One and the same."

"What a prick. I can't believe he grabbed you like that. What is wrong with people? At least Griffin took him to task. I saw him beat the shit out of a guy once during sophomore year. Some drunk tried to hit another bartender with an empty beer bottle after he was cut off. Griffin was escorting him out when the guy got belligerent and took a swing at Griff. For a big guy he sure can move fast."

"You're telling me! You should have seen him fly over the bar to save me. It was Superman-esque, or maybe more Batman-esque. Superman was an alien, and I'm fairly certain Griffin is human. One complex human." It felt good to laugh about it.

"What else is new? Seeing anyone?"

"You're just asking all the wrong questions today." I was only partially joking and Linc laughed. "It's complicated. I just started dating a guy from my martial arts class. It's casual. He is extremely nice and would be good for me."

"But?"

"But I made the monumental mistake of falling in love with my best friend."

"Sam?" Linc asked, appearing simultaneously confused and aroused.

I slapped his arm.

"No, you perv. I'm talking about my other best friend, Hunter."

"Right, the guy from The Stop, I remember now. He was giving me the 'cut you' eyes."

"The what?"

"You know the look. The one that says—if you look at her again I'm gonna cut you and bury the body where no one will ever find it. Maybe you have to be a guy to understand."

"Exaggerate much?" I asked while laughing at his theatrical translation of a look.

"Definitely not exaggerating. The guy had castrated me in his mind, and that's painful even if only imagined. He definitely sent the message that you were his and I best back off. Let me tell you, message received—loud and clear."

I rolled my eyes.

"So where is the problem? You're into him, he is into you. Seems pretty cut and dry to me."

I wish it were so simple.

"That's the complication. We are both insanely attracted to each other. We have chemistry that is off the charts. We are best friends, we understand and trust each other, and we are both single."

"I'm going to have to stop you there. I'm not hearing any impediment."

"He doesn't want a relationship at this 'stage of his life.'"

"Ev, forgive my brutal honesty, but that is bullshit. That's guy code for one of two things: I don't want a relationship with you—ever. Or I can't have a relationship with you because I'm with someone else and I don't intend to leave, and I'm too noble to cheat."

"Geeze, Linc, don't sugarcoat it for me," I answered sarcastically to hide my pain. He was not telling me anything I had not already thought myself, but it was more credible when someone else spoke your thoughts. "I don't think he is seeing anyone else. He's with me a lot."

"If married men who live with their wives can pull it off, then Hunter can. I'm not saying he is, but it's possible."

"I just can't see it. Hunter is trustworthy, honest to a fault. I don't think he would lie or cheat."

"How do you define cheating? You haven't slept together, have you? Have you even kissed?"

"No, nothing." I didn't like that Linc was making sense.

"Maybe he married some girl he knocked up in high school but didn't love. Now he found you, but isn't free to give you his heart, so he resists."

"You should write romance novels," I insulated myself in sarcasm. "I think you're off base with this theory. Sometimes the simple answer is the right one. He just doesn't want me, not forever. He loves me as his friend, would love to practice the horizontal tango, but he is not *in* love with me."

"You may be right, but does it really matter the reason?"

"What do you mean Linc? Of course it matters."

"Do you really want to be with someone who is telling you they don't want to be with you and can't give you forever? You're a catch, Ev, one in a million. You shouldn't settle for anything less than everything. The man you choose to devote your life to should be willing to climb over broken glass—naked—to stand by your side. That is what you deserve."

"Oh, Lincoln," I leaned around the corner of the table to hug him as best I could, "you're a wise man and an amazing friend."

"If you don't remember your value, no one else will. Don't ever settle, Ev. You're too beautiful to waste on someone who doesn't appreciate you."

"If you make me cry I'm going to slap you. Stop being so damn sweet," I joked. "You're a bit of a poet, you know?"

"Shut it, Miss Carsen. Don't you dare spread that filthy rumor around. It would attract the wrong type of women."

"What type would that be?"

"The type you marry."

I left Linc after lunch, grateful for his friendship and unexpected wisdom. As I drove home, I reflected on our conversation. I don't know if my new understanding brought me any peace, but I gained perspective and the resolve to let Hunter go when the time came.

Glancing in my review mirror, I noticed a shiny black pick-up was following me, or at least it appeared to be. The car was familiar, but I couldn't recall from where. I knew my imagination was probably running away with me, but to reassure myself I turned onto a side street to take a roundabout route home. Sure enough, the pick-up followed. Thank God it was daytime or I would have been hyperventilating by now. My eyes were glued to the review mirror, only occasionally glancing at the road ahead as I watched the tail. The driver never got close enough for me to identify him, but I was confident it was a man based on his size.

I was positive I had seen the truck before; the decal on the windshield was distinctive. If it was a Hensley student I may have seen the car in a parking lot, the driver could be a stranger. I was near the entry to the apartment complex and decided to turn in, but not park if the truck followed.

I made a quick left at the last minute and slammed on my brakes while turning to see who was stalking me. Shit! I did know the driver—it was Drew. He must have purchased a new car since we had dated. Damn it, why was he following me?

I parked in front of my building and locked my doors, but didn't exit. I wanted to be sure that Drew didn't turn around. I noticed a neighbor park a few spots over and jumped out. I called a greeting and forced small talk as I entered the building with her.

Once I was locked in my apartment, I dialed Hunter, in need of advice. After explaining what had happened during Drew's initial visit and today, I waited for his guidance.

"Are you ok? Do you need me to come over?" Hunter voice was full of concern.

"No, I'm fine. I have Krav Maga in a little while and I need to study."

"Ev, you are a magnet for dubious characters. It's becoming a full time job worrying about you," he sighed, kidding, I hoped. "Give me his full name and I will call one of the officers I know at Suffolk P.D. to check him out. Maybe he can even have a talk with him."

"I am sorry to heap more problems on your shoulders, but I didn't know who else to call."

"Are you kidding? I would have been furious if I found out about this and you hadn't told me directly. Drew's behavior is extremely disconcerting, I would worry even without the murder. I wish you would have confided about his initial visit sooner, but I understand why you dismissed it. No more benefit of the doubt...for anyone."

"Yes, sir."

"I'll call the cop now and update you later if I hear anything. Be careful."

I felt better after enlisting Hunter's help. I was grateful for his police connection courtesy of the safety seminar. I don't know what I would do when I no longer had Hunter to turn to.

Krav class proved unintentionally arousing once again. Josh and I continued to partner as we worked on ground holds and breaks. When we began working on a technique to break a mount the situation got sticky. I was laying on the ground on my back and Josh was straddling me with a knee on each side of my hips, a mount position. I had to pull my legs up and hook my knees over his shoulders, using my momentum to reverse our positions. It took several attempts before I gained enough speed and fluidity to pin Josh to the ground successfully. The reversal left me straddling Josh's shoulders with a knee on each side of his head; needless to say, my crotch was in his face. Josh tried to maintain focus, but we were both struggling not to laugh or rip each other's clothes off after the third time I completed the move. When we reversed positions, providing Josh a chance to break my mount, the tension only escalated. I believe Josh tried, honestly I do, but he failed to squelch the stirring that occurred when he ultimately straddled my face. He blushed and quickly rose, stating he felt he had mastered the move and we didn't need to practice further. Was the universe trying to communicate a divine plan to me? My face had been in Josh's crotch in public more times than some of my ex-boyfriend's in private. It was getting ridiculous, but there were no female partners available and I felt more comfortable with Josh than any of the other guys in the class.

After class he invited me for coffee, but I declined. The day had taken its toll and I needed to rest. Josh was understanding and confirmed our date for Saturday, and we agreed to a casual dinner at a local Spanish restaurant. I was grateful he didn't offer to pick me up this time. I trusted Josh, but I had promised Hunter I would exercise caution. Josh walked me to my car and placed a kiss on my lips before saying goodbye.

As the week went by, Hunter was markedly absent. I saw him at class, but he missed our weekly clan lunches and didn't linger to chat with me on Tuesday after class. I was feeling pushed aside and began to fear he was distancing himself from me to prepare me for his imminent departure. After class on Thursday, I broached the topic as we exited the building.

"Are you okay? You seem off this week."

"Yeah, I'm just rundown and have a lot going on with work. I feel like I'm being pulled in different directions and beginning to tear."

I recalled hearing that Higosha Dojo was opening three new schools between Suffolk and Nassau Counties, so I took a wild guess.

"Are you having problems with the new dojos?"

He looked surprised by my insight. "We are actually. We have run into complications with the town permits for one of the renovations, and there are staffing issues at another. The third school is progressing smoothly, but it's always stressful opening a new facility, even when everything goes as planned. I can't fathom what my father was thinking when he decided to open three schools at once."

"So you're not avoiding me? Intentionally pushing me away?" I blatantly stated my fears.

Hunter stopped dead in his tracks, grabbing my hand to halt my progress.

"Is that what you think?"

I nodded timidly.

"Hell no, that's not it at all. It's all work related. There have been tons of meetings I've had to attend and problems to solve. I would have preferred to be with you if I could have. Don't you know that by now?"

"I'm not normally the insecure girl, full of self-doubt. You have me twisted into knots trying to figure out what you're thinking. I find myself analyzing the motivations behind your every action. I have no idea what you're feeling, what you want," I vented.

"Everleigh, I've told you where I'm in my life right now. There is no mystery to solve, no reason to second guess yourself or me." He used his hold on my hand to pull me closer. "You're my best friend. I adore spending time with you and I wish I had more time to give you. If I seem distant, it has nothing to do with us. Nothing has changed."

He was trying to comfort me, but his assurances were a rock in my stomach. I wanted his feelings to change; I wanted him to love me, to want to be with me.

I plastered what I hoped was a convincing smile on my face. "Sorry, you're right. I'm just a little more emotional than usual with all the stress around here. The fear is oppressive; I must be developing paranoid tendencies."

"Until they catch the guy, keep the paranoia. It's probably safer even if it makes you a little crazy," he teased as he wrapped an arm around my shoulders and kissed the top of my head. "I have to head to work, again, but why don't we make plans for Saturday night? We can catch up."

I was excited to have some additional time with Hunter and was about to give an enthusiastic yes, when I remembered I had a date with Josh. This was going to take some finesse.

"I would love to, but I have plans Saturday night. How about tomorrow?"

"I can't tomorrow, I have a commitment. What are you doing Saturday?"

"Nothing major. What are you doing Friday?" I countered vaguely.

"I don't want to bore you with the details," he responded equally vague.

We were at an impasse. I couldn't ask him if he had a date on Friday—I was masochistically dying to know—because he would ask me the same in return. This Pandora was not opening that box. Likewise, Hunter couldn't grill me about my plans if he was unwilling to share his own. We were gridlocked. We walked in quiet contemplation for several minutes before Hunter broke the silence.

"How about the following Saturday? Are you free then?"

"In fact I am. What did you have in mind?"

"Dinner, just you and me. It will give us some quality time to catch up and unwind. What do you say?"

"Perfect, sounds great."

I was excited to have him all to myself for more than a half hour here and there. I pushed aside the spiteful voice in my mind who insisted on pointing out that this was an *un*-date with my *un*-boyfriend. I should kick Robbie for that vicious sniglet.

"Want sushi? We'll figure out the time next week once your schedule is set."

"Definitely sushi, as if you need to ask."

"Excellent," he sounded genuinely eager. "I'll attempt to swing by Higher Yearning tomorrow if I can squeeze it in. Otherwise, I'll see you on Monday."

"Sounds good. Talk to you soon."

He gave me a hug and kiss on the forehead before leaving.

All I could think as I walked to my car was that I would have to consult Sam on what one wears on an *un*-date. I sure as hell didn't know.

Saturday night I drove to Café Salamanca to meet Josh. It was located a few towns over, but I didn't mind the drive when the tapas were widely regarded as the best on Long Island. Once again, Josh was waiting in anticipation of my arrival. He greeted me with a kiss in the parking lot and led me to the restaurant.

The atmosphere was casual and we were both in jeans. I had to give credit where credit was due; Josh in jeans was yummy! We decided to order an assortment of tapas to share, which was perfect for my curious palate. We ordered entirely too much food for the two of us, but I loved to try new foods and Josh's adventurous spirit was a fitting match for mine. We gorged ourselves with an assortment of tastiness. The meal was delicious and the conversation pleasant. We lingered over coffee, trading stories and anecdotes about ourselves. It was nice to feel desired by an attractive, intelligent man. Josh walked me to my car after dinner, once again opening my door and kissing me goodnight. As I drove out of the parking lot I saw Josh wave to me with a contented smile.

I was halfway home when struck by exhaustion. Working all day, followed by the gluttony of our dinner was taking its toll. Lost in a fantasy about crawling into bed and sleeping for a week straight, I nearly missed the check engine light illuminated on my dashboard. That little glowing icon was never a good sign. I was still twenty minutes from home, and driving through a winding tree lined section of road where there was little populous. I decided to press on, in hopes of making it home before the problem worsened. My radio abruptly turned off of its own accord moments before my headlights dimmed. I knew these were definitely bad news. I tried to remember my many visits to the mechanic over my five years of driving Papa Smurf to deduce the problem. I suspected my alternator might be the culprit based on a similar experience years prior. I prayed I could make it home without compounding the damage to my car. My optimism proved false when Papa shuddered and became sluggish. I carefully guided the car to the narrow shoulder of the two-lane road. It was midnight and I was stranded fifteen miles from home, alone, in the dark. If it were not for bad luck, I'd have no luck.

I tried to call Sam's phone but it went straight to voicemail. It was Saturday night. Sam and Robbie were on a date, which meant by this time Sam would be indisposed, followed by sleep. She would not be saving me. I dialed Hunter's cell, fingers crossed I would be able to reach him.

"Hello?" a sleepy voice greeted me.

"Hunter, it's Ev. What are you doing right now?"

"It's midnight, I was sleeping. Wait, is something wrong? Are you hurt?"

"I'm fine, but I have a problem and I was hoping you could help me out. You know, don the shining armor and mount your trusty white steed," I joked.

I could hear him dressing through the phone. Didn't that paint a delicious visual for me to cling to in my time of desperation?

"What's up?"

"Papa Smurf died," I replied sadly.

"You're watching cartoons? What are you talking about? Have you been drinking?"

"No you dolt, Papa Smurf is my car and he died. I think it's the alternator; I'm stuck on the side of the road."

"You call your car Papa Smurf? No wonder he died on you."

"Hey don't judge, he loves his moniker. Can we refocus on the issue at hand? I'm stuck on the side of the road several miles from civilization. Are you going to rescue me, or do I need to call one of my other superhero buddies?"

"Why am I stuck being a knight, when your other friends get to be superheroes? That doesn't seem fair. I want cool powers." He was teasing to distract me, and I loved him for it.

"Your magnificence supersedes all super powers. They would be superfluous next to your immense abilities."

"In that case, tell me where you are, and I will come and save the stranded maiden."

I gave him the best description of my location as possible under the circumstances, and he was confident he could find me.

"I'm going to hang up so I can call a tow truck for you. Hang tight and I should be there in fifteen minutes."

I heard his engine roar to life, confirming help was on the way. I sat in my car, trying to stay warm. April on Long Island was comfortable during the day, but nights still dropped to 40°F. I sang songs to myself to keep my mind occupied, not wanting to let fear seep in. Fifteen minutes could be a lifetime if the music from the movie "Psycho" was playing in your head.

Ten minutes later headlights approached me. I strained to see if it was Hunter's Yukon, but all large SUVs looked the same to me, especially in the dark. When the car slowed and made a U-turn behind me, I knew it was Hunter.

I climbed out as he did the same. He held his arms open to me and I walked into them gratefully.

"My hero," I teased, partially serious.

I was appreciative for his aide, especially when it required he drag himself out of bed in the middle of the night. He still appeared sleep deprived most days, making his sacrifice that much more significant. I huddled in the warmth of his arms, snaking my hands under his jacket and shirt to steal his body heat.

He jumped when my frigid hands connected with the warm bare skin of his back. I was only seeking to thaw my paws, but once my hands met his smooth skin, my intentions were diverted. I drew small circles with my pointer finger, my hands drifting to his lower back. He shivered, whether from the cold or my touch I wasn't certain. I dipped the fingertips of one hand under the waistband of his jeans, while I dragged my other hand up his spine and settled it between his shoulder blades. His grip on me tightened and I heard the raggedness of his breathing. I savored the sensation of his bare skin against mine and the familiarity of the moment. I could feel his body's response to me growing, causing my breathing to shallow.

His left hand slowly descended, stopping on the lowest part of my back. His right hand tangled in my hair as he cupped the back of my head. He gently tugged, causing my head to tilt back until we were gazing in each other's eyes. The yearning was palpable between us; I didn't dare breathe and risk breaking the thrall. His lips lowered as I rose on my toes, straining to meet him.

When the tow truck's headlights hit us, Hunter sighed, retreating from our embrace.

"Why don't you warm up in the car? I'll tell the driver what the problem is and where to tow the car."

I nodded, which was all I could manage at the moment. My synapses were enflamed with the enticement that had gone unfulfilled. If Hunter had waited two more minutes before calling, we would not have been disrupted at such an inopportune time. He would have kissed me—possessed me—at last. I climbed into the balmy truck, thwarted and discontent. I focused on slowing my breathing, trying to release the tension from my body. Could a person die from gratification deprivation? It certainly felt like it was a possibility.

Hunter had been as enthralled as I was, closer than ever to capitulating and indulging my inaudible pleas to satiate our desire.

Overcome by my exasperation, I beat the dashboard with clenched fists, needing to vent my disappointment. Hunter chose that moment to open the car door. He raised one eyebrow and chuckled.

"Please don't take your anger at Papa Smurf out on my baby." He had retreated to our familiar banter to displace the previous heat. "Are you worried about the cost to get him fixed?"

"Sure, that's the problem."

He knew damn well that was not the source of my grievance. I decided to play along, as he was begging me to do. Tow the line, stay on course, preserve our friendship. I hated the binds of amiability. Clearly we had journeyed back to Platonicville; I wished I could nuke that place. Obliterate its existence so we never had to return there.

"Where were you coming from?"

"I was at Café Salamanca having dinner. My car died on my way home."

"Oh. You were on a date with Jack?"

"Josh," I corrected what I suspected was his deliberate mistake.

"I see. Did you have a nice time?"

"We did. The food was delicious."

"That's nice," Hunter said blandly.

"It was in fact, Josh really is a nice guy. He's handsome, interesting, chivalrous, and *very* interested in me."

I could see Hunter's jaw clenched, his teeth grinding.

"He's established a successful career already. With that goal accomplished, I think he's ready to find the right woman and settle down, lay the foundation to build a family one day."

I was feeling spiteful; a child whose candy had been taken away, throwing a tantrum.

"Isn't he lucky to be in a position where he is able to offer you so much. It must be nice." Hunter's façade was slipping, "When's the wedding? Can I expect an invite?" He took a page from my book and reverted to sarcasm, "Wait, let me guess—are you going to ask me to walk you down the aisle?"

"Don't be ridiculous, I wouldn't have you walk me down the aisle...that would be Sam's job."

We sat in silence, stewing, each trying to calm our tempers before terse words and sarcastic barbs descended into a full-scale argument.

"Why do you have to push it, Everleigh? Can't you just enjoy our friendship? Can't that be enough for now?"

"Not when you keep teasing me. What was that before? Are you trying to drive me mad? Because it's working."

"The only thing I'm trying to do is preserve our friendship. I'm trying to keep you in my life. Apparently, it isn't as important to you as it is to me."

"Of all the idiotic things to say!" I was incensed. "There is nothing I want more than to keep you in my life. Hell, I'd keep you forever if I could, you just won't let me," I lost my momentum pitifully.

"Everleigh," Hunter said with compassion, "we have the same goal; we are both fighting to keep one another. Let's work together so we can succeed. I'm not your adversary."

"You're right. I'm just tired and frustrated about Papa Smurf." I was not tired at all, and Papa Smurf was low on my list of worries at the present. "Things are good the way they are, I don't want them to change."

Were my pants on fire? That may be the biggest lie I ever told.

"Nite, Hunter." I kissed his cheek before getting out of the car.

I walked into the apartment and fell into my bed fully clothed. I was emotionally drained and broken.

Chapter Thirteen

"I like men to be men, and I like them to care about me and to take care of me. I'm willing to let them do that." -Shelley Long

"They found another body."

Sam's wake-up call was effective. She was standing in my doorway still in her flannel pajamas.

"When?" I whispered as I rubbed the sleep from my squinting eyes.

"Sometime in the middle of the night. She was found on campus, but they haven't said where exactly. It's confirmed she was a student at Hensley. The news is calling him the next Ted Bundy. It's horrible."

"I still can't believe this is happening. I was clinging to hope that the first murder was unrelated, but it seems unlikely now. How can we have a serial killer on campus?"

"According to the news, he isn't a serial killer yet. Supposedly, to be classified a serial killer they must have killed three or more people over a period of more than a month with a cooling off period between the murders. Do you think that's his goal—infamy?" Sam asked as if I could offer insight into the mind of an almost serial killer.

"Who knows? I don't think you can apply rational thought to psychopathy. I just want it to end. All of the lives damaged and lost. The girls who survived will never be the same, nor will the families of those who died. It makes me sick."

"I know. Me too."

I carried the news with me through my day. At work, all of the customers were talking about the tragedy. I noticed less women came in to get coffee by themselves, and Marty's husband even came to stay with us at close and walked us to our cars. When I arrived home, Sam was watching the latest reports, absorbing every detail. Everyone deals with crises differently. Sam wanted to hear every report from every news station, as if knowledge would protect her. I wanted to tune it all out, not to bury my head in the sand, but I couldn't live in a cloud of death either. I let Sam do what she needed and went to my room to work on my final paper for Business Ethics.

The air at Hensley was rife with fear on Monday. I couldn't wait to leave campus and free myself from the stifling despondency. I headed to Krav Maga that evening looking forward to the normalcy that class and Josh would provide; I should have known better. As soon as I walked in Josh pulled me into a hug and kissed me gently.

"I'm so glad you're okay. It's horrible what is going on at your school."

I thanked him, hoping that would be the end of the conversation, but it was futile. Sensei Alex and the whole class decided they needed to work with me to improve my skills. The entire time was focused on developing my defense against multi-person attacks. I appreciated their concern, and it was useful to spar with opponents of differing sizes and abilities, but I was uncomfortable being the center of attention.

After class, Josh walked me to my car. He asked me out for the coming Saturday, but I already had agreed to my *un*-date with Hunter, so instead I consented for the following Saturday. Josh advised me that he would not be at class next week due to a business dinner, but would be looking forward to our date. He gave me a hug and a restrained kiss before watching me drive away.

When I entered the apartment, I was greeted by Sam's shrieking.

"Everleigh Rose Carsen! Get your butt in here."

Whatever was going on was big if Sam was using my middle name.

"I'm here. Our apartment isn't big enough to require shouting under any circumstances."

"Shut your face," her favorite response when I made a valid point to which she had no retort, "you will not believe what I just found out. Tonight Robbie was called to an emergency Kappa meeting. I just got off the phone with him, and he filled me in even though he was told he couldn't speak about it to anyone."

I could tell she was pleased that Robbie had defied his frat in some small way. I couldn't imagine what would be so interesting about a frat meeting that Sam was literally vibrating, but I was about to find out.

"All the frat brothers were called in to go over a list of dates, and they had to report if they had been with Heath on any of the days. They were trying to piece together a comprehensive timeline for hours. Do you know why?"

"No." But, I was sure she was going to tell me.

"Because the police found tire tracks at the scene of the last murder. The tracks were for a Lamborghini. Do you know how many students and faculty at Hensley drive Lamborghinis? One. I will give you one guess who owns the car. His pretentious taste in automotives got him busted. The police brought him in for questioning this morning, and he immediately called his father who sent the family lawyer. He claims he didn't do it, of course, but the police are holding him until they can corroborate his alibis or charge him. Heath's father called Kappa alumni who had sons in the frat to have the emergency meeting to provide him alibis."

"Holy cow!" I was reeling.

"I know. It makes sense if you think about it. Heath is an ass, and he has already proven he has aggressive tendencies with you."

"Heath is a cretin, unquestionably, but it's a huge step from what he did to me to rape and murder."

"I think he fits the profile, he seems deranged to me." Sam definitely watched too much CSI.

"Were the frat brothers able to provide alibis?"

"Robbie said, for the most part, people couldn't remember specifics. His two best friends were able to cover a couple of the dates definitively, but who knows if they are lying."

"I'm sure the police will sort it out. It would be a miracle to have the violence stop, but only if they have the right person."

I feared a convenient suspect with circumstantial evidence would result in hasty charges to pacify the public, leaving the real culprit free to continue his reign of terror.

"It's Heath, I'm telling you. I can feel it in my bones."

The police released Heath the next day with their apologies. The Dean of Students verified that Heath had been present at a university-sponsored meeting between the administration and leading campus groups, including Kappa Sigma Tau, which occurred at the same time as one of the attacks. His family verified he was home during one attack and on a family ski vacation in Vermont during another. His two best friends attested he was with them at the time of several other attacks. Heath was unable to supply an alibi for the nights of the murders. He claimed to be at home both nights while his roommates were out on dates. He implied he had company, but was unable to furnish more than the girls' first names. When asked to explain how tire tracks that matched his rare vehicle was found at the scene, he had no explanation. Sam found out from Robbie that Heath's father called the President of Hensley and the Dean of Students to ensure they promptly responded to the police's inquiry. He then contacted the Commissioner of the Suffolk County Police

Department to berate him for his incompetence in detaining his innocent son. The family was threatening to sue the county and police department for slander and discrimination; Heath was vindicated.

The rest of the week flew by as we all attempted to avoid campus and the news crews camped out around the entrances. Everyone was on edge; the whole campus felt taut, even the teachers seemed leery. I was relieved after my last class on Thursday, anxious to get off campus as quickly as possible. Hunter walked me to my car to ensure my safety, as usual.

"Are we still on for Saturday?" Hunter inquired as he pulled me in for a hug.

"Absolutely," I responded, feeling the first stirring of enthusiasm in days.

"Great. I'll pick you up at eight?"

He gently swayed us to and fro while talking. It soothed me and caused me to snuggle into him further.

"Eight is perfect," I agreed.

He kissed the top of my head with approval.

"I've missed you this week. We've both been so busy and you've been wisely avoiding campus. Work has had me tied up non-stop. We haven't had time to just be us, together. I'm looking forward to having you all to myself so I can soak up my dose of Everleigh-time."

"Ditto. I just want to have a nice night, forget about all the craziness going on around us. I need normalcy."

"That I can do. How about we agree not to discuss the assaults, or murders, or suspects, or motives, or anything remotely relating to violent crime? We will just be Hunter and Everleigh hanging out and having fun. No worries, no pressures, no concerns. We won't talk about school ending or the future. We will remain in the present the whole night. Deal?"

"Oh, you've got yourself a deal alright. That sounds like heaven right now."

He rubbed my back as he held me close, sheltering me from the world. I clung to him, wanting to feel the security of his arms around me and the peace he brought. They provided a sanctuary from the storm around us. I kissed his chest, unable to refrain. He kissed the top of my head in response, sharing the peace of the moment.

"Text me when you go to and from work. Let me know you're safe."

"Text you my every move, copy that," I joked.

"Get going you wise ass."

He placed another kiss on my forehead before letting me go. I was looking forward to our *un*-date. I promised myself I would live in the moment and enjoy my time with Hunter, just as he said.

Friday and Saturday passed quickly at work. The news channels were onto the next big story and life was returning to normal. The threat lingered, but was not as prominent as it had been the previous week. I arrived home from work on Saturday evening feeling lighthearted as I prepared for my *un*-date. I didn't even let the '*un*' attached to the date bother me. At this point, I was just happy to have some Hunter time. I decided to embrace the plan we outlined on Thursday and enjoy the night for what it was with no ulterior motives. I dressed casually with comfort in mind in lieu of seduction.

Hunter arrived promptly and wisely made reservations at our favorite sushi restaurant near campus—Oishii Sushi. We were seated immediately at a traditional Japanese table, as per his request. In a modern twist, there were chairs provided without legs at the low table. It was fun to sit in the traditional position. I had seen this special sitting area when previously dining at the restaurant, but never had the experience. Once we had settled in and ordered our meals, we exchanged a knowing look. This was going to be one delicious dinner.

"I hope you fasted today to make room for everything we just ordered," Hunter warned.

"I did in fact, I figured if you were paying I would indulge."

"Who said I was paying?"

"You invited me, which means you have to pay. It's in the rulebook."

"And what rule book would that be?"

"Proper Etiquette for the Modern World," I answered confidently.

"You made that up."

"Yes, I did," I laughed.

"I know you too well, you can't dupe me that easily."

"I know, you're stealing my thunder. It's only polite to pretend you're my unwitting victim."

"Is that from your book, too?"

"But, of course."

Our green tea and miso soup arrived and we both devoured the flavorful broth before sipping our tea.

"Why is this tea so delicious? I've had green tea a million times, and it's always the best here. There is something different about it."

"It isn't plain green tea. It's actually Genmai-cha, which is green tea with roasted brown rice. It adds a different flavor to the tea."

"It sort of tastes like an ice cream cone, the wafer kind."

"That is the first time I have ever heard it described in that way. Your mind is a scary and fascinating place."

"Just keep your hands and arms inside your cart and you'll be just fine."

Hunter chortled in response. "You always keep me on my toes, Miss Carsen. There is never a boring moment with you."

"That is just the polite way of saying I'm insane—not saying you're wrong, mind you—and I do appreciate your effort to pretty-up my crazy."

"You're nuts," Hunter chuckled.

"I know, I just told you exactly that. Weren't you listening?"

"Touché." Hunter reached across the table and took my hand in his. "Thank you for coming with me tonight. I wasn't exaggerating when I said I had been missing you terribly. Spending time with you rejuvenates me. You're my own personal nirvana."

"Why, do I smell like teen spirit?"

"Nice Nirvana reference, but I'm serious. There were days when the last thing I wanted to do was drive to Hensley in the morning, but when I knew I would see you, it suddenly didn't seem so bad."

"The feeling is mutual, Mr. Charles. You have made a tough semester bearable. More than bearable, you have been an unexpected gift. I contemplated returning you on occasion, but you remain one I will always cherish."

"You can't return me; I was bought on clearance at the end of the season."

"That does explain the defects and irregularities."

"Hey," he protested while slyly throwing an edamame at me. "I'll have you know that even on clearance, I cost a fortune. I'm practically priceless."

"You are priceless, despite your defects and irregularities."

"And you, my dear, are inimitable," he complimented. "For better or worse," he needled.

Our second courses arrived and we each paused to savor our first bite, groaning our pleasure in unison. We loaded our chopsticks for a second bite when he caught my eye, causing me to pause. Hunter carefully guided his chopsticks to my mouth with a bite of his seaweed salad. I opened my mouth to receive the offering and moaned my approval. I returned the favor by feeding him a bit of my kani salad. About halfway through my kani, I began to look longingly at Hunter's seaweed. Noticing my attention, he loaded up another bite to satisfy my craving. I returned the favor. We continued our exchanges until both salads had vanished.

"Now that was delicious," I declared.

"This place never disappoints."

"Are we getting dessert?" I asked suddenly.

"I don't know. I haven't thought about it. We haven't even had our sushi yet."

"But I need to decide now, so I know if I have to save room. If I don't plan, I will stuff myself with sushi, and if you decide to get dessert, I'm going to want dessert too, but I'll be too full. Inevitably, I'll have no restraint when it's in front of me, and in the end I'll wind up feeling like hell. Can you see the importance of planning ahead?"

"You're one strange creature," Hunter mused.

"Be that as it may, I still await your answer about dessert."

"I don't care. Do you want dessert?"

"How do I know? I haven't even had my sushi yet."

"You're making no sense. We could keep going around and around and never reach an answer. It's like the chicken and the egg question. No matter what I answer, it won't be sufficient for you to make a decision."

Hunter was trying hard to appease me, but no matter what he said, it only made matters worse.

I started to laugh at him. I laughed until my sides hurt and tears filled my eyes.

"You did that on purpose, didn't you?"

I nodded, unable to answer through my guffawing.

"I can't believe you; I was prepared to order dessert now to escape the conversation. That was cruel."

"I know," I smiled, infinitely pleased with myself.

The server appeared, carrying a tray laden with dishes. She placed each beautifully prepared plate before us with grace before leaving. We dug into the sushi, sashimi, and rolls with gusto. Hunter made a strange sound I could not interpret.

"You have to try this, it's amazing."

He held a piece of sushi I could not identify by sight. He raised the delicate fish to my lips, waiting for me to open my mouth. As I did so, my lips grazed his fingers and a bolt of electricity shot through my body. Caught in the moment, I gazed into his eyes as he placed the bite on my tongue. I closed my lips too quickly and caught his finger in my mouth. It took everything I had to refrain from circling my tongue around the tip, but I controlled myself. I heard Hunter's sharp intake of breath when my lips captured him. I slowly retracted my head so his finger slid from my mouth. Focusing on the subtle taste of the fish was nearly impossible. I was too busy searching for the taste of Hunter.

"That was delicious," I supplied, not clarifying that I was speaking of my first taste of him. What he didn't know wouldn't hurt me.

Hunter cleared his throat. "Yes, it was amazing. I'll have to ask what type of fish it was. I don't think I've tried it before. Perhaps it's a special from Japan."

He was rambling, buying himself time to recompose. I tried not to revel in the knowledge, it wouldn't do me any good, but it was difficult to forget. We refocused on our food and I struggled to keep up with my half. I had eaten about one-third when I threw in the towel.

"You quitting on me?"

"I have to save room for dessert," I gloated, my earlier triumph still fresh in my mind.

"You are an evil woman indeed."

After Hunter polished off the remaining food, our server returned to take our dessert order. We decided to share, as we were both full. When the trio of ice creams arrived, we both descended on the green tea scoop, our spoons clanked as they met.

"Ladies first," he offered.

"Do you know what I really want to do?"

"Why do I have a feeling I'll regret asking this...what?"

"I desperately want to fill up a bathtub with green tea ice cream and eat my way out of it. That is the depth of my love for it."

"I can't even begin to tell you everything that is wrong with what you just said."

"What? It's that good. You can't tell me you have never thought about it."

"I can honestly say I haven't. It would melt before you ever finished, you would likely make yourself ill, and you would be sticky from head to toe." I saw him struggle to break free from the visual he unintentionally created. "You'd probably end up drowning."

"Ah, but what a way to go."

As we walked to the car after dinner, I leaned heavily against Hunter. His body supported much of my weight and his arm around my waist steadied me.

"It hurts so badly. Why did you let me do it? I should have never eaten the last of the ice cream. I feel like I'm dying."

"You're not allowed to die. You're going to be fine, you just need a little time to digest the tsunami of food you inflicted on your body."

"I'm not kidding; I don't think I'm going to make it. All of the different fishies are fighting in here," I pointed to my stomach.

"Come on, let's get you in the car. You'll feel better soon."

I climbed into the passenger seat and immediately reached for the recline button and lowered myself back as far as it could go. Unable to stand the pain I undid the button on my pants and lowered the zipper. It could not have been an appealing look. Wearing a cropped top had been a huge mistake. My food baby must have appeared mammoth, but the pain overtook my vanity and I let it all hang out.

Hunter's door opened and I heard him climb in. I could feel him staring at me but I didn't care. At this point, anything that relieved the pressure in my stomach was worth the sacrifice of my pride. I stretched my arms over my head, trying to finagle a little more space for my intestines. Hunter started the car, but made no move to put it in gear.

"You can't drive yet, the motion will make me sick. I'm walking a wisp thin line between passive nausea and active hurling," I pleaded

"No problem, we can sit here as long as it takes."

I felt him lower the temperature of the car's climate control, for which I would have hugged him if I could move.

"That's better. Thanks."

"You do realize this is karma. You tortured me inside with your joke about dessert, and now you're sick. I hope you learned your lesson about messing with me. There is a natural order to the universe and you disturbed it by outwitting me."

I laughed at his assessment. Bad move. Really, really bad move. I started panting to stave off the desire to vomit.

"Don't make me laugh, you sadist. I'm dying here."

"I'm sorry, it didn't occur to me. You really are looking green. Do you want me to get you some ginger ale? It might soothe your stomach."

"No! Nothing else is getting inside me tonight. I'm entirely too full already."

I heard his snicker at my unintentional double entendre. I would have laughed too had it not risked the Yukon's interior. His hand gently caressed my head, relaxing me. He remained quiet, letting me focus on my breathing to fight the queasiness.

"Are you feeling any better? You still look clammy."

Ugh, why was he talking about shellfish? That was not helping my circumstances.

"No. Not better, worse. I think you need to euthanize me. Be a friend," I begged, only partially jesting.

"I'm afraid that is out of the question. A world without Everleigh is an unimaginable place. You will have to persevere."

"So I should suffer for your benefit?" I asked with as much indignation as I could muster.

"Yes, also for the good of all mankind. It's a noble thing you do now."

"God, you're good at turning it around. It's one of the things I love about you. So damn quick," I mumbled, only half-aware of what I was saying.

"Wow, it's rare you give me a compliment that isn't backhanded. I will treasure this moment always."

"You don't need me stroking your ego. You're perfectly aware of how amazing you are. We need to make sure your head remains manageable enough to fit through doorways," I volleyed back, but it took effort, causing me to grimace.

"Shhhh. I'm sorry for making you talk. Just be quiet and rest, you'll feel better soon."

He stopped stroking my hair, which was disappointing, but I heard him riffling around in the back seat. The distinct sound of a zipper opening and closing echoed in the car. A few moments later, I felt a damp cool towel on my forehead. It was heavenly.

"Don't worry, it's my gym towel but it's clean. I just poured some bottled water on it."

As if I would care should it have been used. I was drifting on the waves of nausea, praying for an ending, in whichever form it may come. This was worse than any case of the alcohol induced spins I had ever endured. I kept one knee bent so that my foot touched the floor mat, practicing the drinker's theory that the spins will stop if you keep a foot off the bed and on the ground. It had never worked for me before, but I was willing to try anything.

"Make it better, please," I begged pathetically.

I felt Hunter's lips kiss my stomach. At any other time, it would have been wondrously sexual, but right now it was just comforting.

I would have sworn I had food poisoning if Hunter had not eaten everything I had. Never in my life have I been this ill where alcohol or virus were not the cause. The sickness intensified, and I started to worry I would lose the battle.

"Hunter, can you help me sit up? I think I need to get out of the car."

He understood my meaning and walked around to my side, carefully lifted me up, cradling my body. He walked to a grassy area that was private and dark. He placed me on my feet and stood behind me. Wrapping one arm low around my hips, so there was no pressure on my stomach, still able to bend over unencumbered. He held me up with one arm, and with his free hand gathered my hair to hold back in preparation.

"You don't have to..." I could not finish.

I bent at the waist, grateful for Hunter's support and evacuated the contents of my stomach. I heaved several times before the intense waves of sickness began to recede. The cool air against my sweat-dampened face felt amazing. I was weak and tired, too spent to feel embarrassed by what Hunter had witnessed dreadfully up close and personal.

When I had managed to go several minutes without dry heaving, Hunter swept me back into his arms and carried me to the car. Once he had helped me in, he wiped my face with the damp towel, cooling and cleaning me. He gave me a bottle of water to rinse my mouth and sip. When I was finally settled, I chilled as my body temperature dropped after the stress, causing me to shiver. Hunter covered me with his jacket and adjusted the climate control.

"Angel, how are you?" Hunter asked with concern.

"Better. I'm so sorry I—"

"Hush, it's fine. I'm sorry you're feeling so ill. Your color is starting to come back and you're shivering less. I think it's passing now, but you're going to be as weak. Just rest. I'll take care of you."

And he did. I don't remember anything about getting home or into my bed. I have a faint memory of Hunter placing a sweet kiss on my lips, but even that may have been a figment of my imagination. At some point during the night I heard him enter my room to check on me, his hand touched my face and forehead checking for a fever before I drifted back under.

When I awoke in the morning, Hunter was gone. There was a glass of water and a note on the nightstand.

Angel,

I hope you're feeling better when you wake up. Drink water and eat something mild for breakfast. I'm sorry I couldn't stay. I was called into work for an emergency.

Text me when you wake up and let me know how you're feeling. I will be worried until I hear from you.

Do not be mad, I called Marty (found her number in your phone). I explained you were sick and would need the day to rest. I also texted Sam to give her the heads up and she promised to be home from Robbie's by 11 am should you need anything.

Hang in there and rest.

—Hunter

I should be furious that he called my boss without my knowledge, but I wasn't. He had taken such great care of me; there was nothing to justify any complaint. He was right, I was still wiped and needed to rest today and recuperate. I must have succumbed to a twenty-four hour bug because there is no way last night was the result of overeating. I have never been that violently ill in my life. If Hunter had not been there to hold me up, I would have been laying on the ground wrecked.

I flipped back the blankets to find my shoes, jeans, and cardigan gone. I was still in my comfy cropped top, and I was also wearing a pair of old boxer shorts. Evidently, Hunter had prepared me for bed. I was still too fatigued to care.

Other than my mother, no one had ever taken such tender and meticulous care of me. I had a lot to thank Hunter for.

I texted him I was awake and feeling better. I also told him he was once again my hero and I was eternally grateful.

After eating a few slices of toast, I crawled back to bed and slept the rest of the day, recovering from the strain on my body. The long night had taken its toll, but it was all worth it to experience Hunter's unfettered tenderness just once in my life.

Chapter Fourteen

*"In a lot of cop shows, because they have the
restraints of having a new case every episode,
the victims often become these kind of nameless,
faceless plot points, and as an audience we don't
feel anything for those people." -Mireille Enos*

Monday continued the return to the status quo. Everyone at
Hensley seemed to breathe a sigh of relief when no murders
were reported. We had all made it through the weekend
safely. Our group resumed our routine, enjoying lunch
together on campus. I was without a partner at Krav Maga due
to Josh's absence, so all of the guys took turns pairing with me
to continue my lessons in response to varying assailants. Sensei
Alex hovered while I worked the weight bag and instructed me
on proper technique for forward and reverse head-butts. It was
one of my hardest workouts to date, and I was certain I would
be sore. I relished the sore muscles, knowing I earned each
one. I had noticed a subtle tightening of my body after weeks
of class and I carried myself more confidently. I felt
accomplished, having mastered many of the basic skills and
progressing through the more complex throws and
combinations. Hanshi Rosati walked me to my car after class.

"Ev, you're doing well. You should be proud of yourself."

"Thanks Hanshi. I love Krav and I can't thank you enough for having me."

"You're welcome here anytime, free for life."

He placed his hand on my shoulder, in a fatherly gesture. "I want you to know if you ever need any help, if you ever find yourself in trouble, you can call me. You still don't know me well, but you remind me of my daughter, and I want you to know you have someone you can trust. It's difficult to hold everyone you meet under constant suspicion. I'm a retired marine and police officer, you can check me out and know you'll be safe. My wife would welcome you at our house anytime. Just know you have a safe haven if you ever need one."

"I appreciate your offer, and if I ever need help I will take you up on it. I have a couple of people in my life I trust implicitly, but it's always nice to have another. I don't have a father, so I may just adopt you." I smiled my appreciation.

"You're crazy, girl. Okay, get."

Hanshi watched as I drove away, ensuring my safety in the small way he could.

As I walked from my car to my apartment, I felt someone's eyes on me. I glanced around quickly, but saw nothing. I hurried to the door, positive I heard footsteps behind me. My fear was overwhelming, but I remained focused on my goal. As I approached the door, it swung open and another tenant exited. I didn't know him well, but we exchanged courtesy smiles as we passed. I ran to my apartment door and rushed inside, slamming it in my haste.

It was possible the eerie feeling of being watched was my imagination, but I had the same sensation several times over the last month. I hoped Drew wasn't persisting in his quest to reunite. I hadn't seen him since the day he tailed me home, and I had hoped he moved on. I considered calling Hunter, but I didn't know what I would say. 'Hi Hunter, it's Ev, I got the heebie jeebies tonight and want you to come hold my hand.' I needed to stiffen my spine and stop fretting over every little thing. Being cautious was a necessity, but I couldn't allow fear to paralyze me. I continued to scold myself silently as I prepared for bed, promising to be less anxious tomorrow.

When I arrived at school Tuesday morning, Hunter was waiting for me.

"You, Miss, forgot to text me when you left your house this morning," Hunter chided while hugging me tightly. "Don't make me worry more than I already do, please."

"Can't we stop the crazy 'text your friends incessantly so everyone knows where you're at all times' plan yet?"

"That is quite the plan name. You may need to go back to the drawing board."

"It's just the working title," I laughed.

Hunter sounded lighter, but I could see the strain around his mouth and the dark circles beneath his eyes. The schoolwork and job stress had accumulated over the semester and were taking their toll on him. He was still gorgeous, positively stunning, but he was depleted. I didn't want to add to his burdens by causing him to worry about me.

"I'll remember, promise. This is the first time I have forgotten. I swear Sam texts me every move she makes, even potty breaks."

"Well Sam is a good, obedient girl. Maybe she will rub off on you," Hunter poked.

"Har, har, har. I'm essentially a good girl."

"Whatever you say, angel. Whatever you say."

I heard Sam enter my room on Wednesday morning while I was lying in bed, gathering the will to rise and collect my first cup of the day. I knew the news would not be good. She laid down next to me and put her head on my shoulder.

"Another murder?" I asked, knowing the answer.

"Yeah."

"Want to talk about it?"

The fear that had slightly receded over the past two days was crashing down hard on Sam.

"No," she answered in monotone.

"Okay."

We laid there for a while, hiding from the world and the dangerous reality that waited outside my bedroom door. "I don't know why I'm so upset. It should not be shocking anymore. You would think I would be desensitized to the carnage by now," Sam finally shared.

"Thank God you aren't desensitized. Then you would be some callous, self-absorbed bitch. I would no longer be able to call you my bestest friend."

I had upgraded Sam's title to bestest friend when she teased that Hunter was trying to compete for her title. After she suggested a 'Hunger Games' style competition, I understood the need for distinction of Sam's special status. Hunter may be a badass martial arts guy, but Sam could be cutthroat. I feared for Hunter's life in a death match against Sam.

"You'll continue to be a bitch no matter what, but I'm glad you aren't a callous, self-absorbed one," I ribbed to make her smile.

In response, Sam ribbed me, literally, with an elbow to my ribcage. What a bitch.

After class on Thursday, Hunter was giving me a hug goodbye, when it dawned on me, there was only one week left of classes. What would happen after the semester ended? I would begin my full-time position at Higher Yearning and Hensley would no longer be a prominent part of my life. When would I see Hunter? I was accustomed to seeing him at least four days a week, courtesy of classes. Most weeks, I saw him five or six days. Would this mark the end of Hunter in my life? Would we be like so many college friends that drift apart when forced proximity no longer exists? Would our relationship slowly fade to an occasional phone call and 'happy birthday' comment on Facebook?

I must have indicated my distress because Hunter placed his fingers under my chin to tilt my head upward until our eyes met. The uncertainty of our future was creating anxiety that would certainly show in my eyes.

"What's wrong, angel?"

"I just realized there is only one week left of classes. Then my time at Hensley is over."

"You will have accomplished a huge goal and passed a milestone. Why the sad eyes? It's something to be celebrated. Are you feeling nostalgic?"

I shook my head in the negative.

"Then what has you so upset?"

"When will I see you if we don't have class together?"

He smiled at me indulgently. "Is that what has you worried? Everleigh, we'll still see each other. Perhaps a little less frequently, but still on a regular basis. We will develop a new schedule."

"But who will bring me coffee in the mornings and breakfast treats?"

"You're running a coffee shop. You have those items at your disposal," Hunter laughed.

"That is true, but who will give me big bear hugs each day?"

"I'm sure you can persuade Sam to fill in for me when needed."

"She's physically incapable of giving me a bear hug—she can only provide tiny cub hugs."

I averted my eyes, the reality hitting me like a blow.

"Everleigh, look at me. You will not lose me. I won't drift away until I'm just a fond college memory, I promise."

He addressed the heart of my concerns head-on, as was his way.

"You promise?"

"I promise, and you know I've never lied to you. You think I could stand to lose you from my life?" He held me close, kissing the top of my head, whispering into my hair, "I need you. You are not temporary."

I held him to me, my head against his chest, battling a premonition that the end was near. Irrespective of our promises, I had a feeling that Hunter just lied to me for the first time whether he intended to or not.

As I drove to meet Josh on Saturday night, I was struck with how unjustly I was treating him. I liked Josh, as a friend. I enjoyed his company and found him attractive, but I didn't feel any romantic spark. When he held me, it was nice; when he kissed me, it was pleasant. There was no invisible string drawing me to him like a fishing line being reeled in by a rod. When we were apart he didn't cross my mind. Josh's interest in me was more than superficial and, if I continued to date him, I would be implying a future that would never be. Even if Hunter wasn't a distraction, Josh was not going to be my forever.

Poor Josh. He was probably driving to the restaurant right now, thinking the classic third date rule was in effect, and he was going to get lucky tonight. Instead, I was getting ready to bludgeon him with the equally classic "it's not you, it's me" break-up. I had to bite the bullet and end it. I was regretful, aware of what a catch Josh was. He would make a wonderful husband and father one day; he just wouldn't be my husband or the father of my children. I was tempted to delay the inevitable, but in such cases, tearing the Band-Aid off quickly was for the best. After four years of college, I had learned the benefit of being proactive versus procrastinating. Damn maturity and personal growth. It was far easier being irresponsible.

I parked my car in the lot of a local Italian eatery and slowly made my way to the entry. Josh was waiting for me out front, wearing a smile, pleased to see me. When I neared, he drew me into his embrace and kissed my lips. It felt wrong.

"I've missed you," he said with conviction.

"Thanks, you too," I replied softly.

He pulled back and looked at me studying my face, searching for the answer to a question neither of us had asked.

"You're different tonight. You look as lovely as ever, but something is off, you seem dimmer." He led me to a bench in front of the restaurant's garden. "What's troubling you?"

Josh was more astute than I had realized.

"You're entirely too kind to me," he smiled at my compliment. "Josh, as fond as I am of you, I'll never be able to give you my heart. You deserve to know that. I could continue enjoying your company and ingratiating myself in your life—it's tempting, believe me-but it would be incredibly selfish when I know I will never be your forever girl."

I met his eyes and saw the surprise; he had not expected our conversation to take this direction.

"Is there someone else?" he asked neutrally.

"No," I paused, wanting to be honest, "not really."

"Not really?" He raised an eyebrow.

"There is a guy, Hunter, he is my best friend, but it will never be anything more. I'm not ending things with you because of him. I swear. I know I can never have him, I've accepted it. But it would be very easy to allow myself to cling to you to fill the void he will leave. You deserve better than that from me, and I can't offer you more than a temporary distraction. You're far too good to wear an ill-fitted suit. You need to hold out for the custom tailored Armani."

Josh smiled at my analogy and reference to his attire on our first date. He took my hand in his. He was too good, any woman in her right mind would beat me for letting him go.

"I thought we were building something special, that we were well suited. I am surprised to find that you don't feel the same."

I sighed, unsure how to explain. "You are everything I could ever ask for, Josh. Smart, kind, good looking, successful. You are everything I could want. The problem is, I unintentionally gave my heart away, and now I don't have it to give to you. I don't think I will ever get it back, if I'm being honest."

He shook his head, disappointed. "I wish I could change your mind Ev, I could make you happy. You are letting go of someone who wants to open his life to you because you don't believe you will ever fall in love again. I never understand why women do that."

"You could make me very happy, I'm sure, but you would never be able to have all of me. Right now you're convinced time will change that, but I am telling you it won't. You deserve more than most of me, you deserve everything."

I placed my hand on top of his, willing him to accept my words even if he couldn't understand. "Some men may never notice the difference, for some most may be enough, but you would notice and regret having settled."

He nodded his understanding, perhaps not fully agreeing, but taking me at my word. We sat in companionable silence for a short time.

"He is a fool to let you go."

"No, I'm the fool for not hearing him when he told me in no uncertain terms he could not offer me more. I listened, but I didn't hear. I should have let him go in the beginning when I was still strong enough to do so." I breathed through my sorrow. "Some people believe the strongest will cling through the storm with steadfast determination never wavering, but sometimes the strength is in letting go."

Josh lifted my hand and kissed the top. "I can't say I'm thrilled by your decision, but I will respect your wishes. After all, what choice do I have?" He chuckled dryly.

"You're an incredible woman, full of beauty and vitality. You deserve a man who reveres you above all others, who would sacrifice everything for you. I would have liked the opportunity to be that man, but if not, then take your own advice and hold out for everything, Ev, it's the least you deserve."

"Thank you Josh, for everything."

"Come on. Let's go have a delicious meal. No more talk of heartbreak and unfulfilled wishes. I may not have found my future wife in you, but I do hope I have found a friend."

"That I can give you, and it would be my honor to call you a friend."

We had a wonderful meal. Josh did his best to transition from suitor to friend. There were awkward moments, but it was still a pleasant dinner. I was optimistic we could build a friendship from the remnants of our brief romantic attempt. After dinner, I thanked him again, profusely, and gave him a genuine hug.

"If there is ever anything I can do for you, please let me know. I would love to repay your kindness to me."

"Don't be silly. Just keep your eyes peeled for Ms. Right and point her in my direction if you find her. I'll see you Monday. You're still going to be my partner, aren't you?"

"Absolutely."

Driving home, I had an epiphany. I had to be suspicious right now to ensure my safety, but once this siege was over, I would let go of my skepticism. Josh, Hanshi Rosati, Griffin, and so many others had proven that for every horrid, foul, evil person in the world, there were countless others who were selfless and compassionate. I would not let the experiences and fear over the last year alter me permanently. I would retain my awareness that malevolence existed, but I would not live my life expecting the worst. Humanity was, for the most part, good. I would hold that close and retain a touch of the innocence I had before the horrors began.

Our last week of classes brought a flurry of activity—final papers were due, study sessions were attended, and cramming began for the earliest final exams. I was constantly running between classes, Higher Yearning, and review sessions. During lunch on Wednesday, our clan decided to celebrate the end of classes with dancing at The Stop on Saturday night. We all knew this would be one of our last outings as undergrads and wanted to live it up.

I was the lucky one of the bunch. I had a final paper due Thursday, in lieu of a final exam, for Business Strategies. Intro to Acting had no final exam, the class was graded cumulatively from participation and one performance piece to be presented on Wednesday. By Friday, all that remained was my Business Ethics final, for which I was well prepared. I worked all day, supplying a steady stream of stressed and caffeine-dependent students who crammed for finals. Regan and I had fun discerning between the students. Those who were merely refreshing the knowledge they acquired across the semester and those who had started out strong until after mid-terms, began to slack, and were working to catch up. My favorite to watch—those who had not attended a single class since the first day or read a single assignment, and were now trying to cram an entire course into a two-day study session. The last were our best customers, because inevitably they employed the same practice in all of their classes, leaving them with eight days of non-stop studying without sleep and no hope of passing.

At the end of my shift I texted Sam to let her know I was heading home. When I arrived at the apartment, I found it empty. Checking my phone, I saw that Sam was grabbing a quick dinner with Robbie on campus before her final study group for Calculus. I will never understand why Sam had saved the math requirement—her most challenging subject—for her final semester of college. Sam promised to text me when she was heading home and suggested we plan our ensembles for tomorrow night before bed. We were all excited to go dancing, certain it would be a night to remember. I was even considering surpassing my usual happy alcohol buzz for the land of moderately tipsy.

I spent my alone time reviewing my Business Ethics notes again to prepare for my final next week. When I was satisfied I had absorbed as much as was possible, I went to shower off the day. Sam texted me she was leaving study group and heading home, instructing me to have a bottle of wine open and to be ready to select the most spectacular outfits of our college careers. Laughing, I followed her instructions and opened a bottle of Shiraz to let it breathe.

Knowing Sam would only take a few minutes to get home, I entered my bedroom and began to pull options for tomorrow. When I had selected all viable contenders, I decided to pour myself a glass of wine. Where was Sam? I checked to see if she had texted me a pit stop. No new messages. She probably stopped at the 24-hour drugstore to pick up Tylenol for her calculus-induced headache. I could go for rocky road ice cream, I shot her a text telling her as much.

Thirty minutes later, Sam still was not home and I had received no return text. I called her cell to speed her along. It rang four times before the voicemail picked up. I decided to give her five more minutes before I started hounding her. When the time limit expired, I dialed her again. Same as before. A premonition was taking hold of me, causing my stomach to drop. I knew I was overreacting, but I decided to call Robbie. He answered on the first ring.

"Hey Ev. What's up?"

"Is Sam with you?"

"No, we had dinner earlier, but she had a study group tonight," Robbie provided.

"I know, she texted me over an hour ago saying she was on her way home and she still isn't here. I thought you two might have gotten distracted."

"She's not with me Ev, I'm sure she is fine. She probably just stopped at the store," he dismissed my concern.

"No, Robbie, I called her phone twice and she hasn't answered."

"Maybe she left it in the car. Try not to get yourself worked up, she'll be home soon. Have her call or text me when she gets in. Thanks."

I wish I could be as unconcerned as Robbie, but my intuition was screaming at me that Sam was in trouble. I let another five minutes pass before I tried Sam's cell again.

Receiving her voicemail once more I hung up, beginning to feel sick. Something was wrong, I knew it. I had to do something. Picking up my phone, I dialed Hunter.

"Hey angel, you taking a break from Ethics?"

"Hunter," I could hear the panic in my own voice "something is wrong."

"What is going on? You sound terrified," he asked in a controlled voice.

"It's Sam. She texted me over an hour ago and said she was on her way home. She still isn't here. I've called her a bunch of times and she isn't picking up. I called Robbie and she isn't with him, and he made me feel like a paranoid idiot for worrying." I paused to catch my breath, "Hunter, I know I sound crazy, but something is wrong. I know it, Sam is in trouble. Please, believe me." I was prepared for Hunter to dismiss my concerns as Robbie had.

"Okay we are not going to panic, but we are not going to ignore your instincts either. I will call a police officer I know from volunteering at Hensley, you call Campus Security. Do you know where she was last?"

"I know she had a study group for her calculus class. I'm not sure where it was held on campus."

"I'm sure there is a record of what room they were in, Campus Security should have access to the information. Call them now and I'll call you back when I'm off the phone with Detective Norse."

I hung up and immediately dialed Campus Security.

"Campus Security, how can I help you?"

"Hi, my name is Everleigh Carsen, I'm a student at Hensley. My roommate, Samantha Whitney, and I live off campus. She texted me over an hour ago that she was on her way home, but she still is not here. We only live five minutes away, I think something is wrong. She was coming from her calculus study group. Can you please try to find her?"

"I will let the patrol cars know you're concerned and have them keep an eye out. What type of car does she drive?"

"A silver Mercedes coupe."

"Alright, I'll let them know. I'm sure she is fine. We get several of these calls a day and the missing person always turn up. Let me have your number and keep us posted."

I gave him my number and thanked him. I sat on our loveseat with my phone in hand awaiting Hunter's return call, and calling Sam's phone every five minutes. Twenty minutes later, my phone rang.

"Hunter?"

"Hey, sorry that took so long, I tried to give them as much info as I know. They promised to send patrol cars all over campus and search for her. How did it go with campus security?"

"Same, although they did say they are getting a bunch of calls like this every day and the person usually turns up."

"Why don't you see if you can track down someone who was in the study group. Do you have Sam's Facebook password?"

"Of course."

"Maybe they created an event for the session or you can see if a friend mentioned anything. Check her email too, if you can. If you can find anyone who was there with her, find out where the session was, when she was last seen, and what direction she was headed. Either way, I will pick you up in an hour and we will drive the campus if she is still missing. Does that sound like a plan?"

"Yes."

Thank God for Hunter. I had something to do which may be useful and he was going to come with me to search for Sam. He didn't belittle my fears; he just gave me what I needed. "Thank you."

"God willing this will be a huge overreaction, and you will feel silly tomorrow. If not, then we will have done everything we can to help her. I'll see you in an hour."

I tried Sam's cell phone again. Same as before—four rings then voicemail.

I checked Sam's Facebook page with no luck. Frustrated, I logged into her student email to check for any information that would help. I located an email from the TA stating the review session would be from 7:00 pm until 10:00 pm in the Mathematics Building. I tried to find the contact details for other students in the class to no avail. At least I had a lead.

I called campus security back and advised them of Sam's last known location and that she had departed the Mathematics Building at 9:35 pm, according to the text she had sent. They reiterated their promise to check the area and keep me posted.

Fifteen minutes later, there was a knock on my door. I looked through the peephole to confirm it was Hunter before opening the door, he was on his phone finishing a call.

"...I understand. Is the ambulance on the way?" Pause. "Good, I will prepare her. We will be there in five. Thanks for letting me know Detective, I owe you one."

I snapped into action grabbing my jacket and purse, prepared to leave.

"Ev, baby, you need shoes," he said gently.

I looked at my feet realizing I was barefoot. I slid my feet into a pair of ballet flats by the door. I immediately realized they were Sam's because they were two sizes too small, but I was not going to waste time returning to my room. I had overheard enough to know that they had found Sam.

Hunter took my hand and led me out the door, making certain the lock engaged. Once he joined me in the Yukon, I spoke.

"Tell me," I prompted.

"A patrol car located Sam's Mercedes in the parking lot near Mathematics. Everything looked fine, but based on your concerns he looked around. Woods buffer the lot and the officer noticed drag marks through the residual sand in the parking lot leading to the tree line. He found a bag at the periphery of the lot, which led him to search the woods. He located a female who had been assaulted. Based on the description I provided there is a strong possibility it's Sam." Hunter paused, "I'm sorry Everleigh. The detective I spoke with just arrived on scene. She is unconscious and sustained severe injuries. He didn't give me any details, but told me to prepare you. Her condition appears critical, and they believe she was left for dead."

I gasped, focusing on my breathing and trying to clear my mind. I had to keep it together, I couldn't fall apart now. Sam would be okay. She would live. That was all that mattered, the rest we would deal with.

Hunter pulled up to the parking lot next to Mathematics where the police stopped us.

"I'm Hunter Charles. Detective Norse is expecting us." The officer nodded, checking Hunter's identification before letting us through. We drove past several police cars and parked in an area of the lot not blocked by marked cars. I hurried out of the car, seeing an ambulance nearby.

As we approached, I saw a stretcher being carried from the neighboring woods. It was Sam; I felt it from twenty feet away without a doubt. My gasp must have clued Hunter in because he reached to support and restrain me. We were ten feet from the stretcher when a man approached.

"Detective, thank you again for notifying us. This is Everleigh Carsen, Miss Whitney's roommate."

"I'm sorry to meet under such circumstances, Miss Carsen. I will need to get a statement from you, but it can wait until tomorrow. Can you confirm the victim is Samantha Whitney?"

"I can," I responded, straining to get to Sam. "Can I ride with her?"

"Yes," the detective responded kindly.

The stretcher was being loaded into the ambulance as I approached with Hunter.

"She's going to be riding with Miss Whitney."

The paramedic looked at us.

"Are you sure that's a good idea, sir?"

"Yes," Hunter answered with authority.

"Okay, but you need to get in now. We have to go, and you'll need to ride in the front."

I nodded as Hunter guided me to the front passenger side and assisted me in.

"I'll meet you in the hospital waiting room."

I turned to the back of the ambulance trying to see Sam, but the paramedic was obstructing my view. When the driver got in and switched on the sirens, the reality of what had happened came crashing down on me. Sam had been attacked and injured severely. God knows what else had been done to her. My best friend had been brutalized.

If I had agreed to change schools. If I had met her after the review. If I had called for help sooner. A thousand puzzle pieces, if I had moved just one, could I have prevented this?

Countless questions circled my mind. Was she conscious? Did she know she was safe? How much pain was she in? Did she blame me the way I blamed myself?

"How long till we arrive, Jimmy?" the paramedic called from the back.

"We are still five minutes out."

"Shit," I heard him mutter beneath his breath. "Just get there as fast as you can. I'm going to have to intubate en route. Call ahead and advise there is a critical 'Plan Blue' incoming; have them page neuro for TBI, ortho for multi-sites, and general for possible internal—they will need to be on standby for arrival."

I barely understood what he was saying, but none of it was good. He was scared Sam was not going to make it, I could hear it in his voice.

"Got it," I heard the paramedic say to himself with relief.

"One minute out," the driver announced. He turned toward me, "Make sure you take your purse, Miss. You will not be able to go with her when we arrive and you will need to stay out of the way. Head to the waiting room and they will keep you posted."

I nodded, not trusting my voice. As we entered the hospital's emergency bay, I looked back again and finally had a clear view of Sam. My heart stopped.

She was unrecognizable. Her face so battered and swollen, misshapen and covered in blood, she looked inhuman. She appeared naked, but I didn't know if they had removed her clothing for treatment purposes or if that was how she was found. Her left arm and shoulder were at an unnatural angle and it appeared several of her fingers were oddly positioned. I noticed bloodstains on the white sheet draped over her lower half and I could guess the source.

My hands flew to my mouth, trying to keep back the vomit. Oh sweet Jesus. How could this have happened? How could she survive this? My door suddenly opened and Hunter was there, pulling me out of the ambulance. I started gagging as I repressed the urge to vomit. Hunter quickly brought me to the side of the building where I was violently ill. This time food or virus was not the cause.

I was panting, unable to breathe when Hunter picked me up and carried me inside. He brought me to the waiting room and found a loveseat in an isolated corner. He pushed my head between my knees and told me to breathe slowly and deeply. Through my panic, I realized I must have been hyperventilating. I had to get a hold of myself. I focused on drawing air into my lungs and slowly releasing it. I repeated the cycle over and over until I had composed my body and my mind enough to sit up and speak.

"Did you see her?"

"No."

"Did the detective tell you anything?"

"He told me to get to the hospital because you would need me once you saw her." Hunter paused, "He said it was the worst of the attacks thus far. Did she regain consciousness at all?"

"No, and from what I saw, that is a blessing. Hunter, you wouldn't recognize her. He cut her hair, whoever did this to her. There was blood on the sheet covering her...covering her...I think she was raped," I whispered.

Hunter put his arms around me and held me. For the first time since my mom died, I cried. Hunter scooped me onto his lap and held me against his chest, cradled like a baby as sobs wracked my body. He continually reminded me to breathe while telling me to let it out. I ached from a place so deep within, it felt as though my soul was torn apart and would never mend. My anguish was omnipresent, in every molecule of my body, to the essence of my spirit. I registered pain in my hands and I realized I had been beating Hunter's chest and clawing at his shirt. In my hysteria, I was close to pulling my short fingernails from my fingers. I forced myself to relax my fingers, one by one.

As my sobs subsided, and only quiet tears remained, Hunter continued to stroke my back and head. He placed soft kisses anywhere he could reach and whispered words of comfort to me. I do not know how much time passed, but I eventually came back to myself. I unlocked my knees and elbows, trying to regain circulation.

Hunter repositioned me so my butt and legs were resting on the seat, but my upper body was resting across him, with my head in the crook of his elbow.

"Sleep."

I was about to protest but he continued, "You've wiped yourself out. There won't be news for hours. Just sleep for now, so you can be strong when she needs you. I will hold you, and promise to wake you if the doctor comes."

I was unable to speak, so I snuggled into his chest and cried until sleep claimed me.

Chapter Fifteen

"It's true that I have had heartache and tragedy in my life. These are things none of us avoids. Suffering is the price of being alive."
-Judy Collins

I awoke disoriented with my body wrapped around Hunter. He was still holding me, which must have been incredibly painful for him by this point. Then the vile images flooded back into my mind like acid, burning me from the inside out. I hissed at the agony of the memories. I felt Hunter's body shift slightly and I turned my head enough to look up at him. He looked destroyed.

"Hi," I managed to say.

"Angel," he whispered, full of sorrow and anguish.

"Is she—?" I could not say the words.

"No," he understood I was asking if Sam was gone. "She's still in surgery. The doctors haven't come out yet. The nurse just stopped by to let us know."

"How long have I been asleep?"

"Only two hours, not long. You can rest more if you need."

"No I've been selfish, spending this much time wallowing in my grief. I have to call the Whitneys and Robbie. I will need to talk to the police. Do you think they will meet me here, your detective friend?"

"I'm sure he will be willing to meet you here, or I can ask him to delay for a couple of days."

"No, Sam will need me once she wakes up, so it's best if they come here tonight."

"Everleigh, I don't want to say this, I don't even want to think it, but you need to prepare yourself, there is a strong possibility..." I cut him off, refusing to let him finish that thought.

"Don't you even say it," I insisted. "Sam will survive, she is strong. I will not even consider the alternative. I know you're trying to protect me. I love you for it, but I can't let that be a reality in my mind or I will have a nervous breakdown. I have to keep it together now. I had my time to come unhinged, now it's time to be strong and grounded. There is a lot to be done before Sam wakes up."

"That's my girl." He helped me sit up, "Why don't you start on your calls? I will find you a cup of coffee and a little something to eat. I will also call Detective Norse and ask him to come here as soon as possible. I'll swing by the nurses' station on the way back to check if there are any developments."

"Sounds like a good plan." I stretched my muscles and rose, slightly wobbly after my strange position for the last two hours. "Hunter, I can't thank you enough. For believing me when I said something was wrong, for coming with me to find Sam, for following me to the hospital, for holding me while I came unglued, and for helping me now. There are not words for my profound gratitude. You held me together."

"Everleigh, no thanks is needed. I would do anything for you without hesitation or regret. I could never let you go through this alone." He kissed my forehead and hugged me, "I'm glad you pulled the pieces back together so quickly. You scared me for a moment. I thought they might have needed to sedate you."

"I'm alright, no more breakdowns, I promise. Go take care of your to do list, and I'll work on mine. We'll meet back here once you have coffee in hand," I tried to joke.

It was a pitiful attempt, but I could see that Hunter valued my effort. After he left, I called the Whitney residence. Their housekeeper advised me Mr. and Mrs. Whitney were in London for the weekend. I asked her to contact them and tell them it was urgent they phone me. I was dreading the next call—Robbie. I dialed his number and it rang four times before voicemail picked up.

"Robbie, it's Ev. Sam's been attacked. She is at the hospital, it's bad. Hunter and I are here. Call me."

I called Marty next, despite the early hour, and requested the week off work. I explained what had happened and Marty told me to take all the time I needed. God bless her.

I waited for Hunter to return, making lists in my mind of what else needed to be done. I needed to find the contact information for the rape crisis center so Sam could get counseling when she was released. I would need to get her comfortable clothes; Sam wouldn't want to wear those creepy hospital gowns when she awoke. I would have to notify Sam's professors that she needed to delay her finals. I must call Sam's job and let them know she had been injured and would need time off, and get her car back to the apartment. I also needed to make an appointment for her hairdresser to correct the damage. Geeze, I had to get a pair of shoes that fit me at some point, my feet were killing me. Now I knew how Chinese women felt when their feet were bound.

Hunter returned, interrupting my list making. He sat beside me, handed me a cup of coffee and put his arm around my shoulders.

"The nurse told me Sam is still in surgery. I requested that a doctor update us on her condition at their soonest convenience. I spoke to Detective Norse; he will be here within the hour." I nodded my acceptance. "How are you?"

I took a sip of my coffee and nearly spit it out. Seeing my face, Hunter laughed.

"Nothing was open at 2:30 in the morning, so I was reduced to getting you coffee from a vending machine. No food either for a few hours."

"That's okay, I'm not hungry. The coffee on the other hand, I appreciate the gesture, but do not call this sludge coffee. How can it be bitter and weak at the same time?"

"They just don't make vending machine coffee like they used to, huh?"

"I'm setting up a 24-hour coffee cart in the waiting room. People stuck in this limbo waiting for news, are not going to sleep but they are tired. They need caffeine to aid them. We would make millions if the only competition is this despicable brew."

It felt good to exchange meaningless dialogue. I rested my head on Hunter's shoulder, unsure how I would have survived without his strong, reassuring presence. He was doing everything in his power to help without my having to ask. He was a gift I had done nothing to merit. I toed off Sam's shoes and rubbed my toes inelegantly with one hand, sighing at the relief. Hunter batted my hand away, pulling my foot into his lap and began to rub. I groaned my appreciation.

"Shoes hurting you?"

"I grabbed Sam's shoes when you insisted on footwear."

"I'm a tyrant like that."

"I'm getting used to your autocratic demeanor. Oh, right there."

It felt so good. Every muscle and tendon in my foot felt as if they'd been tied in clumsy knots. As Hunter kneaded, each slowly released, abating my suffering. We remained in silence for a long time, Hunter massaging my feet, both of us lost in contemplation. When he finally released my feet I rested my head on his shoulder and drifted off again.

Hunter woke me when Detective Norse arrived. He took my statement and asked several questions regarding Sam's usual routine. He questioned if anyone would want to hurt Sam. Had she been threatened? Was there anyone I could think of that was capable of such violence? My answer to all of his questions was a resounding "no."

Not long after the detective left, my phone rang. I could tell by the international exchange that it was the Whitneys. I took a moment to fortify myself before answering. I spoke to Mrs. Whitney first, but Mr. Whitney took the phone when her emotions overtook her. I explained what had happened and tried my best to answer his questions. I promised to phone with any developments. There was still so much I didn't know. They were going to find the first flight back to the US and would come directly to the hospital. I told them I had not contacted Sam's brothers and Mr. Whitney said he would take care of it. As I ended the call, I understood just a little of what doctors and law enforcement officers must endure each time they had to deliver horrendous news to families and loved ones.

I still had not heard from Robbie, so I tried his cell again. Voicemail. He was clearly enjoying a peaceful night sleep. It may be the last he had for a long while.

Thirty minutes later, five hours after our initial arrival, a nurse found us. She asked that we follow her to a private waiting room to speak with the doctor. I clutched Hunter's hand, fearing the worst. Why would she take us to a separate waiting room unless the doctor was going to deliver the worst outcome possible? Feeling my tension and apprehension, Hunter wound his arm around my waist to support me.

"Don't make any assumptions. They probably just want to speak privately. It won't be long before the news channels find out about the attack, and they must protect Sam's identity and the details. It's going to be okay, I've got you. You can do this."

When we entered the room, the nurse assured me the doctors would arrive shortly. Thankfully, the wait was less than three minutes, but it felt like an eternity. Two men and one woman walked into the room together all dressed in scrubs.

"Are you the family of Samantha Whitney?" the woman asked.

"I'm her best friend; her parents are traveling in Europe and are on their way back now. I'm Sam's emergency contact, if that helps. Please, just let me know how she is."

They exchanged looks, assessing the wisdom of sharing such sensitive information, particularly given the circumstances of her injuries, with a non-family member.

"I believe you have all been briefed by hospital representatives about the nature of the attack and the ongoing investigation. Detective Norse assured me he would speak to administrators to authorize Miss Carsen's knowledge of the full extent of Miss Whitney's injuries. Since Miss Carsen is her emergency contact, I presume there would be no violations of the patient privacy HIPAA Laws. Please, Miss Carsen and Miss Whitney are extremely close, they are like sisters, raised together," Hunter championed my cause.

"Very well," one of the gentlemen replied, "my name is Dr. Halthum, I'm the head of the Neurosurgical Department. Miss Whitney sustained severe intracranial bleeding caused by trauma. I have surgically relieved the pressure, but she will need to remain in a medically induced coma until she has stabilized. We will closely monitor with CT scans to ensure excess blood doesn't pool and create additional pressure. We have prescribed a series of diuretics to reduce swelling and anticonvulsants to prevent further seizures. I believe we were able to treat her in time to prevent any permanent damage. We won't be certain until she wakes, but we are hopeful her cognitive and motor functions will be intact."

"Thank you Dr. Halthum. Will you please keep me posted?" I requested.

"Of course."

He excused himself and left. The next gentleman drew my attention.

"Hello, I'm Dr. Khan from orthopedics. I performed surgery on Miss Whitney after Dr. Halthum, and in tandem with Dr. Spinel," he gestured to the remaining doctor.

"Miss Whitney's injuries were substantial. She has a fractured left clavicle that required the use of plates, rods, and screws. Her left shoulder was dislocated, and her left ulna was also severely fractured requiring plates and screws. Her third and fourth metacarpi were broken and set with pins. Several fingers on her left hand were broken which have also been set. She sustained several fractured ribs that have been wrapped to help reduce her pain. We identified five broken toes, which have been secured to allow proper healing." He paused, his laundry list completed, "She will require physical therapy, but she should make a full recovery with minimal residual effects, physically."

Dr. Kahn excused himself with his apologies.

"As Dr. Kahn said, I'm Dr. Spinel. I'm from plastics. Miss Whitney had a lot of damage to her face, as well. I reconstructed her left zygomatic and maxilla bones–her cheek– as well as her nasal bone. She also had extensive lacerations and contusions on her face, which I cleaned and sutured. I suspect she will have several scars she will want to address once the healing is complete. There is one cut on her left cheek that may require surgical scar revision. There is another scar along her forehead, which I suspect will require cryosurgery. Any remaining scars should be easily corrected with dermabrasion. The good news is Miss Whitney will look like herself again, once she is healed and the swelling recedes."

As she finished speaking, I noticed another female doctor slip into the room. Dr. Spinel excused herself with her well wishes for Sam.

"Hello, I'm Dr. Bilatus. I apologize for my lateness, but I was just checking on Sam."

I liked her already. She was the first doctor to call Sam by her given name.

"She is doing well. While she is still unconscious, in recovery, she has ample pain medication to ensure her comfort. We will keep her in a medically induced coma until she has healed and is able to breathe independently. This will allow her body time to recover."

"Thank you Dr. Bilatus," I could not help but interject.

"Please, call me Lauren. I'm the head of Gynecology and Obstetrics at the hospital. I performed an SOEC kit, a rape kit, on Sam. There is evidence to indicate she has been sexually assaulted. She had extensive vaginal trauma that required internal and external sutures, as did lacerations around her anus. I don't believe her injuries will impede her fertility or ability to carry a child to term, but additional examinations after she has healed will offer more conclusive findings. At this time our biggest gynecological concern will be to guard against infection."

Dr. Bilatus paused, collecting herself. "May I speak frankly?"

"Please," I consented.

"Sam will heal physically, I'm cautiously optimistic she will fully recover from all her injuries after consulting with my colleagues. However, the violence of her assault will leave its own scars, ones that are not visible. She may seem fine, but she won't be. It's not possible to be okay after what happened to her unless she gets professional help. I know you love her and would probably do anything for her. This is not something where your love and support will be enough. You need to ensure she receives professional assistance to process what has happened to her and to help her heal, even if she fights you. I'm sorry to speak so bluntly, but I have seen so much abuse over the years. I don't want Sam to suffer more than she already has."

"Thank you Dr. Bilatus...Lauren. I understand and I promise I will do everything in my power to heal Sam, including dragging her kicking and screaming to counseling, doctors, and whatever else she needs."

"Good." She seemed to debate saying more. "I had a sister who was raped while she was in college." I saw the shadows in her eyes as she said, "She confided in me and made me promise not to tell anyone. She said she was fine every time I asked. I watched her so closely, trying to help. She began to change, became depressed. Two years later, she committed suicide. I know it's not my fault, but I can't help but wonder if I had gotten her the help she needed would her story have had a different ending. I don't want that for Sam, or for you."

On an impulse, I hugged Lauren. She understood the pain I was feeling and my fears for Sam. I could imagine the pain if

I lost Sam because of the attack, whether directly or indirectly—now or later. She returned my embrace and I heard a quiet sniffle before she pulled away.

"I'll be checking on her periodically while she is here, and I'll continue to pray for her after she leaves. Good luck."

She slipped from the room, leaving Hunter and I shell-shocked. Neither of us could find the words for several minutes.

"What hell did she live through?" I asked Hunter.

"The most important thing at this point is that she lived, angel, she lived."

I nodded my agreement outwardly, but internally I was disconsolate. I believed Sam would wake up, she would live, but would she still be the same girl I loved like a sister? Could she be so altered by her horrific experience that she would become someone I couldn't even recognize?

A nurse entered to advise us Sam was out of recovery and relocated to the Intensive Care Unit (ICU). Hunter and I immediately headed for the elevators.

The ICU nurse provided Sam's room number and we navigated the circular pattern of rooms until we located her. Upon entering, I was struck by the heinousness of the attack. She looked slightly better than when I saw her in the ambulance, the blood washed away, her wounds treated and bandaged. I heard Hunter's gasp, reminding me he had yet to see the full extent of the damage. I walked to her bed and lightly kissed her forehead on the one tiny spot that appeared unmarred. I wanted to hold her hand and offer her comfort, even in her unconscious state, but I didn't know where to touch her that would not inflict pain.

Hunter dragged a chair near the bed and sat down, pulling me into his lap. We sat silently together watching Sam, her artificial breathing accompanied by a symphony of machinery. Her unnatural stillness was disconcerting. I began to pray to every deity I had ever heard of for her recovery and healing. I prayed Sam would overcome the brand she would carry on her soul from the violation. In addition, I prayed that the bastard who committed the atrocity would get what he deserved. I prayed he would be found, convicted, and incarcerated. Finally, I prayed he would be an involuntary prison bitch every day for the rest of his life. It may not have been the holiest of prayers, but it was from the heart.

"Why don't I take you home? You can sleep for a few hours, shower, and collect anything Sam might want when she wakes up. I will follow you back to the hospital later so your car will be here just in case you need it. I'll even buy you non-vending machine coffee," Hunter offered sweetly.

"I don't want to leave her. What if she wakes up and I'm not here? She should not wake up alone. She'll be scared and confused. I don't want her to be scared again," I pleaded.

"She's in a medically induced coma for the time being, she won't wake while you're gone. We can even check with the nurse before we leave to verify, and leave your phone number in case there are any changes," Hunter reasoned with me.

"Okay. I could use a little rest and a shower, not necessarily in that order. I was planning on collecting clothes and toiletries for Sam soon, so I would be able to check that off my to-do list."

We stopped by the nurse station and she confirmed Sam would remain in a medically induced coma for at least 72 hours, best-case scenario. With her reassurance to call if there was any change, we headed back to my apartment.

On the way I left a message for Mr. Whitney, providing the information learned about Sam's injuries and the prognosis. I didn't go into any further details. It felt wrong to divulge such personal information, even to her father. It would be Sam's choice who she would and would not tell. Perhaps she would wake up and not even remember any of the attack or rape, some type of trauma-induced amnesia to protect her mind and spirit. Would that be better for her? Would she heal better knowing or wondering? I was too tired to ponder such difficult questions.

Hunter parked near my building and we walked in together. After I unlocked the door, Hunter walked through the apartment inspecting every room and closet for intruders. When he was done, he gave me a thumbs up and headed for the door.

"I'll see you in a little bit. Try to rest."

"Please, stay. I don't want to be alone," I begged.

"I'm just going to run home and get a change of clothes, I will be back in a little while. Take your shower and try to eat something. Why don't you give me your key in case you fall asleep before I return?"

I handed him the spare key from the junk drawer. I didn't want him to leave, but understood the desire for clean clothes. He was not being unreasonable, but that didn't bring me any comfort when I was afraid.

"I know you're scared, understandably. Your apartment is safe, lock the deadbolt behind me. I will have my cell with me at all times," Hunter tried to calm me.

"Alright." I was only mildly pacified.

He kissed the tip of my nose and left, closing the door behind him. I locked the deadbolt and checked it had engaged three times before I was satisfied.

I decided to take a shower first, locking the bathroom door as soon as I was inside. After starting the shower, I quickly stripped to my birthday suit. I was thankful for the glass doors on the shower, if we had a shower curtain I would have left it open, water be damned. My eyes were glued to the door the whole time, causing me to get shampoo in my eyes, which initiated a new flood of tears. They began as shampoo tears, but quickly transitioned into sobs of grief for Sam. I slid down the wall to the floor of the shower, pulling my knees up and wrapping my arms around them protectively, as if I could hold myself together. I repeated "why" like a mantra.

After an indeterminable period, I wiped my face and finished my shower. Coming back to my senses, I noted that the next time I decided to have a breakdown in the shower I should apply my deep-conditioning treatment first. Then I could cry to my heart's content while repairing my hair. If there was nothing I could do to repair my heart, why not fix my hair instead?

Shaving required too much effort, so I washed my face and exited the shower. After wrapping a towel around my hair, I dried my body and moisturized. My teeth felt grimy so I brushed them, too. I debated hiding in the bathroom until Hunter returned, but I decided to put on my big-girl panties and conquer my fear. I unlocked the bathroom, opening it a cranial width and popped my head out. My eyes met Hunter's and I screamed, startled to find him in the hallway only ten feet away. I knew I had startled him too because he tensed. I must have looked like a rabid prairie dog.

"Sorry, you scared me."

"I was just coming to knock on the door to let you know I was back so I didn't scare you. Obviously that plan is moot. You okay?"

"Yes, I'm fine, just a little jumpy. The shock was good for me—once the adrenaline stops coursing through my veins I will crash and actually get some sleep."

"Now that's looking at the bright side. Did you eat?"

"No, I showered first."

He nodded, and was kind enough not to mention my exorbitantly long shower.

"I'll prepare something while you get dressed. I brought decaf coffee, so you wouldn't have to wait for it to brew. Go throw on some pajamas and meet me at the table."

After dressing I headed to the kitchen, but Hunter shooed me out of his way, handing me my cup of coffee and telling me to sit down. Whatever he was concocting smelled delectable. I was not hungry, but my body needed nourishment. It had been more than twenty hours since I had last eaten. I sat, sipping my coffee as Hunter worked efficiently, quickly locating items and utensils he needed. He cleaned as he cooked, leaving the kitchen immaculate. He would make a good roommate, but I already had a roommate and I wanted her back.

Hunter carried two plates to the table before returning to carry in two glasses of water. I studied my plate. An egg white omelet with ham, onions, tomatoes, and cheese, accompanied by two pieces of whole-wheat toast with butter and jam. Perfection.

"This looks fantastic. I didn't know you could cook."

"You don't know everything about me."

"What else don't I know?"

"Ask me anything."

"Nope. I'm looking for random factoids, selected by you."

I took a bite of my omelet. Dang, it was scrumptious!

"Random? Hmmm...I was missing my deciduous upper lateral incisors. Both of them."

"Deciduous upper lateral incisors? What the heck are you talking about?"

"I was missing the baby teeth on top that are supposed to be between the canines and eye teeth."

"That is weird. Finally, proof you're not perfect. You are defective, that is encouraging. Still, *deciduous?*"

"Second factoid: I have a word of the day calendar."

I laughed. He was ridiculous. I love it! This was a perfect distraction from my melancholy, which I was confident was his intention.

"I need more. Keep 'em coming."

"You're greedy." He paused, deep in thought, "I'm double jointed."

"That one was pretty boring."

"If you think you can do better, you try."

"Nope. I want to listen and learn about you. Continue," I gestured my hand regally.

"I can break a 2'x4' wood plank with my hands, feet, or head."

"Predictable." At least for Hunter.

He raised an eyebrow. Yep, I was hard to impress today.

"I speak four languages: English, Spanish, Russian, and Japanese."

"And by speak, I presume you mean more than just curse words?"

"Yes...sí...da...hai," he responded.

"Impressive," I repeated my regal gesture urging him to continue.

"I can wake up, shower, dress, and be out of my house in under five minutes."

"You're a man, that's not impressive."

What was impressive was how good he would look after those five minutes. Now that was unfair.

"You Miss, are a tough audience."

I shrugged, not offended in the least.

"I have perfect vision, literally. I'm 20/5 in both eyes."

"Interesting."

"I turn down the music in the car when I'm not familiar with an area and need to read street signs."

"Because turning the music down improves your vision?"

He shrugged, aware of how silly the habit was.

"I have a tattoo."

"You do? Where? What of?"

"I'm not telling. I need to keep some mystery."

"That's just mean. You know it will drive me nuts not knowing."

"I do," he chuckled.

"Please," I whined.

"I've never heard you whine. It's strangely cute, and persuasive. The tattoo is on my chest, and it's the Japanese word "eien," which means forever or eternal."

"Can I see it?"

I had never seen Hunter's chest before. Screw the tattoo; I just wanted to see bare skin.

"Sure," he sighed, sounding slightly put out, but placating me nonetheless. He lifted his shirt to expose his chest. On his left pectoral was an intricate design in black ink.

The tattoo was interesting. His chest was enthralling. He had perfectly defined pecs. I could glimpse the top of his abs before the table blocked my view. He was ripped. I could wash my clothes on his stomach if there was ever a nuclear event that killed the world's power sources and we were forced to revert to pioneer living. Thank you sir, may I have another?

I cleared my throat. "Very enlightening. More." I really wanted to see more of his body, but I settled for more Hunter particulars.

"I have three testicles."

"What?" I nearly spit out my water.

"Just checking if you were paying attention."

"Ever the comedian, Mr. Hunter."

"I have never said 'I love you' to a woman, excluding family."

"Why not?"

Maybe it wasn't me, maybe he was incapable of love or commitment. That was mildly comforting. It still sucked, but at least I knew it wasn't me.

"Because I didn't, and I was not going to lie."

"That is respectable."

"Last one for today." I nodded my acceptance. "I like to drink pickle juice from the jar once all the pickles are gone."

"That is disgusting, you're a freak. Do you know how much sodium is in that juice? Does it even qualify as juice? Isn't it more of a preserving liquid?" I pondered in disgust.

"Don't judge me," he repeated the command I had given him more than once. "Time for you to rest. Off to bed with you."

He turned me around by my shoulders and directed me toward my bedroom.

"Hunter, will you sleep with me?"

I didn't want to be alone. I saw the conflict in his eyes and realized my poor word choice.

"Let me try that again—will you lay with me, fully clothed, while we both sleep? I don't want to be alone."

"Sure, lead the way."

Hunter followed me into my bedroom and I looked at my unmade bed. There was nothing sexual about what I needed from Hunter, but it was still strange. I was vulnerable, exposed. Reining in my sudden nerves, I walked to the left side of my bed and laid down on my back. Hunter toed off his shoes and climbed in on the right. He rolled onto his side and used his arm to snag me around my ribcage, and pulled my back against him. His head was resting on his right shoulder and he used his free hand to stroke my hair. His left arm wrapped around me and took my hand in his. I was cocooned in Hunter. His scent was warm and spicy with a hint of clean musk. The heat of his body seeped into me, relaxing me. I was encaged in his arms, his strength. I felt protected and precious. He kissed my neck before nuzzling into the back of my head and pulling his knees up so that they tucked behind mine. We were fully aligned. Every inch touching front to back. I sighed my pleasure quietly. In this one moment, the rest of the world forgotten, I was content.

I wanted to stay awake to savor every second, but my exhaustion triumphed, and I fell asleep in Hunter's arms.

Chapter Sixteen

"Between men and women there is no friendship
possible. There is passion, enmity, worship,
love, but no friendship." -Oscar Wilde

After hours wrapped in Hunter's arms I awoke, never wanting to leave his embrace. The sanctuary he provided couldn't last forever and it was time to return to the real world full of tribulations, burdens, and worries.

I looked over my shoulder to find Hunter already awake.

"Did you sleep?" I asked groggily.

"For a couple of hours, I've been up for a bit."

"You could have roused me. Your arms must be asleep."

"You needed rest and I'm totally comfortable." He gently repositioned me on the bed as he rose. "I'll go make some coffee while you get dressed. I presume you have a travel mug?"

I gave him a look that indicated exactly how ridiculous I felt his question was.

"Stupid question, I know," he replied as he left the room.

He had never made coffee for me before—this had disaster potential. It took two years living with Sam before I had her properly trained.

I dressed quickly before entering Sam's room. I steeled myself against the tide of emotions surging and packed her overnight bag with a variety of comfortable clothes, pajamas, socks, and slippers. I returned to the bathroom and added her toiletries and hair accessories. Task completed, I carried the bag to the front door, ensuring it was not forgotten.

Apprehension filled me as I entered the kitchen. There were many things in life I was willing to fake. Interest in prosaic conversation—no problem. Enjoyment of bland food—doable. An orgasm—more often than I cared to admit. However, there is one thing I could not, would not fake—the quality of a cup of coffee. Hunter smiled as he handed me my travel mug, confident he had done well. 'Please, let this be drinkable,' I chanted in my mind as I raised the mug to my lips, inhaling. The aroma was pleasing, a step in the right direction. Tentatively I took my first sip, rolling it across my tongue to taste the flavor and body. It was good, not the best cup of coffee I had ever had, but definitely drinkable.

"You have passed the test. If you ever need a job, you know where to find me. With a bit of training, you could be good."

"I *could* be good? That is a great cup of coffee," Hunter said with self-assurance.

"I appreciate it more than you can imagine, but it's not brilliant. Higher Yearning only serves brilliance. Don't feel bad, you did at least as well as some of the baristas at the big franchise."

"Elitist."

"I prefer connoisseur."

"Come on Madame Connoisseur, let's get to the hospital before you feel the need to educate me on the finer points of brewing you a pot of coffee."

When we arrived in Sam's room, she was exactly as we left her. We stopped to ask the nurse if there had been any changes, and she assured us all was the same. The doctors had checked on her and were comfortable with her progress. Dr. Halthum from neurology would update us within the hour. I was disappointed there had been no progress, but relieved she had not regressed.

I left another message for the Whitneys to provide an update and was shocked that Robbie was still missing in action, but I was not going to chase him down; if he wasn't man enough to face the trials ahead, then good riddance. Hunter and I passed the time talking to Sam. Hunter shared humorous stories and anecdotes, while I reminded her of all the plans and resolutions we had yet to keep. We endeavored to keep the climate of the room positive and encouraging. I would not want to wake up to a bunch of crying and dour individuals, Sam wouldn't either.

When Dr. Halthum arrived, he asked that we step out of the room while he examined Sam, which we obliged. Fifteen minutes later the door opened and Dr. Halthum invited us to return. He spent several more minutes making notes on Sam's chart.

"She is making progress, has responded well to the medications provided, and has not had any additional seizures. There has been a measurable decrease in cranial pressure indicating the course of treatment is effective. We will conduct another CT scan tomorrow and Monday. Depending on the results, we will adjust the treatment plan accordingly. I expect we will keep her in a medically induced coma and on ventilation for approximately one week, if all goes as planned. That is only a projection, so please do not be disappointed if we must make adjustments."

"Thank you, Doctor," Hunter and I said concurrently.

After he departed, we continued talking to Sam, to occupy our minds, and keep the concern at bay. After dinner, I received a call from Mr. Whitney requesting Sam's room number. Hunter excused himself to the waiting room so they could have privacy.

Several minutes later, I heard Mrs. Whitney's distinctive voice echoing down the hall, and braced for their reaction. When they walked in and saw Sam, they both paled. Approaching the bed, Mrs. Whitney lost the battle to remain composed and disintegrated before my eyes. Mr. Whitney caught his limp wife and guided her to the loveseat across the room.

"I'll sit with her," I offered.

Mr. Whitney nodded before returning to Sam's bedside, leaving me to tend to a nearly catatonic Mrs. Whitney. He spent several minutes examining his daughter, clearly distraught but able to control his reaction better than his wife.

"I think it best I bring Beverly home, this is too much for her. I understand Samantha is expected to remain in a coma for at least the next week, which will provide time for her to improve visibly. Once she is awake, I will bring Beverly back to visit. Samantha will not know the difference before she is conscious, and I do not want to overtax my wife. Will you be so kind as to keep us posted on her progress and notify me when she awakens?"

"Certainly," I agreed, too shocked to express my real thoughts.

"Thank you Everleigh, for all you have done for Samantha. I am ever in your debt."

With those parting words, he left his only daughter lying battered and broken in a hospital bed, in my care. The Whitneys were not bad people, I reminded myself, but they were apathetic parents. They were self-absorbed and sacrifice was a foreign concept to them. They believed furnishing opportunities and materialistic possessions was equivalent to love. They loved Sam as best they could, but their love was shallow and finite.

Hunter opened the door to peek in, clearly expecting there to be a full house, foolish man. He inspected the room as if his eyes had deceived him during his preliminary assessment.

"They're gone; they left about ten minutes after they arrived. Mr. Whitney asked that I keep him abreast of any developments. He expects they will return to visit once she is alert."

Hunter, in his wisdom, kept his questions and opinions to himself, permitting me to keep my inner monologue to myself.

We resumed our idle chatter about nothing and anything. I told Hunter about vacations Sam and I had enjoyed together and our many antics. Hunter shared stories of his travels and study in Japan. We passed the time as best we could, reclaiming the optimistic tone from earlier in the evening to leave Sam on a positive note.

When we left for the night, Hunter followed me home in his Yukon. I asked him to stay the night so I would not have to face it alone, and he obliged. I was setting myself up for a much harder fall later, but I didn't care. I was in survival mode and Hunter felt essential to that survival. I would pay the price when the time came. For now, I used my emotional charge card and continued to rack up the debt. I prayed the solace he provided now would be worth the anguish I would suffer later.

I visited Sam every day for hours, talking and reading to her. I didn't know if she could hear me, but in case she could I aimed to entertain. I sat for my Business Ethics final, which I had thankfully prepared for prior to the attack, confident I had at least passed. My college career was officially over and I could not have cared less. The trivial things that previously monopolized my attention were now disregarded entirely. I had learned about priorities in the hardest possible way, but it was a lesson I would never forget.

Hunter worked most days, but came every night to visit with Sam. He was no longer sleeping over, but would always escort me home and hold me on the couch until I was ready for bed. He was my shelter through the storm, the buoy to which I had attached myself to remain afloat. He never complained and rarely needed to ask what I needed, he was there to anticipate and supply.

The doctors continued to be pleased with Sam's progress, optimistic about her prognosis. It was a week following the attack when Dr. Halthum advised they would cease the medication inducing her coma and remove the ventilator the following day. I was overjoyed that her recovery had come so far, but daunted by the new challenges greeting Sam when she regained consciousness. Her physical injuries and pain were only part of her healing. She would also have to confront the emotional baggage that had piled on top of her while she numbly floated.

When Friday arrived, I was the first person in line for a guest pass when visiting hours began. Permission secured, I headed up to Sam's room. Today was the big day—I would get my best friend back, the doctors were going to wake her up. It was better than any Christmas or birthday I ever had. I arrived in Sam's room and kissed her forehead after dropping my paraphernalia. Nothing had changed from the night before, but I felt a new energy in the room.

I spent an hour recounting every detail of how I had spent my night after leaving the hospital. The minute detail with which I had documented my life over the past week should have been enough to rouse Sam, if only for her to tell me to shut the hell up.

When Dr. Halthum arrived in the room I was vibrating with anticipation, and considered shredding the book I had been reading to provide him a ticker tape parade. After a quick assessment of Sam's vitals, he removed one of the drip bags that had been feeding her I.V.

"We have been slowly reducing the medication that maintained Miss Whitney's coma overnight. I have just removed it completely. If you will step out of the room for a moment I will remove her ventilator as well."

I complied immediately, glad they would remove the breathing apparatus while Sam was still unconscious. I imagined it would be distressing to experience while cognizant. She didn't need any more distress with which to contend. When I re-entered the room, I was comforted to find Sam's face no longer obstructed by tubing.

"How long until she wakes up?" I asked Dr. Halthum without patience. It had been a week, I was fresh out.

"It varies. The human brain is still a mystery in many ways. Her cranial swelling has almost completely abated, which is a good indication. She could awake instantly or it could take days. Try not to worry, continue to talk with her as you have been, and I will return to check on Miss Whitney this evening. The nurses will page me if she regains consciousness before my return."

After Dr. Halthum exited, I dug in my purse to find my Burt's Bees and slathered it over Sam's chapped and cracked lips. Satisfied I had aided her physical comfort in the only way I could, I settled into a chair and resumed reading to Sam. I chose a suspenseful and seductive romance, the type Sam would love, full of mystery and naughty bits. I would occasionally pause at a climactic section to see if she would object and argue for me to continue. She didn't.

As the day passed my frustration mounted. By the time Hunter arrived, I was discouraged and irritable.

"Why isn't she waking up?" I demanded, as if Hunter should know more than a neurosurgeon with decades of experience.

"I don't know, Everleigh. She will wake up soon. Keep the faith."

"Well thank you for that," sarcasm dripped from my words.

"Come here," he held out his arms, overlooking my petulance. I walked into his open arms, gluttonously absorbing the ease he afforded.

"Want to help me read a sexy novel to her?"

"Chick-lit, huh? I don't know if I can do it justice."

"We'll read it screenplay style. You just read the male dialogue; I'll take care of the female portions and narration."

"Only for you. I would never consent to such absurdity for anyone else. You better appreciate my sacrifice."

"Come on drama queen, you have noble work yet to do."

When we left several hours later, Sam was still asleep. The time would have been unbearable if not for Hunter's dramatic readings. I had to give it to the guy, when he undertook a challenge, he committed fully. Although not sold on the story, he delivered his lines like a seasoned thespian.

I fell asleep on the couch in Hunter's arms that night, disappointed but not defeated. Sam would be back tomorrow, I was certain, and then we could begin the work of reclaiming that which was stolen from her.

Three days later there was still no change and I was devastated, defeated. The doctors provided no explanation, encouraging me to be patient. Patience–I never realized it was a four-letter word. If one more person told me to have patience, I would go ballistic. I was inconsolable and even Hunter's presence brought no respite.

The nurses and doctors were now avoiding me like the plague. I had brooded, pleaded, agonized, bargained, denied, argued, threatened, and apologized. I even degenerated to the point of yelling at Sam, calling her stubborn and selfish. It was not one of my finer moments. By the end of the third day, Hunter had evidently seen enough.

"Get your things, I'm taking you home."

"The hell you are!"

"You have been here non-stop for three days. You haven't eaten, barely slept and, I'm sorry, but you are in desperate need of a shower. Enough is enough. I can't watch you deteriorate any further. Sam would kill me if she saw how far I've allowed you to descend. You will go home, you will shower, eat, and sleep. Then you can return and take up your vigil. If I have to haul you out of this hospital over my shoulder, I will."

I evaluated Hunter's determination–he was resolute. I debated the virtues of fighting him, quickly determining I was no match for his might or will in my current state. Resigned, I collected my belongings. We stopped at the nurse's station and she looked at me with reticence. I stood mutely as Hunter requested she contact him if there was any change in Sam's condition. She promised to do so sweetly—sure, she was sweet to him—bitch. We exited the hospital and I followed Hunter to his car. I was in no condition to drive.

"I'm sorry," I broke the silence.

"I know. You have been carrying this burden on your own for the past ten days. Endured more than anyone could reasonably expect. You're wound so tightly it was inevitable that you would snap." He paused, allowing me to appreciate his understanding. "Let me take care of you tonight. Recharge and return tomorrow, ready for whatever is thrown at you, even if it's more of the same. You're sleep deprived and depleted. You need this break, angel; you can't ride the edge any longer without tumbling over."

I nodded my acceptance, recognizing the truth of his words.

When we arrived back at my apartment, Hunter's first order of business was to get me in the shower. Feeling refreshed and enlivened, I headed to the dining table to eat the sandwiches Hunter had prepared for us. The food revived me further, I was feeling more coherent and rejuvenated.

"You were right, thank you. I needed the break to revitalize. I feel like a new woman."

"That's great, angel. You may act like a supergirl, but you're still human. You need to meet your body and mind's fundamental needs."

"Definitely."

I got up to carry our plates to the kitchen, but Hunter removed the dishes from my hands to rinse them. I returned to the dining table to collect my purse and keys. I was searching for my shoes when Hunter found me.

"What do you think you're doing?" he asked flabbergasted.

"I'm heading back to the hospital."

"No, you're not. You're going to sleep."

"Hunter, I feel much better. You were right, I needed a break. Now that I've had one, I need to get back to the hospital."

"Everleigh, you're delusional if you think I'm letting you walk out of this apartment before you rest."

He was starting to piss me off. He wasn't my father, hell, he was not even my boyfriend. He was the *un*-boyfriend who didn't want me, but he felt entitled to command my actions. Well screw him!

"I'm a grown woman. You can't dictate my life."

"Then act like one, you're being petulant. You need to sleep, put down your purse and your keys, and go to bed."

I toyed with the keys in my hand. I was closer to the door, Hunter would have to navigate around the table to stop me. If only I had my shoes. I looked around the apartment and spotted a pair of flip-flops near the couch. I walked with confidence across the room, past Hunter, to retrieve them. I placed my hand on the couch for balance as I slid the thongs between my toes.

Then I was airborne. I landed with a thud, my stomach over Hunter's shoulder. He began to walk in the direction of my room. Once my shock faded, I began to struggle, my purse, keys, and shoes lost in the effort.

"What the fuck are you doing?" I shouted into Hunter's back as I used my arms to lever myself up.

"I'm putting you to bed. I will not waste the next hour fighting with you when you could be sleeping."

"Put me down right this minute!"

"Nope."

I began to struggle in earnest. I levered myself enough that I could walk my hands up his back until they reached his shoulders. I was upright and board straight, being held across my hips, braced by his shoulder. I leaned back slightly, forcing Hunter to pause and adjust his hold to prevent me from falling. This provided an opening for me to shimmy downward and lock my legs around his ribcage. He tightened his grasp on me as I continued to wiggle, slipping further down his body until I settled at his waist. We ended up in a reverse piggyback. I tried to push off his shoulders, intending to fling myself back and reach for the ground with my hands. Once I released my leg lock, I could roll to a standing position. My plan was good, but Hunter was prepared. As soon as I released my hold around his neck, I positioned my hands on his shoulders prepared to push off. Anticipating my escape, he spun around and pinned me against the wall. Shit, I was trapped. Having trained to find every possible opportunity for escape, I writhed against him, trying to create enough space to maneuver. Hunter pressed me further into the wall, using his body to secure me fully, freeing his arms. He braced my head with his hands, preventing me from hurting myself or evading him.

"Stay still, dammit, you're going to hurt yourself."

"No! You don't own me, you don't get to tell me what to do." I wiggled as best I could trying to get away. "Why do you even care? You're not my father. You're *not* my boyfriend. You aren't even my lover. You get no say—Put. Me. Down."

"I will not watch idly while you purposelessly destroy yourself. Damn it, stop wiggling!"

"No! And another thing, just because you're some big bad—"

His lips crashed into mine. I suppose his intention was to silence me, but it rapidly transformed into devouring one another. His tongue plunged into my mouth, dueling with mine angrily. We parried and blocked with aggressive desire. I fought my way into his mouth, exploring him, conquering. Slowly, the kiss transitioned from a strategized attack to a choreographed dance. Our mouths glided along one another, sensuously licking and nibbling. He finessed his return, entwining our tongues seductively as he discovered every inch with tantalizing strokes that set me on fire.

Breaking our kiss, I stared into his eyes, begging him, imploring.

"Please," I whispered, "I need you."

"Angel," he groaned full of yearning, but his eyes revealed his inner conflict.

Certain he was going to reject me once again, I prepared to release him. Without warning he spun from the wall, marching purposefully to my room.

I unlocked my ankles and slowly slid down his body until my bare feet reached the floor. Our kiss resumed languidly, with ardent care, savoring every movement. The hands resting on my waist sought the skin beneath my shirt, caressing my sides and stomach before proceeding upward, grazing my breasts as the shirt was removed. He lowered his head, kissing my collarbone while releasing the clasp confining me.

I traced the muscles of his back, drawing patterns with my fingertips, causing him to shiver receptively. Following the planes of his body, my fingers glided over his chest and abdominals like a blind woman learning braille. He gripped my head in his hands, tangling his fingers in my hair, and tilted my head to possess my mouth more fully. He drank me in, drowning me in lust, slowing our progression briefly to increase the suspense as he laid me on the bed.

Everything became sensation and textures; I could no longer isolate a single touch or kiss as we urgently sought the intimacy of skin against skin. Utilizing mouths and hands, we investigated the responsiveness of the other's body. I inhaled him, the intensity of his alluring scent amplified by the increased body temperature, causing my mouth to water.

He lifted himself up, gazing into my eyes. "I wasn't prepared for this, I never expected to..."

Understanding, I reached into my bedside table to provide the solution.

He returned to me, braiding his fingers with mine, as he supported his weight on his forearms, positioning our joined hands on either side of my head. His reassuring mass pressed me into the mattress, enveloping me. He leaned down kissing my forehead, as he had countless times. Traveling downward, he kissed my nose, cheeks, and finally my lips. A kiss that began slow and reverent, progressed to sultry and ardent, escalating to erotic and vehement.

He worshiped my body with his hands and mouth, giving every part of me deliberate attention, arousing each nerve ending, until I felt like an electrical current was coursing through me.

He teased me relentlessly, withholding the fulfillment I craved, preparing me. I reveled in his every touch but feared I would die from wanting if he didn't satisfy my body's demands. I felt him position himself seconds before he slid into me smoothly, my body offering only acceptance and welcome. His breach caused me to convulse with pleasure, gasping at the fullness my body and spirit craved. I had never experienced such completion, a sense of belonging as if I had been made whole.

We rocked together, relishing the closeness our unification brought. I grabbed his head, pulling his mouth back to mine, needing the extra connection to reach my peak. Tasting, pure Hunter, better than the finest Kona, every muscle in my body contracted. I was panting, as the first shimmers lit my eyelids.

"Open your eyes, angel."

My mouth fell open in a silent gasp as I stared into Hunter's intense eyes, experiencing unfettered bliss. His entire being became rigid as he fell over the cliff's edge and my name slipped from his lips. I was barraged, the flimsy walls safeguarding my heart obliterated as I floated in a sea of oxytocin. Our connection was so profound, ruining me for any other. I had found what most spent their lives searching for in countless partners and endless relationships. He was the missing piece, complementing and completing me. My love for him was boundless and infinite—eternal. And I wanted him forever.

He gathered me in his arms, my head resting on his chest. I wrapped myself around him, clinging for dear life. I wanted to tell him I loved him that it would only ever be him, but the words stuck in my throat. I wouldn't risk tainting this perfect moment with honesty.

"Thank you," I said quietly.

"For what?"

"That was. Well...that was everything. It's never been so..." I could not find the world.

"Earth-shattering," he suggested.

"That too," I smiled, uncharacteristically shy.

"I know. I've never—" it was his turn to break off mid-sentence.

"You've never?" I prompted, unable to let the thought go unfinished.

"I've never felt so much, so connected."

I nodded my agreement.

"I've done a terrible job of getting you to rest. Sleep now, angel. I'll be here when you wake. I promise."

I yawned and closed my eyes. I felt him kiss my head and heard him whisper something I couldn't decipher. I wanted to ask him what he had said, but I fell asleep, once again in Hunter's arms.

Chapter Seventeen

*"I never knew until that moment how
bad it could hurt to lose something you
never really had."* -The Wonder Years

I awoke the following morning still wrapped in Hunter's arms,
wanting to stay in bed forever, hidden away from the world. I
wanted more of what we shared last night, but the world was
just outside the door, and I had escaped reality long enough.

"Good morning," Hunter greeted me.

"Morning to you, too."

"You ready to go see Sam?"

"Absolutely. Concern for her is the only thing that could
drag me from this bed."

"I hear you."

He cuddled me closer and kissed my lips before releasing
me. Was this our new normal? I wasn't sure. Were we friends
with benefits or something more? He told me clearly that a
relationship was out of the question, but last night was more
than fucking, more than physical release. It felt like
everything—passion, fire, lust, comfort, freedom,
and...love. Unfortunately, I didn't have time to contemplate
the ramifications of the night prior. It would have to wait until
later.

Hunter had his last exam that day, so I drove my car to the hospital and he followed. When we arrived at the hospital, we proceeded to the ICU where the nurse shared that Sam responded to external stimuli, both physical and verbal. The consensus was that Sam would likely wake in the next day or two.

Sheer joy poured over me, I was near tears at the news. My legs weakened and Hunter drew me closer to aid my balance. We thanked the nurse for the miraculous news and entered the room. Sam looked better than she had in nearly two weeks. Her color was noticeably improved and she seemed to have slight movements, a huge improvement over her death-like stillness.

Hunter pulled the cushioned armchair to the side of the bed and sat, pulling me into his lap. I reached into the side pocket of the chair and extracted the *smexy* book stored there.

"Not again. If she wakes up to us reading dirty books to her, she may pretend to sleep." He leaned in closer to me. "Besides, I may not be able to contain my response to such a scintillating topic with you in the same room—on my lap."

"Nice try, buddy. You aren't getting out of it."

We read to Sam for several hours. Hunter managed to control himself, but whenever he had to read a particularly dirty prose, he looked me in the eyes, reciting the words to me temptingly.

I was in the midst of narrating a wicked chapter where the heroine is tied up and blindfolded, when it finally happened.

"Ev? Are you reading me smut?"

I almost fell out of Hunter's lap. Tears of joy poured down my cheeks, landing on Hunter's arm. I fought to gain the composure to reply.

"I am in fact. Would you like me to continue?"

"It's tempting. I do love filthy literature, but it's usually something I read alone. Plus, I feel like a shitty friend getting off to Hunter's voice talking dirty to me," she opened her eyes. "I'm in the hospital? That explains why I feel like I've been hit by a truck."

"You are, but you're well on your way to recovery. Do you want some water?"

"Yeah, that would be great." She rolled her head toward us, "How long have I been here?"

"About ten days."

I leaned over to assist her in sipping the water.

"I'm so glad you're back, Sam. This one has been driving me nuts without you. You wouldn't believe the things she has talked me into doing." Hunter leaned over and kissed her forehead. "I'm going to get Everleigh a cup of coffee and tell the nurse you have decided to join the party. I'll be back in a bit."

With that, Hunter left us alone.

"How bad is it?"

I hesitated for a moment before deciding honesty was the best course of action. She would find out soon enough when the doctors arrived. At least I could give her the bullet points in plain English. I ran through her list of injuries, her current progress, and the long-term prognosis. She listened carefully.

"I'm alive, that's good news. No permanent damage some minor plastic surgery won't fix. We know that won't be an issue; my mom has her surgeon on speed dial. Some physical therapy," she paused, processing everything again, "It could be worse."

"You're taking this exceptionally well. It's kind of scaring me. Do you remember anything? I'm not pushing you; I just want to...I don't know."

"I don't know what else to do but survive. In order to do that, I need to focus on what matters. I'm alive and have no permanent disabilities or disfigurements. I fared better than many of the other girls. I'm not going to complain."

"That's a great perspective. Still scary, but enlightened. So you do remember?"

"Yes," she said quietly, "I remember everything."

"Okay. When you want to talk about it, you know I'm here. It doesn't have to be now."

"I know you are, Ev. I'm not ready to go there yet, but I will. I just need a little time."

"Fair enough."

"Thank you," Sam said emphatically.

"For what?"

"I'm sure you've been here every day. I would guess you all but moved in. Thank you for taking care of me. For giving me time to process before I start sharing the details. For being you. Thank you." Her eyes misted.

"You would do the same for me."

"You know it."

She looked thoughtful and I wondered what was weighing on her mind. There was so much for her to process.

"You going to tell me what is going on with Hunter before he returns?"

I laughed at her unexpected question.

"He has been amazing through everything. He supported me so I could support you. He has been here every day, almost as much as I have."

"And?" Sam asked, knowing I was editing.

"We slept together last night," I said, barely audible.

"And?" Sam replied impatiently. She would never let me get away with holding back details.

"It was amazing. Earth shattering, mind blowing, it was everything. I'm hopelessly in love with him and destined to be destroyed in the near future."

"Hung like a thoroughbred horse?"

For once, her inappropriate question was welcome, it was a sign she was still herself.

"Oh, yeah. I saved a horse and rode a cowboy," I said dramatically for her benefit.

"Maybe he felt the same. Maybe he changed his mind about the no commitment resolution."

"I doubt it."

"He's in love with you too, Ev."

"I don't think so. He loves me, definitely. Our sexual chemistry is off the charts hot. We are best friends, unquestionably. But, *in* love with me—doubtful." I took a centering breath. "I will keep him for as long as I can and enjoy every nanosecond. Then I will let him go gracefully with a smile. Even if I'm dying inside, shattered beyond repair, I will give him that gift in thanks for all he has given me."

"And you claim that I'm taking things too well, *you're* scaring *me*. Oh well, time will tell. Either way I will be here to share your joy, or sweep up the pieces and Krazy Glue you back together."

"I love you, and I'm so glad you're back."

"Back at ya, sister."

Hunter returned a little while later, followed by a parade of nurses and doctors. Everyone welcomed Sam back. I called Mr. Whitney, who advised me he was in Tokyo on business with Mrs. Whitney and they would return next week. They asked that I give their regards-*their regards*-to Sam, and inform them if a credit card was necessary for expenses. Sam was not surprised with the news, and seemed relieved not to have to deal with her parents for the time being.

The first truly uncomfortable moment arose when Sam asked where Robbie was. I told her it was too painful for him to see her in her previously unconscious state, and I was certain he would be coming to the hospital shortly. Hunter gave me a 'what the heck' look at my explanation, but I felt justified. It was a version of the truth, possibly completely true, in fact. I just had not actually spoken with him to know. A little while later I covertly left a message for Robbie letting him know that Sam was awake and if he didn't get his ass down here and pretend everything was okay, I would castrate him and make him eat his own balls sashimi style.

Hunter left to take his final before dinner. Sam enjoyed a lovely broth of unknown origins from the hospital kitchen while I treated myself to a burger and fries. It was probably cruel to eat real food in front of Sam, but it was our celebration dinner, and it wasn't my fault Sam's diet restrictions were not celebratory. I stayed until late in the night, not wanting to leave Sam. She seemed to be understandably avoiding sleep, and I was hanging in there with her. During the 1:00 am rounds, the nurse finally administered a medication that knocked Sam out. They assured me she would sleep until the morning. She wanted some items from home, so I would have to head to the apartment either way, I might as well sleep comfortably.

I texted Hunter that I was heading home for the night and would return to the hospital in the morning. I was exhausted and it was a twenty-minute drive. With no alternative, I succumbed to the dastardly vending machine coffee. I pressed the button for a large black and waited for it to brew. When the alert announced its completion, I opened the little plastic door and reached in to grab the wannabe coffee. I jostled the cup when removing it from the small opening, causing hot liquid to spill from the mouthpiece, directly onto my hand. Holy shit, it was hot! I most likely received second-degree burns from this sludge. Proof once again, vending machine coffee was bad. It was entirely too hot for me to sip, which defeated the purpose, but I could not throw it out even if it was coffee only in name. I paused to extract my keys from my purse before heading out of the hospital.

There were only a few cars in the parking lot adjacent to the hospital. The owners of those whose cars remained were like me, keeping vigil at a loved one's bedside praying for a miracle. It struck me how incredibly blessed I was to have Sam back, alive and surprisingly well, considering her ordeal. It was a miracle for which I would always be grateful. I stopped halfway across the lot, trying to remember where I had parked this morning. I was so tired I was barely able to remember. I scanned the lot and saw my car over in the furthest corner. Right! We got here late this morning, tired after our exertions the night before. The memory brought a smile to my face. I would have to broach the subject of our relationship with Hunter at some point, I needed clarification as to what we were now, but it could wait a couple of weeks. I wanted to enjoy more mind-blowing orgasms before potentially cutting off my supplier.

I approached my car, wishing I was already home in bed. I set my coffee on the roof while I unlocked the door. Retrieving it, I reached for the door handle when I heard movement behind me. I instinctively spun around and came face-to-face with Heath. Startled, I dropped my keys. I had a bad feeling, my gut was screaming, RUN! I quickly assessed my surroundings—I had parked facing a cement retaining wall, effectively cornered. I would not be able to escape without passing him. Not willing to take my eyes from Heath to locate my keys, I stood still and waited to see what he did.

"Everleigh, what brings you here this evening?" Heath asked congenially.

"I was visiting a friend."

I looked directly into his eyes, hoping I projected the confidence I wasn't feeling.

"Would that friend be Samantha?"

"I'd rather not say."

How did he know it was Sam? It would be a reasonable assumption on anyone's part, but I feared he knew it was Sam for a more sinister reason.

"You don't need to say it, I know it was her."

There it was, all the confirmation I needed. Heath was the one who had attacked Sam. I needed to create an opportunity to get the hell away. I knew Heath was infinitely stronger, so I needed to avoid physical confrontation. I had to stall until I could run.

"You're the one who attacked her," It was a statement, not a question.

"It was you I wanted, but your guard dog was always around. When Robbie warned me off Sam I was not pleased, hence when the opportunity presented itself, I took it," Heath's grin was sinister. "She was a particularly succulent piece of ass, and I don't mean that figuratively." He chuckled at his own depraved joke. "Since she is awake and I'm not being pursued by our friends in blue, I presume she didn't know it was me."

"No, she has no clue," I answered, not wanting him to target Sam again if I didn't make it out alive.

"None of them knew, I used a Lycra hood and they never saw us, I was careful never to speak. It was brilliant really," he mused. "They never saw anything, never heard anything. I wore gloves and a hat, as well as different sized shoes each time. I even wore a weight belt to vary the depth of the footprints each time. I was exceedingly careful not to leave any DNA evidence. You know, I shaved my whole body, even my pubes. Now that is commitment, don't you think?"

He paused thoughtfully, "In the future, I think I will select women based on specific traits, instead of just letting opportunity direct my conquests. A few of those girls were real dogs. I deserve better."

"Why did you kill those three girls but let Sam live?"

I edged away from my car, trying to position myself for an escape. I let my purse slide down my arm, hanging from my wrist.

"The first girl was an accident, I got a little carried away. I realized I limited my risk of exposure if I left no witnesses, it was the sensible decision for the subsequent two. Plus if I'm being honest, I rather enjoyed it—an added rush." He smiled reminiscently, "As for Sam, I didn't *let* her live. The bitch was as good as dead when I left her. If the damn police hadn't stumbled upon her, she would be in the ground already. I won't make that mistake again."

He was certifiable. A complete psychopath. A serial killer, already planning for his future murders with no remorse or guilt.

"Why are you telling me this? Why are you letting me see you? I could identify you."

I knew the answer, but I had to keep him talking. I subtly dropped my purse to the ground. I would not be able to find my cell phone in the jumbled mess and it would only slow me when I ran or hinder me if forced to fight.

"Come now, Everleigh, you're a smart girl. You won't be able to tell anyone because you'll be dead. I don't plan on risking exposure in the future, but for you, I just had to let you know it was me. You're special, you deserve my undivided attention. I couldn't share you."

"How nice," I said drolly.

"There's the fire I love. Would you like to know what I plan to do with you? What I did with the others? We have to hurry; I don't want to risk lingering here much longer. Perhaps just a little preview to whet your appetite. I'm going to incapacitate you and bind your hands with rubber restraints. I will take to you into the woods on the other side of this retaining wall, tie your arms and legs to trees to open you up for me, and then I'm going to fuck you senseless. When I'm done, I will likely rape and sodomize you with a small tree branch, to ensure you bleed out any possible DNA evidence. Never can be too careful, you know. Then I will beat you to death. Inspiration will come and fill in the details, but you get the gist."

"You do realize you're criminally insane?" I had to ask. He just described brutally violating and killing me, as if he was giving me a recipe for lasagna.

"That is certainly what I will claim if I'm ever caught," he smiled maniacally.

He took a step in my direction and I feigned left before moving right. He quickly adjusted and moved closer. He was only four feet away from me, almost within arm's reach. He faked a grab and I jerked. Pain registered on my hand and I realized I was still holding my coffee—my hot coffee. I pried off the lid with my fingernails while taking a step in his direction and threw the coffee in his face.

Heath shrieked in pain. It was not enough to do permanent damage, having cooled slightly, but it was still hot enough to scald. It was all the opening I needed—I ran. I ran for all I was worth, throwing every ounce of energy into propelling my body forward. I only focused on the hospital in front of me, pretending there was no Heath in pursuit. I probably only had a five second head start, but that would be enough. It had to be enough.

My lungs were burning, but I pushed on, twenty feet from the hospital entrance. I registered Heath was closing in on me, but I didn't allow him to distract me. Ten more feet. I was going to make it. Five more feet. Almost there. I was at the door. The stupid mechanical doors cost me precious seconds opening, allowing Heath the opportunity to grab my wrist as I began to cross the threshold. I screamed like a banshee while twisting to break his grip. I continued to call for help and I screamed "rape," as if my life depended on it, because it did. I heard commotion in front of me and I looked up to see a security guard approaching. Heath turned and ran.

I stumbled through the door into the atrium and screamed for the security officer to call the police and tell them the Hensley murderer had just attempted another attack. He followed my instructions immediately. A second guard assisted me to a nearby couch where I continue to fight for breath. I couldn't intake enough oxygen to satisfy my body's need, and my panic was rising.

I was also beginning to feel incredibly nauseous. I realized I was going to be sick and darted to a nearby garbage can, vomiting violently. After several minutes, my stomach was empty and the dry heaves ceased. I felt a hand on my back and jumped, swinging around with my arm in a defensive position. My fisted hand nearly connected with Dr. Bilatus.

"Miss Carsen, it's me, Dr. Bilatus—Lauren." She was safe, I knew she was. "Are you okay?"

I shook my head. She took my arm and guided me back to the couch.

"Tom, grab me a blanket and a pair of scrubs," Lauren requested from a nearby employee.

"Were you attacked, Miss Carsen?"

"Ev. Please call me Ev."

She nodded. "Were you attacked, Ev?

"Yes, in the parking lot. It was Heath. Heath attacked me and he's the one who hurt Sam." The words poured out of me in a staccato rush.

"Okay, the police are on their way. They will find him, and I'll send security up to guard Sam's room."

"Ian, can you please request a guard be stationed outside Samantha Whitney's room, ICU? Urgently."

"Yes, Doctor." He stepped away and radioed the request.

"Were you hurt, Ev?" Lauren returned her focus to me.

"No, I got away. He didn't get me."

"Are you certain?"

"Yes, I was having a hard time breathing and I threw up once I made it here, but I'm okay."

"You were hyperventilating and vomited as a result of the adrenaline surge you experienced. It's to be expected. Just focus on taking a slow deep breath, count to three, and then release. Let's do it together."

She breathed with me several times until she was satisfied with my performance. The orderly returned with a blanket and scrubs a few moments later. He handed them to Lauren along with a plastic bag.

"Ian, can you walk us to the ladies restroom and make sure it's empty, and then guard the door while we are inside?"

"Absolutely," Ian agreed.

"Come on Ev, let's get cleaned up."

Lauren helped me rise and guided me to a restroom around the corner.

After Ian had ensured it was secure, Lauren and I entered.

"Okay. Let's wash your face and rinse your mouth first," she directed me.

I complied without resistance. I was coming back to myself, but it was nice not to have to think for a few minutes under someone else's direction.

"Perfect. Throw your clothes in this bag and put on these scrubs. Wait," she grabbed some paper towels and wet them before handing them to me, "you can use these too."

I looked at her confused. She looked at my pants, and I looked down to find they were wet. Did I spill the coffee on me? No, I would have felt the burn by now. Oh, oh no. I wet my pants. I, a grown woman, wet my pants. Tears of embarrassment filled my eyes.

"No, don't be upset." Lauren put her arm around my shoulders, "It's another side effect of a major adrenaline rush, especially in cases of extreme stress. It's not one of the effects highly publicized, but it's prevalent."

I could not meet her eyes. "It could be worse. Do you know that the common male reaction to an adrenaline rush is an erection? Imagine the show if all those mixed-martial arts fighters weren't wearing groin protection when their adrenaline surged. Female viewership would quadruple."

At that bit of trivia, I laughed. I laughed until my sides hurt and my eyes teared. I looked up and met Lauren's eyes.

"Thank you, thank you so much. You have been incredibly kind to me."

She smiled in return as I entered the bathroom stall to clean up and change. When we finally exited the bathroom, Detective Norse was outside talking to Ian.

"Would you like me to stay with you?" Lauren offered.

"No, I've met Detective Norse before, I'll be fine. I can't thank you enough for all your help." I reached out and hugged Lauren.

"It was my pleasure," Lauren responded before waving goodbye.

"Miss Carsen, I'm sorry we keep meeting under such somber circumstances. It's an occupational hazard, I'm afraid. Do you mind telling me what happened, for the report?"

"Please call me Ev. Yes, I will tell you everything. I think you will want to dispatch someone to track down Heath Varbeck."

"Let's go sit down."

"My purse and keys are in the parking lot," I exclaimed with worry.

"The police units canvassing the area will recover them for you. I will have it brought here before we finish. If you're ready, please tell me what happened."

I told Detective Norse every detail I could remember. I recounted every word Heath uttered. The only thing I omitted was the fact that I had soiled my clothing. I suspect he had figured as much based on my current attire, but he was professional enough to feign ignorance.

"You did exceptionally well, Ev. You kept your cool and kept him talking until you were able to escape. Using the coffee was extremely resourceful. You did everything right. That doesn't always guarantee a positive outcome, but I'm glad it did this time."

"Thank you, Detective."

"Just give me one moment, please."

He walked a few feet away and spoke to a uniformed officer. I heard Heath's name and the order to 'bring him in.' When Detective Norse was done speaking to the officer, he returned to me.

"They're going to pick up Heath. I have an officer stationed outside Sam's room and a squad car will be outside your apartment building as well. We will keep the protection in place until we have apprehended him."

"Thank you that is a definite relief."

"Your belongings should be here momentarily. Is there anyone you can call to pick you up? I do not think it would be wise for you to drive yourself home. You have had quite the ordeal tonight."

"I'll call Hunter once I have my cell phone, it's in my purse."

As if I conjured him, I heard Hunter call my name.

"Everleigh." He strode to my side, "Are you okay? What the hell happened?"

"Heath attacked me. He is insane! He is the one who attacked Sam and all those girls at school. It was him all along."

Hunter's eyes darted to Detective Norse who gave a brief nod. Hunter wrapped an arm around my shoulders and kissed the top of my head.

"Give me a moment to talk to Detective Norse, I want to find out if they intend to protect you and Sam, then I'll take you home."

He walked away before I could assure him that Detective Norse had offered protection for us.

Several minutes later Hunter returned to me, with my purse and keys in hand.

"Are you ready to go?"

"Yes, please." As we began to walk away, I paused. "Wait. I need to ask a favor of Detective Norse."

"Detective Norse," I called.

"Yes, Miss Carsen?"

"Can you please make sure no one tells Sam anything before I speak with her? She doesn't know who attacked her, and it would be best coming from me." Detective Norse nodded his agreement. "Thank you."

"Okay, time to get you home." Hunter pulled me toward the door.

"It seems silly to leave; Sam will wake up in a few hours."

"I will call the nurses station and ask them to tell her you said you were running late. You need to get some rest before you return. When you come down from your adrenaline high, you're going to be hurting."

I wanted to argue but I didn't have the energy, which probably proved Hunter's point. We walked to his car, parked at the entrance door of the hospital. He studied me for a moment before starting the Yukon.

"You want to hear what happened, but you're trying not to push, aren't you?"

He smiled guiltily. "You don't have to relive it right now," he stated conciliatorily.

"It's fine, if the tables were turned it would drive me bonkers not to know. Maybe if I talk about it I will be able to sleep tonight," I offered. "Wait, are you staying with me tonight?"

"Yes," he said vehemently.

"Thank you."

I proceeded to give Hunter a full account of what had happened from the time I left Sam's room until he arrived at the hospital. Again, the only detail I omitted was my humiliating adrenaline induced accident. At several points, Hunter white-knuckled the steering wheel, clenched his jaw, ground his teeth, or hissed. He never interrupted, letting my thoughts flow undisturbed. When I was done, I waited for his response. He didn't say anything for a couple of minutes.

"So he didn't touch you?" He was wound tight.

"Just grabbed my wrist as I was entering the hospital."

"I'm so sorry this happened to you, angel, but I'm also extraordinarily proud of you. You handled yourself better than many trained professionals. You even managed to get a confession out of him."

"I can't take any credit for the confession. I was only trying to stall him and he felt like bragging. I wish I had been able to hold him for the cops, but I was too scared."

"Baby, are you crazy? You got yourself away from him safely and without injury. That was your only goal. I would have been reaming you out if you had tried to apprehend him. My brave, crazy girl."

We pulled into my complex and Hunter parked in front of my building. As we got out of the Yukon and walked toward my apartment, Hunter nodded at a random car.

"Who's that?"

"That's your unmarked police protection."

"Good catch."

"I was looking for them. Detective Norse guaranteed they would be here."

We walked inside and entered the apartment. Hunter set down a bag I had not realized he was carrying. He must have planned to stay the night before I requested it.

"I'm going to take a quick shower."

"I'll be here. Are you hungry?"

"No, there's no way I could eat. Be right back."

I brushed my teeth and took a record setting shower. When I exited the bathroom, Hunter rose from the couch and walked toward me. He took me in his arms, hugging me close. This was what I needed; I needed him to hold me, to love me. I wanted to feel him against me, to know everything was all right, that life would go on.

I kissed his chest, working my way up his neck until I reached his lips. I dragged my lips across his, applying light pressure. On my second pass, I peeked my tongue out to lick the seam of his mouth, requesting entrance. He denied me access, and instead leaned back to look into my eyes.

"You need your rest."

"I need you."

"You had an incredibly difficult night, your emotions are still all over the map. You need to go to bed, and you will feel better in the morning."

"I'm fully aware of how difficult my night was, how raw I feel. I know what I need, what I'm feeling. Right now, I need to be in your arms, to feel your body pressed against mine, inside mine. I need to be reminded that I'm alive and there are a lot more good moments than bad."

"Everleigh, we can't. Please just go to bed and get some rest. I will be out here all night to protect you."

"Out here?" I asked confused.

"I'm going to sleep on the couch."

"Why are you sleeping on the couch? Do you not want to sleep with me?"

I could not wrap my mind around what he was saying. Hadn't it been last night he slept in my bed after we had the most indescribably intimate sex?

"No, I'm not going to be sleeping with you tonight. What happened last night was astonishing. It was truly special, but it can't happen again."

I pulled back as if struck. Did he just say it would never happen again? I knew it was not the right time for this conversation. I had run the gamut of emotions and I was still tender. Hadn't I just told Sam I was going to enjoy my time with Hunter, and when the time came I would let him go with a smile? But that was before. Tonight scared the bejesus out of me, I learned life was precious and fleeting.

"What are you saying, Hunter? What changed between yesterday and today?" I asked contemptuously.

"Nothing has changed. Yesterday should never have happened. I have told you all along that I can't be with you, I've never wavered from my position. You're my best friend, and I never should have slept with you. Things got out of hand last night, for both of us. As spectacular as it was between us, best friends cannot screw each other if they want to remain friends. I don't have sex with my best friend and I'm not interested in having casual sex with you. I'm hoping we can put it behind us and not lose what we have. I don't know how many times I can say it. I'm not at a place in my life where a relationship with you is a possibility."

"You keep saying you can't *right now*, it's not a possibility *right now*. What does that mean? Are you implying you want to pursue something in the future?" I continued before he could even respond, "Let me make sure I'm clear on your position—you would like to have a relationship with me, you could see having a future together, but you're too young to commit to something that serious? Is that the bullshit you're trying to feed me?"

Hunter groaned his frustration. "Why are you pushing this conversation now? Can't we just let things be? Everything was going so well before yesterday. I know I confused you. I should not have slept with you. I already admitted my mistake. Can't you forgive me so we can move past it?"

"Why am I pushing this? Because I fucking love you, you idiot, and I can't hide my feelings anymore," I screamed at him. "I'm in love with you. I love you so much it eclipses everything else around me. You're the star I can never reach. I can wish and dream, stretch and strain, but you're always just out of my grasp. I need something I can hold, I can count on. I need something tangible."

Hunter looked stunned, unprepared for my sentiment or anger.

"There is no man more perfect for me, no one I'd rather spend my life with, no one I will ever want more. But I need someone who wants me equally in return. I love you with every ounce that I am, down to the smallest molecule of my being, but that isn't enough if you won't reciprocate."

I paused to take a deep breath, praying he would interject, tell me he would reciprocate. Instead, he said nothing.

"I would do anything for you...anything. The only thing I can't do is pretend I'm not in love with you. I have given you everything you would accept, but I can't make you love me. I can't create feelings in you that are not there. Can you imagine what it's like to want something so desperately and know you can never have?"

Still, he said nothing.

"There are times when it feels real, when I fool myself into believing you are feeling what I am. But you're not, are you?"

He shook his head, refusing to answer. That was an answer in itself as far as I was concerned.

"It's now or never, Hunter. This is the time to make your decision. It's all or nothing for me. I'm already all-in, I have been for months, but it's irrelevant unless you're ready to take the risk with me. There was a time I would have settled for the half-life we have been living, but it's not enough anymore. Our *un*-relationship is not enough for me. I have a boyfriend in every aspect except the actual commitment. You know what...I want the damn title, I want the fucking commitment."

"Please don't do this, Ev, not right now. Don't push me, I don't want to lose you," he sounded so desolate.

"You need to let me go. Let me move on if you do not want me–if you don't want us. I'm your hostage right now. You keep me tied to you because you don't want to lose me, our friendship, but you're being selfish." I fought back the tears that threatened to fall. "Hunter, you're tearing me to shreds so that you can keep the pieces of me you want and discard the rest, and you're destroying me in the process. You don't get to keep my heart anymore if you refuse to give me yours in return. It's time to stop holding me in limbo. It's time to decide."

"You're asking me for something I can't give you. I wish I could, you have no idea how much, but if the only option you're leaving me is all or nothing you're leaving me no choice." His eyes looked damp and he was struggling to get the words out, "I can't do it, angel. I can't give you everything."

I nodded, not trusting myself with words. Tears were running down my face like rivers, but I didn't care. He took a step toward me, reaching out. I help up my hand to stop him, shaking my head.

"I need you to go now, Hunter, you have to leave. Maybe someday I can find a way to be your friend again, but that day is not today. I'm sorry, I'm just not strong enough." I stifled a sob, choking slightly. "Take care of yourself, and don't regret this, regardless of the outcome, I will never regret having you in my life-even if only briefly. You have been a good friend to me, and I thank you."

"Everleigh, I'm not leaving you alone right now. Heath is out there, Sam is in the hospital, I don't feel ri—"

"Go. You've made your choice, and you can't have it both ways. Let me go, so I can try and find a way to do the same," I said more firmly.

"I will tomorrow, for tonight just let me stay to make sure your sa—"

"Go!" I shouted.

Sobs wracked my body, but I remained standing. I walked to the door and opened it for him. He reluctantly picked up his overnight bag. As he passed me, he placed a kiss on my forehead, the last of many. I closed the door behind him and leaned my back against it, sliding down toward the ground in a heap, where I cried myself to sleep.

Chapter Eighteen

"You kept quiet... When these victims wanted
your help to survive, you kept quiet."
-Paul Kagame

I awoke several hours later on the floor at the foot of my front door. Talk about a bad start to the day, every muscle in my body hurt. Remembering the night before, I drew a shuddering breath and pressed against my chest as if I could physically restrict the pain that had blossomed. I wanted to crawl into bed and hide from life. I let Hunter go; more accurately—I threw him out of my home and my life. I demanded what I knew he couldn't give, and I had finally lost him. I knew it would come, but it was too soon, I wasn't ready.

Maybe a little tough love was all he needed. We would take some time apart, and he would realize that he did love me. He would come back to me. I was deluding myself but I needed to cling to the false hope that we were not done, especially if I was ever going to get off the floor today. I would allow myself hope, pretend it was all a bad dream, just for today.

I hurried to dress and headed to the hospital. I had to get to Sam before anyone told her what happened yesterday. I didn't know what the information would do to her, and I would be damned if she found out without me there to hold her together if she needed it. Remembering I didn't have my car and unable to call Hunter, I was forced to call a taxi to get to the hospital.

As I rode to the hospital, I ruminated about Sam's progress. Physically, Sam was healing well, the doctors were pleased and she would be able to go home as early as this weekend. I wondered if we should find a home nurse to stay with her while I was at work for the next few weeks. I could help Sam dress and bathe, but she may need additional assistance when I could not be there. I would have to download as many e-books as possible on her iPad to keep her mind occupied for the next month. She needed to rest so her bones could heal properly. Mentally, Sam was infinitely better than anyone had a right to expect. She had begun to deal with what had happened, but she was resolved to survive, to fight not to lose herself. That had to be a good sign. I wanted to cover her in emotional bubble wrap to ensure nothing impinged on her time to process and heal. I still needed to find a counselor for her, as she would need to talk about what happened soon. I would give her until she was released from the hospital and then I would begin my push. The doctors warned me that there could be psychological side effects from having been in a coma and in the ICU for an extended period, especially when combined with the intensity of her injuries from the attack. They instructed me to watch her carefully for anxiety, restlessness, nightmares, paranoia, disorientation, agitation, delusions, and abnormal behavior. I was also to alert them of fluctuating levels of consciousness, which include aggressive or passive behavior. It had only been a day, but Sam was displaying none of the symptoms they had indicated, which was a huge relief.

The taxi dropped me off at the front door. I flashed back to last night, to Heath, as I entered. I focused on my breathing, trying to calm myself. I was safe; everything was fine. I tried to relax all my muscles while waiting for the elevator. Slowly, my panic receded; I suspected I would have random moments of anxiety in the foreseeable future. If I was experiencing the emotional effects of my incident, what must Sam be experiencing?

As I approached Sam's room I nodded to the police officer standing outside.

"Hi Officer, I'm Everleigh Carsen. Everything good?"

"Hello Miss Carsen. Yes, everything has been fine. There is a young man who arrived a little while ago to visit Miss Whitney, she confirmed he was her boyfriend. I cleared him, but requested they keep the door open."

"Thank you."

I was about to enter when I heard crying, but it was not from Sam. Peeking in, I saw Robbie sitting in a chair next to Sam's bed. He was holding her hand with his head resting where they were joined. I listened, wanting to give them their privacy, but not willing to trust anyone with Sam's wellbeing except myself.

"I'm so sorry, Sam. I should have come sooner, but I was a mess. When I heard you had been attacked, I was sick with worry, physically ill. I can only imagine what they did to you, I should have protected you. I felt so guilty for not taking better care of you."

Sam began stroking Robbie's hair, soothing him. What a selfish ass; he should be comforting, soothing, and reassuring her. Robbie was such a twit sometimes.

"Robbie, it's alright, I know you must have been scared. I was not even conscious. It doesn't matter, you're here now. I love you. Do you still love me? Can you be with me despite what..." Sam trailed off. "Can you still be with me despite what happened? Does that change how you feel about me?" Sam asked in a small voice.

"Of course I still love you. Nothing could change that. Whatever they did, it does not change who you are. I'm just so sorry. We will be okay; we will make it through this. Can you forgive me? I love you, Sam; I want to marry you, I planned to ask after graduation. Say you forgive me, please," Robbie pleaded desperately.

"There is nothing to forgive, babe. You didn't do anything wrong. Nothing you could have done would have prevented what happened. It was a random attack. I hate that it happened, but if it did have to happen, I prefer it was me instead of some other girl who may not have the love and support of people like you and Ev. I love you as I always have. I want to marry you, too. I'm not going to forgive you, because there is nothing to forgive."

"You have to forgive me Sam. It won't work if you don't forgive me." Robbie was getting irrationally upset. "Please, just say you forgive me. I need to hear you say it, and then we can move on and try to forget everything that happened."

"Robbie, calm down. This is just your male instinct to protect driving you crazy. If it means that much to you, of course I forgive you." She leaned over and kissed him gently on his head.

"Oh, thank God. I was sick with worry that you would never forgive me for failing you. I never thought they would attack you. I told him to stay away from you or I would kill him. I tried to protect you, but I failed. I'm so sorry. I couldn't live without you, Sam," Robbie rambled thoughtlessly.

Heath had told me he targeted Sam because Robbie had warned him off. Robbie had just inadvertently admitted Heath had attacked Sam. How did Robbie know? I intended to get the answer, now. I stepped into the room.

"How did you know Robbie? How did you know it was Heath?"

They both looked at me—Robbie terrified and Sam confused.

"What do you mean, Ev? Heath was the one who attacked me?"

"Yes," I answered evenly.

"You can't know that," Robbie said in desperation, realizing his mistake.

"Yes, I can. He tried to attack me when I left the hospital last night. I was able to escape, but first he confessed everything to me."

"Why would he do such a thing? Was it because of the bar incident?" Sam asked bewildered.

"Heath was the one attacking and murdering all the girls, Sam—he's a psycho. He was targeting me, but I was proving difficult to isolate. Robbie threatened him to stay away from you, which in Heath's twisted mind was a challenge. When he found you alone near Mathematics he took the opportunity."

"Oh my God," Sam muttered to herself, "but you're safe. He didn't hurt you?"

"No Sam, he didn't get me. I threw a hot cup of coffee in his face and ran. It was close, but I was lucky."

"Thank God," Sam said with conviction, "but what does that have to do with Robbie? He didn't know Heath was killing people. He was just trying to protect us because he knew Heath was a creep."

"Is that true, Robbie?" I questioned him for Sam's benefit. I didn't want to break her, but she needed to know the truth.

"I was trying to protect Sam, I love her. I never wanted her or anyone to be hurt," Robbie replied defensively.

"But how did you know Sam needed protection? What made you so certain he was dangerous? You knew, didn't you?"

"No," Sam gasped. "No way, Ev. Robbie couldn't have known. He wouldn't have let him hurt all those girls."

"Robbie?" I prompted when he remained silent.

"Sam, love, it's not what it sounds like. It all started as some stupid frat prank. Heath instituted a competition amongst the brothers to see how many women would agree to be tied up and spanked during sex. With all those kinky romance books girls are reading now, he thought it would be a fun twist to the classic notch in the bedpost competition the frat ran every year. The entire fraternity had to participate, each brother was required to get at least one. I didn't even do it; I lied and said I did. I didn't do anything wrong."

"But Heath did," I stated calmly.

"Look, Heath has never been right in the head. I don't know how many complaints Hensley received from girls about him, but there must be a ton. He never was good at hearing 'no.' After the competition ended Heath didn't stop. He was always bragging about his exploits, the things he got women to do. He was spouting lunacy about women wanting to be dominated and controlled. He said women wanted the pain— as in *all* women. I know some girls like kink and, if she is into it then it's all good, but Heath was adamant all women wanted it. He said they would tell him 'no' as part of the game, to push him so he'd give them more of what they craved; he's twisted. When the attacks started, I was suspicious. He would boast about encounters with 'enthusiastic' women, and then there would be news of a violent attack. A couple of the brothers actually bought into his rhetoric and would watch. I never witnessed any attacks, but I heard about them. I never, not in a million years, thought he would hurt you. I would have done something. I only warned him off you because he was fixated on Ev and I didn't want him to turn his attentions to you."

"You knew he was hurting those girls?" Sam asked horrified.

"I didn't *know*, I suspected," Robbie argued.

"And you thought he might hurt Ev, but you still did nothing about it? You didn't tell anyone? Not the university? Not the cops?" She shook her head in disgust. "Even if you didn't have the balls to come forward yourself, you could have done it anonymously. You just sat back and let it happen."

"He would have figured out it was me. He never trusted me; he would have killed me and gotten away with it. His father gets him out of everything." Robbie defended himself pathetically.

"And that's justification for letting him continue to hurt people? To kill them?" Sam shrieked, "You could have stopped this. Prevented the attacks and all of the murders. You could have protected those girls–you could have protected me," Sam finished quietly.

"No, baby, I would have never let him hurt you if I had known. I love you. It kills me that I wasn't there to protect you," Robbie disputed.

"You didn't need to be there to protect me, you just needed to speak up. Tell the truth," she shuddered. "Do you know what he did to me? I prayed for death, Robbie. I prayed that you and Ev would be okay when I was gone. He took everything from me I was not willing to give. I'm terrified of everything now, broken—in pieces. He broke me and you let him."

"Sam, please, please baby. I lov—" Robbie begged, but Sam was done.

"Don't you finish that sentence, don't you dare. You do not love me; you're not capable of love. Love is selfless, self-sacrificing—you are selfish and self-serving. You are a coward and your inaction rendered you just as bad as him. You are equally accountable for what happened to all of us as if you had done it yourself." Sam steadied herself, grabbing the bedrail, "Get out."

"Sam," Robbie tried again.

"I said get the fuck out of my room you conscienceless bastard. Get out. Get out! Get. The. Fuck. Out!" Sam screamed like a lunatic before dissolving into body-shaking sobs.

The officer ran into the room, ready to intervene. He surveyed the drama, assessing if there was any threat.

"Officer, this man has information regarding crimes committed by Heath Varbeck. You may want to let Detective Norse know," I advised, not caring what happened to Robbie at this point. Sam had been right about every word she spoke, every accusation. I would never forgive him for hurting Sam by his neglect; he had betrayed her with his silence. On top of everything else she had gone through, I was afraid this would be the final straw that broke her irrevocably.

"Sir, why don't you step outside with me so we can speak? I'll need to get all of your contact details," the officer addressed Robbie with revulsion.

When they left the room, I sat on the edge of Sam's bed and held her as best I could with her injuries. She cried on my shoulder for hours, muttering nonsensically. If anyone other than me tried to touch her, she would shriek and fight. She was like a wild animal, incapacitated and petrified. When Sam began to scream that Heath was in the room I called the nurses. I was having a hard time restraining her as she thrashed and fought, defending herself from a ghost. The nurse quickly took inventory of her condition and administered a sedative. A short time later the doctor from the psychiatric unit came in.

"I will need to evaluate Miss Whitney when she wakes. I don't believe we will need to hold her for psychiatric observation, provided she has calmed when she awakens. I suspect she was experiencing ICU psychosis, which is common for patients confined for more than a few days. The combination of medication, environment, and the stress of healing can be potent. Most patients are fully recovered within 24-hours with no further episodes after they are discharged," he explained.

"Doctor, she was hallucinating, convinced her attacker was in the room with us. Is that normal?"

"Hallucinations are common, yes. I believe the added emotional strain from the attack and sexual abuse are the cause. I understand she also had a highly charged exchange with her significant other right before the episode. That would also be a contributing factor, and most likely the trigger. She needs a safe, calm environment to heal—physically and mentally. She has been through a terrible tragedy and is fragile. I will return this evening to evaluate her further. Stay with her; familiar people, loved ones, bring the greatest relief."

I kept vigil by Sam's bedside, reading to her, talking to her, and offering comfort as she slept. I had no idea what to expect when she awoke, I prayed she would be calm and coherent. The words she had spoken to Robbie about her attack haunted me. They replayed in my mind on loop, tormenting me with her devastation. She felt tainted and forsaken.

Sam finally awoke several hours later. When she blinked her eyes open, I offered her a smile that she didn't reciprocate.

"How are you feeling, girlie?"

Nothing.

"Are you in any pain?"

Silence.

"Do you understand me?"

She nodded once.

"Are you taking a mental health break from words?"

She nodded once again.

"Fair enough, you have more than earned a vacation day. How about I read to you?"

She nodded once.

Everything was fine until I reached a juicy section of the book, which depicted a graphic sex scene, and Sam slapped the book out of my hands. I guess we were done reading.

"I was getting tired of that book, too. Are you hungry?"

Silence.

"Would you like to watch TV? I turned the cable on for you earlier today."

No response.

"Do you want to sit in companionable silence?"

Nada.

"Do you want to hear about how Hunter tore out my heart and stomped on it before returning it to me as if nothing had happened?" I tried, knowing under any other circumstances that would grab Sam's attention.

She nodded once.

So, I told her. I recounted every single word, every tear, every look, and gesture. She listened intently. I shared my pain, rejection, sense of loss, and the fear I would never find anyone I loved as much as Hunter. She squeezed my hand at my confession, offering me comfort in the only way she was able. When the psychiatrist returned to examine Sam, she remained mute. She was skittish and panicked when he tried to touch her. Finally, she seemed to separate from her environment, staring blankly into space, disassociated.

I spoke to the doctor in the hallway after his examination. He was concerned about her regression. I shared with him that she communicated with me non-verbally, listened, and offered comfort. The doctor believed our friendship provided her a sense of security, enabling her to interact with me. It was his opinion that she had retreated into a shell like a turtle, to protect herself after all she had endured. Like the turtle, she would pop her head out when she felt it was safe, but crawl back inside at any perceived threat. He suggested several therapists for her to consider upon her discharge. Though he felt this was a psychological defense and not a cognitive impairment, he advised me that if she didn't reestablish verbal communications in the next several days, he suggested I consider finding an intensive treatment program. He suspected she was suffering from PTSD, Post Traumatic Stress Disorder, but it was premature to officially diagnosis, especially on the heels of her ICU psychosis. I thanked him for his guidance and returned to Sam. It was three hours before she would acknowledge me again.

Two days later, Sam remained nonverbal. She would communicate by nodding to me if no one else was there, but hid herself away in the presence of anyone else. She wouldn't permit anyone but me to touch her, sedation was required when the doctors examined her injuries. It was heartbreaking to watch my once vivacious best friend become a shadow. The turtle analogy was perfect—she would pop out for me, allowing me to feed and pet her. With strangers she would hide away and, if forced from her shell, would snap and bite viciously.

By day three of the silent treatment, I was desperate. I finally deciphered her plan—if she didn't speak, she couldn't talk about what happened. If she didn't talk about it then she could pretend it was not reality. She didn't have to confront the pain and emotions running through her like a tornado, leaving destruction in its wake. The doctors advised me that Sam would be physically ready to leave in two days, however they had concerns about her mental stability. They wouldn't release her unless there was a plan in place for intensive mental health care; I did not disagree.

I would do anything for Sam, but I was not qualified to help her through this. I would love and support her, but I didn't have the tools to get her talking. I didn't know the proper way to help her walk through her memories without risk of her being consumed by them. She needed professional, experienced help. This was complicated because she also needed significant physical therapy. I only had one recourse, but I hated it.

When I returned home that evening, I called the rape crisis center and explained what had transpired. They gave me the name of several therapists they recommended. One of the names they provided had been included in the list from the hospital psychiatrist. I called her and left a message briefly outlining the situation. She called me back thirty minutes later. It was 11:30 at night, at least I knew she was committed.

"Hello?"

"Hello, I'm Dr. Cynthia Veritus. Is this Everleigh?"

"Hello Dr. Veritus. Thank you so much for calling me back."

"It's no problem. Tell me a little more about what happened with Sam, and her current state."

I told her everything, including the turtle analogy and my theory that she was silent to avoid dealing with the rape. I ended with my belief she needed an intensive therapeutic environment that could address her psychological needs as well as her physical requirements. I felt strongly that a psychiatric hospital would be detrimental in the long-term progress.

"You're a good friend and I concur. Sam needs a specific type of facility to address her complex needs at this time. A colleague and friend of mine has a live-in facility for women, which specializes in rape trauma syndrome, RTS, which is a sub-set of PTSD. Due to the nature of her specialty, she is accustomed to addressing medical needs concurrently. She collaborates with physicians and medical specialists to ensure continued physical recovery. There is a physical therapy suite on-site and a clinic, so all examinations and treatments take place on property. The staff, including the visiting doctors, are exclusively female. Those in residence do not encounter any males until deemed mentally prepared, and the reintroduction of masculine presence is a part of the treatment course. The facility is spectacular. It has a spa-vibe, posh. The only issue may be the cost, the facility caters to the ultra-wealthy, those who want the best treatment with the utmost privacy."

"That would be a good fit, actually. Sam's family will not want to risk publicity, and money is inconsequential to them."

"Great. I'm confident I can pull some strings to secure her a spot. She will be discharged in two days, correct?"

"Yes."

"She will need to go directly to the facility upon discharge. They will have a nurse and a counselor fly out to meet her and bring her back to San Diego."

"San Diego? That far?"

I didn't like the idea of Sam being so far from me when I was entrusting her care to strangers, but if this was the premier facility to address her needs, then so be it.

"I can fly with her," I immediately offered.

"No, that will not be possible. She needs to establish trust relationships with the therapeutic team as a part of her treatment. This will be the first step. If for any reason it doesn't pan out, let me know and I can suggest alternatives. When she completes the program, if she chooses to return to New York, please feel free to contact me for her continued care."

"Thank you so much, Dr. Veritus. If I can just ask one more question—how long will she be at the facility?"

"It varies by patient, but I would estimate sixty days."

"Wow, that long," I was stunned.

I thanked Dr. Veritus again before saying goodnight. It was nearly 1:30 am and I was exhausted. I showered and dressed for bed, desperate for the oblivion of sleep.

Chapter Nineteen

"The friend who can be silent with us in a
moment of despair or confusion, who can stay
with us in an hour of grief and bereavement,
who can tolerate not knowing...not healing,
not curing...that is a friend who cares."
-Henri Nouwen

My phone rang early the next morning.

"Hello?" I grumbled, frustrated by the intrusion into my now rare REM cycle.

"Miss Carsen, it's Detective Norse. I'm sorry to call so early, but I wanted to let you know that we have apprehended Heath Varbeck. His arraignment is scheduled for tomorrow. I anticipate he will be remanded without bail. I wanted to confirm that you're willing to testify when the time comes."

"Morning Detective, thank you for letting me know. Yes, I will absolutely testify. I can't be certain, but I would anticipate Sam would also be willing, if needed."

"Thank you. Take care of yourself and send my best wishes to Miss Whitney as well."

After we disconnected I laid in bed unable to return to sleep. I was elated the police had apprehended Heath—truly ecstatic—the news could have waited two more hours. Accepting the disappointing reality that sleep would remain elusive, I got out of bed to make myself a cup of coffee.

I sat on the couch with my cell phone nested in my lap as I sipped my coffee, desperately wanting to procrastinate the phone call that had to be made. I longed for a personal assistant to whom I could delegate unpleasant tasks. Steeling my spine, I lifted my cell phone.

It rang twice before a clipped tone answered, "Whitney."

Reminding myself of the necessity precipitating the call I began, "Good morning Mr. Whitney, it's Everleigh, I was hoping to have a minute of your time."

"Is it urgent, Everleigh? I'm terribly busy this morning."

"I'm afraid it is. Sam will be discharged from the hospital tomorrow and I don't believe I'm equipped to address the full spectrum of her needs."

He cut me off dismissively, "Fine, fine. Just let me know the specifics and I will have our driver pick her up. My assistant can arrange for nursing care at our home until she is able to return to her apartment."

"I don't believe that would be the best option at this time. I have consulted several professionals who recommended a facility that can best address Sam's needs during her recovery."

"That would be preferable, actually. Have the facility direct the bills to my office. I will ensure they are paid. Please spare no expense, no cost is too much for Samantha's care and comfort.

I restrained myself from pointing out his parental neglect, "I will be sure to let you know when it would be appropriate to visit Samantha so you can be assured of the standard of care being provided to her."

There was no way the Whitneys would fly to San Diego to inspect Sam's care when they couldn't be bothered to drive to the nearby hospital to do so.

"Everleigh, please make certain you stress our desire for confidentiality as it pertains to the details of Samantha's wellbeing. I don't want her life to incur any further interruptions as a result of the incident."

He didn't want any further '*interruptions*'? What he didn't want was for his country club cronies to discover his daughter was damaged goods—soiled. Pretentious prick!

"I will see to it, Mr. Whitney."

He ended the call with no further commentary.

Checking my email, I found the admission packet from the facility Dr. Veritus had suggested. I printed the attachment, reviewing the pages as my printer expelled them. Several forms needed to be completed by Sam's physicians. I would need the paperwork to be completed today and returned to—I didn't even know the name of the place I was sending Sam. I scanned the papers—Phoenix Center: A Restorative Haven. It sounded awfully 'new age.' Feeling resourceful, I contacted the San Diego area rape crisis center to inquire about the Phoenix Center. The hotline volunteer enthusiastically recommended the center provided I could: A) secure a spot, and B) afford the exorbitant cost. Able to meet both of the stipulations I thanked the volunteer for her time. I decided to call, feeling more confident in the facility, but still wanting to speak directly with the person in charge of Sam's care,

I spoke with Dr. Michelle Drake—Shelly, as she insisted I call her—for an hour discussing the center's general philosophy, therapeutic programs and techniques, medical care, physical therapy, daily routine, and amenities. Shelly put me at ease effortlessly earning my confidence.

"Shelly, I'm entrusting you with the care of my best friend, my sister, please don't let me down."

"Have faith, Everleigh. If Sam is as strong as you believe, the program will provide her the tools to heal and reclaim her life. The road won't be easy, but given time she will heal."

"Thank you, Shelly. I will have the doctors send the required forms. You have all the details to arrange for the flights tomorrow?"

"I do. We had to charter a flight due to Sam's injuries as well as prevent further trauma from exposure during a commercial flight. The nurse and therapist will be with her every step of the way to ensure health, comfort, and safety. I will keep you appraised of her progress on a weekly basis and let you know when it's appropriate to visit. Take care."

I was confident I had made the right choice by the time I ended the call. Now for the hardest part—I had to tell Sam and I was clueless as to how she would respond.

When I entered Sam's room, she was alone staring blankly into space. She appeared lost.

"Good morning Sam. I have good news, they caught Heath. The detective said it was unlikely that the judge would grant bail. Isn't that a relief?"

She continued to gaze at the wall.

"How are you?"

She turned to look at me but offered no reply.

"I need to talk to you. You're scheduled to be discharged tomorrow, but the extent of your injuries require more professional care than I am capable of providing. I suspect your parent's home would not be conducive to recuperating either."

Sam nodded her agreement vigorously.

"I found an amazing center that can provide the medical attention and rehabilitation you need during your recovery. They specialize in women who have been through similar experiences."

Sam shook her head in protest.

"Sam, I know you want to come home and hide under your covers. I get it, I would probably feel the same, but I can't let you do that. I love you enough to give you what you need—even if it isn't what you want."

Sam slammed her fist on the bed in response.

"Don't give me attitude! You refuse to speak, you can only tolerate my touch, you're broken—you said it yourself. You need to get better, I need you to get better, but I don't have the skills to help you with this. Please, Sam, you are the only family

I have. I can love you and support you, but that will not be enough. I don't know what to do other than to send you to the most qualified professionals."

Sam turned her head, refusing to look at me.

"You're mad at me. Fine, I'll accept your anger and you can hate me if you want to, but you are going to Phoenix Center. You may have experienced a tragedy, but I will not let you *become* a tragedy." I stopped, wanting to guide the conversation in a more positive direction.

"The center is outside San Diego, on the beach. It's a private complex that has every amenity you could want and need—they even have a salon and spa on site. Their reputation is stellar and I spoke to the director myself, you will love Shelly."

Sam still refused to look at me.

"I'm going to miss you like crazy but I will come visit soon and you will be back before we know it." I was swimming in guilt as if I too had betrayed her, "You can't make the right decisions for yourself at this point, so I will make them for you, until you're stronger. Please do this, give it a real chance—for me. You always said that you would do anything you could for me and this is what I'm asking of you. Go and heal, get better because I need you. You're my bestest friend, my sister, and I can't live without you. Please," I finished on a whisper with tears glistening on my face.

Sam finally looked at me and nodded her agreement. She held out her uninjured arm inviting me near, and I went without hesitation and hugged her gently.

"Thank you," I kissed the top of her head as if she was a small child.

"Only for you," she whispered in return.

With those three small words, my hope was restored. Sam would come through this, scarred but living again.

I slept at the hospital that night, not willing to leave Sam alone. She didn't speak again until she was leaving with the staff from Phoenix Center. I bent down to her wheelchair to hug her when she whispered, "love you" in my ear. Yeah, Sam would find her way. She may have to claw and fight to come back, and she may not be the same Sam she used to be, but the new Sam would be stronger than ever before.

I returned to work the day after Sam left, Marty was overjoyed to have me back. Her patience was unparalleled while I was attending to Sam but she was ready to get back to the usual routine. I threw myself into work needing the distraction it provided. It was odd not to spend all my time at the hospital. I still worried about Sam incessantly, but was confident she was well cared for. School was over; I had graduated. The actual commencement Friday would not include me. I had no desire to accept my diploma on stage with no one there to care or cheer for me. My solitude was too depressing to emphasize by walking in the ceremony.

Heath was arraigned and bail had been denied, despite the protests of his lawyer and father. Police revealed Heath's two best friends were accomplices in his crimes, usually as voyeurs but they had also committed several of the attacks. Heath had cleverly planned his absence during several of the assaults ensuring he had undeniable alibis should he ever become a suspect. His friends apparently confessed once arrested in order to obtain leniency for their testimonies.

A commercial for the evening news caught my attention the week after Heath's arrest. It promoted an exposé including "untold details about the conspiracy and capture of 'Heath, the Hensley Hunter'." Great, Heath had a new alliterated moniker. I'm sure the twisted psycho loved it.

I didn't want to watch, but I could not stop myself. I had lived the horror but like every motorist driving by a car wreck, I couldn't look away. I folded myself on the couch with coffee in hand. The program began with a recapitulation of the events at Hensley and of Heath's alleged crimes. Thankfully, the victims' names were withheld. The reporter surprised me when he disclosed that Hensley had received over thirty complaints from female students about Heath over the past four years—ranging from obsessive behavior to non-consensual sex, which Hensley had either ignored or willfully buried. The reporter speculated that the university turned a blind eye to his troublesome and illegal actions due to the influence and monetary contributions made by Mr. Varbeck. Several Hensley administrators had stepped down or suddenly retired this week, including the president of the university. I was shocked to learn of Hensley's complicities and the volume of complaints registered against Heath. The reporter praised the dedication and determination of the Suffolk County Police Department, mentioning Detective Norse by name, in the eventual capture of Heath. Credit was also given to the FBI for their assistance in providing resources and manpower to the investigation over the past four months, at the request of the police.

"Our sources have confirmed that Special Agent Hunter Charles of the FBI New York Field Office was instrumental to the investigation as an undercover operative. Special Agent Charles is the son of William Charles—founder of the Higosha Dojo, a popular and profitable chain of martial arts schools." A photo of Hunter dressed in a dark suit exiting the police headquarters was shown full screen.

"What the—" I muttered to myself as I struggled to process the information.

That lying son of a bitch—I really should not disparage Hunter's mother, she was probably a lovely woman. That deceitful, two-faced, duplicitous, liar liar pants on fire! He must have marveled at my naiveté. No wonder he *couldn't* have a relationship with me, he was too busy using me for his investigation. Was any of it real? I had heard undercover DEA agents sometimes had to use drugs to maintain their cover—was having sex with me the equivalent in this operation? Could our friendship have been nothing more than an avenue to gain access to students and blend into academia? Every word out of his mouth, every promise, was a lie. I had been alarmingly wrong about Hunter an absurd number of times, but this was the icing on the cake.

I had thrown myself at him; I had begged him to love me, to want me. I was going to be sick. I was in love with a character—he was not real, merely playing a role to catch the villain.

Plato said, "Love is a serious mental disease." Damn that guy was smart. I had spent the last four months of my life losing my heart to a man who didn't want it—who told me he didn't want it—but I insisted he didn't know his own mind. We played hot potato with my heart—me throwing it to him, him tossing it back to me. But every time the music stopped, I was always the one holding my bruised organ—out of the game.

Why did I let myself succumb to the temptation of him? He had a skull and crossbones label on him, but I drank his poison nevertheless and loved it; now I needed an antidote. I was a fool, alone and angry, preparing to do what every fool did at such times—I was going to a bar to drink myself smart. I changed my clothes and drove to The Stop. Thankfully the bar was nearly empty, providing a nearly private venue to drink myself to understanding.

Selecting the bar stool I calculated was closest to the liquor I craved, I settled in for a long night; the only way I was leaving this stool was when I fell off. Griffin spotted me and approached.

"Hey pretty lady, how are you?"

"I'm in need of a double-shot of tequila."

"That good? Give me a minute and I'll get your anesthetic."

He was a good man. I watched as he spoke to another bartender before pouring my drink. With shot and bottle in hand, he rounded the bar and approached.

"Come on girl, there is a table in the corner with our names on it."

I debated following him, I had already made a commitment to my stool, and I was not one to break a vow. Persuaded by the full bottle of tequila in his hand, I hopped down and marched to the booth. Finding a comfortable position, I recommitted myself to not moving from my seat until I had fallen to the floor, and reached for the shot he set down. I tossed my head back, letting the burn course through me, welcoming the fire. I reached for the bottle to refill but Griffin snatched it first.

I grunted my displeasure like an ornery caveman, "More. Now!"

"You talk, I pour. You don't talk, I don't pour. The choice is yours."

"I'm in love with Hunter."

I nodded to the bottle in his hand demanding recompense for my five words.

"Tell me something I don't know."

"I'm in love with Hunter and he doesn't reciprocate. He is an FBI agent, undercover at Hensley to catch Heath. Every moment I spent with him was a fabrication, part of his cover."

Griffin whistled his surprise while he poured me a shot, which I raised to my lips without hesitation.

"Both of my best friends are gone. I'm alone." Griffin cleared his throat with a reproachful look. "You're right, thank you, Griff. You have been a good friend to me and I'm sorry for diminishing you. Tequila?"

"No harm, Ev. I know you're feeling rejected and isolated, but I am your friend, too." I smiled my appreciation while reaching for the shot he refilled. "Your friend who is giving you a limit. Three shots are all you're getting tonight. Do you want to consider keeping the last on reserve?"

I grabbed the shot and swallowed before he could offer any further wisdom.

"I find myself wondering where he is and what he's doing. Does he have a girlfriend or a wife who is celebrating his return? Is he sharing drinks with his FBI buddies, swapping stories of the dumb women who fell for them during an operation?"

"He wasn't faking it, Ev."

"Yes he was. I offered myself to him, begged him to want me and he patted me on the head like a faithful collie and declined. It was all a lie; he was pretending to be my friend."

"Cut the crap. He was never just your friend," Griffin shook his head. "When people feign emotions they only emote when there is an audience to witness their performance. Hunter displayed the most unbridled feelings when he thought no one was looking. It was not fake, Ev, he was not pretending."

The tequila was making its presence known. The warm tingles were encompassing my body, providing the companionship my lonely heart required. I wanted more of the goodness, but Griffin had made my quota clear.

"I miss Sam," I lamented.

"Where is your lovely partner-in-crime? I haven't seen either of you ladies for the last month. I was afraid she was avoiding me."

"She's not avoiding you, Griff. She has been...indisposed, on an extended vacation. She will probably be gone a couple more months." I aimed for nonchalance, trying to hide my concern.

"She just took off for a couple of months and left you behind?" He was skeptical.

I shrugged, "I have to work."

Griffin studiously read my reaction to his queries, determining there was more to learn.

"What about loverboy?"

"That's through. Sam learned some things about Robbie she couldn't live with. She kicked him to the curb a couple of weeks ago."

"We had a deal Miss, you promised to notify me when she became a free-agent," Griffin reminded me.

"It isn't the right time Griff. She's working through some issues," I hedged.

"So she took off on an extended vacation to mend her broken heart. That doesn't ring true. You two have one of the most symbiotic friendships I have ever seen. If she was hurting you're the first place she would go—and remain—until she was restored. You draw strength from one another, support one another. What aren't you telling me?"

He was right and each of his words prodded a wound that had yet to scab over. My eyes filled with tears that clung to the rim before spilling over onto the table.

Griffin took my hand in his, consoling me, "Ev, honey, what happened?"

I shook my head, unwilling to break Sam's trust. Griffin drew a sharp breath and clenched the table's edge in his huge hands.

"No," he muttered to himself. "Ev, please tell me it's not the horror I'm imagining."

I averted my eyes, unable to meet his stare. I heard the shot glass rattle on the table and raised my eyes to find Griffin trembling with rage. I gasped at the fury emanating from him.

"Is she ok?" he gritted through clenched teeth.

I shrugged, and then shook my head.

"Is she getting help?" he asked softly.

I nodded.

He released a ragged breath before asking, "Tell me what you can, please."

Jose had loosened my tongue, curse him, the ninety proof bastard. I told him what happened, omitting only the details of Sam's attack, because it was not my story to tell. Griffin never interrupted me, but there were many points where he returned his grasp to the table as if restraining himself from action. When I finished, he sat unnervingly still.

After several minutes passed I interceded, "Griffin, have I lost you? I have developed quite the aversion to catatonic behaviors over the last month."

"Don't joke. I'm not ready to joke yet, Everleigh," Griffin said fiercely.

He was not handling the knowledge I had imparted with the objectivity so intrinsic to him. His speculation to the brutality Sam had endured and her subsequent breakdown was a burden he was struggling to bear.

"She will survive this and come back to us soon," I reassured.

Griffin snapped into clinical mode, "Has she regressed since entering the facility? Is she exhibiting appropriate emotional responses? Is she interacting with other patients and staff? Is she participating in group sessions?"

Whoa, that was a whole lot of questions, many of which I didn't know the answer.

"Shelly, the director of the center, said she is integrating well. She is building a trust bond with one counselor in particular. She will acknowledge the attack now and recount factual details, but not express consequential emotions. She attends group sessions willingly, but has yet to participate." I hated talking about Sam in detached terms. "She's made a lot of progress in her short time there, we have every reason to be optimistic."

Griffin nodded his agreement. "Heath is exceedingly lucky he's in prison. If provided the opportunity—"

"You would have to take a number. I understand the queue is longer than the line to the women's restroom after a chick flick."

That earned me a chuckle.

"It would be best if Robbie went into hiding. I won't seek him out, but if we come face-to-face...I won't be able to control myself—he has a lot to answer for."

We sat in silence for a while, both wishing to rewrite history with a different outcome.

"Come on pretty lady, I was supposed to take one of the bar backs home after his shift tonight. I'll drive your car and have him follow us; it'll save you the cab fare tomorrow."

When we arrived at my apartment, Griffin took my hand in his benignly. "I know you're missing your confidants. I want you to know you have a friend in me. Do not isolate yourself, you know where to find me most nights."

"You're one in a million, Griffin Evensen. If you weren't like a brother I'd likely be smitten."

"Goodnight, sis."

I entered my apartment feeling lighter, having unloaded on Griffin. My trip to the bar provided the opportunity to re-establish my friendship with Griffin when I needed it most.

Over the weeks that followed, I spent much of my leisure time at The Stop, keeping Griffin company during his shifts in an effort to avoid the solitude of home. He listened to my whining about Hunter, my concerns for Sam—he was always eager for her progress reports, my growing responsibilities at Higher Yearning, and every random thought that popped into my head. At times, he provided distraction but often he pushed me to confront my tangled emotions. I suspected our friendship initiated from a mutual caring for Sam, but it had grown to be independent of the initial commonality we shared.

While Griffin was wiping down the bar one night, he broached the topic I had been avoiding as of late.

"Ev, have you considered reaching out to Hunter now that your temper has cooled? He may be waiting for you to approach him."

That was Griff, always picking at my scabs—I would need to buy stock in Neosporin to prevent infection and scaring—but I had learned he would not be ignored.

"It would be easy to delude myself into believing you. Hunter was abundantly clear he doesn't love me and we have no future. Even if I put aside his lies, which I can't fathom doing, I begged and he denied me...repeatedly. What is the definition of insanity, psych boy? The act of repeating the same behaviors with the expectation of a different outcome. I've had enough crazy to last a lifetime, now I want stability."

"I'm convinced what you shared was genuine. You could consider the possibility," he chided. "You miss him. Everything about you is dimmer—much of it is the consequence of your concern for Sam—but an equal part is Hunter's absence from your life."

He was correct, but the solution was not to invite Hunter back into my life.

"I stepped off the merry-go-round for a reason, Griff. It made me dizzy and I kept ending up in the same spot. It may have been fun for a short ride, but was never headed anywhere."

"Your biggest problem is that you are pigheaded—you assemble the facts and draw your conclusions—but once you make a determination you are unwilling to reconsider. Be careful not to tie yourself so tightly to your assumptions that you cut off possibility."

"Thank you, oh wise one. I will keep that in mind," I replied sarcastically.

⊱ ⋯ ❦ ⋯ ⊰

At least once a week we rehashed the conversation. Griffin would spring the attack inopportunely, and I would circumvent his efforts. It would have been gratifying if it were not reminiscent of my banter with Hunter.

"For all that is holy. If Hunter was here right now I would disrobe and climb aboard the love train shouting 'choo-choo' just to get you to shut it. You're inexorable; I can't even remember why I like you."

"Not exactly the result I was hoping for, but it will do. At least you're beginning to relent," he laughed. "By the way, I will be sure to remind you why you like me soon, since you seem to have forgotten."

I rolled my eyes and changed topics before he could continue his preaching. The man could persuade a vegan to nosh on bacon cheeseburger sliders. He was right though—I would be lost without him.

The following Sunday I had received amazing news; Sam was recovering well and finally beginning to share her experience and feelings in personalized terms. This was a huge victory, a foundation upon which the rest of her recovery could be built. I texted Griffin as soon as I was off the phone, and he insisted we celebrate the following evening.

Chapter Twenty

"Love recognizes no barriers. It jumps hurdles,
leaps fences, penetrates walls to arrive at its
destination full of hope." -Maya Angelou

I arrived at The Stop, my second home, to find the bar vacant; it was eerie. Griffin caught my eye and an unknown object sailed toward me. Much to my satisfaction, I caught the projectile before it struck me. I unclenched my hand to find a silver whistle on a rope—the kind gym teachers wear—shining in my palm.

"Where is everyone?" I prodded. "And what the heck is with the whistle missile?"

"The bar is closed for a private party tonight," he winked, "and you're the one who said you needed a whistle."

I had said no such thing; I would recall such an outlandish request, wouldn't I? Griffin came around the bar and headed for the stage, which I noticed was illuminated by the spotlight. He climbed the stairs, picked up his guitar, and stood in front of the microphone. What the hell, were we having a concert?

Griff began to strum a familiar chord progression as I focused on the sound identifying the tune—"Open Arms" by Journey. It was a strange choice for our celebration.

As Griffin picked an extended intro, I feared that he was using the moment to communicate his romantic intentions to me—damn, that would be tragic. I shook off the thought quickly.

I stood frozen until a hand grasped mine, causing me to turn. There he was...

"Hunter," I breathed like a prayer.

"Angel," he said smiling, "will you dance with me?"

I was too flabbergasted to process his question or offer a response. Sensing my quandary, Hunter took the lead. Placing his hand on my lower back, he guided me closer to him until our bodies met.

"Listen," Hunter commanded gently as he cradled me to his chest.

Griffin began to sing the lyrics to a song I had known all my life, but heard for the first time. I absorbed every syllable, every word, registering the meaning, and understanding this was Hunter's opening dialogue. I shut out every doubt and question for the time being, content to savor the feeling of his arms around me.

When the song ended Griffin slipped off the stage and out the back door.

"It's time we talk, angel. There's been too much left unsaid."

"Are you wearing a wire? Should I call my attorney?" Evidently, my joy at finally seeing him again had abated, leaving me insolent.

He sighed. "No I'm not wearing a wire, would you like to conduct a strip search?" he offered mischievously.

His impish reply was usually an aphrodisiac but was not winning him any points tonight.

"Cut the cutesy routine. You lied to me and used me. Other than an apology, I can't fathom what more there is to say." If he wanted to make amends, he was going to have to work for it.

"Cutesy? I have never been called that before," he mused, before turning serious. "I have never lied to you,

Everleigh. There were times it was damn near impossible, but I promised myself I'd never lie to you, and I haven't. I have withheld a pertinent detail about my job, hurt you through my inaction, and failed to protect you when you needed me, but I never lied to you."

"A lie by omission is still a lie!" I corrected his supposition.

"Then we disagree. I withheld the nature of my job by necessity, but it wasn't really pertinent."

"Not pertinent, are you out of your mind? There was nothing more relevant. You were using me to assimilate at Hensley for your undercover operation. You forged a sham friendship with me to ingratiate into the student body. That may make you a resourceful agent, but it makes you a shit friend and a shittier lover. Speaking of which—did you screw me to further the operation or was it a fringe benefit? Get your rocks off with the gullible undergrad?"

Hunter took a step back as if I had struck him.

"Is that what you believe—that I used you to gain access to Hensley—that I made love to you to garner intel? What kind of man do you think I am?"

"The type of man who pretended to be someone he wasn't, who fucked me and then left. I guess that makes you no different from every other manwhore barfly, except they don't pretend to care about their prey. Evidently they have more integrity."

"First, if I needed to befriend and seduce a woman to acclimate at Hensley I would be a pitiful agent. I had already gained exposure through the self-defense seminar and undergrad classes. Second, I didn't fuck and leave you. I made love to you, and you gave me an ultimatum. When I could not provide everything you wanted from me, you kicked me out of your life. Third, I have not pretended to be anything other than myself. I was not undercover—if I were, I would have assumed a false identity—it was a plain-clothes operation. I was always me, I just didn't specify my profession or how it related to my presence at Hensley. Fourth, I have not ever lied to you. Don't challenge my integrity."

He made several valid points. Was I really upset that he suppressed his ties to the FBI or was I resentful of his chronic rejection? It was the latter. I understood his need to conceal his purpose at Hensley. What had me incensed was his inability to recognize what we had was precious, rare, and scarce, and he cast it off like junk mail.

"You're right; for the most part you were only doing your job, an honorable job, trying to protect the women of Hensley and solve a case. The criminals are behind bars and the operation was a success. I commend you, mission accomplished. The rest is just details—the end justified the means. If you came for my forgiveness, you have it; I wish you nothing but the best in life. Take care of yourself, Hunter." I smiled so he would see my sincerity.

I was proud of myself. I let him go with dignity and a smile this time. I finally put his needs ahead of my wants. He needed absolution to find closure and I had given it to him. My final act of love for the man I could never have. Hunter and I appeared to have divergent perspectives on my noble sacrifice.

"Are you freakin' kidding me? You're dismissing me with trite well wishes? We are not done discussing this, Everleigh. We haven't even begun to reach an understanding."

I stared at him confused.

"I officially closed my portion of the case—debriefing done, reports filed, actions accounted for. I can finally say what has been gnawing at me for months. At last, I can have an uncensored conversation with you, and you want to pat me on the head saying 'Good boy Fido, now go pee in someone else's yard'? I don't think so. You're going to listen to me, and for once you're going to hear what I say and not read between lines that aren't there."

"What else is there to say, Hunter? You explained your reasons for omitting your law enforcement status, and I granted my forgiveness. There is no reason to beat a dead horse." He may be feeling chatty, but I needed to leave while I was still able to let him go.

"Everything! There is everything left to say. You could try the patience of a saint, do you know that? You are going to sit down and be silent while I say what I need to say without interruptions. You get me?"

"Hunter, let's walk away now. Our issues are resolved. We can look back one day and smile with fondness when reminiscing about the time we shared."

"That's it," he muttered, and suddenly I was over his shoulder...again. He really had a thing with manhandling me. He dropped me unceremoniously on the edge of the stage.

"You will sit there and you will remain silent. You will listen—and hear. You will not move a single muscle until I'm finished. Do you understand me?" I was about to speak when he held up his hand to stop me, "It was a rhetorical question. Don't speak, don't move."

Hello, Alpha-Hunter. I was beginning to fear I had pushed the man passed the edge of reason. Watching him pace before me, I decided to follow his directive to sit still and silent, awaiting his monologue.

"I'm going to tell you a story. It will be a 'Choose Your Own Adventure'—did you ever read one of those books as a kid? They were my favorite—you have control over the story and will choose how it ends."

I nodded my acceptance. He tossed me a warning look; apparently, he was serious about me not moving a muscle.

"There was once a man who thought he was happy. He volunteered to investigate a string of heinous crimes because he wanted to protect people and hopefully save lives. He also volunteered to teach women how to protect themselves because he knew he couldn't personally protect them all. He met a woman—a sarcastic, stubborn, stunning woman—and he was intrigued, captivated by her. She didn't like him at first, but then she made it her mission to make him her friend. He laughed at her determination because he was already taken with her. They became friends, best friends, but their relationship grew complicated."

They became something more than friends, something undefined, which confused the girl and would occasionally cause her to do something crazy. He wanted to explain his feelings, but he couldn't. He had to keep his job a secret to make sure the bad guys didn't get away with their crimes when he caught them. He tried to be just her friend, but it was hard, monumentally hard. He wanted to hold her, touch her...he wanted more. But, he wasn't able to give her more until his job was completed. One night she was sad, hurting. He intended to comfort her and take care of her, but he wanted her so badly he lost control. He made love to her. It was a life-changing, revelatory experience, but he knew he made a mistake because the timing was wrong. He had opened a door that he could not yet walk through, and he couldn't close the door afterwards because they had splintered the frame."

She asked him to give her everything. He wanted to do just that, but he couldn't until his mission was complete. He asked her to wait but couldn't offer an explanation as to why. With no explanation, she *assumed* he was rejecting her and promptly kicked him out of her life; he was devastated. He rushed to catch the bad guys and ensure they wouldn't get away with their crimes. He wanted to return to the girl, but he had hurt her so deeply he didn't know if she would forgive him or give him another chance. He conspired with a mutual friend to re-win her heart. When his co-conspirator told him it was time, he went to the girl—his girl. She was still angry and tried to send him away, but this time he refused to leave. He told her a story about a man very much like himself and a woman very much like her, and then he waited to learn how the story would end."

I stared, mouth agape, absorbing all he had just said. He concisely recapped our entire relationship. I had been wrong. I was so stupid, impatient, stubborn, presumptuous, and—in love with him. I was prepared to jump off the stage and tackle him, but he had ordered me to stay put and be silent. I decided to obey for a change.

"Do you remember my tattoo? I had it inked at the end of March."

I was confused by his non sequitur, but nodded. As if I could forget the brand on his left pectoral. Why we had descended into the history of his body art, I didn't know.

"Do you remember what it means?"

I nodded. He looked at me expectantly, granting me permission to speak.

"Forever. You said it was the Japanese word forever, eternal."

"Exactly. Forever."

He looked at me expectantly again. But I shrugged, still not comprehending his point.

He put his hand over his heart and repeated himself, separating the words, "For—Ever."

Shut your—what? Did he just say what I think he said?

"I already knew, for me there is only you. No matter what happened between us in the future, it would only ever be you. I was made for you—only for you."

Yes, he was in fact saying what I thought he said. I was dumbfounded, rendered mute.

"I have been in love with you for months, Everleigh. I wanted to tell you every day, but it would have been selfish to verbalize my love when I wasn't at liberty to give you anything else at the time. I hoped to be able to keep us in the friend-zone until I closed the case, at which time I could give you everything if you still wanted me. Then you started dating that shmuck from Krav. I was terrified I would lose you, but my hands were tied. Like an idiot, I fucked things up royally by sleeping with you."

That was not complimentary, and he must have read my thought because he hurried to continue.

"Don't misunderstand—there was nothing I wanted more than to have you wrapped around me, watching you come apart in my arms. It was spectacular, and I would have given anything to have spent the last month repeating the experience over and over again. I could never get enough of you. I wanted to taste you and try you on, in all the ways I had fantasized, but the timing was all wrong. I still couldn't be with you, give you what we both needed. I desperately wanted to say I love you that night."

Now, I was hot and bothered which was not conducive to deep meaningful confessions.

"It was torture, watching your heart break, being thrown out on my ass because I couldn't give you the one thing in the world I wanted above all else. If it had just been about the job, I would have said 'screw it' and quit, rather than risk losing you. But it wasn't just the job. We were so close to stopping him and if I had told you everything, jeopardized a conviction, I would never have been able to live with myself. There were too many women who deserved justice, Sam especially."

He finally approached me, placing his hands on either side of my hips, leaning in close.

"Catching Heath was the only cause worthy enough to keep me from you. I thought I was happy before you, but you lit up my world. You challenged me, made me laugh, and aroused me beyond reason. Everything before you and without you was dim and monotonous. I may be able to live without you, but I don't want to, it would be bland and uninspiring. Existing, not thriving."

"Everleigh Rose Carsen, I'm irrevocably in love with you, I have been for quite some time and I will always be. You're what I want exclusively. It's an irreversible condition. Please, angel, give me a chance to finally give you the everything you asked for. Let me love you."

Screw his rules! I grabbed Hunter's head and pulled it down to mine. I whispered against his lips, "I love you" before kissing him with all the fullness of emotion I had previously restrained.

His hands left the stage, one cradling the back of my head with care, the other cupping my face. Languorously his lips and tongue mingled with mine. He took control of the kiss, demanded it, building a wealth of passion and fervor. Forced to break our connection when I began to feel faint, his lips traveled down the column of my neck, nipping and sucking gently as he went.

I enfolded Hunter with my arms and legs, needing him closer.

He stepped back, taking me with him as he walked to the game room. Hunter looked around to consider all options. Making a decision, he sat me gently on the edge of a pool table and placed a reverent kiss on my forehead.

He shrugged, "I'll buy Griffin a new table if he complains."

When considering making love to the man of my dreams, a pool table had not figured in, but it was perfect for us in this moment. I wondered if I should feel guilty at the prospect of desecrating the table. The thought was pushed aside as Hunter's lips grazed the shell of my ear.

"I need you now, knowing you're really mine, not having to censor my words or shutter my emotions. I need you to see and feel how deeply I love you. Can I have you, angel? Can I take all of you and keep it?"

"Please," I begged.

He undressed me slowly with great care, kissing every inch as he exposed it, as if memorizing my topography with his lips. He whispered words of love and praise, listing the ways I had stolen his heart with each kiss. When he was finished, I returned the favor, following his lead and sharing every facet of my abiding love for him. When we were finally exposed to one another, bared body and soul, he climbed up beside me and wrapped me soundly in his arms, kissing me until my only thoughts were of him. With an inarticulate utterance, he entered me, and we both gasped as we melded into one being. We had an intrinsic understanding of one another, two halves creating a whole that moved and breathed as one.

Ensuring he had my eyes, he stroked my cheek. "I love you, with everything I am. My heart beats for you...only for you."

He moved with deliberate slowness, finding the spot that caused my eyes to roll back in my head, showing me with his body the truth of his words, making me melt. Under his expert care, I soared through time and space, there was not gravity holding me to earth, no laws of physics to restrain me. Every second felt like an hour as if time had lost all meaning. Hunter followed me with words of love pouring from his mouth as he stared into my eyes shaking with exertion and release.

I was encased in Hunter's arms, my head resting on his chest as I regained my breath and my wits. Oh my, how I loved this man.

"I think I'm bleeding," he shared unexpectedly.

"Did I scratch you?"

"No—well, yes you did, but that was welcome. I hit my head a few times on the drop light above the pool table."

"Are you okay?"

"With you, it's a full contact sport. I may need headgear next time." He teased while placing strategic kisses along my nape and shoulder.

I laughed, "Why didn't you move? It would have put a damper on my fun if you had been knocked unconscious."

"I didn't register what had happened until just now. I was too distracted by the beautiful woman putting on a spectacular show beneath me."

"Your performance garnered some pretty rave reviews, too."

"I heard the critics were fairly difficult to win over, I'm glad I appeased them."

I swatted at his arm playfully.

"How are you feeling?"

"I have loved you so long—never believing we could be together—I'm afraid I will wake up alone again in my bedroom."

"This is not a dream, angel—this is beyond my most fantastic dreams. I have my best friend back, my lover in my arms, and my heart where it always wanted to be."

He kissed me again with a new reverence. I gave my soul to his kiss with every touch. We lay together for a long time, cuddling and enjoy the freedom to be with one another fully.

Sometime later, I heard the back door open and shot upright, yelling "choo-choo" at the top of my lungs. Hunter looked at me as if I was the mad hatter.

"Do I even want to know?"

"It's probably best if you don't."

I laid back down and snuggled with him a little while longer. Griff could wait.

"How is Sam?" Hunter inquired.

"She is struggling to crawl out of the hole she dug to survive, but she will be okay. She has a difficult journey ahead, the road will be treacherous at times, but her will is strong."

"We owe Griffin big time, you know. He was the mastermind behind our reunion. I think he has a bit of the romantic in him."

I would like to dismiss Hunter's comment as merely a tangent, but I knew he was plotting.

"Love, she is not ready—she may never be ready for him. Her wounds are so deep, when they finally heal the scars that remain may be too thick to penetrate. I love Sam with all my heart and want her to be happy and to find love when she is ready, if she's ready. But, I love Griffin too, and I'm not sure Sam will ever be able to fully give herself to another person after what she has been through—definitely not anytime soon. Griffin deserves more than a piece of her. He deserves everything."

Epilogue

*"The phoenix hope, can wing her way through
the desert skies, and still defying fortune's spite;
revive from ashes and rise."*
-Miguel de Cervantes

Finally she was home, safe and sound. The ride from the
airport had been treacherous, both navigating the highway and
conversation with Sam. I tried to keep it light—updating her on
the progress of my flourishing relationship with Hunter since
our last visit at the Phoenix Center. Sam 'ohh'-ed and 'ahh'-ed
in all the right places, laughed at my funny anecdotes, and
defended me against his stupid man behavior. She did
everything right, but everything felt off. She was Sam-lite, not
the same girl as before the attack, which was to be
expected. Her responses seemed computer generated, less
human and more android—it was disconcerting.

The therapists had cautioned me that Sam may initially
regress as she acclimated into life at home.

"Any changes in environment and routine can be jarring to
those with PTSD. It's normal, so try not to worry too
much. She has gained the tools to survive and thrive—you just
have to let her do it on her terms and at her own pace."

I hoped sessions with Dr. Veritus would help her regain
any ground she had lost in her homecoming. I mentioned that

Hunter offered to bring us dinner when we arrived home, unsure of Sam's reaction.

"I would love to see Hunter, please have him come over. I have missed him almost as much as I missed you. Plus, I still have to berate him for the whole FBI secret and breaking your heart."

That was my first glimpse of the real Sam—I almost cried.

I decided to press my luck. "Griffin wanted to come, too. He said he would understand if you needed time to settle in first, but wanted to be a part of the welcome home dinner if you were up for it."

Sam paused for a long time.

"I think I would rather keep it to just the three of us...so we can catch up. I appreciate Griffin's support, but I need a few days before I tackle the rest of the world."

I nodded my understanding; Griffin had suspected as much and told me so. I knew I should not push them together, I was the one who had told Griffin he deserved more than the broken pieces of Sam. I couldn't help but feel that Griff was the one person with the understanding and perseverance that Sam could trust one day.

"You're right. I didn't really want to share you—even with Hunter—but he won't stay long," I validated her feelings.

"Ev, I'm sure you and Hunter are screwing like bunnies in the apartment and everywhere else with a modicum of privacy, he doesn't need to head home tonight and sleep alone for my benefit."

"Tonight is Sunday, that's chick time. Hunter only received permission to attend dinner due to the celebratory nature of the event. Plus, he is the one providing the sustenance."

"It's your call, but I'm fine with him staying over. I would actually feel safer with him in the apartment."

That was a relief; Hunter had become a regular fixture during Sam's absence. He even had his own toothbrush. What concerned me was Sam's potential reaction to hearing Hunter and I dirty dancing—we were not the quietest of folks. I didn't want to trigger any unpleasant memories.

As if reading my mind she interjected, "And don't worry about working on your *ground and pound* when I'm at home—the girl in the room next to me really embraced the whole male re-emersion therapy concept. She fucked her way to being comfortable in a man's presence again. I think she had a sign-up sheet on her door. I'm not ready to dance the horizontal mambo yet, but you won't set me off if you do."

"Just tell me if anything bothers you and we will re-evaluate." I could not help my relief at being able to enjoy all of the benefits of Hunter.

"Besides, Shelly strongly encouraged masturbation to help disassociate negative thoughts from the rape with healthy sexual gratification. Having Hunter around and hearing him enjoying himself can serve as inspiration for me."

I stared at her wide-eyed for as long as possible without crashing the car. "You are not going to use my boyfriend as fodder for your private time."

"Oh, but I am," Sam smirked, "and you, my bestest friend in the world, can do nothing to stop me."

She was teasing me and I was thrilled that she was joking about sexual situations comfortably.

"The visuals you are implanting in my head may ruin my sex life for the foreseeable future," I was only partially kidding.

"I'm just kidding. Hunter is H.O.T. hot, but I see him in more of a brotherly light. I'll find another muse for my therapy."

Thank heavens for that! Maybe I would be able to have sex again.

"Besides, I can't fantasize about my future brother-in-law. That breaks all kinds of chick rules."

I almost choked on my sip of coffee. "We aren't engaged. We've only been officially together for two months. There is no ring on the horizon, no white dress to be ordered. Slow your roll, crazy lady."

"Whatever you say. I will bet you a Benjamin that he puts a ring on it within six months and you're Mrs. Everleigh Rose Charles this time next year," Sam predicted with confidence.

"Girlfriend...bite your tongue. I just graduated, I'm taking over a business, and I'm enjoying new boyfriend sex. Don't rush me."

"You better enjoy new boyfriend sex because it is soon to be replaced by new fiancé sex quickly followed by new husband sex; mark my words. I may be crazy now, but I'm not clueless."

"You're a sly one you manipulative little twerp. Stop messing with my head. Only one of us can be loco at a time."

Sam laughed, a real Sam laugh for the first time. Again, I almost cried.

She would be okay, she had some huge obstacles to scale, but she would be okay. And I would be here every step of the way to pick her up when she veered off course. She would be great because I would not let her be anything else.

Acknowledgements

To my Momma, you inspired me with your own book and encouraged me to follow my dream. You listened to me on the phone every day sharing my progress as I struggled through the process of writing a novel. You were my first unofficial beta reader, suffering through my typos and patiently correcting them. Only a mother could offer the love and support you have. Thank you, thank you, thank you. I love you with all my heart!

You do *not* want to imagine what this book would have been like without the talents of my editor C.J. Manise. Goose, thank you for embracing this story and caring enough to tell me when changes (or cuts, *gasp*) were necessary to improve the reader experience. You found my grammatical snafus, and ensured I presented the best work possible. I'm sorry for any times I may have argued, bit, spit, punched, or kicked you during the process...oh, I didn't do any of that except for argue...it must have been in my fantasies at the time. Thanks C.J. Ready for round two?

To The Book Bosses, Hildy and JJ—
You two *bossy* ladies were my saving grace while I was preparing to release *Only For You*. Between JJ's rapid-fire real-time messages that offered insight into the reader's mind and experience, and Hildy's priceless feedback on readability and grammar glitches...this book wouldn't have been nearly as polished without you both. So I thank you from the bottom of my EB heart. That's right JJ, I just wrote "EB" in the book. LOL.

To the fabulous Miss Amy Bartol—you sacrificed your time responding to a despairing e-mail of an unknown and unpublished author. Your words of empathy, encouragement, and advice were a gift for which you have my utmost gratitude. You rock! For anyone who hasn't read The Premonition Series by Amy Bartol, I strongly encourage you buy them today—just be sure to clear your schedule because you will not be able to put them down, they are addictive. For more information visit www.amybartol.com.

I was inspired by countless authors, who have swept me away with their stories of life, love, and heartbreak. I can't imagine I would have had the courage to pursue my dream if it weren't for their bravery. Please allow me to thank you all collectively for your talent and pluck. I am compelled to list several authors who were particularly inspiring and motivating, each for their own reasons. Alphabetically (because it just seemed fair), I offer my most sincere gratitude to: Jennifer L. Armentrout, Kristen Ashley, Shelly Crane, Colleen Hoover, M. Leighton, Jamie McGuire, Raine Miller, Jessica Sorensen, Nicole Williams, and Samantha Young.

A special thank you to Hanshi Michael J. Rosati, Sr. In a weird twisted way, you helped inspire this book. You're an amazing teacher! Rosati System of Modern Martial Arts www.rosatimma.com

Thank you to Moshe D Katz for your amazingly helpful website www.your-krav-maga-expert.com/self-defense-tips.html, your self-defense tips were a wonderful resource.

About The Author

Genna Rulon is an up-and-coming contemporary romance author.

During her 15 years in the corporate world, Genna, inspired by her love of reading, fantasized about penning her own stories. Encouraged by her favorite authors, many of whom are indie writers and self-published, she committed to pursue her aspirations of writing her own novels.

Genna was raised on Long Island in New York, where she still resides, surrounded by the most amazing family and friends. Married to a wonderful man who patiently tolerates her ramblings about whichever book she is currently working on, even feigning interest relatively convincingly! Genna is blessed with two little boys who do their best to thwart mommy's writing time with their hilarious antics and charming extrapolations.

You can find Genna online at: www.gennarulon.com

Genna would <u>love</u> to hear from you, and will personally respond to all messages! You can contact her as follows:
Email: genna@gennarulon.com

You can also follow Genna online at:
Twitter: www.twitter.com/GennaRulon
Facebook: www.facebook.com/genna.rulon.author
Goodreads: www.goodreads.com/gennarulo

Other Books by Genna Rulon

Pieces For You

For You Series - Book #2

release date: December 17, 2013

"The phoenix hope, can wing her way through the desert skies, and still defying ortune's spite; revive from ashes and rise." -Miguel de Cervantes

Samantha Whitney survived an unimaginable tragedy only to discover she had been betrayed by the man she loved. With the help of her best friend, she found a safe haven to physically recover and begin the process of healing emotionally.

Sam expected her homecoming to be tumultuous; she thought she was prepared to deal with the ramifications of her assault, but nothing could have prepared her for the battle she faced.

As she reestablishes a life that no longer feels familiar, she finds unwavering support in a familiar face. Despite every effort to distance herself, Griffin manages to take two steps forward for every step she retreats.

When unexplainable accidents plague Sam, she is forced to turn to Griffin.

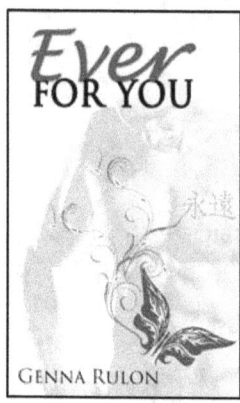

Ever For You
For You, Book #1.5
Expected publication: February 2014

Temper For You
For You, Book #3
Publication date: Sep 24, 2014